## Also by Robert Harris

# DICTATOR

# DICTATOR

## Robert Harris

Alfred A. Knopf | New York | 2016

THIS IS A BORZOI BOOK
PUBLISHED BY ALFRED A. KNOPF

Copyright © 2015 by Robert Harris

All rights reserved. Published in the United States by Alfred A. Knopf,
a division of Penguin Random House LLC, New York. Originally
published in hardcover in Great Britain by Hutchinson, a division of
Penguin Random House Ltd., London, in 2015.

www.aaknopf.com

Knopf, Borzoi Books, and the colophon are registered trademarks of
Penguin Random House LLC.

ISBN: 978-0-307-95794-8 (hardcover) /
ISBN: 978-0-307-95796-2 (eBook)
LCCN: 2015955103

Maps by Neil Gower
Jacket illustration by Matt Buck

Manufactured in the United States of America

First United States Edition

To Holly

The melancholy of the antique world seems
to me more profound than that of the
moderns, all of whom more or less imply that
beyond the dark void lies immortality. But
for the ancients that "black hole" was infinity
itself; their dreams loom and vanish against
a background of immutable ebony. No crying
out, no convulsions—nothing but the fixity of
a pensive gaze. Just when the gods had ceased
to be and the Christ had not yet come, there
was a unique moment in history, between
Cicero and Marcus Aurelius, when man stood
alone. Nowhere else do I find that particular
grandeur.

—Gustave Flaubert, letter to
Mme Roger de Genettes, 1861

Alive, Cicero enhanced life. So can his letters
do, if only for a student here and there,
taking time away from belittling despairs to
live among Virgil's Togaed People, desperate
masters of a larger world.

—D. R. Shackleton Bailey, *Cicero*, 1971

# CONTENTS

NORTH SEA

FURTHER GAUL

NEARER GAUL

ITALY

1.

FURTHER SPAIN

NEARER SPAIN

2.

SARDINIA

MEDITERRA

SICILY

MAURETANIA

NUMIDIA

3.

N.G.

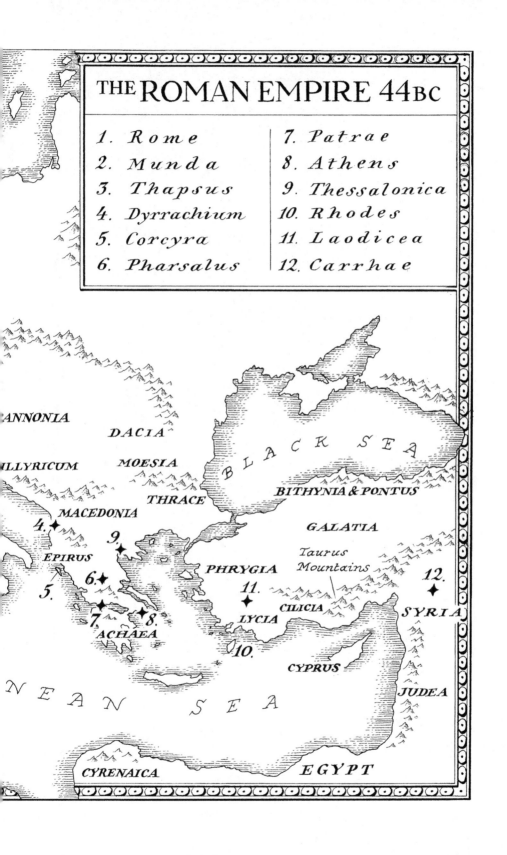

# THE ROMAN EMPIRE 44 BC

1. Rome
2. Munda
3. Thapsus
4. Dyrrachium
5. Corcyra
6. Pharsalus
7. Patrae
8. Athens
9. Thessalonica
10. Rhodes
11. Laodicea
12. Carrhae

ANNONIA

DACIA

ILLYRICUM

MOESIA

MACEDONIA

EPIRUS

THRACE

BLACK SEA

BITHYNIA & PONTUS

GALATIA

Taurus
Mountains

PHRYGIA

LYCIA

CILICIA

SYRIA

CYPRUS

JUDEA

ACHAEA

NEAN SEA

CYRENAICA

EGYPT

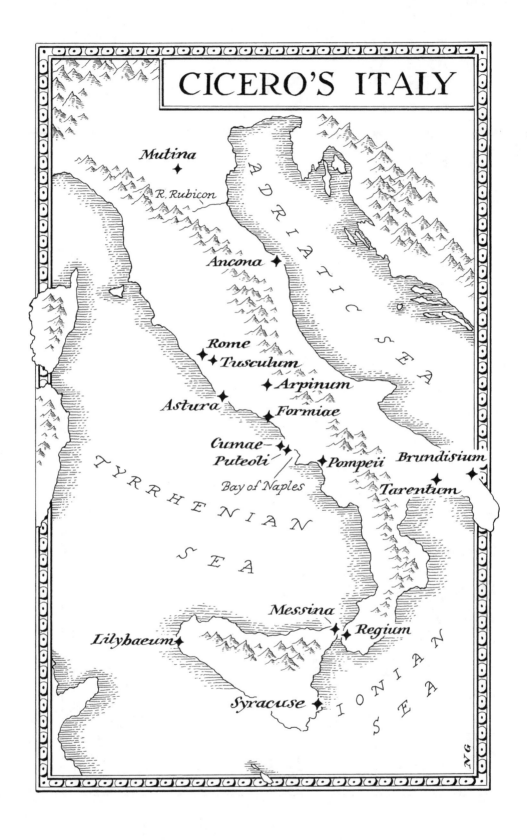

# CICERO'S ITALY

*Mutina* ✦

*R. Rubicon*

*Ancona* ✦

ADRIATIC SEA

*Rome* ✦
✦ *Tusculum*
*Arpinum* ✦
*Astura* ✦
✦ *Formiae*

*Cumae–* ✦
*Puteoli* ✦ *Pompeii*
*Bay of Naples*

*Brundisium*
✦

*Tarentum*

TYRRHENIAN

SEA

*Messina*
✦ *Regium*

*Lilybaeum* ✦

IONIAN SEA

*Syracuse* ✦

NG

# AUTHOR'S NOTE

*Dictator* tells the story of the final fifteen years in the life of the Roman statesman Cicero, imagined in the form of a biography written by his secretary, Tiro.

That there was such a man as Tiro and that he wrote such a book are well-attested historical facts. Born a slave on the family estate, he was three years younger than his master but long outlived him, surviving, according to Saint Jerome, until he reached his hundredth year.

"Your services to me are beyond count," Cicero wrote to him in 50 BC, "in my home and out of it, in Rome and abroad, in private affairs and public, in my studies and literary work..." Tiro was the first man to record a speech in the Senate verbatim, and his shorthand system, known as *Notae Tironianae,* was still in use in the Church in the sixth century; indeed some traces of it (the symbol "&," the abbreviations etc., NB, i.e., e.g.) survive to this day. He also wrote several treatises on the development of Latin. His multivolume life of Cicero is referred to as a source by the first-century historian Asconius Pedianus; Plutarch cites it twice. But, like the rest of Tiro's literary output, the book disappeared amid the collapse of the Roman Empire.

What must it have been like, one wonders? Cicero's life was extraordinary, even by the hectic standards of the age. From relatively lowly origins compared to his aristocratic rivals, and despite his lack of interest in military matters, deploying his skill as an orator and the brilliance of his intellect he rose at meteoric speed through the Roman political system, until, against all the odds, he finally was elected consul at the youngest-permitted age of forty-two.

There followed a crisis-stricken year in office—63 BC—during which he was obliged to deal with a conspiracy to overthrow the republic led by Sergius Catilina. To suppress the revolt, the Senate, under Cicero's presidency, ordered the execution of five prominent citizens—an episode that haunted his career ever afterwards.

When subsequently the three most powerful men in Rome—Julius Caesar, Pompey the Great and Marcus Crassus—joined forces in a so-called triumvirate to dominate the state, Cicero decided to oppose them. Caesar in retaliation, using his powers as chief priest, unleashed the ambitious aristocratic demagogue, Clodius—an old enemy of Cicero's—to destroy him. By allowing Clodius to renounce his patrician status and become a plebeian, Caesar opened the way for his election as tribune. Tribunes had the power to haul citizens before the people, to harass and persecute them. Cicero swiftly decided he had no choice but to flee Rome. It is at this desperate point in his fortunes that *Dictator* begins.

My aim has been to describe, as accurately as I can within the conventions of fiction, the end of the Roman Republic as it might have been experienced by Cicero and Tiro. Wherever possible, the letters and speeches and descriptions of events have been drawn from the original sources.

As *Dictator* encompasses what was arguably—at least until the convulsions of 1933–45—the most tumultuous era in human history, maps, a glossary and a cast of characters have been provided to assist the reader in navigating Cicero's sprawling and collapsing world.

—Robert Harris
Kintbury, 8 June 2015

# DRAMATIS PERSONAE

**Afranius, Lucius** an ally of Pompey's from his home region of Picenum; one of Pompey's army commanders in the war against Mithradates; consul in 60 BC

**Agrippa, Marcus Vipsanius** Octavian's closest associate, aged twenty

**Ahenobarbus, Lucius Domitius** patrician senator; praetor in 58 BC; married to Cato's sister; a determined enemy of Caesar

**Antony, Mark (Marcus Antonius)** renowned as a brave and enterprising soldier under Caesar's command in Gaul; grandson of a famous orator and consul; stepson of one of the Catiline conspirators executed by Cicero

**Atticus, Titus Pomponius** Cicero's closest friend; an equestrian, an Epicurean, immensely wealthy; brother-in-law to Quintus Cicero, who is married to his sister, Pomponia

**Balbus, Lucius Cornelius** wealthy Spaniard originally allied to Pompey and then to Caesar, whose *homme d'affaires* he became in Rome

**Bibulus, Marcus Calpurnius** Caesar's colleague as consul in 59 BC, and his staunch opponent

**Brutus, Marcus Junius** direct descendant of the Brutus who drove the kings from Rome and established the republic in the sixth century BC; son of Servilia, nephew of Cato; the great figure-head of the constitutionalists

**Caesar, Gaius Julius** former consul; a member of the "triumvirate" with Pompey and Crassus; governor of three Roman provinces—Nearer and Further Gaul and Bithynia; six years Cicero's junior; married to Calpurnia, daughter of L. Calpurnius Piso

**Calenus, Quintus Fufius** an old crony of Clodius and Antony; a supporter of Caesar and an enemy of Cicero; father-in-law of Pansa

**Cassius, Gaius Longinus** senator and able soldier; married to Servilia's daughter, Junia Tertia, and thus Brutus's brother-in-law

**Cato, Marcus Porcius** half-brother of Servilia; uncle of Brutus; a Stoic and a stern upholder of the traditions of the republic

**Cicero, Marcus Tullius Junior** Cicero's son

**Cicero, Quintus Tullius** Cicero's younger brother; senator and soldier; married to Pomponia, the sister of Atticus; governor of Asia, 61–58 BC

**Cicero, Quintus Tullius Junior** Cicero's nephew

**Clodia** daughter of one of the most distinguished families in Rome, the patrician Appii Claudii; the sister of Clodius; the widow of Metellus Celer

**Clodius Pulcher, Publius** scion of the leading patrician dynasty, the Appii Claudii; a former brother-in-law of L. Lucullus; the brother of Clodia, with whom he is alleged to have had an incestu-ous affair; at his trial for sacrilege Cicero gave evidence against him; transferred to the plebs at the instigation of Caesar and elected tribune

**Cornutus, Marcus** one of Caesar's officers, appointed urban praetor in 44 BC

**Crassipes, Furius** Tullia's second husband; a senator; a friend of Crassus

**Crassus, Marcus Licinius** former consul; member of the "triumvirate"; brutal suppressor of the slave revolt led by Spartacus; the richest man in Rome; a bitter rival of Pompey

**Crassus, Publius** son of Crassus the triumvir; cavalry commander under Caesar in Gaul; an admirer of Cicero

**Decimus** properly styled **Brutus, Decimus Junius Albinus,** but not to be confused with **Brutus** (above); brilliant young military commander in Gaul; a protégé of Caesar

**Dolabella, Publius Cornelius** Tullia's third husband; one of Caesar's closest lieutenants—young, charming, precocious, ambitious, licentious, brutal

**Fulvia** wife of Clodius; subsequently married to Mark Antony

**Hirtius, Aulus** one of Caesar's staff officers in Gaul, groomed for a political career; a noted gourmet, a scholar who helped Caesar with his *Commentaries*

**Horensius Hortalus, Quintus** former consul, for many years the leading advocate at the Roman bar, until displaced by Cicero; a leader of the patrician faction; immensely wealthy; like Cicero, a civilian politician and not a soldier

**Isauricus, Publius Servilius Vatia** a patrician, son of one of the grand old men of the Senate, who nevertheless chose to support Caesar; elected praetor in 54 BC

**Labienus, Titus** a soldier and former tribune from Pompey's home region of Picenum; one of Caesar's ablest commanders in Gaul

**Lepidus, Marcus Aemilius** patrician senator, married to a daughter of Servilia; member of the College of Pontiffs

**Milo, Titus Annius** a tough street-wise politician, an owner of gladiators

**Nepos, Quintus Caecilius Metellus** consul at the time of Cicero's return from exile

**Octavian, Gaius Julius Caesar** Caesar's great-nephew and heir

**Pansa, Gaius Vibius** one of Caesar's commanders in Gaul

**Philippus, Lucius Marcius** consul soon after Cicero's return from exile; married to Caesar's niece, Atia, and thus the stepfather of Octavian; owner of a villa next door to Cicero's on the Bay of Naples

**Philotimus** Terentia's business manager, of questionable honesty

**Piso, Lucius Calpurnius** consul at the time of Cicero's exile, and thus an enemy of Cicero's; Caesar's father-in-law

**Plancius, Gnaeus** quaestor of Macedonia; his family were friends from the same region of Italy as the Ciceros

**Plancus, Lucius Munatius** close lieutenant of Caesar, appointed governor of Further Gaul in 44 BC

**Pompey, Gnaeus Magnus** born in the same year as Cicero; for many years the most powerful man in the Roman world; a former consul and victorious general who has already triumphed twice; a member of the "triumvirate" with Caesar and Crassus; married to Caesar's daughter, Julia

**Rufus, Marcus Caelius** Cicero's former pupil; the youngest senator in Rome—brilliant, ambitious, unreliable

**Servilia** ambitious and politically shrewd half-sister of Cato; the long-term mistress of Caesar; the mother of three daughters and a son, Brutus, by her first husband

**Servius Sulpicius Rufus** contemporary and old friend of Cicero, famed as one of the greatest legal experts in Rome; married to Postumia, a mistress of Caesar

**Spinther, Publius Cornelius Lentulus** consul at the time of Cicero's return from exile; an enemy of Clodius and friend of Cicero

**Terentia** wife of Cicero; ten years younger than her husband, richer and of nobler birth; devoutly religious, poorly educated, with conservative political views; mother of Cicero's two children, Tullia and Marcus

**Tiro** Cicero's devoted private secretary, a family slave, three years younger than his master, the inventor of a system of shorthand

**Tullia** Cicero's daughter

**Vatinius, Publius** a senator and soldier famed for his ugliness; a close ally of Caesar

Part One

Exile

58 BC–47 BC

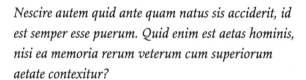

*Nescire autem quid ante quam natus sis acciderit, id est semper esse puerum. Quid enim est aetas hominis, nisi ea memoria rerum veterum cum superiorum aetate contexitur?*

To be ignorant of what occurred before you were born is to remain always a child. For what is the worth of human life, unless it is woven into the life of our ancestors by the records of history?

—Cicero, *Orator*, 46 BC

# I

I REMEMBER THE CRIES OF CAESAR'S WAR-HORNS CHASING US OVER the darkened fields of Latium—their yearning, keening howls, like animals in heat—and how when they stopped there was only the slither of our shoes on the icy road and the urgent panting of our breath.

It was not enough for the immortal gods that Cicero should be spat at and reviled by his fellow citizens; not enough that in the middle of the night he be driven from the hearths and altars of his family and ancestors; not enough even that as we fled from Rome on foot he should look back and see his house in flames. To all these torments they deemed it necessary to add one further refinement: that he should be forced to hear his enemy's army striking camp on the Field of Mars.

Even though he was the oldest of our party Cicero kept up the same fast pace as the rest of us. Not long ago he had held Caesar's life in the palm of his hand. He could have crushed it as easily as an egg. Now their fortunes led them in entirely opposite directions. While Cicero hurried south to escape his enemies, the architect of his destruction marched north to take command of both provinces of Gaul.

He walked with his head down, not uttering a word and I imagined it was because he was too full of despair to speak. Only at dawn, when we rendezvoused with our horses at Bovillae and were about to embark on the second stage of our escape, did he pause with his foot in the doorway of his carriage and say suddenly, "Do you think we should turn back?"

The question caught me by surprise. "I don't know," I said. "I hadn't considered it."

"Well, consider it now. Tell me: why are we fleeing Rome?"

"Because of Clodius and his mob."

"And why is Clodius so powerful?"

"Because he's a tribune and can pass laws against you."

"And who made it possible for him to become a tribune?"

I hesitated. "Caesar."

"Exactly. Caesar. Do you imagine that man's departure for Gaul at that precise hour was a coincidence? Of course not! He waited till his spies had reported I'd left the city before ordering his army to move. Why? I'd always assumed his advancement of Clodius was to punish me for speaking out against him. But what if his real aim all along was to drive me out of Rome? What scheme requires him to be certain I've gone before he can leave too?"

I should have grasped the logic of what he was saying. I should have urged him to turn back. But I was too exhausted to reason clearly. And if I am honest there was more to it than that. I was too afraid of what Clodius's thugs might do to us if they caught us re-entering the city.

So instead I said, "It's a good question, and I can't pretend I have the answer. But wouldn't it look indecisive, after bidding goodbye to everyone, suddenly to reappear? In any case, Clodius has burned your house down now—where would we return to? Who would take us in? I think you'd be wiser to stick to your original plan and get as far away from Rome as you can."

He rested his head against the side of the carriage and closed his eyes. In the pale grey light I was shocked by how haggard he appeared after his night on the road. His hair and beard had not been cut for weeks. He was wearing a toga dyed black. Although he was only in his forty-ninth year, these public signs of mourning made him look much older—like some ancient, mendicant holy man. After a while he sighed. "I don't know, Tiro. Perhaps you're right. It's so long since I slept I'm too tired to think any more."

And so the fatal error was made—more through indecision

than decision—and we continued to press on southwards for the remainder of that day and for the twelve days that followed, putting what we thought was a safe distance between ourselves and danger.

We travelled with a minimal entourage to avoid attracting attention—just the carriage driver and three armed slaves on horseback, one in front and two behind. A small chest of gold and silver coins that Atticus, Cicero's oldest and closest friend, had provided to pay for our journey was hidden under our seat. We stayed only in the houses of men we trusted, no more than a night in each, and steered clear of those places where Cicero might have been expected to stop—for example at his seaside villa at Formiae, the first place any pursuers would look for him, and along the Bay of Naples, already filling with the annual exodus from Rome in search of winter sun and warm springs. Instead we headed as fast as we could towards the toe of Italy.

Cicero's plan, conceived on the move, was to make for Sicily and stay there until the political agitation against him in Rome subsided. "The mob will turn on Clodius eventually," he predicted. "Such is the unalterable nature of the mob. He will always be my mortal enemy but he won't always be tribune—we must never forget that. In nine months his term of office will expire and then we can go back."

He was confident of a friendly reception from the Sicilians, if only because of his successful prosecution of the island's tyrannical governor, Verres—even though that brilliant victory, which launched his political career, was now twelve years in the past and Clodius had more recently been a magistrate in the province. I sent letters ahead giving notice of his intention to seek sanctuary, and when we reached the harbour at Regium we hired a little six-oared boat to row us across the straits to Messina.

We left the harbour on a clear cold winter morning of searing blues—the sea and the sky; one light, one dark; the line dividing them as sharp as a blade; the distance to Messina a mere three miles. It took us less than an hour. We drew so close we could see

Cicero's supporters lined up on the rocks to welcome him. But stationed between us and the entrance to the port was a warship flying the red and green colours of the governor of Sicily, Gaius Vergilius, and as we approached the lighthouse it slipped its anchor and moved slowly forwards to intercept us. Vergilius stood at the rail surrounded by his lictors and, after visibly recoiling at Cicero's dishevelled appearance, shouted down a greeting, to which Cicero replied in friendly terms. They had known one another in the Senate for many years.

Vergilius asked him his intentions.

Cicero called back that naturally he intended to come ashore.

"That's what I'd heard," replied Vergilius. "Unhappily I can't allow it."

"Why not?"

"Because of Clodius's new law."

"And what new law would that be? There are so many, one loses count."

Vergilius beckoned to a member of his staff who produced a document and leaned down to pass it to me and I then gave it to Cicero. To this day I can remember how it fluttered in his hands in the slight breeze as if it were a living thing; it was the only sound in the silence. He took his time and when he had finished reading it he handed it to me without comment.

### LEX CLODIA IN CICERONEM

Whereas M. T. Cicero has put Roman citizens to death unheard and uncondemned; and to that end forged the authority and decree of the Senate; it is hereby ordained that he be interdicted from fire and water to a distance of four hundred miles from Rome; that nobody should presume to harbour or receive him, on pain of death; that all his property and possessions be forfeit; that his house in Rome be demolished and a shrine to Liberty consecrated in its place; and that whoever shall move, speak, vote or take any step towards recalling him shall be treated as a public enemy, unless those whom Cicero unlawfully put to death should first spring back to life.

It must have been the most terrible blow. But he found the composure to dismiss it with a flick of his hand. "When," he enquired, "was this nonsense published?"

"I'm told it was posted in Rome eight days ago. It came into my hands yesterday."

"Then it's not law yet, and can't be law until it's been read a third time. My secretary will confirm it. Tiro," he said, turning to me, "tell the governor the earliest date it can be passed."

I tried to calculate. Before a bill could be put to a vote it had to be read aloud in the Forum on three successive market days. But my reasoning was so shaken by what I had just read I couldn't remember what day of the week it was now, let alone when the market days fell. "Twenty days from today," I hazarded, "perhaps twenty-five?"

"You see?" cried Cicero. "I have three weeks' grace even if it passes, which I'm sure it won't." He stood up in the prow of the boat, bracing his legs against the rocking of the hull, and spread his arms wide in appeal. "Please, my dear Vergilius, for the sake of our past friendship, now that I have come so far, at least allow me to land and spend a night or two with my supporters."

"No, as I say, I'm sorry, but I cannot take the risk. I've consulted my experts. They say even if you travelled to the very western tip of the island, to Lilybaeum, you'd still be within three hundred and fifty miles of Rome, and then Clodius would come after *me*."

At that, Cicero ceased to be so friendly. He said coldly, "You have no right under the law to impede the journey of a Roman citizen."

"I have every right to safeguard the tranquillity of my province. And here, as you know, my word *is* the law ..."

He was apologetic. I dare say he was even embarrassed. But he was immovable, and after a few more angry exchanges there was nothing for it but to turn round and row back to Regium. Our departure provoked a great cry of dismay from the shoreline and

I could see that Cicero for the first time was seriously worried. Vergilius was a friend of his. If this was how a friend reacted then soon the whole of Italy would be closed against him. Returning to Rome to oppose the law was much too risky. He had left it too late. Apart from the physical danger such a journey would entail, the bill would almost certainly pass, and then we would be stranded four hundred miles from the legal limit it prescribed. To comply safely with the terms of his exile he would have to flee abroad immediately. Obviously Gaul was out of the question because of Caesar. So it would have to be somewhere in the East—Greece perhaps, or Asia. But unfortunately we were on the wrong side of the peninsula to make our escape in the treacherous winter seas. We needed to get over to the opposite coast, to Brundisium on the Adriatic, and find a big ship capable of making a lengthy voyage. Our predicament was exquisitely vile—as no doubt Caesar, the original sponsor and creator of Clodius, had intended.

IT TOOK US TWO WEEKS OF ARDUOUS TRAVEL TO CROSS THE mountains, often in heavy rain and mostly along bad roads. Every mile seemed fraught with the hazard of ambush, although the primitive little towns we passed through were welcoming enough. At night we slept in smoky, freezing inns and dined on hard bread and fatty meat made scarcely more palatable by sour wine. Cicero's mood veered between fury and despair. He saw clearly now that he had made a terrible mistake by leaving Rome. It had been madness for him to quit the city and leave Clodius free to spread the calumny that he had put citizens to death "unheard and uncondemned" when in fact each of the five Catiline conspirators had been allowed to speak in his own defence and their execution had been sanctioned by the entire Senate. But his flight was tantamount to an admission of guilt. He should have obeyed his instinct and turned back when he heard Caesar's departing trumpets and first began to realise his error. He wept at the disaster his folly and timidity had brought upon his wife and children.

And when he had finished lashing himself, he turned his scourge on Hortensius "and the rest of the aristocratic gang," who had never forgiven him for rising from his humble origins to the consulship and saving the republic: they had deliberately urged him to flee in order to ruin him. He should have heeded the example of Socrates, who said that death was preferable to exile. Yes, he should have killed himself! He snatched up a knife from the dining table. He *would* kill himself! I said nothing. I didn't take the threat seriously. He couldn't stand the sight of others' blood, let alone his own. All his life he had tried to avoid military expeditions, the games, public executions, funerals—anything that might remind him of mortality. If pain frightened him, death terrified him—which, although I would never have been impertinent enough to point it out, was the principal reason we had fled Rome in the first place.

When finally we came within sight of the fortified walls of Brundisium, he decided not to venture inside. The port was so large and busy, so full of strangers, and so likely to be his destination, he was convinced it was the obvious spot for his assassination. Instead we sought sanctuary a little way up the coast, in the residence of his old friend Marcus Laenius Flaccus. That night we slept in decent beds for the first time in three weeks, and the next morning we went down to the beach. The waves were much rougher than on the Sicilian side. A strong wind was hurling the Adriatic relentlessly against the rocks and shingle. Cicero loathed sea voyages at the best of times; this one promised to be especially treacherous. Yet it was our only means of escape. One hundred and twenty miles beyond the horizon lay the shore of Illyricum.

Flaccus, noticing his expression, said, "Fortify your spirits, Cicero—perhaps the bill won't pass, or one of the other tribunes will veto it. There must be *someone* left in Rome willing to stand up for you—Pompey, surely?"

But Cicero, his gaze still fixed out to sea, made no reply, and a few days later we heard that the bill had indeed become law and that Flaccus was therefore guilty of a capital offence simply by having a convicted exile on his premises. Even so he tried to persuade us to stay. He insisted that Clodius didn't frighten *him*. But Cicero wouldn't hear of it: "Your loyalty moves me, old friend, but that monster will have dispatched a team of his hired fighters to hunt me down the moment his law passed. There is no time to lose."

I had found a merchant ship in the harbour at Brundisium whose hard-pressed master was willing to risk a winter voyage across the Adriatic in return for a huge fee, and the next morning at first light, when no one was around, we went on board. She was a sturdy, broad-beamed vessel, with a crew of about twenty, used to ply the trade route between Italy and Dyrrachium. I was no judge of these things, but she looked safe enough to me. The master estimated the crossing would require a day and a half—but we needed to leave quickly, he said, and take advantage of the favourable wind. So while the sailors made her ready and Flaccus waited on the quayside, Cicero quickly dictated a final message to his wife and children: *It has been a fine life, a great career—the good in me, nothing bad, has brought me down. My dear Terentia, loyalest and best of wives, my darling daughter Tullia, and little Marcus, our one remaining hope—goodbye!* I copied it out and passed it up to Flaccus. He raised his hand in farewell. Then the sail was unfurled, the cables cast off, the oarsmen pushed us away from the harbour wall, and we set off into the pale grey light.

AT FIRST WE MADE GOOD SPEED. CICERO STOOD HIGH ABOVE THE deck on the steersmen's platform, leaning on the stern rail, watching the great lighthouse of Brundisium recede behind us. Apart from his visits to Sicily, it was the first time he had left Italy since his youth, when he went to Rhodes to learn oratory from Molon. Of all the men I ever knew, Cicero was the least equipped by temperament for exile. To thrive he needed the appurtenances of civilised society—friends, news, gossip, conversation, politics, dinners, plays, baths, books, fine buildings; to watch all these dwindle away must have been an agony for him.

Nevertheless, in little more than an hour they had gone, swallowed up in the void. The wind drove us forwards strongly, and as we cut through the whitecaps I thought of Homer's "dark blue wave/foaming at the bow." But then around the middle of the morning the ship seemed gradually to lose propulsion. The great brown sail became slack-bellied and the two steersmen standing at their levers on either side of us began exchanging anxious looks. Soon dense black clouds started to mass on the horizon, and within an hour they had closed over our heads like a trapdoor. The light became shadowy; the temperature dropped. The wind got up again, but this time the gusts were in our faces, driving the cold spray off the surface of the waves. Hailstones raked the heaving deck.

Cicero shuddered, leaned forwards and vomited. His face was as grey as a corpse. I put my arm around his shoulders and indicated that we should descend to the lower deck and seek shelter in the cabin. We were halfway down the ladder when a flash of lightning split the gloom, followed instantly by a deafening, sickening crack, like a bone snapping or a tree splintering, and I was sure we must have lost the mast, for suddenly we seemed to be tumbling over and over while all around us great glistening black mountains of jet towered and toppled in the lightning flashes. The shriek of the wind made it impossible to speak or hear. In the end I simply pushed Cicero into the cabin, fell in after him and closed the door.

We tried to stand, but the ship was listing. The deck was ankle-deep in water. Our feet slid from under us. The floor tilted first one way and then the other. We clutched at the walls as we were pitched back and forth in the darkness amid loose tools and jars of wine and sacks of barley, like dumb beasts in a crate on our way to slaughter. Eventually we wedged ourselves in a corner and lay there soaked and shivering as the boat shook and plunged. I was sure we were doomed and closed my eyes and prayed to Neptune and all the gods for deliverance.

A long time passed. How long I cannot say—certainly it was the remainder of that day, and the whole of the night, and part of the day that followed. Cicero seemed quite unconscious; on several occasions I had to touch his cold cheek to reassure myself he was still alive. Each time his eyes opened briefly and then closed again. Afterwards he said he had fully resigned himself to drowning but such was the misery of his seasickness he felt no fear: rather he saw how Nature in her mercy spares those *in extremis* from the terrors of oblivion and makes death seem a welcome release. Almost the greatest surprise of his life, he said, was when he awoke on the second day and realised the storm was over and his existence would continue after all: "Unfortunately my situation is so wretched, I almost regret it."

Once we were sure the storm had blown itself out, we went back on deck. The sailors were just at that moment tipping over the side the corpse of some poor wretch whose head had been smashed by a swinging boom. The Adriatic was oily-smooth and still, of the same grey shade as the sky, and the body slid into it with scarcely a splash. There was a smell on the cold wind I didn't recognise, of something rotten and decaying. About a mile away I noticed a wall of sheer black rock rising above the surf. I assumed we had been blown back home again and that it must be the coast of Italy. But the captain laughed at my ignorance and said it was Illyricum, and that those were the famous cliffs that guard the approaches to the ancient city of Dyrrachium.

CICERO HAD AT FIRST INTENDED TO MAKE FOR EPIRUS, THE mountainous country to the south, where Atticus owned a great estate that included a fortified village. It was a most desolate region, having never recovered from the terrible fate decreed it by the Senate a century earlier, when, as a punishment for siding against Rome, all seventy of its towns had been razed to the ground simultaneously and its entire population of one hundred and fifty thousand sold into slavery. Nevertheless, Cicero claimed he wouldn't have minded the solitude of such a haunted spot. But just before we left Italy Atticus had warned him—"with regret"—that he could only stay for a month lest word of his presence become known: if it did, under clause two of Clodius's bill, Atticus himself would be liable to the death penalty for harbouring the exile.

Even as we stepped ashore at Dyrrachium, Cicero remained in two minds about which direction to take—south to Epirus, temporary refuge though it would be, or east to Macedonia, where the governor, Apuleius Saturninus, was an old friend of his, and from Macedonia on to Greece and Athens. In the event, the decision was made for him. A messenger was waiting on the quayside—a young man, very anxious. Glancing around to make sure he was not observed, he drew us quickly into a deserted warehouse and produced a letter. It was from Saturninus, the governor. I do not have it in my archives because Cicero seized it and tore it to pieces the moment I had read it out loud to him. But I can still remember the gist of what it said: that "with regret" (that phrase again!), despite their years of friendship, Saturninus would not be able to receive Cicero in his household as it would be "incompatible with the dignity of a Roman governor to offer succour to a convicted exile."

Hungry, damp and exhausted from our crossing, having hurled the fragments of the letter to the ground, Cicero sank on to a bale of cloth with his head in his hands. That was when the messenger said nervously, "Your Excellency, there is another letter . . ."

It was from one of the governor's junior magistrates, the quaestor Gnaeus Plancius. His family were old neighbours of the Ciceros from their ancestral lands around Arpinum. Plancius said that he was writing secretly and sending his letter via the same courier, who was to be trusted; that he disagreed with his superior's decision; that it would be an honour for him to take the Father of the Nation under his protection; that secrecy was vital; that he had already set out on the road to meet him at the Macedonian border; and that in the meantime he had arranged for a carriage to transport Cicero out of Dyrrachium "immediately, in the interests of your personal safety; I plead with you not to delay by so much as an hour; I shall explain more when I see you."

"Do you trust him?" I asked.

Cicero stared at the floor and in a low voice replied, "No. But what choice do I have?"

With the messenger's help I arranged for our luggage to be transferred from the boat to the quaestor's carriage—a gloomy contraption, little better than a cell on wheels, without suspension and with metal grilles nailed over the windows so that its fugitive occupant could look out but no one could see him. We clattered up from the harbour into the city and joined the traffic on the Via Egnatia, the great highway that runs all the way to Byzantium. It started to sleet. There had been an earthquake a few days earlier and the place was wretched in the downpour, with corpses of the native tribespeople unburied by the roadside and here and there little groups of survivors sheltering in makeshift tents among the ruins, huddled over smoking fires. It was this odour of destruction and despair that I had smelt out at sea.

We travelled across the plain towards the snow-covered mountains and spent the night in a small village hemmed in by the encroaching peaks. The inn was squalid, with goats and chickens in the downstairs rooms. Cicero ate little and said nothing. In this strange and barren land, with its savage-looking people, he had at last fallen into the full depths of despair, and it was only with difficulty that I roused him from his bed the next morning and persuaded him to continue our journey.

For two days the road climbed into the mountains, until we came to the edge of a wide lake, fringed with ice. On the far side was a town, Lychnidos, that marked the border with Macedonia, and it was here, in its forum, that Plancius awaited us. He was in his early thirties, strongly built, wearing military uniform, with half a dozen legionaries at his back, and there was a moment when they all began to stride towards us that I experienced a rush of panic and feared we had blundered into a trap. But the warmth with which Plancius embraced Cicero, and the tears in his eyes, convinced me immediately that he was genuine.

He could not disguise his shock at Cicero's appearance. "You need to recover your strength," he said, "but unfortunately, we must leave here straight away." And then he told us what he had not dared put into his letter: that he had received reliable intelligence that three of the traitors Cicero had sent into exile for their parts in Catilina's conspiracy—Autronius Paetas, Cassius Longinus and Marcus Laeca—were all out looking for him, and had sworn to kill him.

Cicero said, "Then there is nowhere in the world where I am safe. How are we to live?"

"Under my protection, as I said. In fact come back with me to Thessalonica, and stay under my very roof. I was military tribune until last year and I'm still on active service, so there'll be soldiers to guard you as long as you stay within the frontiers of Macedonia. My house is no palace, but it's secure and it's yours for as long as you need it."

Cicero stared at him. Apart from the hospitality of Flaccus, it was the first real offer of help he had received for weeks—for months, in fact—and that it should have come from a young man he barely knew, when old allies such as Pompey had turned their backs on him, moved him deeply. He tried to speak, but the words choked in his throat and he had to look away.

THE VIA EGNATIA RUNS FOR ONE HUNDRED AND FIFTY MILES ACROSS the mountains of Macedonia before descending to the plain of Amphaxis, where it enters the port of Thessalonica, and this was where our journey ended, two months after leaving Rome, in a secluded villa off a busy thoroughfare in the northern part of the town.

Five years earlier, Cicero had been the undisputed ruler of Rome, second only to Pompey the Great in the affections of the people. Now he had lost everything—reputation, position, family, possessions, country; even at times the balance of his mind. For reasons of security he was confined to the villa during the hours of daylight. His presence was kept secret. A guard was posted at the entrance. Plancius told his staff that his anonymous guest was an old friend suffering from acute grief and melancholia. Like all the best lies it had the merit of being partly true. Cicero barely ate, or spoke, or left his room; sometimes his fits of weeping could be heard from one end of the house to the other. He would not receive visitors, not even his brother, Quintus, who was passing nearby on his way back to Rome after completing his term as governor of Asia: *You would not have seen your brother the man you knew,* he pleaded in mitigation, *not a trace or semblance of him but only the likeness of a breathing corpse.* I tried my best to console him, without success, for how could I, a slave, understand his sense of loss, having never possessed anything worth losing in the first place? Looking back, I can see that my attempts to offer solace through philosophy must only have added to his aggravation. Indeed on one occasion, when I tried to advance the Stoic argument that possessions and rank are unnecessary, given that virtue alone is sufficient for happiness, he threw a stool at my head.

We had arrived in Thessalonica at the beginning of spring, and I took it upon myself to send letters to Cicero's friends and family letting them know, in confidence, where he was hiding, and asking them to write in response using Plancius as a poste restante. It took three weeks for these messages to reach Rome, and a further three weeks before we started to receive replies, and the news they brought was anything but encouraging. Terentia described how the charred walls of the family house on the Palatine hill had been demolished so that Clodius's shrine to Liberty—the irony!—could be erected on the site. The villa at Formiae had been pillaged, the country estate in Tusculum also invaded, and even some of the trees in the garden carted off by the neighbours. Homeless, at first she had taken refuge with her sister in the House of the Vestal Virgins.

*But that impious wretch Clodius, in defiance of all the sacred laws, broke into the temple, and dragged me to the Basilica Porcia, where in front of the mob he had the impertinence to question me about my own property! Of course I refused to answer. He then demanded that I hand over our little son as a hostage to my good behaviour. In answer I pointed to the painting that shows Valerius defeating the Carthaginians and reminded him that my ancestors fought in that very battle and that as my family had never feared Hannibal, we most certainly would not be intimidated by him.*

It was the plight of his son that most upset Cicero: "The first duty of any man is to protect his children, and I am helpless to fulfil it." Marcus and Terentia were now sheltering in the home of Cicero's brother, while his adored daughter, Tullia, was sharing a roof with her in-laws. But although Tullia, like her mother, tried to make light of her troubles, it was easy enough to read between the lines and recognise the truth: that she was nursing her sick husband, the gentle Frugi—whose health, never robust, seemed to have collapsed under the strain. *Ah, my beloved, my heart's longing!* Cicero wrote to his wife. *To think that you, dearest Terentia, once everybody's refuge in trouble, should now be so tormented! You are before my eyes night and day. Goodbye, my absent loves, goodbye.*

The political outlook was equally bleak. Clodius and his supporters were continuing their occcupation of the Temple of Castor in the southern corner of the Forum. Using this fortress as their headquarters, they could intimidate the voting assemblies and pass or block whatever bills they chose. One new law we heard about, for example, demanded the annexation of Cyprus and the taxation of its wealth, "for the good of the Roman people"—that is, to pay for the free dole of corn Clodius had instituted for every citizen— and charged Marcus Porcius Cato with accomplishing this piece of theft. Needless to say, it passed, for what group of voters ever refused to levy a tax on someone else, especially if it benefited themselves? At first Cato refused to go. But Clodius threatened him with prosecution if he disobeyed the law. As Cato held the constitution to be sacred above all things, he felt he had no choice but to comply. He sailed off for Cyprus, along with his young nephew, Marcus Junius Brutus, and with his departure Cicero lost his most vocal supporter in Rome.

Against Clodius's intimidation, the Senate was powerless. Even Pompey the Great ("the Pharaoh," as Cicero and Atticus privately called him) was now becoming frightened of the over-mighty tribune he had helped Caesar create. He was rumoured to spend most of his time making love to his young wife, Julia, the daughter of Caesar, while all the time his public standing declined. Atticus wrote gossipy letters about him to cheer Cicero up, one of which survives:

*You remember that when the Pharaoh restored the King of Armenia to his throne a few years back, he brought his son to Rome as a hostage to ensure the old man behaved himself? Well, just after your departure, bored of having the young fellow under his own roof, Pompey decided to lodge him with Lucius Flavius, the new praetor. Naturally, our Little Miss Beauty [Cicero's nickname for Clodius] soon got to hear of it, whereupon he invited himself round to Flavius's for dinner, asked to see the prince, and then took him away with him at the end of the meal, as if he were a napkin! Why? I hear you ask. Because Clodius has decided to put the prince on the throne of Armenia in place of his father, and take all the revenues of Armenia away from Pompey and have them for himself! Unbelievable—but it gets better: the prince is duly sent back to Armenia on a ship. There is a storm. The ship returns to harbour. Pompey tells Flavius to get himself down to Antium straight away and recapture his prize hostage. But Clodius's men are waiting. There is a fight on the Via Appia. Many are killed—among them Pompey's dear friend Marcus Papirius.*

*Since then, things have gone from bad to worse for the Pharaoh. The other day, when he was in the Forum attending the trial of one of his supporters (Clodius is prosecuting them left, right and centre), Clodius called together a gang of his criminals and started a chant. "What's the name of the lecherous imperator? What's*

*the name of the man who is trying to find a man? Who is it who*
*scratches his head with one finger?" After each question he made*
*a sign by shaking the folds of his toga—in that way the Pharaoh*
*does—and the mob, like a circus chorus, all roared out the answer:*
*"Pompey!"*

*No one in the Senate lifts a finger to help him, as they all think his*
*harassment is eminently deserved for the way he abandoned you . . .*

But if Atticus thought such news would bring comfort to Cicero, he was wrong. On the contrary, it served only to make him feel more isolated and helpless. With Cato gone, Pompey cowed, the Senate impotent, the voters bribed and Clodius's mob in control of all law-making, Cicero despaired of ever having his exile rescinded. He chafed against the conditions in which we were obliged to exist. Thessalonica may be nice enough for a short stay in the spring-time. But as the months passed, summer came—and Thessalonica in the summer becomes a hell of humidity and mosquitoes. No breath of a breeze stirs the brittle vegetation. The air is suffocating. And because the walls of the town retain the heat, the nights can be even more sweltering than the days. I slept in the room next to Cicero's—or rather, I tried to sleep. Lying in my tiny cubicle, I felt as if I were a roasting pig in a brick oven, and that the sweat pooling beneath my back was my melted flesh. Often after midnight I would hear Cicero stumbling around in the dark, his door opening, his bare feet slapping across the mosaic tiles. Then I would slip out after him and watch from a distance to make sure he was all right. He would sit in the courtyard on the edge of the dried-up pool with its dust-clogged fountain, and stare up at the brilliant stars, as if he could read in their alignment some clue as to why his good fortune had so spectacularly deserted him.

The next morning he would often summon me to his room. "Tiro," he would whisper, his fingers gripping my arm tightly, "I've got to get out of this shithole. I'm losing all sense of myself." But where could we go? He dreamed of Athens, or possibly Rhodes. But Plancius would not hear of it: the danger of assassination, he insisted, was, if anything, even greater than before, as rumours of Cicero's presence in the region spread. After a while I began to suspect that he quite enjoyed having such a famous figure in his power and was reluctant to let us leave. I voiced my suspicions to Cicero, who said: "He's young and ambitious. Perhaps he's calculating that the situation in Rome will change and he might eventually get some political credit for shielding me. If so, he deludes himself."

And then late one afternoon, when the ferocity of the day's heat had subsided a little, I happened to go into town with a packet of letters for dispatch to Rome. It was hard to persuade Cicero even to raise the energy to reply to his correspondence, and when he did so, it was mostly a list of complaints. *I am still stuck here with no one to talk to and nothing to think about. There could be no less suitable spot in which to bear calamity in such a state of grief as I am in.* But write he did, and to supplement the occasional trusted traveller who would carry our letters, I had arranged to hire couriers provided by a local Macedonian merchant named Epiphanes, who ran an import/export business with Rome.

He was an inveterate lazy crook, of course, as are most people in that part of the world. But I reckoned the bribes I paid him ought to have been enough to buy his discretion. He had a warehouse up the slope from the harbour, on the higher ground close to the Egnatian Gate, where a haze of red-grey dust hung permanently over the clustered roofs, thrown up by the traffic from Rome to Byzantium. To reach his office one had to cross a yard where his wagons were loaded and unloaded. And there, that afternoon—with its shafts resting on blocks and its horses unhitched and drinking noisily from a water trough—was a chariot. It was so unlike the usual ox carts that the sight of it brought me up short and I went over to give it a closer look. Obviously it had been ridden hard: it was so filthy from the road it was impossible to tell its original colour. But it was fast and strong and built for fighting—a war chariot—and when I found Epiphanes upstairs I asked him whose it was.

He gave me a crafty look. "The driver did not say his name. He just asked me to look after it."

"A Roman?"

"Undoubtedly."

"Alone?"

"No, he had a companion—a gladiator, perhaps: both young men, strong."

"When did they arrive?"

"An hour ago."

"And where are they now?"

"Who can say?" He shrugged and bared his yellow teeth.

A terrible realisation gripped me. "Have you been opening my letters? Have you had me followed?"

"Sir, I am shocked. Really . . ." He spread his hands to show his innocence and glanced around as if in silent appeal to some invisible jury. "How could such a thing even be suggested?"

Epiphanes! For a man who made his living by lying, he was remarkably bad at it. I turned and ran out of that room and down those steps and didn't stop running until I was within sight of our villa, where a pair of rough-looking villains were loitering in the street. My footsteps slowed as the two strangers turned to look at me and I knew in my bones they had been sent to kill Cicero. One had a puckered scar that split the side of his face from his eyebrow to his jaw (Epiphanes was right: he was a fighter straight from the gladiator barracks), while the other could have been a blacksmith— given his swagger, he could have been Vulcan himself—with bulging sunburnt calves and forearms and a face as black as a Negro's. He called out to me, "We're looking for the house where Cicero is living!" And when I started to plead ignorance, he cut me off and added, "Tell him Titus Annius Milo has come to pay his compliments, all the way from Rome."

CICERO'S ROOM WAS DARK, HIS CANDLE EXPIRING FOR WANT OF AIR. He lay on his side, facing the wall.

"Milo?" he repeated in a monotone. "What sort of a name is that? Is he Greek, or what?" But then he rolled over on to his back and raised himself up on his elbows. "Wait—hasn't a candidate of that name just been elected tribune?"

"It's the same man. He's here."

"But if he's a tribune-elect, why isn't he in Rome? His term of office begins in three months."

"He says he wants to talk to you."

"It's a long way to come just for a chat. What do we know of him?"

"Nothing."

"Maybe he's come to kill me?"

"Maybe—he has a gladiator with him."

"That doesn't inspire confidence." Cicero lay back and thought it over. "Well, what does it matter? I might as well be dead in any case."

He had skulked in his room so long that when I opened the door, the daylight blinded him and he had to put up his hand to protect his eyes. Stiff limbed and waxen, half starved, with straggling grey hair and beard, he looked like a corpse freshly risen from its tomb. It was scarcely surprising that when he first came into the room, supported on my arm, Milo failed to recognise him. It was only when he heard that familiar voice bidding him good day that our visitor gasped, pressed his hand to his heart, bowed his head and declared this to be the greatest moment and the greatest honour of his life, that he had heard Cicero speak countless times in the law courts and from the rostra but had never thought to meet him, the Father of the Nation, in person, let alone be in a position (he dared to hope) to render him some service . . .

There was a lot more in this vein, and eventually it elicited from Cicero something I had not seen from him in months: laughter. "Yes, very well, young man, that's enough. I understand: you're pleased to see me! Come." And with that he stepped forward, arms open, and the two men embraced.

In later years, Cicero was to be much criticised for his friendship with Milo. And it is true that the young tribune-elect was headstrong, violent and reckless, but there are times when these

traits are more to be prized than prudence, calmness and caution—
and these were such times. Besides, Cicero was touched that Milo
should have come so far to see him; it made him feel he was not
entirely finished. He invited him to stay for dinner and to save
whatever he had to say until then. He even tidied himself up a little
for the occasion, combing his hair and changing into less funereal
garb.

Plancius was away upcountry in Tauriana, judging the local
assizes, so therefore only the three of us gathered to eat. (Milo's
gladiator, a murmillo named Birria, took his meal in the kitchen;
even a man as easy-going as Cicero, who had been known occasionally to tolerate the presence of an actor at his dinner table, drew the
line at a gladiator.) We lay in the garden in a kind of fine-mesh tent
designed to keep out the mosquitoes, and over the next few hours
we learned something of Milo, and why he had made such an arduous journey of seven hundred miles. He came, he said, of a noble
but hard-up family. He had been adopted by his maternal grandfather. Even so, there was little money and he had been obliged
to earn a living as the owner of a gladiator school in Campania,
supplying fighters for funeral games in Rome. ("No wonder we've
never heard of him," Cicero remarked to me afterwards.) His work
brought him often to the city. He had been appalled, he claimed,
by the violence and intimidation unleashed by Clodius. He had
wept to see Cicero harried and pilloried and eventually driven from
Rome. Given his occupation, he fancied himself to be in a unique
position to help restore order, and through intermediaries he had
approached Pompey with an offer.

"What I am about to disclose is in the strictest confidence," he
said, with a sideways glance at me. "No word of it must go beyond
us three."

"Who am I to tell?" retorted Cicero. "The slave who empties my
chamber pot? The cook who brings my meals? I assure you I see
no one else."

"Very well," said Milo, and then he told us what he had offered
Pompey: to place at his disposal one hundred pairs of highly trained

fighting men to recapture the centre of Rome and end Clodius's control of the legislative assembly. In return he had asked for a certain sum to cover expenses, and also Pompey's support in the elections for tribune: "I couldn't just do this as a private citizen, you understand—I'd be prosecuted. I told him I needed the invio-lability of the office."

Cicero was studying him closely. He had barely touched his food. "And what did Pompey say to that?"

"At first he brushed me off. He said he'd think about it. But then came the business with the Prince of Armenia, when Papirius was killed by Clodius's men. Did you hear about that?"

"We heard something of it."

"Well, the killing of his friend seemed to make Pompey do that bit of extra thinking, because the day after Papirius was put on the pyre, he called me to his house. 'That idea of your becoming tribune—you've got yourself a deal.'"

"And how has Clodius reacted to your election? He must know what you have in mind."

"Well, that's why I'm here. And this you won't have heard about, because I left Rome straight after it happened, and no messenger could have got here quicker than I." He stopped and held out his cup for more wine. He had come a long way to tell his story; he was obviously a raconteur; he meant to do it in his own time. "It was about two weeks ago, not long after the elections. Pompey was doing a little business in the Forum when he ran into a gang of Clodius's men. There was some pushing and shoving, and one of them dropped a dagger. A lot of people saw it, and a great shout went up that they were going to murder Pompey. His attendants hustled him out of there fast, and back to his house, and barricaded him in—and that's where he is still, as far as I know, with only the Lady Julia for company."

Cicero said in astonishment, "Pompey the Great is barricaded in his own house?"

"I don't blame you if you find it funny. Who wouldn't? There's rough justice in it, and Pompey knows it. In fact he said to me that the greatest mistake of his life was letting Clodius drive you out of the city."

"Pompey said that?"

"That's why I've raced across three countries, barely stopping to eat or sleep—to give you the news that he's going to do everything he can to get your exile overturned. His blood is up. He wants you back in Rome, you and me and him, fighting side by side, to save the republic from Clodius and his gang! What do you say to that?"

He was like a dog that has just laid a kill at its master's feet; if he'd had a tail, it would have been thumping against the fabric of the couch. But if Milo had expected either delight or gratitude, he was to be disappointed. Depressed in spirit and ragged in appearance though he might be, Cicero had nevertheless seen straight through to the heart of the matter. He swilled his wine around in his cup, frowning before he spoke.

"And does Caesar agree to this?"

"Ah now," said Milo, shifting slightly on his couch, "that's for you to settle with him. Pompey will play his part, but you must play yours. It would be hard for him to campaign to bring you back if Caesar were to object very strongly."

"So he wants me to reconcile with him?"

"His word was to *reassure* him."

It had grown dark while we were talking. The household slaves had lit lamps around the perimeter of the garden; their gleams were clouded with moths. But no light was on the table, so I couldn't properly make out Cicero's expression. He was silent for a long while. It was terrifically hot as usual, and I was conscious of the night sounds of Macedonia—the cicadas and the mosquitoes, the occasional dog bark, the voices of local people in the street, speaking in their strange, harsh foreign tongue. I wondered if Cicero was thinking the same as I was—that another year in such a place as this would kill him. Perhaps he was, because eventually he let out a sigh of resignation and said, "And in what terms am I supposed to 'reassure' him?"

"That's up to you. If any man can find the right words, it's you.

But Caesar has made it clear to Pompey that he needs something in writing before he'll even think of reconsidering his position."

"Am I supposed to give you a document to take back to Rome?"

"No, this part of the arrangement has to be between you and Caesar. Pompey thinks it would be best if you sent your own private emissary to Gaul—someone you trust, who could deliver some form of written undertaking into Caesar's hands personally."

Caesar—everything seemed to come back to him eventually. I thought again of the sound of his trumpets leaving the Field of Mars, and in the stifling gloom I sensed rather than saw that both men had turned to look at me.

# II

———•◦•———

HOW EASY IT IS FOR THOSE WHO PLAY NO PART IN PUBLIC AFFAIRS to sneer at the compromises required of those who do. For two years Cicero had stuck to his principles and refused to join with Caesar, Pompey and Crassus in their "triumvirate" to control the state. He had denounced their criminality in public; they had retaliated by making it possible for Clodius to become a tribune; and when Caesar had offered him a legateship in Gaul that would have given him legal immunity from Clodius's attacks, Cicero had refused it, because acceptance would have made him Caesar's creature.

But the price of upholding those principles had been banishment, poverty and heartbreak. "I have made myself powerless," he said to me, after Milo had gone off to bed, leaving us alone to discuss Pompey's offer, "and where is the virtue in that? What use am I to my family or my principles stuck in this dump for the rest of my life? Oh, no doubt one day I could become some kind of shining example to be taught to bored pupils: the man who refused ever to compromise his conscience. Perhaps after I'm safely dead they might even put up a statue of me at the back of the rostra. But I don't want to be a monument. My skill is statecraft, and that requires me to be alive and in Rome." He fell silent. "Then again, the thought of having to bend the knee to Caesar is scarcely bearable. To have suffered all this, and then to have to go creeping back to him like some dog that's learnt its lesson . . ."

He was still undecided when he retired for the night, and the following morning, when Milo called to ask him what answer he should take back to Pompey, I could not have predicted what he would say. "You can tell him this," responded Cicero. "That my whole life has been dedicated to the service of the state, and that if the state demands of me that I should reconcile with my enemy— then reconcile I shall."

Milo embraced him and then immediately set off back to the coast in his war chariot with his gladiator standing beside him— such a pair of brutes longing for a fight that one could only tremble for Rome and all the blood that was bound to be spilt.

IT WAS SETTLED THAT I SHOULD LEAVE THESSALONICA ON MY mission to Caesar at the end of the summer, as soon as the military campaigning season was over. To have set off before then would have been pointless, as Caesar was with his legions deep inside Gaul, and his habit of rapid forced marches made it impossible to say with any certainty where he might be.

Cicero spent many hours working on his letter. Years later, after his death, our copy was seized by the authorities, along with all the other correspondence between Cicero and Caesar, presumably in case it contradicted the official history that the Dictator was a genius and that all who opposed him were stupid, greedy, ungrateful, short-sighted and reactionary. I assume it has been destroyed; at any rate, I have never heard of it since. However, I still possess my shorthand notes, covering most of the thirty-six years I worked for Cicero—such a vast mass of unintelligible hieroglyphics that the ignorant operatives who ransacked my archive doubtless assumed them to be harmless gibberish and left them untouched. It is from these that I have been able to reconstruct the many conversations, speeches and letters that make up this memoir of Cicero— including his humiliating appeal to Caesar that summer, which is not lost after all.

*Thessalonica*

*From M. Cicero to G. Caesar, Proconsul, greetings.*

*I hope you and the army are well.*

*Many misunderstandings have unfortunately arisen between us in recent years but there is one in particular which, if it exists, I wish to dispel. I have never wavered in my admiration for your qualities of intelligence, resourcefulness, patriotism, energy and command. You have justly risen to a position of great eminence in our republic, and I wish only to see your efforts crowned with success both on the battlefield and in the counsels of state, as I am sure they will be.*

*Do you remember, Caesar, that day when I was consul, when we debated in the Senate the punishment of those five traitors who were plotting the destruction of the republic, including my own murder? Tempers were high. Violence was in the air. Each man distrusted his neighbour. Suspicion even unjustly fell upon you, astonishingly, and had I not intervened, the flower of your glory might have been cut off before it had a chance to bloom. You know this to be true; swear otherwise if you dare.*

*The wheel of fate has now reversed our positions, but with this difference: I am not a young man now, as you were then, with golden prospects. My career is over. If the Roman people were ever to vote for my return from exile, I should not seek any office. I should not put myself at the head of any party or faction, especially one injurious to your interests. I should not seek to overturn any of the legislation enacted during your consulship. In what little earthly time remains to me, my life will be devoted solely to restoring the fortunes of my poor family, supporting my friends in the law courts, and rendering such service as I can to the well-being of the commonwealth. On this you may rest assured.*

*I am sending you this letter via my confidential secretary M. Tiro, whom you may remember, and who can be relied upon to convey in confidence any reply you may wish to make.*

"Well, there it is," said Cicero, when it was finished, "a shameful document, and yet if one day it were to be read aloud in court, I don't believe I would need to blush too deeply." He copied it out carefully in his own hand, sealed it and handed it to me. "Keep your eyes open, Tiro. Observe how he seems and who is with him. I want an exact account. If he asks after my condition, hesitate, speak with reluctance, and then confide that I am utterly broken in body and spirit. The more certain he is I'm finished, the more likely he is to let me return."

By the time the letter was done, our situation had in fact become much more precarious again. In Rome, the senior consul, Lucius Calpurnius Piso, who was Caesar's father-in-law and an enemy of Cicero's, had been awarded the governorship of Macedonia in a public vote rigged by Clodius. He would take office at the start of the new year: an advance guard from his staff was expected in the province shortly. If they caught Cicero they might kill him on the spot. Another door was starting to close on us. My departure could no longer be put off.

I dreaded the emotion of our parting, and so, I knew, did Cicero; therefore we colluded to avoid it. On the night before I left, when we had dined together for the final time, he pretended to be tired and retired to bed early, while I assured him I would wake him in the morning to say a final goodbye. In fact I slipped away before dawn, while the house was still in darkness, without a fuss, as he would have wanted.

Plancius had arranged an escort to conduct me back over the mountains to Dyrrachium, and there I took ship and sailed to Italy—not straight across to Brundisium this time, but northwest, to Ancona. It was a much longer voyage than our original crossing and took almost a week. But it was still quicker than going overland, with the added advantage that I would not encounter any of Clodius's agents. I had never before travelled such a long distance on my own, let alone by ship. My terror of the sea was not the same as Cicero's—of shipwreck and of drowning. It was rather of the vast emptiness of the horizon during the day and the glittering, indifferent hugeness of the universe at night. I was at this time forty-six, and conscious of the void into which we all are voyaging; I thought of death often while sitting out on deck. I had witnessed so much; ageing in body though I was, in spirit I was even older. Little did I realise that actually I had lived less than half my life, and was destined to see things that would make all the wonders and dramas that had gone before seem quite pallid and insignificant.

The weather was favourable, and we landed at Ancona without incident. From there I took the road north, crossing the Rubicon two days later and formally entering the province of Nearer Gaul. This was territory familiar to me: I had toured it with Cicero six years earlier, when he was seeking election as consul and canvassing the towns along the Via Aemilia. The vineyards beside the road had all been harvested weeks before; now the vines were being cut back for winter, so that as far as one could see, columns of white smoke from the burning vegetation were rising over the flat terrain, as if some retreating army had scorched the earth behind it.

In the little town of Claterna, where I stayed the night, I learned that the governor had returned from beyond the Alps and had set up his winter headquarters in Placentia, but that with typical restless energy he was already touring the countryside holding assizes: he was due in the neighbouring town of Mutina the next day. I left early, reached it at noon, passed through the heavily fortified walls, and made for the basilica on the forum. The only clue to Caesar's presence was a troop of legionaries at the entrance. They made no attempt to ask my business, and I went straight inside. A cold grey light from the clerestory windows fell upon a hushed queue of citizens waiting to present their petitions. At the far end—too far away for me to make out his face—seated between pillars, dispensing judgement from his magistrate's chair, in a toga so white it stood out brightly amid the locals' drab winter plumage, was Caesar.

Uncertain how to approach him, I found myself joining the line of petitioners. Caesar was issuing his rulings at such a rate that we shuffled forwards almost continuously, and as I drew closer I saw that he was doing several things at once—listening to each supplicant, reading documents as they were handed to him by a secretary, and conferring with an army officer who had taken off his helmet and was bending down to whisper in his ear. I took out Cicero's letter so that I would have it ready. But then it struck me that this was not perhaps the proper place to hand over the appeal: that it was unconducive somehow to the dignity of a former consul for his request to be considered alongside the domestic complaints of all these farmers and tradespeople, worthy folk though they no doubt were. The officer finished his report, straightened, and was just walking past me towards the door, fastening his helmet, when his eyes met mine and he stopped in surprise. "Tiro?"

I glimpsed his father in him before I could put a name to the young man himself. It was M. Crassus's son, Publius, now a cavalry commander on Caesar's staff. Unlike his father he was a cultured, gracious, noble man, and an admirer of Cicero, whose company he used to seek out. He greeted me with great affability—"What brings you to Mutina?"—and when I told him, he volunteered at once to arrange a private interview with Caesar and insisted I accompany him to the villa where the governor and his entourage were staying.

"I'm doubly glad to see you," he said as we walked, "for I've often thought of Cicero, and the injustice done to him. I've talked to my father about it and persuaded him not to oppose his recall. And Pompey, as you know, supports it too—only last week he sent Sestius, one of the tribunes-elect, up here to plead his cause with Caesar."

I could not help observing, "It seems that everything these days depends upon Caesar."

"Well, you have to understand his position. He feels no personal animosity towards your master—very much the opposite. But unlike my father and Pompey, he's not in Rome to defend himself. He's concerned about losing political support while his back is turned, and being recalled before his work here is complete. He sees Cicero as the greatest threat to his position. Come inside—let me show you something."

We passed the sentry and went into the house, and Publius con-ducted me through the crowded public rooms to a small library where, from an ivory casket, he produced a series of dispatches, all beautifully edged in black and housed in purple slip-cases, with the word *Commentaries* picked out in vermilion in the title line.

"These are Caesar's own personal copies," Publius explained, handling them carefully. "He takes them with him wherever he goes. They are his record of the campaign in Gaul, which he has decided to send regularly to be posted up in Rome. One day he intends to collect them all together and publish them as a book. It's perfectly marvellous stuff. See for yourself."

He plucked out a roll for me to read:

There is a river called the Saone, which flows through the territories of the Aedui and Sequani into the Rhone with such incredible slowness that it cannot be determined by the eye in which direction it flows. This the Helvetii were crossing by rafts and boats joined together. When Caesar was informed by spies that the Helvetii had already con-veyed three parts of their forces across that river, but that the fourth part was left behind on this side of the Saone, he set out from the camp with three legions. Attacking them, encumbered with baggage, and not expecting him, he cut to pieces a great part of them ...

I said, "He writes of himself with wonderful detachment."

"He does. That's because he doesn't want to sound boastful. It's important to strike the right note."

I asked if I might be allowed to copy some of it, and show it to Cicero. "He misses the regular news from Rome. What reaches us is sparse, and late."

"Of course—it's all public information. And I'll make sure you get in to see Caesar. You'll find he's in a tremendously good mood."

He left me alone and I settled to work.

Even allowing for a degree of exaggeration, it was plain from the

*Commentaries* that Caesar had enjoyed an astonishing run of military successes. His original mission had been to halt the migration of the Helvetii and four other tribes who were trekking westwards across Gaul to the Atlantic in search of new territory. He had followed their immense column, which consisted both of fighting men and of the elderly and women and children, with a new army he had mostly raised himself of five legions. Finally he had lured them into battle at Bibracte. As a guarantee to his new legions that neither he nor his officers would abandon them if things went wrong, he had all their horses sent far away to the rear. They fought on foot with the infantry, and in the event Caesar, by his own account, did not merely halt the Helvetii—he slaughtered them. Afterwards a list giving the total strength of the migration had been discovered in the enemy's abandoned camp:

| | |
|---|---|
| Helvetii | 263,000 |
| Tulingi | 36,000 |
| Latobrigi | 14,000 |
| Rauraci | 23,000 |
| Boii | 32,000 |
| | 368,000 |

Of these, according to Caesar, the total number who returned alive to their former homeland was 110,000.

Then—and this was what no one else surely would have dreamed of attempting—he had force-marched his weary legions back across Gaul to confront 120,000 Germans who had taken advantage of the Helvetii's migration to cross into Roman-controlled territory. There had been another terrific battle, lasting seven hours, in which young Crassus had commanded the cavalry, and by the end of it the Germans had been entirely annihilated. Hardly any had been left alive to flee back across the Rhine, which for the first time became the natural frontier of the Roman Empire. Thus, if Caesar's account was to be believed, almost one third of a million people had either died or disappeared in the space of a single summer. To round off the year, he had left his legions in their new winter camp, a full one hundred miles north of the old border of Further Gaul.

By the time I had finished my copying it was beginning to get dark, but the villa was still noisy with activity—soldiers and civilians wanting an appointment with the governor, messengers rushing in and out. As I could no longer see to write, I put away my tablet and stylus and sat in the gloom. I wondered what Cicero would have made of it all had he been in Rome. To have condemned the victories would have seemed unpatriotic; at the same time, such sweeping cleansing of populations and adjustments to the frontier, without the authorisation of the Senate, were illegal. I also pondered what Publius Crassus had said: that Caesar feared Cicero's presence in Rome lest he be "recalled before his work here is complete." What did "complete" mean in this context? The phrase seemed ominous.

My reverie was interrupted by the arrival of a young officer, barely more than thirty, with tight blond curls and an improbably immaculate uniform, who introduced himself as Caesar's aide-de-camp, Aulus Hirtius. He said that he understood I had a letter for the governor from Cicero, and that if I would be so kind as to give it to him, he would see that he received it. I replied that I was under firm instructions to give it to Caesar personally. He said that was impossible. I said that in that case I would follow the governor from town to town until such time as I got the chance to speak to him. Hirtius scowled at me and tapped his neatly shod foot, then went away again. An hour passed before he reappeared and curtly asked me to follow him.

The public part of the house was still thronged with callers, even though it was now night-time. We went down a passage, through a stout door and into a warm, heavily scented, thickly carpeted room, brilliantly lit by a hundred candles, in the centre of which on a table lay Caesar, flat on his back and entirely naked, having oil worked into his skin by a Negro masseur. He glanced at me briefly and held out his hand. I gave Cicero's letter to Hirtius, who broke the seal and handed it to Caesar. I directed my gaze to the floor as a mark of respect.

Caesar said, "How was your journey?"

I replied, "Good, Excellency, thank you."

"And are you being looked after?"

"I am, thank you."

I dared then to look at him properly for the first time. His body was glistening, well muscled, and plucked entirely hairless in every respect—a disconcerting affectation which had the effect of emphasising his numerous scars and bruises, presumably picked up on the battlefield. His face was undeniably striking—angular and lean, dominated by dark and penetrating eyes. The overall effect was one of great power, of both the intellect and the will. One could see why men and women alike fell easily under his spell. He was then in his forty-third year.

He turned on to his side towards me—there was no spare flesh, I noticed: his stomach was entirely hard—propped himself up on his elbow and gestured to Hirtius, who produced a portable inkstand and carried it over to him.

He said, "And how is Cicero's health?"

"It's very poor, I'm afraid."

He laughed. "Oh no, I don't believe a word of *that*! He'll outlive us all—or me, at any rate."

He dipped his pen in the inkpot, scrawled something on the letter, and gave it back to Hirtius, who sprinkled sand on the wet ink, blew away the residue, rolled the document up again, and returned it to me without expression.

Caesar said, "If you need anything during your stay, be sure to ask." He lay on his back once more and the masseur resumed his kneading.

I hesitated. I had come such a long way. I felt there should be something more, if only by way of an anecdote for me to take back to Cicero. But Hirtius touched my arm and nodded towards the door.

As I reached it, Caesar called after me, "Do you still practise that shorthand of yours?"

"I do."

He made no further comment. The door closed and I followed Hirtius back up the passage. My heart was pounding, as if I had survived a sudden fall. It wasn't until I had been shown to the room where I was to sleep overnight that I thought to check what he had written on the letter. Two words only—either elegantly brief or typically contemptuous, depending on how you chose to interpret them: *Approved. Caesar.*

WHEN I ROSE THE FOLLOWING MORNING, THE HOUSE WAS SILENT; Caesar had already left with his entourage for the next town. My mission concluded, I too set off on my long return journey.

When I reached the harbour at Ancona, I found a letter from Cicero waiting for me: the first of Piso's soldiers had just arrived in Thessalonica and therefore as a precaution he was departing immediately for Dyrrachium—which, as it lies in the province of Illyricum, was beyond Piso's influence. He hoped to meet me there. Depending on Caesar's answer and on developments in Rome, we would then decide where to go next: *Like Callisto, it seems we are doomed to wander throughout eternity.*

I had to wait ten days for a favourable wind and did not reach Dyrrachium until the festival of Saturnalia. The City Fathers had placed at Cicero's disposal a well-defended house up in the hills with a view across the sea, and this was where I found him, gazing at the Adriatic. He turned at my approach. I had forgotten how much exile had aged him. My dismay must have shown in my expression, because his own face fell the moment he saw me, and he said bitterly, "So I take it the answer was no?"

"On the contrary."

I showed him his original letter with Caesar's scrawl in the margin. He held it in his hands and studied it for a long while.

"'Approved. Caesar,'" he said. "Will you look at that? 'Approved.

Caesar'! He's doing something he doesn't want to do and he's as sulky about it as a child."

He sat on a bench under an umbrella pine and made me recount my visit in every detail, and then he read the extracts I had copied from Caesar's *Commentaries*. When he had finished, he said, "He writes very well in his brutal way. Such artlessness requires some art—it will add to his reputation. But where will his campaigning take him next, I wonder? He could grow strong—very strong. If Pompey is not careful, he will wake up to find a monster on his back."

THERE WAS NOTHING WE COULD DO NOW BUT WAIT, AND whenever I think of Cicero at this time, I always picture him in the same way: on that terrace, leaning over the balustrade, a letter bearing the latest news from Rome clenched in his hand, staring grimly at the horizon, as if somehow by sheer willpower he could see all the way to Italy and impose himself on events.

First we heard from Atticus of the swearing-in of the new tribunes, eight of whom were Cicero's supporters and only two his declared enemies—but two was enough to impose a veto on any law repealing his exile. Then from Cicero's brother, Quintus, we learned that Milo, as tribune, had brought a prosecution against Clodius for violence and intimidation, and that Clodius's response had been to order his bullies to attack Milo's house. On New Year's Day the new consuls took office. One, Lentulus Spinther, was already a firm supporter of Cicero. The other, Metellus Nepos, had long been considered his enemy. But someone must have got at him, because in the inaugural debate of the new Senate, Nepos declared that while he still did not care for Cicero personally, he would not oppose his recall. Two days later, a motion to repeal Cicero's exile, drawn up by Pompey, was laid by the Senate before the people.

At that moment it was possible to believe that Cicero's banishment would soon be over, and I began to make discreet preparations for our departure to Italy. But Clodius was a resourceful and vindictive enemy. On the night before the people were due to meet, he and his supporters occupied the Forum, the comitium, the rostra—in sum, the whole legislative heart of the republic— and when Cicero's friends and allies arrived to vote, they attacked them without mercy. Two tribunes, Fabricius and Cispius, were set upon and their attendants murdered and flung in the Tiber. When Quintus tried to get up on to the rostra, he was dragged off and beaten up so badly he only survived by pretending to be dead. Milo responded by unleashing his own squad of gladiators. Soon the centre of Rome was a battlefield, and the fighting went on for days. But although Clodius for the first time suffered severe punish- ment, he was not entirely driven out, and he still had the two tri- bunes with their vetoes. The law to bring Cicero home had to be abandoned.

When Cicero received Atticus's account of what had happened, he fell into a despair almost as great as that which had gripped him in Thessalonica. *From your letter,* he wrote back, *and from the facts themselves I see that I am utterly finished. In matters where my family needs your help I beg you not to fail us in our misery.*

However, there is always this to be said for politics: it is never static. If the good times do not last, neither do the bad. Like Nature, it follows a perpetual cycle of growth and decay, and no states- man, however cunning, is immune to this process. If Clodius had not been so arrogant, reckless and ambitious, he never would have achieved the heights he did. But being all those things, and subject to the laws of politics, he was bound to overreach and topple even- tually.

In the spring, during the Festival of Flora, when Rome was crowded with visitors from all over Italy, Clodius's mob found itself for once outnumbered by ordinary citizens who despised their bullying tactics. Clodius himself was actually jeered at the theatre. Unused to anything other than adulation from the peo- ple, according to Atticus he looked around him in astonishment at the slow handclapping, taunts, whistles and obscene gestures, and realised—almost too late—that he was in danger of being lynched.

He retreated hastily, and that was the beginning of the end of his domination, for the Senate now recognised how he could be beaten: by appealing over the heads of the urban plebs to the population at large.

Spinther duly laid a motion calling for the entire citizenry of the republic to be summoned together in its most sovereign body, the electoral college of one hundred and ninety-three centuries, and for them to determine the fate of Cicero once and for all. The motion passed in the Senate by four hundred and thirteen votes to one, the one being Clodius. It was further agreed that the vote on Cicero's recall should take place at the same time as the summer elections, when the centuries would already be assembled on the Field of Mars.

The moment he heard what had been decided, Cicero was so certain he was reprieved he arranged for a sacrifice to be made to the gods. Those tens of thousands of ordinary citizens from across Italy were the solid, sensible foundation on which he had built his career; he was sure they would not let him down. He sent word to his wife and family asking them to meet him in Brundisium, and rather than lingering in Illyricum to await the result, which would take two weeks to reach us, he decided to sail for home on the day the vote was held. "If there is a tide flowing in one's direction, one must catch it early, and not allow it time to ebb. Besides, it will look good if I show confidence."

"If the vote goes against you, you will be breaking the law by returning to Italy."

"But it won't. The Roman people will never vote to keep me in exile—and if they do, well, there's no point in going on, is there?"

And so, fifteen months to the day after we had landed in Dyrra-chium, we went down to the harbour to begin the journey back to life. Cicero had shaved off his beard and cut his hair and had put on a white toga with the purple stripe of a senator. As chance would have it, our return crossing was on the same merchant ship that had brought us over. But the contrast between the two journeys could not have been more marked. This time we skimmed across a flat sea all day with a favourable wind, spent the night lying out on the open deck, and the following morning came in sight of Brundisium. The entrance to the greatest harbour in Italy opens like an immense pair of outstretched arms, and as we passed between the booms and approached the crowded quayside, it felt as if we were being clasped to the heart of a dear and long-lost friend. The whole town seemed to be at the harbour and *en fête,* with pipes and drums playing, young girls carrying flowers, and youths waving boughs decorated with coloured ribbons.

I thought they were for Cicero, and said so in great excitement, but he cut me off and told me not to be a fool. "How would they have known we were coming? Besides, have you forgotten everything? Today is the anniversary of the founding of the colony of Brundisium, and therefore a local holiday. You would have known that once, when I was running for office."

Nevertheless, some of the people had noticed his senatorial toga and quickly realised who he was. The word was passed. Soon a sizeable crowd was shouting his name and cheering. Cicero, standing on the upper deck as we glided towards our berth, raised his hand in acknowledgement and turned this way and that so all could see him. Among the multitude I spotted his daughter, Tullia. She was waving with the rest and calling out to him, even jumping up and down to attract his attention. But Cicero was sunning himself in the applause, his eyes half closed, like a prisoner released from a dungeon into the light, and in the noise and tumult of the crowd he did not see her.

# III

---·•·---

THAT CICERO DID NOT RECOGNISE HIS ONLY DAUGHTER WAS LESS peculiar than it may seem. She had changed greatly in the time we had been away. Her face and arms, once plump and girlish, were thin and pale; her fair hair was covered by the dark headdress of mourning. The day of our arrival was her twentieth birthday, although I am ashamed to say that I had forgotten it and so had failed to remind Cicero.

His first act on stepping down from the gangplank was to kneel and kiss the soil. Only after this patriotic act had been loudly cheered did he look up and notice his daughter watching him in her widow's weeds. He stared at her and burst into tears, for he truly loved her, and he had loved her husband too, and now he saw by the colour and style of her dress that he was dead.

He enfolded her in his arms, to the crowd's delight, and after a long embrace took a step back to examine her. "My dearest child, you cannot imagine how much I have yearned for this moment." Still holding her hands, he switched his gaze to the faces behind her and scanned them eagerly. "Is you mother here, and Marcus?"

"No, Papa, they're in Rome."

This was hardly surprising—in those days it was an arduous journey, especially for a woman, of two or three weeks from Rome to Brundisium, with a serious risk of robbery in the remoter stretches; if anything, the surprise was that Tullia *had* come, and come alone at that. But Cicero's disappointment was obvious although he tried to hide it.

"Well, it's no matter—no matter at all. I have you, and that's the main thing."

"And I have you—and on my birthday."

"It's your birthday?" He gave me a reproachful look. "I almost forgot. Of course it is. We shall celebrate tonight!" And he took her by the arm and led her away from the harbour.

Because we did not yet know for certain that his exile had been repealed, it was decided that we should not set off for Rome until we had official confirmation, and once again Laenius Flaccus volunteered to put us up at his estate outside Brundisium. Armed men were stationed around the perimeter for Cicero's protection, and he spent much of the next few days with Tullia, strolling through the gardens and along the beach, learning at first hand how difficult her life had been during his exile—how, for example, her husband, Frugi, had been set upon by Clodius's henchmen when he was trying to speak on Cicero's behalf, stripped naked and pelted with filth and driven from the Forum, and how his heart had ceased to beat properly afterwards until, a few months later, he died in her arms; how, because she was childless, she had been left with nothing except a few pieces of jewellery and her returned dowry, which she had given to Terentia to help pay off the family's debts; how Terentia had been obliged to sell a large part of her own property, and had even steeled herself to plead with Clodius's sister to intercede with her brother to grant her and her children some mercy, and how Clodia had mocked her and boasted that Cicero had tried to have an affair with her; how families they had always thought of as friends had closed their doors on them in fear; and so on and so forth.

Cicero told me all this sadly one night after Tullia had gone to bed. "Little wonder Terentia isn't here. It seems she avoids going out in public as much as she can and prefers to stay cooped up in my brother's house. As for Tullia, we need to find her a new husband as soon as possible, while she's still young enough to give a man some children safely." He rubbed his temples, as he always did at times of stress. "I'd thought that coming back to Italy would mark the end of my troubles. Now I see it is merely the beginning."

It was on our sixth day as Flaccus's guests that a messenger arrived from Quintus with the news that despite a last-minute demonstration by Clodius and his mob, the centuries had voted unanimously to restore to Cicero his full rights of citizenship, and that he was accordingly a free man once more. Oddly, the news did not seem to give him much joy, and when I remarked on his indifference he replied: "Why should I rejoice? I have merely had returned to me something that should never have been taken away in the first place. Otherwise, I am weaker than I was before."

We began our journey to Rome the next day. By then the news of his rehabilitation had spread among the people of Brundisium, and a crowd of several hundred had gathered outside the gates of the villa to see him off. He got down from the carriage he was sharing with Tullia, greeted each well-wisher with a handshake, made a short speech, and then we resumed our journey. But we had not gone more than five miles when we encountered another large group at the next settlement, also clamouring for the opportunity to shake his hand. Once again he obliged. And so it went on throughout that day, and the days that followed, always the same, except that the crowds grew steadily larger as word preceded us that Cicero would be passing through. Soon people were coming from miles around, even walking down from the mountains to stand by the roadside. By the time we reached Beneventum, the numbers were in their thousands; in Capua, the streets were entirely blocked.

To begin with, Cicero was touched by these unfeigned demonstrations of affection, then delighted, then amazed, and finally thoughtful. Was there some means, he wondered, of turning this astonishing popularity among the ordinary citizens of Italy into political influence in Rome? But popularity and power, as he well knew, are separate entities. Often the most powerful men in a state can pass down a street unrecognised, while the most famous bask in feted impotence.

This was brought home to us soon after we left Campania, when Cicero decided we should call in at Formiae and inspect his villa on the seashore. He knew from Terentia and Atticus that it had been attacked, and was braced to find a ruin. In fact, when we turned off the Via Appia and entered the grounds, the shuttered property appeared perfectly intact, albeit the Greek statuary had gone. The garden was neatly tended. Peacocks still strutted between the trees and we could hear the distant motion of the sea. As the carriage halted and Cicero climbed out, members of the household began to materialise from various parts of the property, as if they had been in hiding. Seeing their master again, they flung themselves to the ground, crying with relief. But when he began to move towards the front door, several tried to block his path, pleading with him not to go inside. He gestured to them to move out of the way and ordered the door to be unlocked.

The first shock to confront us was the smell—of smoke and damp and human waste. And then there was the sound—empty and echoing, broken only by the crunch of plaster and pottery beneath our feet, and the cooing of the pigeons in the rafters. As the shutters started to come down, the summer afternoon sunlight revealed a vista of room after room stripped bare. Tullia put her hand to her mouth in horror and Cicero gently told her to go and wait in the carriage. We moved on into the interior. All the furniture was gone, all the pictures, the fixtures. Here and there sections of the ceilings were hanging down; even the mosaic floors had been prised up and carted away; weeds grew out of bare earth amid the bird shit and human faeces. The walls were scorched where fires had been lit, and covered with the most obscene drawings and graffiti, all executed in dripping red paint.

In the dining room a rat scuttled along the side of the wall and squeezed itself down a hole. Cicero watched it disappear with a look of infinite disgust on his face. Then he marched out of the house, clambered back into his carriage, and ordered the driver to rejoin the Via Appia. He did not speak for at least an hour.

Two days later we reached Bovillae, on the outskirts of Rome.


WE WOKE THE NEXT MORNING TO FIND YET ANOTHER CROWD waiting to escort us into the city. As we stepped out into the heat of that summer morning, I was apprehensive: the state of the villa at Formiae had unnerved me. It was also the eve of the Roman Games, a public holiday. The streets would be packed, and reports had already reached us of a shortage of bread that had led to rioting. I was sure Clodius would use the pretext of the disorder to attempt some kind of ambush. But Cicero was calm. He believed the people would protect him. He asked for the roof to be removed from the carriage, and with Tullia holding a parasol seated beside him, and me stationed up on the bench next to the driver, we set off.

I do not exaggerate when I say that every yard of the Via Appia was lined with citizens and that for nearly two hours we were borne northwards on a wave of continuous applause. Where the road passes over the River Almo, by the Temple of the Great Mother, the crowd was three or four deep. Further on, they occupied the steps of the Temple of Mars so densely it resembled a stand at the games. And just outside the city walls, along that stretch where the aqueduct runs beside the highway, young men were perched precariously on the tops of the arches, or clinging to the palm trees. They waved, and Cicero waved back. The din and the heat and the dust were terrific. Eventually we were forced to a halt just outside the Capena Gate, where the press of humanity was simply too great for us to go on.

I jumped down with the intention of opening the door, and tried to push my way round to the side of the carriage. But a surge of people, desperate to get closer to Cicero, pinned me against it so hard I could neither move nor breathe. The carriage shifted and threatened to topple, and I do believe that Cicero might have been killed by an excess of love just ten paces short of Rome, had not his brother, Quintus, appeared at that moment from the recesses of the gate along with a dozen attendants who pushed the crowd back and cleared a space for Cicero to descend.

It was four years since the two had last met, and Quintus no longer appeared the younger brother. His nose had been broken during the fighting in the Forum. He was obviously drinking too much. He looked like a beaten-down old boxer. He held out his arms to Cicero and they locked hold of one another, unable to speak for emotion, tears pouring down their cheeks, each silently pounding the back of the other.

When they separated, Quintus told him what he had arranged, and then we entered the city on foot, Cicero and Quintus walking hand in hand, with Tullia and me behind them, a file of attendants on either side. Quintus, who used to be Cicero's campaign manager, had devised the route in order to show off his brother to as many supporters as possible. We passed the Circus Maximus, its flags already flying in anticipation of the games, and as we progressed slowly along the crowded valley between the Palatine and the Caelian hills, it seemed as if everyone Cicero had ever represented in the law courts, or helped out with a favour, or even just shaken hands with at election time had come out to bid him welcome. Even so, I noticed that not all were cheering, and that here and there small groups of sullen plebeians scowled at us or turned their backs, especially as we drew close to the Temple of Castor, where Clodius had his headquarters. Fresh slogans had been daubed across it, in the same angry red paint that had been used at Formiae: *M. CICERO STEALS THE PEOPLE'S BREAD; WHEN THE PEOPLE ARE HUNGRY THEY KNOW WHO TO BLAME.* One man spat at us. Another slyly drew back the folds of his tunic to show me his knife. Cicero affected not to notice.

A crowd of several thousand cheered us all the way across the Forum and up the Capitoline steps to the Temple of Jupiter, where a fine white bull was waiting to be sacrificed. At every moment I feared an assault, despite my reason telling me it would have been suicidal: any attacker would have been torn apart by Cicero's supporters, even assuming he could have got close enough to strike a blow. Nevertheless, I would have preferred it if we could have got into a place with walls and a door. But that was impossible: on this day Cicero belonged to Rome. First we had to listen to the priests recite their prayers, then Cicero had to cover his head and step forward to deliver his ritual thanks to the gods, and stand and watch while the beast was killed and its entrails examined until the auspices were pronounced propitious. Then he entered the temple and laid offerings at the feet of a small statue of Minerva he had placed there before his exile. Finally, when he emerged, he was surrounded by many of those senators who had campaigned hardest for his restoration—Sestius, Cestilius, Curtius, the Cispius brothers and the rest, led by the senior consul, Lentulus Spinther—each of whom had to be thanked individually. Many were the tears shed and the kisses exchanged, and it must have been well after noon before he was able to start walking home, and even then Spinther and the others insisted on accompanying him; Tullia, unnoticed by any of us, had already gone on ahead.

"Home" of course was no longer his own fine mansion on the slopes of the Palatine: looking up, I could see that it had been entirely demolished to make room for Clodius's shrine to Liberty. Instead we were to be lodged just below it, in the house of Quintus, where we would live until such time as Cicero could get the site restored to him and begin rebuilding. This street, too, was packed with well-wishers, and Cicero had to struggle to reach the threshold. Beyond it, in the shade of the courtyard, waited his wife and children.

I knew, because he had so often spoken of it, how much Cicero had looked forward to this moment. And yet there was an awkwardness to it that made me want to hide my face. Terentia, decked out in her finery, had plainly been waiting for him for several hours, and in the interim little Marcus had grown bored and fretful. "So, husband," she said, with a thin smile, tugging savagely at the boy to make him stand up properly, "you are home at last! Go and greet your father," she instructed Marcus, and pushed him forwards, but immediately he darted around her and hid behind her skirts. Cicero stopped some distance short, his arms outstretched to the boy, uncertain how to respond, and in the end the situation was only retrieved by Tullia, who ran to her father, kissed him, led him over to her mother and gently pressed her parents together, and in this way at last the family was reunited.

QUINTUS'S VILLA WAS LARGE, BUT NOT SUFFICIENTLY SPACIOUS TO accommodate two full households in any comfort, and from that first day there was friction. Out of respect for his brother's superior age and rank, Quintus, with typical generosity, had insisted that Cicero and Terentia should take over the master's quarters, which he usually shared with his wife, Pomponia, the sister of Atticus. It was clear she had objected bitterly to this, and could barely bring herself to give Cicero a civil greeting.

It is not my intention to dwell on personal gossip: such matters fall beneath the dignity of my subject. Nevertheless, I cannot give a proper account of Cicero's life without mentioning what happened, for this was when his domestic unhappiness really started, and it was to have an effect upon his political career.

He and Terentia had been married for more than twenty years. They had often argued. But underlying their disputes was a mutual respect. She was a woman of independent wealth: that was why he had married her; it was certainly not for her looks or the sweetness of her temper. It was Terentia's fortune that had enabled him to enter the Senate. In return, his success had increased her social standing. Now the disaster of his fall had exposed the inherent weaknesses of this partnership. Not only had she been obliged to sell a good part of her property in order to protect the family in his absence, she had been reviled and insulted and reduced to lodging with her in-laws—a family she snobbishly considered far beneath her own. Yes, Cicero was alive and he was back in Rome and I am sure she was glad for that. But she made no secret of her view that his days of political power were over, even if he—still floating on the clouds of popular adulation—had failed to grasp the fact.

I was not asked to dine with the family that first evening, and given the tensions between them, I cannot say I minded especially.

I was, however, dismayed to find that I had been given a bed in the slaves' quarters in the cellar, sharing a cubicle with Terentia's steward, Philotimus. He was an oily, avaricious creature of middle age: we had never liked one another, and I should guess he was no happier to see me than I him. Still, his love of money at least made him a diligent manager of Terentia's business affairs, and it must have pained him to see her fortune depleted month after month. The bitterness with which he assailed Cicero for placing her in this situation infuriated me, and after a while I told him curtly to shut his mouth and show some respect, or I would make sure the master gave him a whipping. Later, as I lay awake listening to his snores, I wondered how many of the complaints I had just heard were his, and how many he was merely repeating from the lips of his mistress.

The next day, because of my restlessness, I overslept and woke in a panic. Cicero was due to attend the Senate that morning to express his formal thanks for their support. Normally he learnt his speeches by heart and delivered them without a note. But it was so long since he had spoken in public he feared he might stumble over his words, therefore this oration had had to be dictated and written out during the journey from Brundisium. I took it from my dispatch box, checked I had the full text, and hurried upstairs, at the same time as Quintus's secretary, Statius, was showing two visitors into the tablinum. One was Milo, the tribune who had visited us in Thessalonica; the other was Lucius Afranius, Pompey's principal lieutenant, who had been consul two years after Cicero.

Statius said to me, "These gentlemen wish to see your master."

"I'll see if he's available."

At which Afranius remarked, in a tone I didn't much care for, "He'd better be available!"

I went at once to the principal bedroom. The door was closed. Terentia's maid put her finger to her lips and told me Cicero wasn't there. Instead she directed me along the passage to the dressing room, where I found him being helped into his toga by his valet. As I was describing who had come to see him, I noticed over his shoulder a small makeshift bed. He caught my glance and muttered, "Something's wrong but she won't tell me what it is," and then, perhaps regretting his candour, brusquely ordered me to go and fetch Quintus so that he too could hear what his visitors had come to say.

At first the meeting was friendly. Afranius announced that he brought with him the warmest regards of Pompey the Great, who hoped soon to welcome Cicero back to Rome in person. Cicero thanked him for the message and thanked Milo for all that he had done to bring about his recall. He described the enthusiasm of his reception in the countryside and of the crowds that had turned out to see him in Rome the previous day: "I feel it is a whole new life that I am beginning. I hope Pompey will be in the Senate to hear me praise him with such poor eloquence as I can muster."

"Pompey won't be attending the Senate," Afranius said bluntly.

"I'm sorry to hear it."

"He doesn't feel it appropriate, in view of the new law that is to be proposed." Whereupon he opened a small bag and handed over a draft bill, which Cicero read with evident surprise and then gave to Quintus, who eventually handed it to me.

Whereas the people of Rome are being denied access to a sufficient supply of grain; and to the extent that this constitutes a grave threat to the well-being and security of the state; and mindful of the principle that all Roman citizens are entitled to the equivalent of at least one free loaf of bread per day—it is hereby ordained that Pompey the Great shall be granted the power as Commissioner of Grain to purchase, seize or similarly obtain throughout the entire world enough grain to secure a plentiful supply for the city; that this power should be his for a term of five years; and that to assist him in this task he shall have the right to appoint fifteen lieutenant commissioners of grain to carry out such duties as he directs.

Afranius said, "Naturally, Pompey would like you to have the honour of proposing the legislation when you address the Senate today."

Milo said, "It's a cunning stroke, you must agree. Having retaken the streets from Clodius, we shall now remove his ability to buy votes with bread."

"Is the shortage really so serious it demands an emergency law?" asked Cicero. He turned to Quintus.

Quintus said, "It's true, there's little bread to be had, and what there is has risen to an extortionate price."

"Even so, these are astonishing, unprecedented powers over the nation's food supply to bestow upon one man. I'd really need to find out more about the situation before I offered an opinion, I'm afraid."

He tried to hand the draft bill back to Afranius, who refused to take it. He folded his arms and glared at Cicero. "I must say, we expected a little more gratitude than that—after all we've done for you."

"It goes without saying," added Milo, "that you'd be one of the fifteen lieutenant commissioners." And he rubbed his finger and thumb together to indicate the lucrative nature of the appointment.

The ensuing silence became uncomfortable. Eventually Afranius said, "Well, we'll leave the draft with you, and when you address the Senate we'll listen to your words with interest."

After they had gone, it was Quintus who spoke first. "At least now we know their price."

"No," said Cicero gloomily, "this isn't their price. This is merely the first instalment of their price—a loan that in their eyes will never be repaid, however much I give them."

"So what will you do?"

"Well, it's a devil's alternative, is it not? Propose the bill, and everyone will say I'm Pompey's creature; say nothing, and he'll turn against me. Whatever I do, I lose."

As was often the case, he had not decided which course to take even when we set off to attend the Senate. He always liked to take the temperature of the chamber before he spoke—to listen to its heartbeat like a doctor with a patient. Birria, the scarred gladiator who had accompanied Milo when he visited us in Macedonia, acted as a bodyguard, along with three of his comrades. In addition, I suppose there must have been twenty or thirty of Cicero's clients, who served as a human shield; we felt quite safe. As we walked, Birria boasted to me of their strength: he said that Milo and Pompey had a hundred pairs of gladiators on standby in a barracks on the Field of Mars, ready to deploy at a moment's notice if Clodius tried any of his tricks.

When we reached the Senate building, I handed Cicero the text of his speech. On entering he touched the ancient doorpost and looked around him at what he called "the greatest room in the world" in thankful amazement that he should have lived to see it again. As he approached his customary position on the front bench nearest to the consuls' dais, the neighbouring senators rose to shake his hand. It was an ill-attended house—not just Pompey was absent, I noticed, but also Clodius, and Marcus Crassus, whose pact with Pompey and Caesar was still the most powerful force in the republic. I wondered why they had stayed away.

The presiding consul that day was Metellus Nepos, the long-standing enemy of Cicero who was nevertheless now publicly reconciled with him—albeit only grudgingly and under pressure from the majority of the Senate. He made no acknowledgement of Cicero's presence but instead rose to announce that a new dispatch had just arrived from Caesar in Further Gaul. The chamber fell silent and the senators listened intently as he read out Caesar's account of yet more brutal encounters with savage and exotically named tribes—the Viromandui, the Atrebates and the Nervii—fought out amid those gloomy echoing forests and swollen impassable rivers. It was clear that Caesar had pushed much further north than any Roman commander before him, almost to the cold north sea, and again his victory was little short of an annihilation: of the sixty thousand men who had made up the army of the Nervii, he claimed to have left alive only five hundred. When Nepos had finished, the house seemed to let out its breath; only then did the consul call on Cicero to speak.

It was a difficult moment to make a speech, and in the event Cicero mostly restricted himself to a list of thanks. He thanked the consuls. He thanked the Senate. He thanked the people. He thanked the gods. He thanked his brother. He thanked just about everybody except Caesar, whom he did not mention. He thanked especially Pompey ("whose courage, fame and achievements are unapproached in the records of any nation or any age") and Milo ("his whole tribunate was nothing but a firm, unceasing, brave and undaunted championship of my well-being"). But he did not raise either the grain shortage or the proposal to give Pompey extra powers, and as soon as he sat down, Afranius and Milo promptly got up from their places and left the building.

Afterwards, as we walked back to Quintus's house, I noticed that Birria and his gladiators were no longer with us, which I thought was odd, for the danger had hardly gone away. There were a great many beggars among the streams of spectators milling around, and perhaps I was mistaken, but it seemed to me that the number of hostile looks and gestures Cicero attracted was substantially greater than before.

Once we were safely indoors, Cicero said, "I couldn't do it. How could I take the lead in a controversy I know nothing about? Besides, it wasn't the proper occasion to make a proposal of that sort. All anyone could talk about was Caesar, Caesar, Caesar. Perhaps now they'll leave me alone for a while."

The day was long and sunny, and Cicero spent much of it in the garden reading or throwing a ball for the family dog, a terrier named Myia, whose antics greatly delighted young Marcus and his nine-year-old cousin, Quintus Junior, the only child of Quintus and Pomponia. Marcus was a sweet, straightforward lad whereas Quintus, spoilt by his mother, had a streak of something nasty in him. But they played together happily enough. Occasionally the roar of the crowd in the Circus Maximus carried up from the valley on the other side of the hill—a hundred thousand voices crying out or groaning in unison: a sound at once exhilarating and frightening, like the growl of a tiger; it made the hairs tingle on my neck and arms. In the middle of the afternoon Quintus suggested that perhaps Cicero should go down to the Circus and show himself to the audience and watch at least one of the races. But Cicero preferred to stay where he was: "I am tired of exhibiting myself to strangers."

Because the boys were reluctant to go to bed and Cicero, having been away so long, wished to indulge them, dinner was not served until late. This time, to Pomponia's obvious irritation, he invited me to join them. She did not approve of slaves eating with their masters, and doubtless felt it was her prerogative, not her brother-in-law's, to decide who should be present at her own table. In the event we were six: Cicero and Terentia on one couch, Quintus and Pomponia on another, Tullia and I on the third. Normally Pomponia's brother, Atticus, would have joined us. He was Cicero's closest friend. But a week before Cicero's return he had abruptly left Rome for his estates in Epirus. He pleaded urgent business but I suspect he foresaw the looming family arguments. He always preferred a quiet life.

It was dusk and the slaves were just bringing in tapers to light the lamps and candles when from somewhere in the distance arose a cacophony of whistles, drums, horn blasts and chanting. At first we dismissed it as a passing procession connected with the games. But the noise seemed to come from directly outside the house, where it remained.

Finally Terentia said, "What on earth is that, do you suppose?"

"You know," replied Cicero, in a tone of scholarly interest, "I wonder if it might not be a *flagitatio*. Now there's a quaint custom! Tiro, would you take a look?"

I don't suppose such a thing exists any more, but back in the days of the republic, when people were free to express themselves, a *flagitatio* was the right of citizens who had a grievance, but were too poor to use the courts, to demonstrate outside the house of the person they held responsible. Tonight the target was Cicero.

I could hear his name mingled among their chants, and when I opened the door I got the message clear enough:

*Whoreson Cicero where's our bread?*
*Whoreson Cicero stole our bread!*

A hundred people packed the narrow street, repeating the same phrases over and over, with occasional and saltier variations on the word "whoreson." When they noticed me looking at them, a terrific jeer went up. I closed the door, bolted it and went back to the dining room to report.

Pomponia sat up in alarm. "But what shall we do?"

"Nothing," said Cicero calmly. "They're entitled to make their noise. Let them get it off their chests, and when they tire of it they'll go away."

Terentia asked, "But why are they accusing *you* of stealing their bread?"

Quintus said, "Clodius blames the lack of bread on the size of the crowds coming into Rome to support your husband."

"But the crowds aren't here to support my husband—they've come to watch the games."

"Brutally honest, as always," agreed Cicero, "and even if they *were* here for me, the city has never to my knowledge run short of food on a festival day."

"So why has it happened now?"

"I imagine someone has sabotaged the supply."

"Who would do that?"

"Clodius, to blacken my name; or perhaps even Pompey, to give himself a pretext to take over distribution. In any case, there's nothing we can do about it. So I suggest we eat our meal and ignore them."

But although we tried to carry on as if nothing was happening, and even made jokes and laughed about it, our conversation was strained, and every time there was a lull, it was filled by the angry voices outside:

*Cocksucker Cicero stole our bread!*
*Cocksucker Cicero ate our bread!*

Eventually Pomponia said, "Will they go on like that all night?"
Cicero said, "Possibly."

"But this has always been a quiet and respectable street. Surely
you can do something to stop them?"

"Not really. It's their right."

"Their right!"

"I believe in the people's rights, if you remember."

"Good for you. But how am I to sleep?"

Cicero's patience finally gave in. "Why not put some wax in your
ears, madam?" he suggested, then added under his breath, "I'm sure
I'd put some in mine if I were married to you."

Quintus, who had drunk plenty, tried to stifle his laughter.
Pomponia turned on him at once. "You'll allow him to speak to me
in that way?"

"It was only a joke, my dear."

Pomponia put down her napkin, rose with dignity from her
couch and announced that she would go and check on the boys.
Terentia, after a sharp look at Cicero, said that she would join her.
She beckoned to Tullia to follow.

When the women had gone, Cicero said to Quintus, "I'm sorry.
I shouldn't have spoken in that way. I'll go and find her and apologise. Besides, she's right: I've brought trouble on your house. We'll
move out in the morning."

"No you won't. I'm master here, and my roof will be your roof for
as long as I'm alive. Insults from that rabble are of no concern to me."

We listened again.

*Bumfucker Cicero where's our bread?*
*Bumfucker Cicero sold our bread!*

Cicero said, "It's a marvellously flexible metre, I'll give them that.
I wonder how many more versions they can come up with."

"You know we could always send word to Milo. Pompey's gladiators would clear the street in no time."

"And put myself even further in their debt? I don't think so."

We went our separate ways to bed, although I doubt any of us slept much. The demonstration did not cease as Cicero had predicted; if anything, by the following morning it had increased in volume, and certainly in violence, for the mob had started digging up the cobblestones and were hurling them against the walls, or lobbing them over the parapet so that they landed with a crash in the atrium or the garden. It was clear our situation was becoming parlous, and while the women and children sheltered indoors, I climbed up on to the roof with Cicero and Quintus to estimate the danger. Peering cautiously over the ridge tiles, it was possible to see down into the Forum. Clodius's mob was occupying it in force. The senators trying to get to the chamber for the day's session had to run a gauntlet of abuse and chanting. The words drifted up to us, accompanied by the banging of cooking utensils:

> *Where's our bread?*
> *Where's our bread?*
> *Where's our bread?*

Suddenly there was a scream from the floor beneath us. We scrabbled down from the roof and descended to the atrium in time to see a slave fishing out a black-and-white object, like a pouch or a small bag, that had just dropped through the aperture in the roof and fallen into the impluvium. It was the mangled body of Myia, the family dog. The two boys crouched in the corner of the atrium, hands over their ears, crying. Heavy stones battered against the wooden door. And now Terentia turned on Cicero with a bitterness I had never before witnessed: "Stubborn man! Stubborn, foolish man! Will you do something at last to protect your family? Or must I crawl out yet again on my hands and knees and plead with this scum not to hurt us?"

Cicero swayed backwards in the face of her fury. Just then there was a fresh bout of childish sobbing and he looked across to where Tullia was comforting her brother and cousin. That seemed to settle the issue. He said to Quintus, "Do you think you can smuggle a slave out through a window at the back?"

"I'm sure we can."

"In fact best send two, in case one doesn't get through. They should go to Milo's barracks on the Field of Mars and tell the gladiators we need help immediately."

The messengers were dispatched, and in the meantime Cicero went over to the boys and distracted them by putting his hands around their shoulders and telling them stories of the bravery of the heroes of the republic. After what seemed a long interval, during which the assault on the door increased in fury, we heard a fresh wave of roars from the street, followed by screaming. The gladiators controlled by Milo and Pompey had arrived, and in this way Cicero saved himself and his family, for I do believe that Clodius's men, finding they were unopposed, were fully intending to break into the house and massacre us all. As it was, after only a short battle in the street, the besiegers, who were not nearly so well armed or trained, fled for their lives.

Once we were sure the street was clear, Cicero, Quintus and I went up on to the roof again and watched as the fighting spilled down into the Forum. Columns of gladiators ran in from either side and started laying about them with the flats of their swords. The mob scattered but did not break entirely. A barricade built of trestle tables, benches and shutters from the nearby stores was thrown up between the Temple of Castor and the Grove of Vesta. This line held, and at one point I saw the blond-headed figure of Clodius himself directing the fighting, wearing a cuirass over his toga and brandishing a long iron spike. I know it was him because he had his wife, Fulvia, beside him—a woman as fierce and cruel and fond of violence as any man. Here and there fires were lit, and the smoke drifting in the summer heat added to the confusion of the melee. I counted seven bodies, although whether they were dead or merely injured I could not tell.

After a while, Cicero could not bear to watch any longer. Leaving the roof, he said quietly, "It is the end of the republic."

We stayed in the house all day as the skirmishing continued in the Forum, and what is most striking to me now is that throughout all this time, less than a mile away, the Roman Games continued uninterrupted, as if nothing unusual were happening. Violence had become a normal part of politics. By nightfall it was peaceful again, although Cicero prudently decided not to venture out of doors until the following morning, when he walked together with Quintus and an escort of Milo's gladiators to the Senate house. The Forum now was full of citizens who were supporters of Pompey. They called out to Cicero to make sure they had bread again by sending for Pompey to solve the crisis. Cicero, who carried with him the draft of the bill to make Pompey commissioner of grain, made no response.

It was another ill-attended house. Because of the unrest, more than half the senators had stayed away. The only former consuls on the front bench apart from Cicero were Afranius and M. Valerius Messalla. The presiding consul, Metellus Nepos, had been hit by a stone while crossing the Forum the previous day and was wearing a bandage. He brought up the grain riots as the first item on the order paper, and several of the magistrates actually suggested that Cicero himself should take control of the city's supply, at which Cicero made a modest gesture and shook his head.

Nepos said reluctantly, "Marcus Cicero, do you wish to speak?"

Cicero nodded and rose. "We none of us needs to be reminded," he began, "least of all the gallant Nepos, of the frightful violence that gripped the city yesterday—violence which has at its core a shortage of that most basic of human needs, bread. Some of us believe it was an ill day when our citizens were granted a free dole of corn in the first place, for it is human nature that what starts as gratitude quickly becomes dependency and ends as entitlement. This is the pass we have reached. I do not say we should rescind Clodius's law—it is too late for that: the public's morals are already corrupted, as no doubt he intended. But we must at least ensure that the supply of bread is continuous if we are to have civil order. And there is only one man in our state with the authority and genius of organisation to ensure such a thing, and that is Pompey the Great. Therefore I wish to propose the following resolution ..."

And here he read out the draft bill I have already quoted, and that part of the chamber which was packed with Pompey's lieutenants rose in acclamation. The rest sat solemn-faced, or muttered angrily, for they had always feared Pompey's lust for power. The cheering was heard outside and taken up by the crowds waiting in the Forum. When they learned that it was Cicero who had proposed the new law, they started clamouring for him to come and address them from the rostra, and all the tribunes—save for two supporters of Clodius—duly sent an invitation to him to speak. When the request was read out in the Senate, Cicero protested that he was not prepared for such an honour. (In fact I had with me a speech he had already written out, and which I was able to give him just before he mounted the steps to the platform.)

He was met by a tremendous ovation, and it was some time before he could make himself heard. When the applause died away, he started to speak, and had just reached the passage in which he thanked the people for their support—*Had I experienced nothing but an unruffled tranquillity, I should have missed the incredible and well-nigh superhuman transports of delight which your kindness now permits me to enjoy*—when who should appear at the edge of the crowd but Pompey. He stood ostentatiously alone—not that he had any need of bodyguards when the Forum was full of his gladiators—and pretended that he had come merely as an ordinary citizen to listen to what Cicero had to say. But of course the people would not permit that, so he allowed himself to be thrust forward to the rostra, which he mounted, and where he embraced Cicero. I had forgotten what a massive physical presence he was: that majestic torso and manly bearing, the famous thick quiff of still-dark hair rising like the beak of a warship above his broad and handsome face.

The occasion demanded flattery, and Cicero rose to it. "Here is a man," he said, lifting Pompey's arm, "who has had, has, and will have, no rival in virtue, sagacity and renown. He gave to me all that he had given to the republic, what no other has ever given to a private friend—safety, security, dignity. To him, fellow citizens, I owe a debt such as it is scarce lawful for one human being to owe to another."

The applause was prolonged, and Pompey's beam of pleasure was as wide and warm as the sun.

Afterwards he consented to walk back with Cicero to Quintus's house and take a cup of wine. He made no reference to Cicero's exile, no enquiries after his health, no apology for his failure years before to help Cicero stand up to Clodius, which was what had opened the door to the whole disaster in the first place. He talked only of himself and of the future, childlike in his eager anticipation of his grain commissionership and the opportunities it would give him for travel and patronage. "And you, of course, my dear Cicero, must be one of my fifteen legates—whichever one you like, wherever you want to go. Sardinia? Sicily? Egypt? Africa?"

"Thank you," said Cicero. "It is generous of you, but I must decline. My priority now has to be my family—restoring us to our property, comforting my wife and children, revenging us on our enemies and trying to recover our fortune."

"You'll recover your fortune quicker in the grain business than any other, I assure you."

"Even so, I must remain in Rome."

The broad face fell. "I'm disappointed, I can't pretend otherwise. I want the name of Cicero attached to this commission. It will add weight. What about you?" he said, turning to Quintus. "You could do it, I suppose."

Poor Quintus! The last thing he wanted, having returned from two tours of duty in Asia, was to go abroad again and deal with farmers and grain merchants and shipping agents. He squirmed. He protested his unfitness for the office. He looked to Cicero for support. But Cicero could hardly deny Pompey a second request, and this time he said nothing.

"All right: it's done." Pompey clapped his hands on the armrests

of his chair to signal that the matter was settled, and pushed himself up on to his feet. He grunted with the effort and I noticed
he was getting rather stout. He was in his fiftieth year, the same
age as Cicero. "Our republic is passing through the most strenuous
times," he said, putting his arms around the brothers' shoulders.
"But we shall come through them, as we always have, and I know
that you will both play your part." He clasped the two men tightly,
squeezed them, and held them there, pinned on either side of his
commodious chest.

# IV

———•◦•———

EARLY THE FOLLOWING MORNING, CICERO AND I WALKED UP THE
hill to inspect the ruins of his house. The palatial building in
which he had invested so much of his wealth and prestige had been
entirely pulled down; nine tenths of the huge plot was weeds and
rubble; it was barely possible to discern the original layout of the
walls through the tangled overgrowth. Cicero stooped to pick up
one of the scorched bricks poking from the ground. "Until this
place is restored to me, we shall be entirely at their mercy—no
money, no dignity, no independence . . . Every time I step outdoors
I shall have to look up here and be reminded of my humiliation."
The edges of the brick crumbled in his hands and the red dust
trickled through his fingers like dried blood.

At the far end of the plot a statue of a young woman had been
set up on top of a high plinth. Fresh offerings of flowers were piled
around the base. By consecrating the site as a shrine to Liberty,
Clodius believed he had made it inviolable and thus impossible
for Cicero to reclaim. The marble figure was shapely in the morning light, with long tresses and a diaphanous dress slipping down
to expose a naked breast. Cicero regarded her with his hands on
his hips. Eventually he said, "Surely Liberty is always depicted as
a matron with a cap?" I agreed. "So who, pray, is this hussy? Why,
she is no more the embodiment of a goddess than I am!"

Until that moment he had been sombre, but now he started to
laugh, and when we returned to Quintus's house he set me the task
of discovering where Clodius had acquired the statue. That same
day he petitioned the College of Pontiffs to return his property to
him on the grounds that the site had been improperly consecrated.

A hearing was fixed for the end of the month, and Clodius was summoned to defend his actions.

When the day arrived, Cicero admitted he felt ill-prepared and out of practice. Because his library was still in storage, he had been unable to consult all the legal sources he needed. He was also, I am sure, nervous at the prospect of confronting Clodius face to face. To be beaten by his enemy in a street brawl was one thing; to lose to him in a legal dispute would be a calamity.

The headquarters of the pontifical college were then in the old Regia, said to be the most ancient building in the city. It stood like its modern successor at the point where the Via Sacra divides and enters the Forum, although the noise of that busy spot was entirely deadened by the thickness of its high and windowless walls. The candlelit gloom of the interior made one forget that outside it was bright and sunny. Even the chilly, tomblike air smelt sacred, as if it had been undisturbed for more than six hundred years.

Fourteen of the fifteen pontiffs were seated at the far end of the crowded chamber, waiting for us. The only absentee was their chief, Caesar: his chair, grander than the others, stood empty. Among the priests were several I knew well—Spinther, the consul; Marcus Lucullus, brother of the great general, Lucius, who was said to have lately lost his reason and to be confined to his palace outside Rome; and the two rising young aristocrats Q. Scipio Nasica and M. Aemilius Lepidus. And here at last I saw the third triumvir, Crassus. The curious conical hat of animal fur the pontiffs were required to wear robbed him of his most distinctive feature, his baldness. His crafty face was quite impassive.

Cicero took a seat facing them while I sat on a stool at his back, ready to pass any documents he required. Behind us was an audience of eminent citizens, including Pompey. Of Clodius there was no sign. Whispered conversations gradually ceased. The silence grew oppressive. Where was he? Perhaps he might not come. With Clodius one never knew. But then at last he swaggered in, and I felt myself turn cold at the sight of the man who had caused us so much anguish. "Little Miss Beauty," Cicero used to call him, but in middle age he had outgrown the insult. His luxuriant blond curls were nowadays cut as tight to his skull as a golden helmet; his thick red lips had lost their pout. He appeared hard, lean, disdainful— a fallen Apollo. As is often the case with the bitterest of enemies, he had started out as a friend. But then he had outraged law and morality once too often, by disguising himself as a woman and defiling the sacred rite of the Good Goddess. Cicero had been obliged to give evidence against him, and from that day on Clodius had sworn vengeance. He sat on a chair barely three paces from Cicero, but Cicero continued to stare straight ahead, and the two men never once looked at one another.

The senior pontiff by age was Publius Albinovanus, who must have been eighty. In a quavering voice he read out the point at issue—"Was the shrine to Liberty, lately erected on the property claimed by M. Tullius Cicero, consecrated in accordance with the rites of the official religion or not?"—and invited Clodius to speak first.

Clodius left it just long enough to indicate his contempt for the whole proceeding, and then slowly got to his feet. "I am appalled, holy fathers," he began in his slangy patrician drawl, "and dismayed, but not surprised, that the exiled murderer Cicero, having brazenly slaughtered Liberty during the time of his consulship, should now seek to compound the offence by tearing down her image . . ."

He brought up every slander that had ever been made against Cicero—his illegal killing of the Catiline conspirators ("the sanction of the Senate is no excuse for executing five citizens without a trial"), his vanity ("if he objects to this shrine, it is mostly out of jealousy since he regards himself as the only god worth worshipping") and his political inconsistency ("this is the man whose return was supposed to mean the restoration of senatorial authority, and yet whose first act was to betray it by winning dictatorial powers for Pompey"). It was not without impact. It would have played well in the Forum. But it failed entirely to address the legal point at issue: was the shrine properly consecrated or not?

He argued for an hour, and then it was Cicero's turn, and it was a measure of how effective Clodius had been that he was obliged to speak extempore to begin with, defending his support for Pompey's grain commission. Only after he had answered that could he turn to making his main case: that the shrine could not be held to be consecrated because Clodius was not legally a tribune when he dedicated it. "Your transfer from patrician to pleb was sanctioned by no decree of this college, was entered upon in defiance of all pontifical regulations, and must be held to be null and void; and if that is invalid your entire tribunate falls to the ground." This was dangerous territory: everyone knew it was Caesar who had organised Clodius's adoption as a pleb. I saw Crassus lean forwards listening intently. Sensing the danger, and perhaps remembering his undertaking to Caesar, Cicero swerved away: "Does this mean I am saying that all Caesar's laws were illegal? By no means; for none of them any longer affects my interests, apart from those aimed with hostile intent against my own person."

He pressed on, switching to an attack on Clodius's methods, and now his oratory took flight—his arm outstretched, his finger pointing at his enemy, the words almost tumbling from his mouth in his passion: "Oh, you abominable plague spot of the state, you public prostitute! What harm had you suffered at the hands of my unhappy wife that you harassed, plundered and tortured her so brutally? Or from my daughter, who lost her beloved husband? Or from my little son, who still lies awake weeping at night? But it was not just my family you attacked—you waged a bitter war against my very walls and doorposts!"

However his real coup was to reveal the origins of the statue Clodius had set up. I had tracked down the workmen who had erected it and learnt that the piece had been donated by Clodius's brother Appius, who had carried it off from Tanagra, in Boeotia, where it had graced the tomb of a well-known local courtesan.

The whole room roared with laughter when Cicero revealed this fact. "So this is his idea of Liberty—a courtesan's likeness, erected over a foreign tomb, stolen by a thief and set up again by a sacrilegious hand! And *she* is the one who drives me from my house?

Holy fathers, this property cannot be lost to me without inflicting disgrace upon the state. If you believe that my return to Rome has been a source of pleasure to the immortal gods, to the Senate, to the Roman people and to all of Italy, then let it be your hands that reinstall me in my home."

Cicero sat to loud murmurs of approval from the distinguished audience. I stole a look at Clodius. He was scowling at the floor. The pontiffs leaned in to confer. Crassus seemed to be doing most of the talking. We had expected a decision at once. But Albinovanus straightened and announced that the college would need more time to consider their verdict: it would be relayed to the Senate the following day. This was a blow. Clodius stood, bent down to Cicero as he passed and hissed, through a false smile, just loud enough for me to hear, "You will die before that place is rebuilt." He left the chamber without another word. Cicero pretended nothing had happened. He lingered to chat with many old friends, with the result that we were among the last to leave the building.

Outside the chamber was a courtyard containing the famous white board on which the chief priest by tradition in those days published the state's official news. This was where Caesar's agents posted his *Commentaries,* and here was where we found Crassus standing—ostensibly reading the latest dispatch but in truth waiting to intercept Cicero. He had taken off his cap; here and there little wisps of brown fur still adhered to his high-domed skull.

"So, Cicero," he said in his unsettlingly jovial manner, "you were pleased with the effect of your speech?"

"Reasonably, thank you. But my opinion has no value. It's for you and your colleagues to decide."

"Oh, I thought it effective enough. My only regret is that Caesar wasn't present to hear it."

"I shall send him a copy."

"Yes, be sure that you do. Mind you, reading is all very well. But how would he *vote* on the issue? That's what I have to decide."

"And why do you have to decide that?"

"Because he wishes me to act as his proxy and cast his vote as I think fit. Many colleagues will follow my lead. It is important I get it right."

He grinned, showing yellow teeth.

"I have no doubt you will. Good day to you, Crassus."

"Good day, Cicero."

We passed out of the gate, Cicero cursing under his breath, and had gone only a few paces when Crassus suddenly called out after him, and hurried to catch us up. "One last thing," he said. "In view of these tremendous victories that Caesar has won in Gaul, I wondered if you would be good enough to support a proposal in the Senate for a period of public celebration in his honour."

"Why does it matter if I support it?"

"Obviously it would add weight, given the history of your relations with Caesar. People would notice. And it would be a noble gesture on your part. I'm sure Caesar would appreciate it."

"How long would this period of celebration last?"

"Oh ... fifteen days should just about do it."

"*Fifteen days?* That's nearly twice as long as Pompey was voted for conquering Spain."

"Yes, well one could argue that Caesar's victories in Gaul are twice as important as Pompey's in Spain."

"I'm not sure Pompey would agree."

"Pompey," retorted Crassus with emphasis, "must learn that a triumvirate consists of three men, not one."

Cicero gritted his teeth and bowed. "It would be an honour."

Crassus bowed in return. "I knew you would do the patriotic thing."

THE FOLLOWING DAY, SPINTHER READ OUT THE PONTIFFS' judgement to the Senate: unless Clodius could provide written proof that he had consecrated the shrine on instructions from the Roman people, "the site can be restored to Cicero without sacrilege."

A normal man now would have given up. But Clodius wasn't

normal. Though he might pretend to be a pleb, he was still a Claudian—a family who took pride in hounding their enemies to the grave. First he lied and told a meeting of the people that the judgement had actually gone in his favour and called on them to defend "their" shrine. Then, when the consul-designate Marcellinus proposed a motion in the Senate to return to Cicero his three properties—in Rome, Tusculum and Formiae, "with compensation to restore them to their former state"—Clodius tried to talk out the session, and would have succeeded had he not, after three hours on his feet, been howled down by an exasperated Senate. Nor were his tactics entirely without effect. Frightened of antagonising the plebs, and to Cicero's dismay, the Senate agreed to pay compensation of only two million sesterces to rebuild the house on the Palatine, and just half a million and a quarter of a million respectively for the repairs at Tusculum and Formiae—far below the actual costs.

For the past two years most of Rome's builders and craftsmen had been employed on Pompey's immense development of public buildings on the Field of Mars. Grudgingly—because anyone who has ever employed builders learns quickly never to let them out of one's sight—Pompey agreed to transfer a hundred of his men to Cicero. Work on restoring the Palatine house began at once, and on the first morning of construction Cicero had the great pleasure of swinging an axe at the head of Liberty and smashing it clean off, then crating up the remains and having them delivered to Clodius with his compliments.

I knew Clodius would retaliate, and one morning soon afterwards, when Cicero and I were working on some legal papers in Quintus's tablinum, we heard what sounded like heavy footsteps clumping across the roof. I went out into the street and was lucky not to be struck on the head by bricks dropping from the sky. Panicking workmen came running round the corner and shouted that a gang of Clodius's toughs had overrun the site and were demolishing the new walls and hurling the debris down on to Quintus's house. Just then Cicero and Quintus came out to see what the trouble was, and yet again they had to send a messenger to Milo to request the assistance of his gladiators. It was just as well, for no sooner had the runner gone than there was a series of flashes overhead, and burning brands and lumps of flaming pitch started landing all around us. Fires broke out on the roof. The terrified household had to be evacuated, and everyone, including Cicero and even Terentia, was pressed into service to pass buckets of water, drawn from the street fountains, from hand to hand to try to prevent the house from burning down.

Crassus had a monopoly of the city's fire services, and fortunately for us, he was at his home on the Palatine. He heard the commotion, came out into the street, saw what was going on, and turned up himself in a shabby tunic and slippers, with one of his teams of fire slaves dragging a water tender equipped with pumps and hoses. But for them the building would have been lost; as it was, the damage caused by the water and smoke rendered the place uninhabitable, and we had to move out while it was repaired. We loaded our luggage into carts and, with night coming on, made our way across the valley to the Quirinal hill, to seek temporary refuge in the house of Atticus, who was still away in Epirus. His narrow, ancient house was fine for an elderly bachelor of fixed and moderate habits; it was less ideal for two families with extensive households and warring spouses. Cicero and Terentia slept in separate parts of the building.

Eight days later, as we were walking along the Via Sacra, we heard an outburst of shouts and the sound of running feet behind us, and turned to see Clodius and a dozen of his henchmen flourishing cudgels and even swords, sprinting to attack us. We had the usual bodyguard of Milo's men and they hustled us into the doorway of the nearest house. In their panic, Cicero was pushed to the ground and gashed his head and twisted his ankle but otherwise was unharmed. The startled owner of the house in which we sought refuge, Tettius Damio, took us in and gave us a cup of wine, and Cicero talked calmly to him of poetry and philosophy until we were told that our attackers had been driven off and the coast was clear; then he said his thanks and we continued on our way home.

Cicero was in that state of elation that sometimes follows a close brush with death. His appearance, however, was a different matter—limping, with a bloodied forehead and torn and dirty clothes—and the instant Terentia saw him she cried out in shock. Useless for him to protest that it was nothing, that Clodius had been put to flight, and that his descent to such tactics showed how desperate he was becoming: Terentia would not listen. The siege, the fire and now this: she insisted that they all should leave Rome at once.

Cicero replied mildly, "You forget, Terentia: I've tried that once, and see where it left us. Our only hope is to stay here and win back our position."

"And how are you to do that when you can't even walk in safety down a busy street in broad daylight?"

"I shall find a way."

"And in the meantime, what lives do the rest of us have?"

"Normal lives!" Cicero suddenly shouted back at her. "We defeat them by leading normal lives! We sleep together as man and wife for a start."

I glanced away in embarrassment.

Terentia said, "You wish to know why I keep you from my room? Then look!"

And to Cicero's astonishment and certainly to mine, this most pious of Roman matrons began to unfasten the belt of her dress. She called to her maid to come and help. Turning her back to her husband, she opened her gown and her maid pulled it down all the way from the nape of her neck to the base of her spine, expos-ing the pale flesh between her thin shoulders, which was savagely criss-crossed by at least a dozen livid red welts.

Cicero stared at the scars, transfixed. "Who did this to you?"

Terentia pulled the dress back up and her maid knelt to fasten her belt.

"Who did this?" repeated Cicero quietly. "Clodius?"

She turned to face him. Her eyes were not wet but dry and full of fire. "Six months ago I went to see his sister, as one woman to another, to plead on your behalf. But Clodia is not a woman: she is a Fury. She told me I was no better than a traitor myself—that my presence defiled her house. She summoned her steward and had him whip me off the premises. She had her louche friends with her. They laughed at my shame."

"*Your* shame?" cried Cicero. "The only shame is theirs! You should have told me!"

"Told *you*? You, who greeted the whole of Rome before he greeted his own wife?" She spat out the words. "You may stay and die in the city if you wish. I shall take Tullia and Marcus to Tusculum and see what lives we can have there."

The following morning, she and Pomponia left with the children, and a few days later, amid much mutual shedding of tears, Quintus also departed to buy grain for Pompey in Sardinia. Prowling round the empty house, Cicero was keenly aware of their absence. He told me he felt every blow that Terentia had endured as if it were a lash upon his own back, and he tortured his brain to find some means of avenging her, but he could see no way through, until one day, quite unexpectedly, the glimmer of an opportunity presented itself.

IT HAPPENED THAT AROUND THIS TIME, THE DISTINGUISHED philosopher Dio of Alexandria was murdered in Rome while under the roof of his friend and host, Titus Coponius. The assassination caused a great scandal. Dio had come to Italy supposedly with diplomatic protection, as the head of a delegation of one hundred prominent Egyptians to petition the Senate against the restoration of their exiled pharaoh, Ptolemy XII, nicknamed "the Flute Player."

Suspicion naturally fell on Ptolemy himself, who was staying with Pompey at his country estate in the Alban hills. The Pharaoh, detested by his people for the taxes he levied, was offering the stupendous reward of six thousand gold talents if Rome would secure his restoration, and the effect of this bribe upon the Senate was as dignified as if a rich man had thrown a few coins into a crowd of starving beggars. In the scramble for the honour of overseeing Ptolemy's return, three main candidates had emerged: Lentulus Spinther, the outgoing consul, who was due to become governor of Cilicia and therefore would legally command an army on the borders of Egypt; Marcus Crassus, who yearned to possess the same wealth and glory as Pompey and Caesar; and Pompey himself, who feigned disinterest in the commission but behind the scenes was the most active of the three in trying to secure it.

Cicero had no desire to become embroiled in the affair. There was nothing in it for him. He was obliged to support Spinther, in return for Spinther's efforts to end his exile, and lobbied discreetly behind the scenes on his behalf. But when Pompey asked him to come out and meet the Pharaoh to discuss the death of Dio, he felt unable to turn the summons down.

The last time we had visited the house was almost two years earlier, when Cicero had gone to plead for help in resisting Clodius's attacks. On that occasion Pompey had pretended to be out to avoid seeing him. The memory of his cowardice still rankled with me, but Cicero refused to dwell on it: "If I do, I shall become bitter, and a man who is bitter hurts no one but himself. We must look to the future." Now, as we rattled up the long drive to the villa, we passed several groups of olive-skinned men wearing exotic robes and exercising those sinister yellowish prick-eared greyhounds so beloved of the Egyptians.

Ptolemy awaited Cicero with Pompey in the atrium. He was a short, plump, smooth figure, dark-complexioned like his courtiers, and so quietly spoken that one found oneself bending forward to catch what he was saying. He was dressed Roman-style in a toga. Cicero bowed and kissed his hand, and I was invited to do the same. His perfumed fingers were fat and soft like a baby's, but the nails I noticed with disgust were broken and dirty. Coyly peering around him with her arms clasped across his stomach was his young daughter. She had huge charcoal-black eyes and a painted ruby mouth—an ageless slattern's mask even at the age of eleven, or so it seems to me now, but perhaps I am being unfair and allowing my memory to be distorted by what was to come, for this was the future Queen Cleopatra, later to cause such mischief.

Once the niceties were out of the way and Cleopatra had departed with her maids, Pompey came to the point: "This killing of Dio is starting to become embarrassing, both to me and to His Majesty. And now to cap it all, a murder charge has been brought by Titus Coponius, Dio's host when he was killed, and by his brother Gaius. The whole thing is ridiculous, of course, but apparently they are not to be persuaded out of it."

"Who is the accused?" enquired Cicero.

"Publius Asicius."

Cicero paused to remember the name. "Isn't he one of your estate managers?"

"He is. That's what makes it embarrassing."

Cicero had the tact not to ask whether Asicius was guilty or not. He considered the matter purely as a lawyer. He said to Ptolemy, "Until this matter blows over, I would strongly advise Your Majesty to remove yourself as far away from Rome as possible."

"Why?"

"Because if I were the Coponius brothers, the first thing I should do is issue a subpoena summoning you to give evidence."

"Can they do that?" asked Pompey.

"They can try. To save His Majesty the embarrassment, I would advise him to be miles away when the writ is served—out of Italy, if possible."

"But what about Asicius?" said Pompey. "If he's found guilty, that could look very bad for me."

"I agree."

"Then he must be acquitted. You'll take the case, I hope? I'd regard it as a favour."

This was not what Cicero wanted. But Pompey was insistent, and in the end, as usual, he had no option but to accede. Before we left, Ptolemy, as a token of his thanks, presented Cicero with a small and ancient jade statue of a baboon, which he explained was Hedj-Wer, the god of writing. I expect it was quite valuable, but Cicero couldn't abide it—"What do I want with their primitive mud gods?" he complained to me afterwards, and he must have thrown it away; I never saw it again.

Asicius, the accused man, came to see us. He was a former legionary commander who had served with Pompey in Spain and the East. He looked eminently capable of murder. He showed Cicero his summons. The charge was that he had visited Coponius's house early in the morning with a forged letter of introduction. Dio was in the act of opening it when Asicius whipped out a small knife he had concealed in his sleeve and stabbed the elderly philosopher in the neck. The blow had not been immediately fatal. Dio's cries had brought the household running. According to the writ, Asicius had been recognised before he managed to slash his way out of the house.

Cicero did not enquire about the truth of the matter. He merely advised Asicius that his best chance of acquittal lay in a good alibi. Someone would need to vouch that he was with them at the time of the murder—and the more witnesses he could produce and the less connection they had with Pompey, or indeed Cicero, the better.

Asicius said, "That's easy enough. I have just the fellow lined up: a man known to be on bad terms both with Pompey and yourself."

"Who?"

"Your old protégé Caelius Rufus."

"Rufus? What's he doing mixed up in this business?"

"Does it matter? He'll swear I was with him at the hour the old man was killed. And he's a senator nowadays, don't forget—his word carries weight."

I half expected Cicero to tell Asicius to find another advocate, such was his distaste for Rufus. But to my surprise he said, "Very well, tell him to come and see me and we'll depose him."

After Asicius had gone, Cicero said, "Surely Rufus is a close friend of Clodius? Doesn't he live in one of his apartments? In fact, isn't Clodia his mistress?"

"She certainly used to be."

"That was what I thought." The mention of Clodia made him thoughtful. "So what is Rufus doing offering an alibi to an agent of Pompey?"

Later that same day, Rufus came to the house. At twenty-five, he was the youngest member of the Senate, and very active in the law courts. It was odd to see him swaggering through the door wearing the purple-striped toga of a senator. Only nine years before, he had been Cicero's pupil. But then he had turned on his former mentor, and eventually beaten him in court by prosecuting Cicero's consular colleague, Hybrida. Cicero could have forgiven him that—he always liked to see a young man on the rise as an advocate—but his friendship with Clodius was a betrayal too far. So he greeted him very icily and pretended to read various documents while Rufus dictated his statement to me. Cicero must have been listening keenly, however, for when Rufus described how he was entertaining Asicius in his house at the time of the killing, and gave as his home address a property on the Esquiline, Cicero suddenly looked up and said, "But don't you rent a property from Clodius on the Palatine?"

"I've moved," replied Rufus casually, but there was something too offhand in his tone, and Cicero detected it at once.

He pointed his finger at him and said, "You've quarrelled."

"Not at all."

"You've quarrelled with that devil and his sister from hell. That's why you're doing this favour for Pompey. You always were the most hopeless liar, Rufus. I see through you as clearly as if you were made of water."

Rufus laughed. He had great charm: he was said to be the most handsome young man in Rome. "You seem to forget, I don't live in your house any more, Marcus Tullius. I don't have to give an account of my friendships to you." He swung himself easily on to his feet. He was also very tall. "Now I've given your client his alibi, as was requested, and our business here is done."

"Our business will be done when I say it is," Cicero called after him cheerfully. He did not bother to rise. I showed Rufus out, and when I returned, he was still smiling. "This is what I've been waiting for, Tiro. I can feel it. He's fallen out with those two monsters, and if that's the case, they won't rest until they've destroyed him. We need to ask around town. Discreetly. Spread some money around if we have to. But we must find out why he's left that house!"

THE TRIAL OF ASICIUS ENDED THE DAY IT BEGAN. THE CASE BOILED down to the word of a few household slaves against that of a senator, and on hearing Rufus's affidavit, the praetor directed the jury to acquit. This was the first of many legal victories for Cicero following his return, and he was soon in high demand, appearing in the Forum most days, just as in his prime.

Throughout this time the violence in Rome worsened. On some days the courts could not sit because of the risks to public safety. A few days after setting upon Cicero in the Via Sacra, Clodius and his followers attacked the house of Milo and attempted to burn it down. Milo's gladiators drove them off and retaliated by occupying the voting pens on the Field of Mars in a vain attempt to prevent Clodius's election as aedile.

Cicero sensed opportunity in the chaos. One of the new tribunes, Cannius Gallus, laid a bill before the people demanding that Pompey alone should be entrusted with restoring Ptolemy to the throne of Egypt. The bill so incensed Crassus that he actually paid Clodius to organise a popular campaign against Pompey. And when Clodius eventually won the aedileship, he used his powers as a magistrate to summon Pompey to give evidence in an action he brought against Milo.

The hearing took place in the Forum in front of many thousands. I watched it with Cicero. Pompey mounted the rostra, but had hardly uttered more than a few sentences when Clodius's supporters started to drown him out with catcalls and slow handclaps. There was a kind of heroism in the way that Pompey simply put his shoulders down and went on reading out his text, even though no one could hear him. This must have gone on for an hour or more, and then Clodius, who was standing a few feet along the rostra, started really working up the crowd against him.

"Who's starving the people to death?" he shouted.

"Pompey!" roared his followers.

"Who wants to go to Alexandria?"

"Pompey!"

"Whom do you want to go?"

"Crassus!"

Pompey looked as if he had been struck by lightning. Never had he been insulted in such a way. The crowd started heaving like a stormy sea, one side pushing against the other, with little eddies of scuffles breaking out here and there, and suddenly from the back, ladders appeared and were passed rapidly over our heads to the front, where they were thrown up against the rostra and a group of ruffians began scaling it—Milo's ruffians, it transpired, for the moment they reached the platform they charged at Clodius and hurled him off it, a good twelve feet down on to the spectators. There were cheers and screams. I didn't see what happened after that, as Cicero's attendants hustled us out of the Forum and away from danger, but we learned later that Clodius had escaped unharmed.

The following evening, Cicero went off to dine with Pompey and came home rubbing his hands with pleasure. "Well, if I'm not mistaken, that's the beginning of the end of our so-called triumvirate, at least as far as Pompey's concerned. He swears Crassus is behind a plot to murder him, says he'll never trust him again, threatens that if necessary Caesar will have to return to Rome to answer for his mischief in creating Clodius in the first place and destroying the constitution. I've never seen him in such a rage. As for me, he couldn't have been friendlier, and assures me that whatever I do, I can rely on his support.

"But better even than that—when he was deep in his cups, he finally told me why Rufus has switched allegiance. I was right: there's been the most tremendous falling-out between him and Clodia—so much so that she's claiming he tried to poison her! Naturally, Clodius has taken his sister's side, thrown Rufus out of his house and called in his debts. So Rufus has had to turn to Pompey in the hope of some Egyptian gold to pay off what he owes. Isn't it all marvellous?"

I agreed it was all marvellous, though I couldn't see why it warranted quite such ecstasies of joy.

Cicero said, "Bring me the praetors' lists, quick!"

I went and fetched the schedule of court cases that were due to be heard over the next seven days. Cicero told me to look up when Rufus was next due to appear. I ran my finger down the various courts and cases until I found his name. He was scheduled to begin a prosecution in the constitutional court for bribery in five days' time.

Cicero said, "Who is he prosecuting?"

"Bestia."

"Bestia! That villain!"

Cicero lay back on the couch in his familiar posture when cooking up a scheme, with his hands clasped behind his head, staring at the ceiling. L. Calpurnius Bestia was an old enemy of his, one of Catilina's tame tribunes, lucky not to have been executed for treason with his five fellow conspirators. Yet here he was, apparently still active in public life, being prosecuted for buying votes during the recent praetorian elections. I wondered what possible interest Bestia could hold for Cicero, and after a long period during which he said nothing, I ventured to ask him.

His voice seemed to come from a long way away, as if I had interrupted him in a dream. "I was just thinking," he said slowly, "that I might offer to defend him."

# V

---

THE NEXT MORNING, CICERO WENT TO CALL ON BESTIA, TAKING ME with him. The old rogue had a house on the Palatine. His expression when Cicero was shown in was comical in its astonishment. He had with him his son Atratinus, a clever lad who had only just donned the toga of manhood and was eager to begin his career. When Cicero announced that he wished to discuss his impending prosecution, Bestia naturally assumed he was about to receive another writ and grew quite menacing. It was only thanks to the intervention of the boy, who was in awe of Cicero, that he was persuaded to sit down and listen to what his distinguished visitor had to say.

Cicero said, "I have come here to offer my services in your defence."

Bestia gaped at him. "And why in the name of the gods would you do that?"

"I have undertaken later in the month to appear on behalf of Publius Sestius. Is it true that you saved his life during the fighting in the Forum when I was in exile?"

"I did."

"Well then, Bestia, chance for once throws us on the same side. If I appear for you, I can describe the incident at great length and that will help me lay the ground for Sestius's defence, which will be heard by the same court. Who are your other advocates?"

"Herennius Balbus to open, and then my son here to follow."

"Good. Then with your agreement I'll speak third and do the winding-up—my usual preference. I'll put on a good show, don't worry. We should have the whole thing wrapped up in a day or two."

Bestia by this time had moved from an attitude of deep suspicion to one of hardly being able to believe his luck that the greatest advocate in Rome was willing to speak on his behalf. And when Cicero strolled into court a couple of days later, his appearance provoked gasps of surprise. Rufus in particular was stunned. The very fact that Cicero, of all people—whom Bestia had once plotted to murder—should now appear as his supporter more or less guaranteed his acquittal. And so it proved. Cicero made an eloquent speech, the jury voted, and Bestia was found not guilty.

As the court was rising, Rufus came over to Cicero. For once his normal charm was gone. He had been counting on an easy victory; instead his career had been checked. He said bitterly, "Well, I hope you're satisfied, although such a triumph brings you nothing but dishonour."

"My dear Rufus," replied Cicero, "have you learnt nothing? There is no more honour in a legal dispute than there is in a wrestling match."

"What I've *learnt,* Cicero, is that you still bear me a grudge and will stop at nothing to gain revenge on your enemies."

"Oh my dear, poor boy, I don't regard *you* as my enemy. You're not important enough. I have bigger fish to catch."

That really infuriated Rufus. He said, "Well, you can tell your client that as he insists on continuing as a candidate, I shall bring a second charge against him tomorrow—and the next time you rise in his defence, if you dare, I give you fair warning: I shall be waiting for you!"

He was as good as his word: very soon afterwards, Bestia and his son brought the new writ round to show Cicero. Bestia said hopefully, "You'll defend me again, I hope?"

"Oh no, that would be very foolish. One can't spring the same surprise twice. No, I'm afraid I can't be your advocate again."

"So what's to be done?"

"Well, I can tell you what *I'd* do in your place."

"And what's that?"

"I'd lay a counter-suit against him."

"For what?"

"Political violence. That takes precedence over bribery cases. Therefore you'll have the advantage of putting him on trial first, before he can get you into court."

Bestia conferred with his son. "We like the sound of it," he announced. "But can we really make a case against him? Has he actually committed political violence?"

"Of course," said Cicero. "Didn't you hear? He was involved in the murder of several of those Egyptian envoys. Ask around town," he continued. "You'll find lots of people willing to tell tales. There's one man in particular you should go to see, although of course you never heard the name from me: you'll understand why the moment I say it. You should talk to Clodius, or better still to that sister of his. I hear Rufus used to be her lover, and when his ardour cooled, he tried to get rid of her with poison. You know what that family is like—they love their vengeance. You should offer to let them join your suit. With the Claudii beside you, you'll be unbeatable. But remember—you never got any of this from me."

I had worked very closely with Cicero for many years. I had grown used to his clever tricks. I did not think him capable of surprising me any more. That day proved me wrong.

Bestia thanked him profusely, swore to be discreet and went off full of purpose. A few days later, a notice to prosecute was posted in the Forum: he and Clodius had combined forces to charge Rufus with both the attacks on the Alexandrian envoys and the attempted murder of Clodia. The news caused a sensation. Almost everyone believed that Rufus would be found guilty and sentenced to exile for life, and that the career of Rome's youngest senator was over.

When I showed him the list of charges, Cicero said, "Oh dear. Poor Rufus. He must be feeling very wretched. I think we should visit him and cheer him up."

And so we set off to find the house that Rufus was renting. Cicero, who at the age of fifty was starting to feel stiff in his limbs on cold winter mornings, rode in a litter, while I walked alongside him. Rufus turned out to be lodging on the second floor of an apartment block in the less fashionable part of the Esquiline, not far from the gate where the undertakers ply their trade. The place was gloomy even at midday, and Cicero had to ask the slaves to light candles. In the dim light we discovered their master in a drunken sleep, curled up beneath a pile of blankets on a couch. He groaned and rolled over and begged to be left alone, but Cicero dragged away his covers and told him to get up on his feet.

"What's the point? I'm finished!"

"You're not finished. Quite the contrary: we have that woman exactly where we want her."

"We?" repeated Rufus, squinting up at Cicero through bloodshot eyes. "When you say 'we,' does that imply you're on my side?"

"Not merely on your side, my dear Rufus. I am going to be your advocate!"

"Wait," said Rufus. He touched his hand gently to his forehead, as if checking it was still intact. "Wait a moment—did you *plan* all this?"

"Consider yourself to have been given a political education. And now let us agree that the slate is wiped clean between us, and concentrate on beating our common enemy." Rufus began to swear. Cicero listened for a while, then interrupted him. "Come, Rufus. This is a good bargain for us both. You'll get that harpy off your back once and for all, and I'll satisfy the honour of my wife."

Cicero held out his hand. At first Rufus recoiled. He pouted and shook his head and muttered. But then he must have realised he had no choice. At any rate, eventually he extended his own hand, Cicero shook it warmly, and with that the trap he had laid for Clodia snapped shut.

THE TRIAL WAS SCHEDULED TO TAKE PLACE AT THE START OF APRIL, which meant it would coincide with the opening of the Festival of the Great Mother, with its famous parade of castrated holy men. Even so, there was no doubting which would be the greater attraction, especially when Cicero's name was announced as one of Rufus's advocates. The others were to be Rufus himself, and Crassus, in whose household Rufus had also served an internship as a young man. I am certain Crassus would have preferred not to have performed this service for his former protégé, especially given the presence of Cicero on the bench beside him, but the rules of patronage placed him under a heavy obligation. On the other side once again were young Atratinus and Herennius Balbus— both furious at Cicero's duplicity, not that he cared a fig for their opinion—and Clodius, representing the interests of his sister. No doubt he too would have preferred to be at the Great Mother's festivities, which he, as aedile, was supposed to oversee, but he could hardly have backed out of the trial when his family's honour was at stake.

I cherish my memories of Cicero at this time, in the weeks before Rufus's trial. He seemed once again to hold all the threads of life in his hands, just as he had in his prime. He was active in the courts and in the Senate. He went out to dinner with his friends. He even moved back in to the house on the Palatine. True, it was not entirely finished. The place still reeked of lime and paint; workmen trailed mud in from the garden. But Cicero was so delighted to be back in his own home, he did not care. His furniture and books were fetched out of storage, the household gods were placed on the altar, and Terentia was summoned back from Tusculum with Tullia and Marcus.

Terentia entered the house cautiously and moved between the rooms with her nose wrinkled in distaste at the pungent smell of fresh plaster. She had never much cared for the place from the start, and was not about to change her opinion now. But Cicero persuaded her to stay: "That woman who caused you so much pain will never harm you again. She may have laid a hand on you. But I promise you: I shall flay her alive."

He also, to his great delight, after two years' separation, heard that Atticus had at last returned from Epirus. The moment he reached the city gates, he came straight round to inspect Cicero's rebuilt house. Unlike Quintus, Atticus had not changed at all. His smile was still as constant, his charm as thickly laid-on—"Tiro, *my dear fellow,* thank you *so much* for taking care of my oldest friend *so devotedly*"—his figure as trim, his silvery hair as sleek and well cut. The only difference was that now he trailed a shy young woman at least thirty years his junior, whom he introduced to Cicero . . . as his fiancée! I thought Cicero might faint with shock. Her name was Pilia. She was of an obscure family, with no money and no particular beauty either—just a quiet, homely country girl. But Atticus was besotted. At first Cicero was greatly put out. "It's ridiculous," he grumbled to me when the couple had gone. "He's three years older even than I am! Is it a wife he's after or a nurse?" I suspect he was mostly offended because Atticus had never mentioned her before, and worried that she might disrupt the easy intimacy of their friendship. But Atticus was so obviously happy, and Pilia so modest and cheerful, that Cicero soon came round to her, and sometimes I saw him glancing at her in an almost wistful way, especially when Terentia was being shrewish.

Pilia quickly became a close friend and confidante of Tullia. They were the same age and of similar temperaments, and I often saw them walking together, holding hands. Tullia had been a widow by this time for a year and encouraged by Pilia now declared herself ready to take a new husband. Cicero made enquiries about a suitable match and soon came up with Furius Crassipes—a young, rich, good-looking aristocrat, of an ancient but undistinguished family, eager for a career as a senator. He had also recently inherited a handsome house and a park just beyond the city walls. Tullia asked me for my opinion.

I said, "What I think doesn't matter. The question is: do you like him?"

"I think I do."

"Do you *think* you do or are you sure?"

"I'm sure."

"Then that is enough."

In truth I thought Crassipes was more in love with the idea of Cicero as a father-in-law than Tullia as a wife. But I kept this view to myself. A wedding date was fixed.

Who knows the secrets of another's marriage? Certainly not I. Cicero, for example, had long complained to me of Terentia's peevishness, of her obsession with money, of her superstition and her coldness and her rude tongue. And yet the whole of this elaborate legal spectacle he had contrived to be enacted in the centre of Rome was for her—his means of making amends for all the wrongs she had suffered because of the failure of his career. For the first time in their long marriage, he laid at her feet the greatest gift he had to offer her: his oratory.

Not that she wanted to listen to it, mind you. She had hardly ever heard him speak in public, and never in the law courts, and had no desire to start now. It took considerable amounts of Cicero's eloquence simply to persuade her to leave the house and come down to the Forum on the morning he was due to speak.

By this time the trial was in its second day. The prosecution had already laid out its case, Rufus and Crassus had responded, and only Cicero's address remained to be heard. He had sat through the other speeches with barely concealed impatience; the details of the case were irrelevant to him and the advocates bored him. Atratinus, in his disconcertingly piping voice, had portrayed Rufus as a libertine, addicted to pleasure, sunk in debt, "a pretty-boy Jason in perpetual search of a golden fleece" who had been paid by Ptolemy to intimidate the Alexandrian envoys and arrange the murder of Dio. Clodius had spoken next and described how his sister, "this chaste and distinguished widow," had been tricked by Rufus into giving him gold out of the goodness of her heart—money she had thought was to finance public entertainment but which he had used to bribe Dio's assassins—and how Rufus had then provided poison to her slaves to kill her and so cover his traces. Crassus, in his plodding way, and Rufus, with typical verve, had rebutted each of the charges. But the balance of opinion was that the prosecution had made its case and that the young reprobate was likely to be found guilty. This was the state of play when Cicero arrived in the Forum.

I conducted Terentia to her seat while he made his way through the thousands of spectators and went up the steps of the temple to the court. Seventy-five jurors had been empanelled. Beside them sat the praetor Domitius Calvinus with his lictors and scribes. To the left was the prosecution, with their witnesses arrayed behind them. And there in the front row, modestly attired but very much the centre of attention, was Clodia. She was almost forty but still beautiful, a grande dame with those famous huge dark eyes of hers that could invite intimacy one moment and threaten murder the next. She was known to be excessively close to Clodius—so much so that they had often been accused of incest. I saw her head turn very slightly to follow Cicero as he walked across to his place. Her expression was one of disdainful indifference. But she must have wondered what was coming.

Cicero adjusted the folds of his toga. He had no notes. A hush fell over the vast throng. He glanced across to where Terentia was sitting. Then he turned to the jury. "Gentlemen, anyone who doesn't know our laws and customs might wonder why we are here, during a public festival, when all the other courts are suspended, to judge a young man of hard work and brilliant intellect—especially when it turns out he is being attacked by a person he once prosecuted, and by the wealth of a courtesan."

At that, a great roar went rolling around the Forum, like the sound the crowd makes at the start of the games when a famous gladiator makes his first thrust. This was what they had come to see! Clodia stared straight ahead as if she had been turned to marble. I am sure that she and Clodius would never have brought their prosecution if they had thought there was a chance of Cicero being against them; but there was no escape now.

Having laid down a marker of what was to come, Cicero then proceeded to build his case. He conjured a picture of Rufus that was unrecognisable to those of us who knew him—of a sober, hard-working servant of the commonwealth whose main misfortune was to be "born not unhandsome," and thus to have come to the attention of Clodia, "the Medea of the Palatine," into whose neighbourhood he had moved. He stood behind the seated Rufus and clasped his hand on his shoulder. "His change of residence has been for this young man the cause of all his misfortunes and of all the gossip, for Clodia is a woman not only of noble birth but of notoriety, of whom I will say no more than what is necessary to refute the charges."

He paused to allow the sense of anticipation to build. "Now, as many of you will know, I am on terms of great personal enmity with this woman's husband ..." He stopped and snapped his fingers in exasperation. "I meant to say brother: I always make that mistake."

His timing was perfect, and to this day even people who otherwise know nothing of Cicero still quote that joke. Almost everyone in Rome had felt the arrogance of the Claudii at some point down the years; to see them ridiculed was irresistible. Its effect not just on the audience but on the jury and even the praetor was wonderful to behold.

Terentia turned to me in puzzlement. "Why is everyone laughing?"

I did not know what to reply.

When order was restored, Cicero continued, with menacing friendliness: "Well, I am truly sorry to have to make this woman an enemy, especially as she is every other man's friend. So let me first ask her whether she prefers me to deal with her severely, in the old-fashioned manner, or mildly, in the modern way?"

And then, to her evident horror, Cicero actually started walking across the court towards her. He was smiling, hand extended, inviting her to choose—the tiger playing with its prey. He halted barely a pace away from her.

"If she prefers the old method, then I must call up from the dead one of those full-bearded men of antiquity to rebuke her ..."

I have often pondered what Clodia should have done at this point. On reflection I believe her best course would have been to laugh along with Cicero—to try to win over the sympathy of the crowd by some piece of pantomime that would have shown she was entering into the spirit of the joke. But she was a Claudian. Never before had anyone dared openly to laugh at her, let alone the common people in the Forum. She was outraged, probably panicking, and so she responded in the worst way possible: she turned her back on Cicero like a sulky child.

He shrugged. "Very well, let me call up a member of her own family—to be specific, Appius Claudius the Blind. He will feel the least sorrow since he won't be able to see her. If he were to appear, this is what he would say ..."

And now Cicero addressed her in a ghostly voice, his eyes closed, his arms raised straight out in front of him; even Clodius started laughing. "Oh woman, what hast thou to do with Rufus, this stripling who is young enough to be thy son? Why hast thou been either so intimate with him as to give him gold, or caused such jealousy as to warrant the administering of poison? Why was Rufus so closely connected with thee? Is he a kinsman? A relative by marriage? A friend of thine late husband? None of these! What else could it have been then between you two except reckless passion? O woe! Was it for this that I brought water to Rome, that thou mightest use it after thy incestuous debauches? Was it for this that I built the Appian Way, that thou mightest frequent it with a train of other women's husbands?"

With that, the ghost of old Appius Claudius evaporated and Cicero addressed Clodia's turned back in his normal voice. "But if you prefer a more congenial relative, let us speak to you in the voice of your youngest brother over there, who loves you *most* dearly— who, as a boy, in fact, being of a nervous disposition and prey to night terrors, always used to get into bed with his big sister. Imagine him saying to you"—and now Cicero perfectly imitated Clodius's fashionable slouching stance and plebeian drawl—"what's there to worry about, sister? So what if you fancied some young fellow. He was handsome. He was tall. You couldn't get enough of him. You knew you were old enough to be his mother. But you were rich. So you bought him things to purchase his affection. It didn't last long. He called you a hag. Well, forget him—just find yourself another one, or two, or ten. After all, that's what you usually do."

Clodius was no longer laughing. He looked at Cicero as if he would like to clamber over the benches of the court and strangle him. But the audience were laughing right enough. I glanced around and saw men and women with tears running down their cheeks. Empathy is the essence of the orator's art. Cicero had that immense crowd entirely on his side, and after he had made them laugh with him, it was easy for him to make them share his outrage as he moved in for the kill.

"I am now forgetting, Clodia, the wrongs you have done me; I am putting aside the memory of what I have suffered; I pass over your cruel actions towards my family during my absence; but I ask you this: if a woman without a husband opens her house to all men's desires, and publicly leads the life of a courtesan; if she is in the habit of attending dinner parties with men who are perfect strangers; if she does this in Rome, in her park outside the city walls, and amid all those crowds on the Bay of Naples; if her embraces and caresses, her beach parties, her water parties, her dinner parties, proclaim her to be not only a courtesan, but also a shameless and wanton courtesan—if she does all that and a young man should be discovered consorting with this woman, should he be considered the corrupter or the corrupted, the seducer or the seduced?

"This whole charge arises from a hostile, infamous, merciless, crime-stained, lust-stained house. An unstable and angry wanton of a woman has forged this accusation. Gentlemen of the jury: do not allow Marcus Caelius Rufus to be sacrificed to her lust. If you restore Rufus in safety to me, to his family, to the state, you will find in him one pledged, devoted and bound to you and to your children; and it is you above all, gentlemen, who will reap the rich and lasting fruits of all his exertions and labours."

And with that it was over. For a moment Cicero stood there—one hand stretched towards the jury, the other towards Rufus—and there was silence. Then some great subterranean force seemed to rise from beneath the Forum, and an instant later the air began to tremble as several thousand pairs of feet stamped the ground and the crowd roared their approval. Someone started pointing repeatedly at Clodia and shouting, "Whore! Whore! Whore!" and very quickly the chant was taken up all around us, the arms flashing out again and again: "Whore! Whore! Whore!"

Clodia looked out blank-faced with incredulity across this sea of hatred. She didn't seem to notice that her brother had moved across the court and was standing beside her. But then he grasped her elbow and that seemed to jolt her out of her reverie. She glanced up at him, and finally, after some gentle coaxing, she allowed herself to be led off the platform and out of sight and into an obscurity from which it is fair to say she never again emerged as long as she lived.

THUS DID CICERO EXACT HIS REVENGE ON CLODIA AND RECLAIM HIS place as the dominant voice in Rome. It is hardly necessary to add that Rufus was acquitted and that Clodius's loathing of Cicero was redoubled. "One day," he hissed, "you will hear a sound behind you, and when you turn, I shall be there, I promise you." Cicero laughed at the crudeness of the threat, knowing he was too popular for Clodius to dare to attack him—at least for now. As for Terentia, although she deplored the vulgarity of Cicero's jokes and was appalled by the rudeness of the mob, nevertheless she was pleased by the utter social annihilation of her enemy, and as she and Cicero walked home, she took his arm—the first time I had witnessed such a public gesture of affection for years.

The following day, when Cicero went down the hill to attend a meeting of the Senate, he was mobbed both by the ordinary people and by the scores of senators waiting outside the chamber for the session to begin. As he received the congratulations of his peers, he looked exactly as he had done in his days of power, and I could see that he was quite intoxicated by his reception. As it happened, this was the Senate's final meeting before it rose for its annual vacation, and there was a febrile mood in the air. After the haruspices had ruled the heavens propitious, and just as the senators started to file in for the start of the debate, Cicero beckoned me over and pointed on the order paper to the main subject to be discussed that day: the grant of forty million sesterces from the treasury to Pompey, to finance his grain purchases.

"This could be interesting." He nodded to the figure of Crassus, just then stalking into the chamber, wearing a grim expression. "I had a word with him about it yesterday. First Egypt, now this—he's in a rage at Pompey's megalomania. The thieves are at one another's throats, Tiro: there could be an opportunity for mischief here."

"Be careful," I warned him.

"Oh dear, yes: 'Be careful!'" he mocked, and tapped me on the head with the rolled-up order paper. "Well, I have a little power after yesterday, and you know what I always say: power is for using."

With that he went off cheerfully into the Senate building.

I had not been intending to stay for the session, having much work to do in preparing Cicero's speech of the previous day for publication. But now I changed my mind and went and stood at the doorway. The presiding consul was Cornelius Lentulus Marcellinus, a patriotic aristocrat of the old sort—hostile to Clodius, supportive of Cicero and suspicious of Pompey. He made sure to call a series of speakers who all denounced the granting of such a huge sum to Pompey. As one pointed out, there was no money available in any case, every spare copper being swallowed up implementing Caesar's law that gave the Campanian lands to Pompey's veterans and the urban poor. The house grew rowdy. Pompey's supporters heckled his opponents. His opponents shouted back. (Pompey himself was not allowed to be present, as the grain commission conveyed imperium—a power that barred its holders from entering the Senate.) Crassus looked gratified with the way things were going. Finally, Cicero indicated that he wished to speak, and the house became quiet as senators leaned forwards to hear what he had to say.

"Honourable members," he said, "will recall that it was on my proposal that Pompey was given this grain commission in the first place, so I am hardly going to oppose it now. We cannot order a man to do a job one day, and then deny him the means with which to accomplish it the next." Pompey's supporters murmured loud assent. Cicero held up his hand. "However, as has been eloquently pointed out, our resources are finite. The treasury cannot pay for everything. We cannot be expected to buy grain all over the world to feed our citizens for nothing and at the same time give free farms to soldiers and plebs. When Caesar passed his law, even he, with all his great powers of foresight, can hardly have imagined that a day was coming—and coming very soon—when veterans and the urban poor would have no need of farms to grow grain, because the grain would simply be given to them for nothing."

"Oh!" shouted the benches of the aristocrats in delight. "Oh! Oh!" And they pointed at Crassus, who, along with Pompey and Caesar, was one of the architects of the land laws. Crassus was staring hard at Cicero, although his face was impassive and it was impossible to tell what he was thinking.

"Would it not be prudent," continued Cicero, "in the light of changing circumstances, for this noble house to look again at the legislation passed during the consulship of Caesar? Now is obviously not the right occasion to discuss it fully, complex as the question is, and conscious as I am that the house is eager to rise for the recess. I would therefore propose that the issue be placed on the order paper at the first available opportunity when we reconvene."

"I second that!" shouted Domitius Ahenobarbus, a patrician who was married to Cato's sister, and who hated Caesar so much he had recently called for him to be stripped of his command in Gaul.

Several dozen other aristocrats also jumped up clamouring to add their support. Pompey's men seemed too confused to react: after all, the main thrust of Cicero's speech had seemed to be in support of their chief. It was indeed a tidy piece of mischief that Cicero had wrought, and when he sat down and glanced along the aisle in my direction, I almost fancy he winked at me. The consul held a whispered conference with his scribes and then announced that in view of the obvious support for Cicero's motion, the issue would be debated on the Ides of May. With that the house was adjourned and the senators started moving towards the exit— none quicker than Crassus, who almost knocked me flying in his eagerness to get away.

CICERO, TOO, WAS DETERMINED TO HAVE A HOLIDAY, FEELING HE deserved one after seven months of non-stop strain and labour, and he had in mind the ideal destination. A wealthy tax farmer for whom he had done much legal work had lately died, leaving Cicero some property in his will—a small villa on the Bay of Naples, at Cumae, between the sea and the Lucrine Lake. (In those days, I should add, it was illegal to accept direct payment for one's services as an advocate, but permissible to receive legacies; the rule was not always strictly observed.) Cicero had never seen the place but had heard that it enjoyed one of the loveliest aspects in the region. He proposed to Terentia that they should travel to inspect it together, and she agreed, although when she discovered I was to be included in the party, she plunged into another of her sulks.

"I know how it will be," I overheard her complaining to Cicero. "I shall be left alone all day while you are closeted with your official wife!"

He made some soothing reply to the effect that no such thing would happen, and I was careful to keep out of her way.

On the eve of our departure, Cicero gave a dinner for his future son-in-law, Crassipes, who happened to mention that Crassus, to whom he was very close, had left Rome in a hurry the previous day, telling no one where he was going. Cicero said, "No doubt he's heard of some elderly widow in a remote spot who is at death's door and who might be persuaded to part with her property cheaply."

Everyone laughed apart from Crassipes, who looked very prim. "I am sure he is simply taking a vacation, like everyone else."

"Crassus doesn't take holidays—there's no profit in them." Then

Cicero raised his cup and proposed a toast to Crassipes and Tullia. "May their union be long and happy and blessed with many children—for preference I should like three at least."

"Father!" exclaimed Tullia. She laughed and blushed and looked away.

"What?" asked Cicero, with an air of innocence. "I have the grey hairs and now I need the grandchildren to go with them."

He rose from the table early. Before he left for the south he wanted to see Pompey. In particular he wanted to plead the case for Quintus to be allowed to relinquish his legateship and return home from Sardinia. He travelled to Pompey's in a litter but ordered the porters to go slowly so that I could walk alongside and we could have some conversation. It was getting dark. We had to travel a mile or so, beyond the city walls, to the Pincian hill, where Pompey had his new suburban villa—or palace would be a better word for it—looking down on his vast complex of temples and theatres then nearing completion on the Field of Mars.

The great man was dining alone with his wife, and we had to wait for them to finish. In the vestibule a team of slaves was busy transferring piles of luggage to half a dozen wagons drawn up in the courtyard—so many trunks of clothes and boxes of tableware and carpets and furniture and even statues that it looked as if Pompey were planning to set up a new home somewhere. Eventually the couple appeared and Pompey presented Julia to Cicero, who in turn presented me to her.

"I remember you," she said to me, although I'm sure she didn't. She was only seventeen but very gracious. She possessed her father's exquisite manners, and also something of his piercing way of looking at one, so that I had a sudden, disconcerting memory of Caesar's naked hairless torso reclining on the massage table at his headquarters in Mutina: I had to shut my eyes to banish it.

She left almost at once, pleading the need to get a good night's sleep before her travels the next day. Pompey kissed her hand—he was famously devoted to her—and took us through into his study. This was a vast room the size of a house, crammed with trophies from his many campaigns, including what he insisted was the cloak of Alexander the Great. He sat on a couch made out of a stuffed crocodile, which he said Ptolemy had given him, and invited Cicero to take the seat opposite.

Cicero said, "You look as though you are embarking on a military expedition."

"That's what comes of travelling with one's wife."

"Might I ask where you're going?"

"Sardinia."

"Ah," said Cicero, "that's a coincidence. I wanted to ask you about Sardinia." And he proceeded to make an eloquent case for his brother to be allowed home, citing three reasons in particular—the length of time he had been away, his need to spend time with his son (who was turning into a troubled boy) and his preference for military rather than civil command.

Pompey heard him out, stroking his chin, reclining on his Egyptian crocodile. "If that's what you want," he said. "Yes, he can come back. You're right anyway—he isn't much good at administration."

"Thank you. I'm obliged to you, as always."

Pompey regarded Cicero with crafty eyes. "So I hear you caused a stir in the Senate the other day."

"Only on your behalf—I was simply trying to secure the funds for your commission."

"Yes, but by challenging Caesar's laws." He wagged his finger in reproach. "That's naughty of you."

"Caesar is not a god, infallible; his laws have not come down to us from Mount Olympus. Besides, if you'd been there and seen the pleasure Crassus was taking in all the attacks on you, I believe you would have wanted me to find some way to wipe the smile from his face. And by criticising Caesar, I certainly did that."

Pompey brightened at once. "Oh well, I'm with you there!"

"Believe me, Crassus's ambition and disloyalty to you have been far more destabilising to the commonwealth than anything *I* have done."

"I agree entirely."

"In fact I'd suggest that if your alliance with Caesar is threatened by anyone, it's him."

"How is that?"

"Well, I don't understand how Caesar can stand back and allow him to plot against you in this way, especially letting him employ Clodius. Surely as your father-in-law he owes his first duty to you? If Crassus carries on like this, he will sow much discord, I predict it now."

"He will." Pompey nodded. He looked crafty again. "You're right, of course." He stood, and Cicero followed suit. He took Cicero's hand in both his immense paws. "Thank you for coming to see me, my old friend. You have given me much food for thought during my voyage to Sardinia. We must write to one another often. Where exactly will you be?"

"Cumae."

"Ah! I envy you. Cumae—the most beautiful spot in Italy."

Cicero was well pleased with his night's work. On the way home he said to me, "This triple alliance of theirs can't last. It defies nature. All I have to do is keep chipping away at it, and sooner or later the whole rotten edifice will come crashing down."

We left Rome at first light—Terentia, Tullia and Marcus all in the same carriage, along with Cicero, who was in great good humour—and made quick progress, stopping first for a night at Tusculum, which Cicero was glad to find habitable again, and then at the family estate in Arpinium, where we remained for a week. Finally from those cold high peaks of the Apennines we descended south to Campania.

With every mile the clouds of winter seemed to lift, the sky became bluer, the temperature warmer, the air more fragrant with the scent of pines and herbs, and when we joined the coastal road, the breeze off the sea was balmy. Cumae was then a much smaller and quieter town than it is today. At the Acropolis I gave a description of our destination and was directed by a priest to the eastern side of the Lucrine Lake, to a spot low in the hills, looking out across the lagoon and the narrow spit of land to the variegated

blueness of the Mediterranean. The villa itself was small and dilapidated, with half a dozen elderly slaves to look after it. The wind
blew through open walls; a section of the roof was missing. But it
was worth every discomfort simply for the panorama. Down on the
lake, little rowing boats moved among the oyster beds, while from
the garden at the back there rose a majestic view of the lush green
pyramid of Vesuvius. Cicero was enchanted, and set to work at
once with the local builders, commissioning a great programme of
renovation and redecoration. Marcus played on the beach with his
tutor. Terentia sat on the terrace and sewed. Tullia read her Greek.
It was a family holiday of a sort they had not taken for many years.

There was one puzzle, however. That whole stretch of coast from
Cumae to Puteoli, then as now, was dotted with villas belonging to
members of the Senate. Naturally Cicero assumed that once word
spread he was in residence, he would begin to receive callers. But
nobody came. At night he stood on the terrace and looked up and
down the seashore and peered up into the hills and complained he
could see hardly any lights. Where were the parties, the dinners?
He patrolled the beach, a mile in either direction, and not once did
he spot a senatorial toga.

"Something must be happening," he said to Terentia. "Where are
they all?"

"I don't know," she replied, "but speaking for myself, I am happy
there is no one with whom you can discuss politics."

The answer came on our fifth morning.

I was on the terrace answering Cicero's correspondence when I
noticed that a small group of horsemen had turned off the coastal
road and were coming up the track towards the house. My immediate thought was *Clodius*! I stood to get a better view and saw to my
dismay that the sun was glinting on helmets and breastplates. Five
riders: soldiers.

Terentia and the children had gone off for the day to visit the
sibyl who was said to live in a jar in a cave at Cumae. I ran inside
to alert Cicero, and by the time I found him—he was choosing the
colour scheme for the dining room—the horsemen were already

clattering into the courtyard. Their leader dismounted and took off his helmet. He was a fearsome apparition: dust-rimed, like some harbinger of death. The whiteness of his nose and forehead was in contrast to the grime of the rest of his face. He looked as if he wore a mask. But I knew him. He was a senator, albeit not a very distinguished one—a member of that tame, dependable class of pederii who never spoke but merely voted with their feet. Lucius Vibullius Rufus was his name. He was one of Pompey's officers from Pompey's home region of Picenum naturally.

"Could I have a word?" he said gruffly.

"Of course," said Cicero. "Come inside, all of you. Come and have something to eat and drink, I insist."

Vibullius said, "I'll come in. They'll wait out here and make sure we're not disturbed." He moved very stiffly, a clay effigy come to life.

Cicero said, "You look all in. How far have you ridden?"

"From Luca."

"Luca?" repeated Cicero. "That must be three hundred miles!"

"More like three hundred and fifty. We've been on the road a week." As he lowered himself to a seat, he gave off a shower of dust. "There's been a meeting concerning you, and I've been sent to inform you of its conclusions." He glanced at me. "I need to speak in confidence."

Cicero, baffled and plainly wondering if he was dealing with a madman, said, "He's my secretary. You can say all you have to say in front of him. What meeting?"

"As you wish." Vibullius tugged off his gloves, unbuckled the side of his breastplate, reached under the metal and pulled out a document, which he carefully unwrapped. "The reason I've come from Luca is because that's where Pompey, Caesar and Crassus have been meeting."

Cicero frowned. "No, that's impossible. Pompey is going to Sardinia—he told me so himself."

"A man can do both, can he not?" replied Vibullius affably. "He can go to Luca and then go to Sardinia. I can tell you in fact how it came about. After your little speech in the Senate, Crassus travelled up to see Caesar in Ravenna to tell him what you'd said. Then they both crossed Italy to intercept Pompey before he took ship at Pisa. The three of them spent several days together, discussing many matters—among them what's to be done about *you*."

I felt suddenly queasy. Cicero was more robust: "There's no need to be impertinent."

"And the gist of it is this: *shut up, Marcus Tullius!* Shut up in the Senate about Caesar's laws. Shut up trying to cause trouble between the Three. Shut up about Crassus. Shut up generally, in fact."

"Have you finished?" asked Cicero calmly. "Do I need to remind you—you are a guest in my house?"

"Not quite finished, no." Vibullius paused and consulted his notes. "Also present for part of the conference was Sardinia's governor, Appius Claudius. He was there to make certain undertakings on behalf of his brother, the upshot of which is that Pompey and Clodius are to be publicly reconciled."

"Reconciled?" repeated Cicero. Now he sounded uncertain.

"In future they will stand together in the best interests of the commonwealth. Pompey wishes me to tell you that he's very unhappy with you, Marcus Tullius: very unhappy. I am quoting his exact words now. He believes he demonstrated great loyalty to you in campaigning for your recall from exile, in the course of which he made certain personal undertakings about your future conduct to Caesar—undertakings, he reminds you, which you repeated to Caesar in writing, and have now broken. He feels let down. He feels embarrassed. He insists, as a test of friendship, that you withdraw your motion on Caesar's land laws from the Senate, and that you do not pronounce on the issue again until you have consulted him in person."

"I only spoke as I did in Pompey's interest—"

"He would like you to write him a letter confirming that you will do as he asks." Vibullius rolled up his document and tucked it away under his cuirass. "That's the official part. What I am about to tell you next is strictly confidential. You understand what I'm saying?"

Cicero made a weary gesture. He understood.

"Pompey wishes you to appreciate the scale of the forces at work: that is why the others gave him permission to inform you. Later this year, both he and Crassus will put their names forward in the consular elections."

"They'll lose."

"If the elections were to be held as usual in the summer, you might be right. But the elections will be postponed."

"Why?"

"Because of violence in Rome."

"What violence?"

"Clodius will provide the violence. As a result, the elections won't take place until the winter, by which time the campaigning season in Gaul will be over and Caesar will be able to send thousands of his veterans to Rome to vote for his colleagues. *Then* they will be elected. At the end of their terms as consul, Pompey and Crassus will both take up proconsular commands—Pompey in Spain, Crassus in Syria. Instead of the usual one year, these commands will last for five years. Naturally, in the interests of fairness, Caesar's proconsular command in Gaul will also be extended for another five years."

"This is quite unbelievable—"

"And at the end of his extended term, Caesar will come back to Rome and be elected consul in his turn—Pompey and Crassus making sure *their* veterans are on hand to vote for him. Those are the terms of the Luca Accord. It is designed to last for seven years. Pompey has promised Caesar you will abide by it."

"And if I do not?"

"He will no longer guarantee your safety."

# VI

---·-•-·---

"SEVEN YEARS," SAID CICERO WITH GREAT CONTEMPT AFTER VIBUL-
lius and his men had gone. "Nothing in politics can be planned in
advance for *seven years.* Is Pompey entirely lacking in sense? Does
he not see how this devils' pact works entirely in Caesar's favour?
In effect, he promises to protect Caesar's back until such time as
Caesar has finished pillaging Gaul, whereupon the conqueror will
return to Rome and take control of the whole republic—Pompey
included."

He sat slumped on the terrace in despair. From the shore below
came the lonely cries of seabirds as the oyster fishermen landed
their catch. We knew now why the neighbourhood was so deserted.
According to Vibullius, half the Senate had got wind of what was
happening in Luca and more than a hundred had gone north to try
to get their share of the spoils. They had forsaken the sun of Campania to bask in the warmest sun of all: power.

"I am a fool," said Cicero, "to be counting the waves down here
while the future of the world is being decided at the other end of
the country. Let's face it, Tiro. I am a spent force. Every man has his
season, and I have had mine."

Later in the day Terentia returned from her visit to the sibyl's
cave in Cumae. She noticed the dust on the carpets and the furniture and asked who had been in the house. Reluctantly Cicero
described what had happened.

Her eyes shone. She said excitedly, "How strange that you should
tell me this! The sibyl prophesied this very outcome. She said that
first Rome would be ruled by three, and then by two, and then by
one, and then by none."

Even Cicero, who regarded the notion of a sibyl living in a jar and predicting the future as entirely fatuous, was impressed. "Three, two, one, none . . . Well, we know who the three are—that's obvious. And I can guess who the one will be. But who will be the two? And what does she mean by none? Is that her way of predicting chaos? If so, I agree—that's what will follow if we allow Caesar to tear up the constitution. But for the life of me I can't see how I am to stop him."

"Why should *you* be the one to stop him?" demanded Terentia.

"I don't know. Who else is there?"

"But why does it always fall to *you* to block Caesar's ambitions when Pompey, the most powerful man in the state, will do nothing to assist you? Why is it your responsibility?"

Cicero fell silent. Eventually he responded, "It's a good question. Perhaps it's just conceit on my part. But can I really, with honour, stand back and do nothing, when every instinct tells me the nation is heading for disaster?"

"Yes!" she cried with passion. "Yes! Absolutely! Haven't you suffered enough for your opposition to Caesar? Is there another man in the world who has endured more? Why not let others take up the fight? Surely you've earned the right to some peace at last?" Then quietly she added, "I am sure that I have."

Cicero did not answer for a long time. The truth, I suspect, is that from the moment he learnt about the Luca agreement, he knew in his heart that he could not continue opposing Caesar—not if he wanted to live. All he needed was for someone to put the issue to him bluntly, as Terentia had just done.

Finally he sighed with a weariness I had never before heard. "You're right, my wife. At least no one will ever be able to reproach me for not having seen Caesar for what he is, and for not trying to stop him. But you are right—I'm too old and tired to fight him any longer. My friends will understand and my enemies will denounce me whatever I do, so why should I care what they think? Why shouldn't I enjoy some leisure at last down here in the sun with my family?"

And he reached over and took her hand.

. . .

NEVERTHELESS, HE WAS ASHAMED OF HIS CAPITULATION. I KNOW that, because although he wrote a long letter to Pompey in Sardinia setting out his change of heart—his "palinode," he called it—he never let me see it and kept no copy. Nor did he show it to Atticus. At the same time he wrote to the consul Marcellinus announcing that he wished to withdraw his motion calling on the Senate to re-examine Caesar's land laws. He offered no explanation; he did not need to; everyone recognised that the political firmament had shifted and the new alignment was against him.

We returned to a Rome full of rumours. Few knew for sure what Pompey and Crassus were planning, but gradually word got around that they were intending to run on a joint ticket for the consul-ship, just as they had in the past, even though everyone knew they had always loathed one another. Some senators, however, were determined to fight back against the cynicism and arrogance of the Three. A debate was scheduled on the allocation of consular provinces, and one motion called for Caesar to be stripped of both Nearer and Further Gaul. Cicero knew that if he attended the chamber, he would be asked his views. He considered staying away. But then he reasoned that he would have to recant publicly sooner or later: he might as well get it over with. He began working on his speech.

And then, on the eve of the debate, after more than two years away in Cyprus, Marcus Porcius Cato returned to Rome. He arrived in fine style, in a flotilla of treasure ships, sailing up the Tiber from Ostia, accompanied by his nephew, Brutus, a young man of whom great things were expected. The whole of the Senate, and all of the magistrates and priests, as well as most of the population, turned out to welcome Cato home. There was a landing stage with painted poles and ribbons where he was supposed to disembark and meet the consuls, but he sailed on past them, standing in the prow of a royal galley that had six banks of oars, his bony profile fixed straight ahead, wearing a shabby black tunic. The crowds at first gasped and groaned with disappointment at his high-handedness, but then his treasure started to be unloaded—ox wagon after ox wagon of it, seven thousand silver talents' worth in all, that wound in procession from the Navalia all the way to the state treasury in the Temple of Saturn. With this one contribution, Cato transformed the finances of the nation—it was enough to provide free grain to the citizenry for five years—and the Senate went into immediate session to vote him an honorary praetorship, together with the right to wear a special purple-bordered toga.

Called upon by Marcellinus to respond, Cato scornfully denounced what he called "these corrupt baubles": "I have discharged the duty placed upon me by the Roman people—an assignment I never requested and would have preferred not to have undertaken. Now that it is done, I need no Eastern flattery or showy garments to puff myself up: the knowledge that I have performed my duty is reward enough for me, as it should be for any man."

He was back in the chamber for the next day's debate on the provinces, as if he had never been away—sitting in his customary position, going through a set of the treasury's accounts as he always did to make sure there was no waste in public expenditure. Only when Cicero rose to speak did he put them aside.

It was quite late on in the session and most ex-consuls had already given their opinions. Even so, Cicero managed to spin out the suspense a little longer by devoting the first part of his speech to an attack on his old enemies Piso and Gabinius, governors of Macedonia and Syria respectively. Then the consul, Marcius Philippus, who was married to Caesar's niece, and who was growing restless like many others, interrupted him to ask why he spent all his time attacking those two puppets when the man who had really instigated the campaign that led to his exile was Caesar. This gave Cicero precisely the opening he wanted. "Because," he said, "I am taking account of the public welfare rather than my own grievances. It is this old and unfailing loyalty of mine to the republic which restores, reconciles and reinstates me in friendship with Gaius Caesar.

"For me," he went on, having to shout now to be heard above the jeers, "it is impossible not to be the friend of one who renders good service to the state. Under Caesar's command we have fought a war in Gaul, whereas before we merely repelled attacks. Unlike his predecessors he believes the whole of Gaul should be brought under our rule. And so he has, with brilliant success, crushed in battle the fiercest and greatest tribes of Germania and Helvetia; the rest he has terrified, checked and subdued and taught to submit to the rule of the Roman people.

"But the war is not yet won. If Caesar is removed, the embers may yet burst out again into flame. Therefore, as a senator—even as the man's personal enemy, if you like—I must lay aside private grievances for the sake of the state, for how can I be the enemy of this man, whose dispatches, whose fame, whose envoys fill our ears every day with fresh names of races, peoples and places?"

It was not his most convincing performance, and towards the end he rather tripped himself up by trying to pretend that he and Caesar had never really been enemies at all, a piece of sophistry that was greeted with derision. Still, he got through it. The motion to replace Caesar was defeated and at the end of the session, even though the most passionate anti-Caesareans—men like Aheno-barbus and Bibulus—pointedly turned their backs on him in con-tempt, Cicero walked towards the exit with his head unbowed. That was when Cato intercepted him. I was waiting by the door and was able to overhear their whole exchange.

Cato: "I am beyond disappointed in you, Marcus Tullius. Your desertion has just cost us what may have been our last chance to stop a dictator."

Cicero: "Why should I want to stop a man who is winning vic-tory after victory?"

Cato: "But who is he winning these victories for? Is it for the republic or is it for himself? And when did it become national pol-icy to conquer Gaul in any case? Has the Senate or the people ever authorised this war of his?"

Cicero: "Then why don't you put down a motion to end it?"

Cato: "Perhaps I shall."

Cicero: "Yes—and see how far it gets you! Welcome home, incidentally."

But Cato was in no mood for such pleasantries and stamped off to talk to Bibulus and Ahenobarbus. From this time on it was he who led the opposition to Caesar, while Cicero retreated to his house on the Palatine, and to a quieter life.

THERE WAS NOTHING HEROIC IN WHAT CICERO HAD DONE. HE realised his loss of face. *Good night to principle, sincerity and honour!* was how he summed it up in a letter to Atticus.

Yet even after all these years, and even with the wisdom of hindsight, I do not see what else he could have done. It was easier for Cato to spit defiance at Caesar. He was from a rich and powerful family, and he did not have the constant threat of Clodius hanging over him.

Everything now proceeded exactly as the Three had planned, and Cicero could not have stopped it even if he had sacrificed his life. First, Clodius and his ruffians disrupted the canvassing for the consular elections so that the campaign came to a stop. Then they threatened and intimidated the other candidates until they withdrew. Finally the elections had to be postponed. Only Ahenobarbus, with the support of Cato, had the courage to continue to stand for the consulship against Pompey and Crassus. Most of the Senate put on mourning in protest.

That winter, for the first time, the city was filled with Caesar's veterans—drinking, whoring and threatening any who refused to salute the effigy of their leader when they set it up at crossroads. On the eve of the postponed poll, Cato and Ahenobarbus went down by torchlight to the voting pens to try to stake out their canvassing position. But they were attacked en route, either by Clodius's men or Caesar's and their torchbearer was killed. Cato was stabbed in his right arm, and although he entreated Ahenobarbus to stand firm, the candidate fled back to his house and barricaded the door and refused to come out. The next day Pompey and Crassus were elected consuls, and soon after that, as agreed at Luca, they made sure they were allotted the provinces they desired to govern at the end of their joint term of office: Spain for Pompey, Syria for Crassus, both commands awarded for five years instead of the normal one, with a further five-year extension for Caesar as proconsul in Gaul. Pompey never even left Rome, but governed Spain through his subordinates.

Throughout all this, Cicero kept clear of politics. On the days when he had no engagements in the law courts, he stayed at home and supervised the schooling of his son and nephew in grammar, Greek and rhetoric. He dined quietly most evenings with Terentia. He composed poetry. He began to write a book on the history and practice of oratory.

"I am still an exile," he remarked to me, "only now my exile is in Rome."

Caesar quickly heard reports of Cicero's about-face in the Senate and immediately sent him a letter of thanks. I recall Cicero's surprise when it arrived, delivered by one of Caesar's superbly swift and reliable military couriers. As I have explained, nearly all their correspondence has since been seized. But I remember the opening, because it was always the same:

> From: G. Caesar, Imperator, to M. Cicero, greetings.
>    I and the army are well . . .

And this particular letter had one other passage I have never forgotten: *It pleases me to know I have a place in your heart. There is not a man in Rome whose opinion I prize more than yours. You may rely on me in all things.* Cicero was torn between feelings of gratitude and shame, relief and despair. He showed the letter to his brother, Quintus, who had just returned from Sardinia.

Quintus said, "You have done the right thing. Pompey has proved a fickle friend. Caesar may be more loyal." And then he added, "To be honest, Pompey treated me with such contempt while I was away that I wondered if I might not do better to throw in my own lot with Caesar."

"And how would you do that?"

"Well, I am a soldier, am I not? Perhaps I could ask for a position on his staff. Or perhaps you could ask for a commission on my behalf."

At first Cicero was uncertain: he had no desire to beg for favours from Caesar. But then he saw how unhappy Quintus was to be back in Rome. There was his miserable marriage to Pomponia, of course, but it was more than that. He was not an advocate or orator like his elder brother. Neither the law courts nor the Senate held much appeal. He had already served as praetor and as a governor in Asia. The sole remaining step for him in politics was a consulship, and he would never gain that unless he enjoyed some spectacular stroke of good fortune or patronage. And then again, the only sphere in which such a transformation might come his way was on the battlefield . . .

The possibility seemed remote, but by such reasoning the brothers convinced themselves that they should further tie their fortunes to those of Caesar. Cicero wrote to him requesting a commission for Quintus, and Caesar replied at once that he would be delighted to oblige. Not only that: he asked Cicero in return if he would help supervise the great rebuilding programme he was planning in Rome to rival Pompey's. Some hundred million sesterces was to be spent on laying out a new forum in the centre of the city and creating a covered walkway a mile long on the Field of Mars. As recompense for his efforts Caesar gave Cicero a loan of eight hundred thousand sesterces at two and a quarter per cent interest, half the market rate.

That was how he was. He was like a whirlpool. He sucked men in by the sheer force of his energy and power until almost the whole of Rome was mesmerised by him. Whenever his *Commentaries* were posted up outside the Regia, crowds would gather and remain there all day reading of his exploits. That year his young protégé Decimus defeated the Celts in a great naval battle in the Atlantic, after which Caesar caused their entire nation to be sold into slavery and their leaders executed. Brittany was conquered, the Pyrenees pacified, Flanders suppressed. Every community in Gaul was required to pay a levy, even after he had sacked their towns and carted off all their ancient treasures. A vast but peaceful German migration of 430,000 members of the Usipetes and Tencteri tribes crossed the Rhine and was lulled by Caesar into a false sense of security when he pretended to agree to a truce; then he annihilated them. His engineers erected a bridge across the Rhine and he and his legion rampaged about through Germany for eighteen days before withdrawing back into Gaul and dismantling the bridge behind them. Finally, as if this were not enough, he put to sea with two legions and landed on the barbarian shores of Britain—a place that many in Rome had refused to believe even existed, and which certainly lay beyond the limits of the known world—burned a few villages, captured some slaves, and then sailed home before the winter storms trapped him.

To celebrate his victories Pompey summoned a meeting of the Senate to vote his father-in-law a further twenty days of public supplication, whereupon a scene ensued that I have never forgotten. One after another the senators rose to praise Caesar, Cicero dutifully among them, until at last there was no one left for Pompey to call except Cato.

"Gentlemen," said Cato, "yet again you have all taken leave of your senses. By Caesar's own account he has slaughtered four hundred thousand men, women and children—people with whom we had no quarrel, with whom we were not at war, in a campaign not authorised by a vote either of this Senate or of the Roman people. I wish to lay two counter-proposals for you to consider: first, that far from holding celebrations, we should sacrifice to the gods that they do not turn their wrath for Caesar's folly and madness upon Rome and the army; and second, that Caesar, having shown himself a war criminal, should be handed over to the tribes of Germany for them to determine his fate."

The shouts of rage that greeted this speech were like howls of pain: "Traitor!" "Gaul-lover!" "German!" Several senators jumped up and started shoving Cato this way and that, causing him to stumble backwards. But he was a strong and wiry man. He regained his balance and stood his ground, glaring at them like an eagle. A motion was proposed that he be taken directly by the lictors to the Carcer and imprisoned until such time as he apologised. Pompey, however, was too shrewd to permit his martyrdom. "Cato by his words has done himself more harm than any punishment we can inflict," he declared. "Let him go free. It does not matter. He will stand forever condemned in the eyes of the Roman people for such treacherous sentiments."

I too felt that Cato had done himself great damage among all moderate and sensible opinion; I remarked as much to Cicero as we walked home. Given his new-found closeness to Caesar, I expected him to agree. But to my surprise he shook his head. "No, you are quite wrong. Cato is a prophet. He blurts out the truth with the clarity of a child or a madman. Rome will rue the day it tied its destiny to Caesar's. And so shall I."

I MAKE NO CLAIM TO BE A PHILOSOPHER, BUT THIS MUCH I HAVE observed: that whenever a thing seems at its zenith, you may be sure its destruction has already started.

So it was with the triumvirate. It towered above the landscape of politics like some granite monolith. Yet it had weaknesses that none could see and which were only to be revealed with time. Of these the most dangerous was the inordinate ambition of Crassus.

For years he had been feted as the richest man in Rome, with a fortune of some eight thousand talents, or nearly two hundred million sesterces. But latterly this had come to seem almost paltry compared to the wealth of Pompey and Caesar, who each had the resources of entire countries at their disposal. Therefore Crassus had set his heart on going out to Syria not to administer it but to use it as a base from which to mount a military expedition against the Parthian empire. Those who knew anything of the treacherous sands and cruel peoples of Arabia thought the plan was hugely risky—not least, I am sure, Pompey. But such was his detestation of Crassus that he did nothing to dissuade him. As for Caesar, he too encouraged him. He sent Crassus's son Publius—whom I had met in Mutina—back to Rome from Gaul with a detachment of one thousand highly trained cavalry so that he could join his father as deputy commander-in-chief.

Cicero despised Crassus more than he did any other man in Rome. Even for Clodius he could occasionally summon a certain reluctant respect. But Crassus he considered cynical, grasping and duplicitous, all traits that he covered over with a slippery and false bonhomie. The two had a furious argument in the Senate around this time, when Cicero denounced the retiring governor of Syria, Gabinius—his old enemy—for finally succumbing to Ptolemy's bribe and restoring the Pharaoh to the Egyptian throne. Crassus defended the man he was about to replace. Cicero accused Crassus of putting his personal interests above those of the republic. Crassus jeered that Cicero was an exile. "Sooner an honourable exile," retorted Cicero, "than a pampered thief." Crassus stalked over to him and thrust out his chest, and the two ageing statesmen had to be physically prevented from exchanging blows.

Pompey took Cicero aside and told him he would not tolerate such abuse of his consular colleague. Caesar wrote a stern letter from Gaul that he regarded any attack on Crassus as an insult to himself. What worried them, I believe, was that Crassus's expedition was proving so unpopular with the people, it was beginning to undermine the authority of the Three. Cato and his followers denounced it as illegal and immoral to make war on a country with which the republic had treaties of friendship; they produced auguries to show it was offensive to the gods and would bring ruin down on Rome.

Crassus was sufficiently concerned to seek a public reconciliation with Cicero. He approached him via Furius Crassipes, his friend who was also Cicero's son-in-law. Crassipes offered to host a dinner for them both on the eve of Crassus's departure. To have refused the invitation would have shown disrespect to Pompey and Caesar; Cicero had to go. "But I want you to be on hand as a witness," he said to me. "This villain will put words in my mouth and invent endorsements I never gave."

Naturally I was not present for the meal itself. Still, I remember some parts of the evening very clearly. Crassipes had a fine suburban house set in the middle of a park about a mile south of the city, on the banks of the Tiber. Cicero and Terentia were the first to arrive so that they could spend some time with Tullia, who had recently miscarried. She looked pale, poor child, and thin, and I noticed how coldly her husband treated her, criticising her for such domestic oversights as the wilting flower arrangements and the poor quality of the canapés. Crassus turned up an hour later in a veritable convoy of carriages that clattered to a halt in the courtyard. With him was his wife, Tertulla—an elderly sour-faced lady, almost as bald as he was—together with their son Publius and Publius's new bride, Cornelia, a very gracious seventeen-year-old, the daughter of Scipio Nasica and considered to be the most eligible heiress in Rome. Crassus also trailed a retinue of adjutants and secretaries who seemed to have no function except to hurry back and forth with messages and documents, conveying a general impression of importance. When the principals went in to dinner and the coast was clear, they lolled about on Crassipes's furniture and drank his wine, and I was struck by the contrast between these unmilitary amateurs and Caesar's efficient, battle-hardened staff.

After the meal, the men went into the tablinum to discuss military strategy—or rather Crassus held forth and the others listened. He was very deaf by this time—he was sixty—and talked too loudly. Publius was embarrassed—"It's all right, Father, there's no need to shout, we're not in the other room"—and once or twice he glanced at Cicero and raised his eyebrows in silent apology. Crassus announced that he would head east through Macedonia, then Thrace, the Hellespont, Galatia, and the northern part of

Syria, traverse the desert of Mesopotamia, cross the Euphrates and thrust deep into Parthia.

Cicero said, "They must be well aware you're coming. Aren't you worried you will lack the element of surprise?"

Crassus scoffed, "I have no need of the element of surprise. I prefer the element of certainty. Let them tremble as we approach."

He had his eye on various rich pickings along the way—he cited the temples of the goddess Derceto at Hierapolis and of Jehovah at Jerusalem, the jewelled effigy of Apollo at Tigraocerta, the golden Zeus of Nicephorium and the treasure houses of Seleucia. Cicero joked that it sounded less a military campaign than a shopping expedition, but Crassus was too deaf to hear.

At the end of the evening the two old enemies shook hands warmly and expressed profound satisfaction that any slight misunderstandings that might have arisen between them had been put to rest at last. "These are mere figments of the imagination," declared Cicero, with a twirl of his fingers. "Let them be utterly eradicated from our memories. Between two such men as you and I, whose lot has fallen on the same political ground, I would hope that alliance and friendship will continue to the credit of both. In all matters affecting you during your absence, my devoted and indefatigable service and any influence I command are absolutely and unreservedly at your disposal."

"What an utter villain that fellow is," said Cicero as we settled into the carriage to drive home.

A day or so later—and a full two months before the expiry of his term as consul, so eager was he to be off—Crassus left Rome wearing the red cloak and full uniform of a general on active service. Pompey, his fellow consul, came out of the Senate house to see him off. The tribune Ateius Capito attempted to arrest him in the Forum for his illegal war-making, and when he was knocked aside by Crassus's lieutenants he ran ahead to the city gate and set up a brazier. As Crassus passed by he threw incense and libations on to the flames and called down curses on him and upon his expedition, mingling his incantations with the names of strange and terrible deities. The superstitious people of Rome were appalled and cried out to Crassus not to go. But he laughed at them, and with a final jaunty wave turned his back on the city and spurred his horse.

SUCH WAS CICERO'S LIFE AT THIS PERIOD, WALKING ON TIPTOE between the three great men in the state, endeavouring to keep on good terms with all of them, doing their bidding, privately despairing of the future of the republic, but waiting and hoping for better times.

He sought refuge in his books, especially philosophy and history, and one day, soon after Quintus had gone off to join Caesar in Gaul, he announced to me that he had decided to produce a work of his own. It was too dangerous, he said, to write an open attack on the current state of politics in Rome. But he could approach it in a different way, by updating Plato's *Republic* and setting out what an ideal state might look like: "Who could object to that?" The answer, I thought, was a large number of people, but I kept my opinion to myself.

I look back on the writing of that work, which took us in the end almost three years, as one of the most satisfying periods of my life. Like most literary compositions, it entailed much heartbreak and many false starts. Originally he planned to write it in nine rolls, but then reduced that to six. He decided to cast it in the form of an imagined conversation between a group of historical characters—chief among them one of his heroes, Scipio Aemilianus, the conqueror of Carthage—who gather in a villa on a religious holiday to discuss the nature of politics and how societies should be organised. He reasoned that no one would mind if dangerous notions were placed in the mouths of the legendary figures of Roman history.

He started dictating it in his new villa in Cumae during the senatorial recess. He consulted all the ancient texts, and on one particularly memorable day we rode over to the villa of Faustus Cornelius Sulla, the son of the former dictator, who lived a little way along the coast. Cicero's ally Milo, who was rising in politics, had just married Sulla's twin sister Fausta, and at the wedding breakfast, which Cicero attended, Sulla had invited him to use his library whenever he liked. It was one of the most valuable collections in Italy. The volumes had been carted back by Sulla the Dictator from Athens almost thirty years earlier, and amazingly included most of the original manuscripts of Aristotle, written in his own hand three centuries earlier. I shall never forget as long as I live the sensation of unrolling each of the eight books of Aristotle's *Politics*: tiny cylinders of minute Greek characters, the edges slightly damaged by damp from the caves in Asia Minor where they had been hidden for many years. It was like reaching back through time and touching the face of a god.

But I am wandering too far from my subject. The essential point was that Cicero for the first time laid out his political credo in black and white, and I can summarise it in a sentence: that politics is the most noble of all callings ("there is really no other occupation in which human virtue approaches more closely the august function of the gods"); that there is "no nobler motive for entering public life than the resolution not to be ruled by wicked men"; that no individual, or combination of individuals, should be allowed to become too powerful; that politics is a profession, not a pastime for dilettantes (nothing is worse than rule by "clever poets"); that a statesman should devote his life to studying "the science of politics, in order to acquire in advance all the knowledge that it may be necessary for him to use at some future time"; that authority in a state must always be divided; and that of the three known forms of government—monarchy, aristocracy and people—the best is a mixture of all three, for each one taken on its own can lead to disaster: kings can be capricious, aristocrats self-interested, and "an unbridled multitude enjoying unwonted power more terrifying than a conflagration or a raging sea."

Often today I reread *On the Republic*, and always I am moved, especially by the passage at the end of book six, when Scipio describes how his grandfather appears to him in a dream and takes him up into the heavens to show him the smallness of the earth in comparison to the grandeur of the Milky Way, where the spirits of dead statesmen dwell as stars. The description was inspired by the vast, clear night skies above the Bay of Naples:

> I gazed in every direction and all appeared wonderfully beautiful. There were stars which we never see from earth, and they were all larger than we have ever imagined. The starry spheres were much greater than the earth; indeed the earth itself seemed to me so small that I was scornful of our empire, which covers only a single point, as it were, upon its surface.

"If only you will look on high," the old man tells Scipio, "and contemplate this eternal home and resting place, you will no longer bother with the gossip of the common herd or put your trust in human reward for your exploits. Nor will any man's reputation endure very long, for what men say dies with them and is blotted out with the forgetfulness of posterity."

Composing such passages was Cicero's chief comfort in the lonely days of his wilderness years. But the prospect that he might ever again have the chance to put his principles into effect seemed remote indeed.

THREE MONTHS AFTER CICERO BEGAN WRITING *ON THE REPUBLIC*, IN the summer of Rome's seven hundredth year, Pompey's wife, Julia, gave birth to a baby boy. The moment he was brought the news at his morning levee, Cicero hastened round to see the happy couple bearing a gift, for the son of Pompey and the grandson of Caesar would be a mighty presence in the years to come, and he wanted to be among the first with his congratulations.

It was not long after dawn yet already hot. In the valley beneath Pompey's house loomed his newly opened theatre, with its temples and gardens and porticoes, its fresh white marble dazzling in the sun. Cicero had attended its dedication ceremony just a few months earlier—a spectacle that had included fights involving five hundred lions, four hundred panthers, eighteen elephants and the first rhinoceros ever seen in Rome. He had found it all revolting, especially the slaughter of the elephants: *What pleasure can a cultivated man get out of seeing a weak human being torn to pieces by a powerful animal or a noble creature transfixed by a hunting spear?* But naturally he had kept his feelings to himself.

From the moment we entered the immense house it was clear something terrible had occurred. Senators and clients of Pompey stood in worried, silent groups. Someone whispered to Cicero that no announcement had been made, but Pompey's failure to appear, and an earlier glimpse of several of Julia's maids fleeing, weeping, across an inner courtyard, suggested the worst. Suddenly from the interior there was a flutter of activity, a curtain parted and Pompey emerged in the midst of a retinue of slaves. He stopped, as if shocked by the number of people waiting for him, and searched for a familiar face. His eye fell on Cicero. He raised his hand and walked towards him. Everyone watched. At first he seemed entirely calm and clear-eyed. But then as he reached his old ally the effort at self-control abruptly became too much. His whole body and face seemed to sag and with a terrible choking sob he cried out, "She's dead!"

A great groan went round the vast room—of genuine shock and grief, I have no doubt, but also of alarm, for these were politicians and this was a much bigger thing than the death of one young woman, tragic though it was. Cicero, in tears himself, put his arms round Pompey and tried to comfort him, and after a few moments Pompey asked him to come and see the body. Knowing how squeamish Cicero was about death, I thought he might try to refuse. But that would have been impossible. He was not being invited purely as a friend. He was to be an official witness on behalf of the Senate in what was a matter of state. He went off holding Pompey's hand, and when he returned shortly afterwards, the others gathered round.

"She started bleeding again soon after the birth," reported Cicero, "and the flow could not be stopped. The end was peaceful and she was brave, as befits her lineage."

"And the child?"

"He will not last the day."

More groans greeted this announcement and then everyone left to spread the news across the city. Cicero said to me, "The poor girl was whiter than the sheet in which they'd wound her. And the boy was blind and limp. I am truly sorry for Caesar. She was his only child. It's as if Cato's prophecies of the gods' rage are starting to come true."

We went back to the house and Cicero wrote Caesar a letter of consolation. As ill luck would have it, Caesar was in the most inaccessible place it was possible for him to be, having crossed over to Britain again, this time with an invasion force of twenty-seven thousand men, including Quintus. It was not until he returned to Gaul several months later that he found the packets of letters informing him of his daughter's death. He showed by all accounts not a tremor of emotion but retired to his quarters, never spoke of it, and after three days of official mourning went on with his normal duties. It was, I guess, the secret of his achievements that he was quite indifferent to the death of anyone—enemy or friend, his only child or even ultimately himself—a coldness of nature that he concealed beneath his famous layers of charm.

Pompey was at the opposite end of the human spectrum. All his depths were on the surface. He loved his various wives with great (some said excessive) tenderness, and Julia most of all. At her funeral—which was, despite Cato's objections, a state occasion held in the Forum—he found it hard to deliver the eulogy through his tears, and generally gave every appearance of being broken in spirit. The ashes were afterwards interred in a mausoleum in the precincts of one of his temples on the Field of Mars.

It must have been perhaps two months later that he asked Cicero to come and see him and showed him the letter he had just received from Caesar. After commiserating with him on the loss of Julia, and thanking him for his condolences, Caesar proposed a new marital alliance, but of double the strength: he would give his sister's granddaughter, Octavia, to Pompey, and Pompey in return would give him the hand of his daughter, Pompeia.

"What do you make of this?" demanded Pompey. "I believe the barbarian air of Britain must have affected his brain! For one thing, my daughter's already betrothed to Faustus Sulla—what am I supposed to tell him? 'Very sorry, Sulla, someone more important has just come along?' And then Octavia of course is married—and not to just some nobody, either, but to Caius Marcellus: how's he going to feel about my stealing his wife? Damn it all, Caesar's married himself, come to that, to that poor little drab Calpurnia! All these lives to be turned upside down, and meanwhile dear little Julia's side of our bed is not yet cold! Do you know, I haven't even had the heart to clear out her hairbrushes?"

Cicero for once found himself speaking up for Caesar: "I'm sure he's only thinking of the stability of the republic."

But Pompey was not to be pacified. "Well, I shan't do it. If I marry for a fifth time, it will be to a woman of my choice; and as for Caesar, he will have to find himself a different bride."

Cicero, who loved gossip, could not resist describing Caesar's letter to several friends, swearing each to secrecy. Naturally, after extracting a similar oath, each friend mentioned it to several others, and so it went on until the news of Caesar's proposal was the talk of Rome. Marcellus especially was outraged that his wife was being spoken of by Caesar as if she were his chattel. Caesar was embarrassed when he heard what was being said; he blamed Pompey for revealing his plans. Pompey was unapologetic; he in turn blamed Caesar for the clumsiness of his matchmaking. Another crack had appeared in the monolith.

# VII

———·•·———

THE FOLLOWING YEAR DURING THE SENATE RECESS CICERO SET OFF
as usual with his family for Cumae in order to continue work on
his political book; and I, as usual, went with him. It was not long
before my fiftieth birthday.

For most of my life I had enjoyed good health. But when, to break
the journey, we reached the cold mountain heights of Arpinum, I
started to shiver, and the next morning I could barely move my
limbs. When I tried to continue with the others I fainted and had to
be carried to bed. Cicero could not have been kinder. He postponed
his departure in the hope I would recover. But my fever worsened
and I was told afterwards he spent long hours at my bedside. In
the end he had to leave me behind, along with instructions to the
household slaves that I should receive exactly the same care they
would give to him. From Cumae two days later he wrote to say that
he was sending me his Greek doctor, Andricus, and also a cook: *If
you care for me, see that you get well and join us when you are thoroughly
strong again. Goodbye.*

Andricus purged and bled me. The cook produced delicious
meals that I was too ill to eat. Cicero wrote constantly.

*You cannot imagine how anxious I feel about your health. If you
relieve my mind on this score, I shall relieve yours of every worry.
I should write more if I thought you could read with any pleasure.
Put your clever brain, which I value so highly, to the job of
preserving yourself for us both.*

After about a week, the fever eased. By then it was too late to travel to Cumae. Cicero wrote telling me to join him instead at Formiae, on his way back to Rome.

*Let me find you there, my dear Tiro, well and strong. My (our) literary brainchildren have been drooping their heads missing you. Atticus is staying with me, enjoying himself in cheerful mood. He wanted to hear my compositions but I told him that in your absence my tongue of authorship is tied completely. You must get ready to restore your services to my Muses. My promise will be performed on the appointed day. Now mind you get thoroughly well. I shall be with you soon. Goodbye.*

*I shall relieve your mind of every worry . . . My promise will be performed on the appointed day . . .* I read the letters over and over, trying to make sense of those two phrases. I deduced that he must have said something to me when I was delirious, but I had no recollection of what it was.

As arranged, I arrived at the villa in Formiae on the afternoon of my fiftieth birthday, the twenty-eighth day of April. It was cold and blustery, not at all propitious, with rain gusting off the sea. I still felt frail. The effort of hurrying into the house so as not to be soaked left me dizzy. The place appeared deserted and I wondered if I had misunderstood my instructions. I went from room to room, calling out, until I heard a young boy's stifled laughter coming from the triclinium. I pulled back the curtain and discovered the whole dining room crammed full of people trying to stay silent: Cicero, Terentia, Tullia, Marcus, young Quintus Cicero, all the household staff, and (even more bizarrely) the praetor Caius Marcellus with his lictors—that same noble Marcellus whose wife Caesar had tried to bestow on Pompey, and who had a villa nearby. At the sight of my astonished face they all started laughing, then Cicero took me by the hand and led me into the centre of the room while the others made space for us. I felt my knees weaken.

Marcellus said, "Who wishes this day to free this slave?"

Cicero replied, "I do."

"You are the legal owner?"

"I am."

"Upon what grounds is he to be freed?"

"He has shown great loyalty and given exemplary service to our family ever since he was born into the condition of slavery, and to me in particular, and also to the Roman state. His character is sound and he is worthy of his freedom."

Marcellus nodded. "You may proceed."

The lictor briefly touched his rod of office to my head. Cicero stepped in front of me, grasped my shoulders and recited the simple legal formula: "This man is to be free." He had tears in his eyes; so had I. Gently he turned me round until I had my back to him, and then he let me go, as a father might release a child to take its first steps.

It is difficult for me to describe the joy of becoming free. Quintus expressed it best when he wrote to me from Gaul: *I could not be more delighted, my dear Tiro, believe me. Before you were our slave but now you are our friend.* Outwardly, nothing much changed. I continued to live under Cicero's roof and to perform the same duties. But in my heart I was a different man. I exchanged my tunic for a toga—a cumbersome garment that I wore without ease or comfort, but with intense pride. And for the first time I began to make plans of my own. I started to compile a comprehensive dictionary of all the symbols and abbreviations used in my shorthand system, together with instructions on how to use it. I drew up a scheme for a book on Latin grammar. I also went back through my boxes of notes whenever I had a spare hour and copied down particularly amusing or clever quotations thrown out by Cicero over the years. He greatly approved of the idea of a book of his wit and wisdom. Often after a particularly fine remark he would stop and say, "Note that down, Tiro— that's one for your compendium." Gradually it became understood between us that if I outlived him, I would write his biography.

I asked him once why he had waited so long to set me free,

and why he had decided to do it at that moment. He answered, "Well, you know I can be a selfish man, and I rely on you entirely. I thought to myself, 'If I free him, what's to stop him going off and transferring his allegiance to Caesar or Crassus or someone? They'd certainly pay him plenty for all he knows about me.' Then when you fell ill in Arpinum I realised how unjust it would be if you died in servitude, and so I made my pledge to you, even though you were too feverish to understand it. If ever there was a man who deserved the nobility of freedom, it is you, dear Tiro. Besides," he added with a wink, "nowadays I have no secrets worth selling."

Love him though I did, I nevertheless wanted to end my days under my own roof. I had some savings and now was paid a salary; I dreamed of buying a smallholding near Cumae where I could keep a few goats and chickens and grow my own vines and olives. But I feared loneliness. I suppose I could have gone down to the slave market and bought myself a companion, but the idea repulsed me. I knew with whom I wanted to share this dream of a future life: Agathe, the Greek slave girl whom I had met in the household of Lucullus and whose freedom I had asked Atticus to purchase on my behalf before I went into exile with Cicero. Atticus confirmed he had done as I asked and that she had been manumitted. But although I made enquiries as to what had happened to her, and always kept an eye out whenever I walked through Rome, she had vanished into the teeming multitudes of Italy.

I DID NOT HAVE LONG TO ENJOY MY FREEDOM IN TRANQUILLITY. MY modest plans, like everyone else's, were about to be mocked by the immensity of events. As Plautus has it:

> Whatever the mind may hope for
> The future is in the hands of the gods.

A few weeks after my liberation, in the month that was then named Quintilis but that we are now required to call July, I was hurrying along the Via Sacra, trying not to trip over my new toga, when I saw a crowd gathered ahead. They were deathly still—not at all animated as they usually were when news of one of Caesar's victories was posted on the white board. I thought immediately that he must have suffered a terrible defeat. I joined the back of the throng and asked the man in front of me what was happening. Irritated, he glanced over his shoulder and muttered in a distracted voice, "Crassus has been killed."

I stayed just long enough to pick up the few details that were available. Then I hastened back to tell Cicero. He was working in his study. I gasped out the news and he quickly stood up, as if such grave information should not be acknowledged sitting down.

"How did it happen?"

"In battle, it's reported—in the desert, near a town in Mesopotamia named Carrhae."

"And his army?"

"Defeated—wiped out."

Cicero stared at me for a few moments. Then he shouted to one slave to bring his shoes and another to arrange a litter. I asked him where he was going. "To see Pompey, of course—come too."

It was a sign of Pompey's pre-eminence that whenever there was a major crisis in the state, it was to his house that people always flocked—be it the ordinary citizens, who that day crowded the surrounding streets in silent, watchful multitudes; or the senior senators, who even now were arriving in their litters and being ushered by Pompey's attendants into his inner sanctum. As luck would have it, both the elected consuls, Calvinus and Messalla, were under indictment for bribery and had been unable to take up office. Present instead was the informal leadership of the Senate, including senior ex-consuls such as Cotta, Hortensius and the elder Curio, and prominent younger men like Ahenobarbus, Scipio Nasica and M. Aemilius Lepidus. Pompey took command of the meeting. No one knew the eastern empire better than he: after all, much of it he had conquered. He announced that a dispatch had just been received from Crassus's legate, G. Cassius Longinus, who had managed to escape from enemy territory and get back into Syria, and that if everyone was in agreement he would now read it out.

Cassius was a cold, austere man—"pale and thin," as Caesar later complained—not given to boastfulness or lying, so his words were heard with all the greater respect. According to him, the Parthian king, Orodes II, had sent an envoy to Crassus on the eve of the invasion to say that he was willing to take pity on him as an old man and allow him to return in peace to Rome. But Crassus had boastfully replied that he would give his answer in the Parthian capital, Seleucia, at which the envoy had burst out laughing and pointed to the palm of his upturned hand, saying, "Hair will grow here, Crassus, before you set eyes on Seleucia!"

The Roman force of seven legions, plus eight thousand cavalry and archers, had bridged the Euphrates at Zeugma in a thunderstorm—itself a bad omen—and at one point during the traditional offerings to placate the gods, Crassus had dropped the entrails of the sacrificial animal into the sand. Although he had tried to make a joke of it—"That's what comes of being an old man, lads, but I can grip my sword tightly enough!"—the soldiers groaned, remembering the curses that had accompanied their departure from Rome. *Already,* wrote Cassius, *they sensed that they were doomed.*

*From the Euphrates* [he continued] *we advanced ever deeper into the desert, with insufficient supplies of water and no clear sense of a route or objective. The land is trackless, flat, with no living tree to offer shade. After wading for fifty miles with full packs through soft sand in desert storms during which hundreds of our men succumbed to thirst and heat, we reached a river called the Balissus. Here for the first time our scouts sighted elements of the enemy's forces on the opposite bank. On the orders of M. Crassus we crossed the river at noon and set off in pursuit. But by now the enemy had entirely disappeared again. We marched for several more hours until we were in the midst of a wilderness. Suddenly from all around us we heard the beating of kettle drums. At that moment, as if springing*

*out of the sand, arose in every direction an immense horde of
mounted archers. The silken banners of the Parthian commander,
Sillaces, were visible behind.*

*Against the advice of more experienced officers, M. Crassus
ordered the army to be drawn up in a single large square, twelve
cohorts across. Our archers were then sent forward to engage the
enemy. However, they were soon obliged to retreat in the face of
the Parthians' vastly superior forces and speed of manoeuvre.
Their arrows spread much slaughter through our packed ranks.
Nor did death come easily or quickly. In the convulsion and agony
of their pain, our men would writhe as the arrows struck them;
they would snap them off in their wounds and then lacerate their
flesh by trying to tear out the barbed arrowheads that had pierced
through their veins and muscles. Many died in this way, and even
the survivors were in no state to fight. Their hands were pinioned to
their shields and their feet nailed through to the ground so that they
were incapable of either running away or defending themselves.
Any hopes that this murderous rain would exhaust itself were
dashed by the sight of fresh supplies of arrows appearing on the
battlefield on heavily laden camel trains.*

*Apprehending the danger that the army would soon be entirely
wiped out, P. Crassus applied to his father for permission to take
his cavalry, together with some infantry and archers, and pierce
the encircling line. M. Crassus endorsed the plan. This breakout
force of some six thousand men moved forwards and the Parthians
quickly withdrew. But although Publius had been expressly ordered
not to pursue the enemy, he disobeyed these instructions. His men
advanced out of sight of the main army, whereupon the Parthians
reappeared behind them. Rapidly surrounded, Publius withdrew his
men to a narrow ridge, where they presented an easy target. Once
again the enemy's archers did their murderous work. Perceiving the
situation to be hopeless and fearing capture, Publius bade his men
farewell and told them to look after their own safety. Then, since he
was unable to use his hand, which had been pierced through with
an arrow, he presented his side to his shield-bearer and ordered him*

to run him through with his sword. Most of his officers followed his example and put themselves to death.

Once they had overrun the Roman position, the Parthians cut off the head of Publius and mounted it on a spear. They then carried it back to the main Roman army and rode up and down our lines, taunting M. Crassus to come and look upon his son. Seeing what had happened, he addressed our men as follows: "Romans, this grief is a private thing of my own. But in you, who are safe and sound, abide the great fortune and the glory of Rome. And now, if you feel any pity for me, who have lost the best son that any father has ever had, show it in the fury with which you face the enemy."

Regrettably, they paid no heed. On the contrary, this sight more than all the other dreadful things that had happened broke the spirit and paralysed the energies of our forces. The airborne slaughter resumed, and it is a certainty that the entire army would have been annihilated had not night fallen and the Parthians withdrawn, shouting that they would give Crassus the night to grieve for his son and would return to finish us off in the morning.

This provided us with an opportunity. M. Crassus being prostrate with grief and despair, and no longer capable of issuing orders, I took over the direction of our forces, and in silence and under cover of darkness those who could walk made a forced march to the town of Carrhae, leaving behind, amidst the most piteous cries and pleadings, some four thousand wounded who were either massacred or enslaved by the Parthians the following day.

At Carrhae our forces divided. I led five hundred men in the direction of Syria while M. Crassus took the bulk of our surviving army towards the mountains of Armenia. Intelligence reports indicate that outside the fortress of Sinnaca he was confronted by an army led by a subordinate of the Parthian king, who offered a truce. M. Crassus was compelled by his mutinous legionaries to go forward and negotiate, even though he believed it to be a trap. As he went, he turned and spoke these words: "I call upon all you Roman officers present to see that I am being forced to go this way. You are eyewitnesses of the shameful and violent treatment that I have *received. But if you escape and get home safely, tell them all that Crassus died because he was deceived by the enemy, not because he was handed over to the Parthians by his own countrymen."*

*These are his last known words. He was killed along with his legionary commanders. I am informed that afterwards his severed head was delivered personally to the king of the Parthians by Sillaces during a performance of* The Bacchae *and that it was used as a prop on stage. Afterwards the king caused Crassus's mouth to be filled with molten gold, remarking: "Gorge yourself now with that metal for which in life you were so greedy."*

*I await the Senate's orders.*

When Pompey finished reading, there was silence.

Finally Cicero said, "How many men have we lost, do we have any idea?"

"I estimate thirty thousand."

There was a groan of dismay from the assembled senators. Some-one said that if that were true, then it was the worst defeat since Hannibal had wiped out the Senate's army at Cannae, one hundred and fifty years before.

"This document," said Pompey, waving Cassius's dispatch, "must go no further than this room."

Cicero said, "I agree. Cassius's frankness is admirable in private, but a less alarming version must be prepared for the people, stress-ing the bravery of our legionaries and their commanders."

Scipio, who was Publius's father-in-law, said, "Yes, they all died heroes—that's what we must tell everyone. That's what I'm going to tell my daughter, certainly. The poor girl is a widow at nineteen."

Pompey said, "Please give her my condolences."

Then Hortensius spoke up. The ex-consul was in his sixties and mostly retired, but still listened to with respect. "What happens next? Presumably the Parthians won't leave it at that. Knowing our weakness, they'll invade Syria in retaliation. We can barely muster a legion in its defence and we have no governor."

"I would propose we make Cassius acting governor," said Pompey. "He's a hard, unsparing man—exactly what this emergency demands. As for an army—well, he must raise and train a new one locally."

Ahenobarbus, who never lost an opportunity to undermine Caesar, said, "All our best fighting men are in Gaul. Caesar has ten legions—a huge number. Why don't we order him to send a couple to Syria to fill the breach?"

At the mention of Caesar's name there was a perceptible stirring of hostility in the room.

"He recruited those legions," pointed out Pompey. "I agree they would be more useful in the east. But he regards those men as his own."

"Well, he needs to be reminded they are not his own. They exist to serve the republic, not him."

Looking round at the senators all nodding vigorously in agreement, Cicero said afterwards that it was only at that moment that he realised the true significance of Crassus's death. "Because, dear Tiro, what have we learned while writing our *Republic*? Divide power three ways in a state and tension is balanced; divide it in two and sooner or later one side must seek to dominate the other—it is a natural law. Disgraceful as he was, Crassus at least preserved the equilibrium between Pompey and Caesar. But with him gone, who will do it now?"

AND SO WE DRIFTED TOWARDS CALAMITY. AT TIMES, CICERO WAS shrewd enough to see it. "Can a constitution devised centuries ago to replace a monarchy, and based upon a citizens' militia, possibly hope to run an empire whose scope is beyond anything ever dreamed of by its framers? Or must the existence of standing armies and the influx of inconceivable wealth inevitably destroy our democratic system?"

And then at other times he would dismiss such apocalyptic talk as excessively gloomy and argue that the republic had endured all manner of disasters in the past—invasions, revolutions, civil wars—and had always somehow survived them: why should this time be any different?

But it was.

The elections that year were dominated by two men. Clodius sought to be praetor. Milo ran for the consulship. The violence and the bribery of the campaign were beyond anything the city had ever seen, and yet again polling day had to be postponed repeatedly. It was now more than a year since the republic had elected legitimate consuls. The Senate was presided over by an interrex, often a nonentity, on a rolling five-day mandate; the fasces of the consuls were placed symbolically in the Temple of Libitina, goddess of the dead. *Hurry back to Rome,* Cicero wrote to Atticus, who was on another of his business trips. *Come and look at the empty husks of the real old Roman Republic we used to know.*

It was a measure of how desperate things were becoming that Cicero vested all his hopes in Milo, even though Milo was entirely his opposite: crude and brutal, lacking in eloquence or indeed any political skill apart from the staging of gladiatorial games to enthuse the voters, the costs of which had left him bankrupt. Milo had outlived his usefulness to Pompey, who would have nothing more to do with him, and who was supporting his opponents, Scipio Nasica and Plautius Hypsaeus. But Cicero still needed him. *I have firmly concentrated all my efforts, all my time, care, diligence and thought, my whole mind in short, on winning the consulship for Milo.* He saw him as the best bulwark against the eventuality he dreaded most: Clodius's election to the consulship.

Cicero often asked me to perform small services for Milo during that campaign. For example, I went back through our files and prepared lists of our old supporters for him to canvass. I also set up meetings between him and Cicero's clients in the various tribal headquarters. I even took him bags of money that Cicero had raised from wealthy donors.

One day in the new year, Cicero asked me, as a favour, if I would spend a short time observing Milo's campaign at first hand. "To put the matter bluntly, I'm worried he's going to lose. You know elections as well as I do. Watch him with the voters. See if anything can be done to improve his prospects. If he loses and Clodius wins, I don't need to tell you it will be a disaster for me."

I cannot pretend that I was delighted with the assignment, but I did as I was asked, and on the eighteenth day of January I turned up at Milo's house, which was on the steepest part of the Palatine, behind the Temple of Saturn. A listless crowd was gathered outside, but of the would-be consul himself there was no sign. I knew then that Milo's candidacy was in trouble. If a man is standing for election and feels himself to have a chance of winning, he works every hour of the day. But Milo did not emerge until the middle of the morning, and when he did, he took me to one side to complain about Pompey, who he said was entertaining Clodius that very morning at his country house in the Alban Hills.

"The man's ingratitude is unbelievable! Do you remember how he used to be so frightened of Clodius and his gang that he daren't even set foot out of doors until I brought in my gladiators to clear the streets? And now he has taken that snake under his roof, yet he won't even bid me good morning!"

I sympathised—we all knew what Pompey was like: a great man, but entirely preoccupied with himself—and then tried tactfully to steer the conversation back to Milo's campaign. There was not long until polling day. Where did he plan to spend these precious final hours?

"Today," he announced, "I am going to Lanuvium, my adopted grandfather's ancestral home."

I could scarcely believe it. "You're leaving Rome, this close to the actual vote?"

"It's only twenty miles. A new priest is to be nominated for the Temple of Juno the Saviour. She is the municipal deity, which means that the ceremony will be huge—you'll see, hundreds of voters will be there."

"Even so, surely these voters are already committed to you,

given your family connection to the town? Wouldn't your time be better spent pursuing voters who are undecided?"

But Milo refused to discuss it further. Indeed his refusal was so absolute that now, when I look back on it, I wonder if he hadn't already given up hope of winning the election in the voting pens and decided to go looking for trouble instead. After all, Lanuvium is also in the Alban Hills, and the road to it would take us practically past Pompey's gates. He must have calculated there was a good chance we would meet Clodius on the way. It would have been just the sort of opportunity for a fight he relished.

By the time we set out that afternoon he had gathered together a considerable wagon train of luggage and servants, protected by his usual small private army of slaves and gladiators armed with swords and javelins. Milo rode in a carriage at the head of this menacing column together with his wife, Fausta. He invited me to join them but I preferred the discomfort of horseback to sharing a carriage with those two, whose tempestuous relationship was notorious. We clattered off down the Via Appia, arrogantly forcing all the other traffic out of our way—again, I noted, poor electoral tactics—and had been going for about two hours when of course, on the outskirts of Bovillae, we duly encountered Clodius heading in the opposite direction, back to Rome.

Clodius was on horseback with perhaps thirty attendants—less well armed than Milo's, and far less numerous. I was in the middle of our column. As he passed, he caught my eye. He knew me pretty well as Cicero's secretary. He certainly gave me a foul look.

The rest of his party followed him. I averted my gaze. I wanted no trouble. But moments later, from behind me, there was a shout and then the clash of steel hitting steel. I turned and saw that a fight had broken out between our gladiators, who were bringing up the rear, and some of Clodius's men. Clodius himself had already gone a little way further along the road. He drew up his horse and turned, and at that moment Birria, the gladiator who had sometimes acted as a bodyguard to Cicero, hurled a javelin at him. It did not hit him full on, but rather in his side as he was in the act of turning, and the force of it almost knocked him from his saddle. The barbed tip buried itself deep in his flesh. He looked at it in astonishment, and screamed and clutched at the shaft with both hands, his whitened toga turning crimson with blood.

His bodyguards spurred their horses and surrounded him. Our convoy halted. I noticed we were close to a tavern—the same place, by bizarre coincidence, where we had stopped to pick up our horses on the night Cicero fled Rome. Milo jumped out of his carriage with his sword drawn and walked down the side of the road to see what was going on. All along the column men were dismounting. By now Clodius's attendants had pulled the javelin from his ribs and were helping him towards the tavern. He was sufficiently conscious to be able to half walk supported on the arms of his companions. Meanwhile small groups of men were fighting hand-to-hand along the road and in the fields next to it—desperate, hacking struggles, some on horseback, some on foot—such a confused melee that I could not at first distinguish our men from theirs. But gradually I perceived that ours were winning, for we outnumbered them three to one. I saw several of Clodius's men, despairing of victory, fling up their arms in surrender or fall to their knees. Others simply threw aside their weapons, turned and ran, or galloped off. No one bothered to pursue them.

The struggle over, Milo, with his arms akimbo, surveyed the carnage, then gestured to Birria and a few others to go and fetch Clodius from the tavern.

I got down from my horse. I had no idea what would happen next. I walked towards Milo. Just then there was a shout, or rather a scream from the tavern, and Clodius was carried out by four gladiators, each holding an arm or a leg. Milo had a calculation to make: would he let Clodius live and take the consequences, or kill him and have done with it? They laid him on the road at his feet. Milo took a javelin from the man standing next to him, checked the tip with his thumb, placed it in the centre of Clodius's chest, grasped the shaft and plunged it in with all his force. Clodius's mouth fountained blood. After that, they all took turns in slashing at the corpse, but I could not bring myself to watch.

I WAS NO HORSEMAN, YET I BELIEVE I GALLOPED BACK TO ROME AT a speed a cavalryman would have been proud of. I urged my exhausted mount up to the Palatine, and for the second time in half a year I found myself blurting out to Cicero the news that one of his enemies—the greatest of them all—was dead.

He gave no sign of pleasure. He was ice-cold, calculating. He drummed his fingers and then said, "Where is Milo now?"

"I believe he carried on to Lanuvium for the ceremony as planned."

"And Clodius's body?"

"The last time I saw it, it was still by the roadside."

"Milo made no attempt to conceal it?"

"No, he said there was no point—there were too many witnesses."

"That's probably true—it's a busy spot. Were *you* seen by many people?"

"I don't think so. Clodius recognised me, but not the others."

He gave a hard smile. "Clodius at least we no longer have to worry about." He thought it over and nodded. "That's good—good that you weren't seen. I think it would be better if we agree you were here with me all afternoon."

"Why?"

"It wouldn't be wise for me to be implicated in this business, even indirectly."

"You anticipate this will cause you trouble?"

"Oh, I am quite certain of it. The question is: how much?"

We settled down to wait for word of what had happened to reach Rome. In the fading light of the afternoon I found it difficult to banish from my mind the image of Clodius dying like a stuck pig.

I had witnessed death before, but that was the first time I had seen a man killed in front of me.

About an hour before darkness, a woman's piercing shriek arose from some place nearby. It went on and on—a frightening, other-worldly ululation.

Cicero walked over and opened the door to his terrace and listened. "The Lady Fulvia," he said judiciously, "if I am not mistaken, has just learned she is a widow."

He sent a servant up the hill to find out what was happening. The man came back and reported that Clodius's body had arrived in Rome on a litter belonging to the senator Sextus Tedius, who had discovered it beside the Via Appia. The corpse had been conveyed to Clodius's house and received by Fulvia. In her grief and fury she had stripped it naked, apart from its sandals, propped it up, and was now sitting beside it in the street beneath flaming torches, crying out that everyone should come and see what had been done to her husband.

Cicero said, "She means to whip up the mob." He ordered the guard on the house to be doubled overnight.

The following morning it was judged far too dangerous for Cicero or any other prominent senator to venture out. We watched from the terrace as a huge crowd led by Fulvia escorted the body on its bier down to the Forum and placed it on the rostra, and then we listened as Clodius's lieutenants worked the plebs up to a fury. At the end of the bitter eulogies the mourners broke into the Senate house and carried Clodius's corpse inside, then went back across the Forum to the Argiletum and started dragging out benches and tables and chests full of volumes from the booksellers' shops. To our horror we realised they were constructing a funeral pyre.

Around midday, smoke began to issue from the small windows set high up in the walls of the Senate chamber. Sheets of orange flame and scraps of burning books whirled against the sky, while from inside came a terrifying and uninterrupted roar, as if a vent had been opened to the underworld. An hour later the roof split from end to end; thousands of tiles and spars of fiery timber plunged soundlessly from view; there was a strange interval of silence; and then the noise of the crash passed over us like a hot wind.

The fountain of smoke and dust and ashes lingered above the centre of Rome in a pall for several days, until the rain washed it away; and in this manner the last mortal vestiges of Publius Clodius Pulcher and the ancient assembly building he had reviled all his life vanished together from the face of the earth.

# VIII

———•◦•———

THE DESTRUCTION OF THE SENATE HOUSE HAD A POWERFUL EFFECT on Cicero. He went down the next day under heavy guard, grasping a stout stick, and clambered around the smouldering ruins. The blackened brickwork was still warm to the touch. The wind howled through the gaping holes, and from time to time from above our heads some piece of debris would dislodge and fall with a soft thump into the drifts of ash. Six hundred years that temple had stood there—a witness to the greatest moments in Rome's existence, and his own—and now it had gone in less than half an afternoon.

Everyone, including Cicero, assumed that Milo would now go into voluntary exile, or at any rate that he would keep well clear of Rome. But that was to underrate the bravado of the man. Far from lying low, he put himself at the head of an even larger force of gladiators and re-entered the city that same afternoon, barricading himself in his house. The grieving supporters of Clodius immediately laid siege to it. But they were easily driven off by arrows. They then went in search of a less formidable fortress on which to vent their anger, and found one in the home of the interrex, Marcus Aemilius Lepidus.

Although he was only thirty-six, and not yet even praetor, Lepidus was a member of the College of Pontiffs, and in the absence of any elected consuls that was enough to make him temporary chief magistrate. The damage inflicted on his property was slight—his wife's nuptial couch was broken up and her weaving destroyed—but the assault created a sense of outrage and panic in the Senate.

Lepidus, ever conscious of his dignity, played up the incident for all it was worth; indeed, this was the beginning of his rise to prominence. (Cicero used to say that Lepidus was the luckiest politician he knew: every time he made a mess of something he was showered with rewards—"He is a sort of genius of mediocrity.") The young interrex summoned a meeting of the Senate to be held outside the city walls, on the Field of Mars, in Pompey's new theatre—a large chamber within the complex had to be specially consecrated for the occasion—and he invited Pompey to attend.

This was three days after the burning of the Senate house.

Pompey duly obliged, sweeping down the hill from his palace surrounded by two hundred legionaries in full battle array—an entirely legal display of force, as he held military imperium as governor of Spain. But still—nothing like it had been seen since the days of Sulla. He left them picketed in the portico of the theatre while he went inside and listened modestly as his supporters demanded that he be appointed dictator for six months so that he could take the steps necessary to restore order: call up all the military reservists in Italy, put Rome under curfew, suspend the imminent elections and bring the killers of Clodius to justice.

Cicero saw the danger at once and rose to speak. "No one has greater respect for Pompey than I," he began, "but we must be careful not to do our enemies' work for them. To argue that to preserve our freedoms we must suspend our freedoms, that to safeguard elections we must cancel elections, that to defend ourselves from dictatorship we must appoint a dictator—what logic is this? We have elections scheduled. We have candidates on the ballot. The canvass is completed. The best way for us to show confidence in our institutions is to allow them to function normally and to elect our magistrates as our ancestors taught us in the olden time."

Pompey nodded, as if he could not have put the issue better himself, and at the end of the session he made an elaborate show of congratulating Cicero on his staunch defence of the constitution. But Cicero was not fooled. He saw exactly what Pompey was up to.

That night, Milo came to visit him for a council of war. Also present was Caelius Rufus, now a tribune and a long-term supporter and close friend of Milo. From down in the valley came the sound of scuffling, of dogs barking and occasional shouts and cries. A group of men carrying flaming torches ran across the Forum. But most citizens were too afraid to venture out and stayed in their houses behind barred doors. Milo seemed to think he had the election in the bag. After all, he had rid the state of Clodius, for which most decent people were grateful, and the burning-down of the Senate house and the violence in the streets had appalled the majority of voters.

Cicero said, "I agree that if there were a ballot tomorrow, Milo, you would probably win it. But there is not going to be a ballot. Pompey will see to that."

"How can he?"

"He'll use the campaign as a cover to manufacture an atmosphere of hysteria so that the Senate and the people will be forced to turn to him to abort the elections."

Rufus said, "He's bluffing. He doesn't have the power."

"Oh, he has the power, and he knows it. All he has to do is sit tight and wait for things to come to him."

Milo and Rufus both dismissed Cicero's fears as the nervousness of an old man, and the next day resumed campaigning with fresh energy. But Cicero was right: the mood in Rome was too jittery for normal electioneering and Milo walked straight into Pompey's trap. One morning soon after their meeting Cicero received an urgent summons to see Pompey. He found the great man's house ringed with soldiers and Pompey himself in an elevated part of the garden with double his normal bodyguard. Seated in the portico with him was a man Pompey introduced as Licinius, the owner of an eating house near the Circus Maximus. Pompey ordered Licinius to repeat his tale to Cicero, and Licinius duly described how he had overheard a group of Milo's gladiators plotting at his counter to murder Pompey, and how, when they realised he was listening, they had tried to silence him by stabbing him: as proof he showed Cicero a minor flesh wound just beneath his ribs.

Of course, as Cicero said to me afterwards, the whole story was absurd. "For a start, whoever heard of such feeble gladiators? If that kind of man wishes to silence you, you are silenced." But it didn't matter. The eating-house plot, as it became known, joined all the other rumours now circulating about Milo—that he had turned his house into an arsenal filled with swords, shields and javelins; that he had stocks of brands hidden throughout the city in order to burn it down; that he had shipped arms along the Tiber to his villa at Ocriculum; that the assassins who had murdered Clodius would be turned loose on his opponents in the election . . .

The next time the Senate met, no less a figure than Marcus Bibulus, Caesar's former consular colleague and passionate lifelong enemy, rose to propose that Pompey should hold office by emergency decree as sole consul. This was remarkable enough; what no one had anticipated was the reaction of Cato. A hush fell over the chamber as he got to his feet. "I would not have proposed this motion myself," he said, "but seeing as it has been laid before us, I propose we accept it as a sensible compromise. Some government is better than no government; a sole consulship is better than a dictatorship; and Pompey is more likely to rule wisely than anyone else."

Coming from Cato, this was almost unbelievable—he had used the word "compromise" for the first time in his life—and no one looked more stunned than Pompey. Afterwards, so the story went, he invited Cato back to his house to thank him personally and to ask him in future to be his private adviser in all matters of state. "You have no need to thank me," replied Cato, "for I only did what I believed to be in the best interests of the republic. If you wish to talk to me alone I shall certainly be at your disposal. But I shall say nothing to you in private that I wouldn't say anywhere else, and I shall never hold my tongue in public to please you."

Cicero observed their new closeness with deep foreboding. "Why do you think men like Cato and Bibulus have suddenly thrown in their lot with Pompey? Do you imagine they believe all this nonsense about a plot to murder him? Do you think they've suddenly changed their minds about him? Not at all! They've given him sole authority because they see him as their best hope of checking the ambitions of Caesar. I'm sure Pompey recognises this and believes he can control them. But he's wrong. Don't forget I know him. His vanity is his weakness. They will flatter him and load him down with powers and honours, and he won't even notice what they're doing, until one day it will be too late—they will have set him on a collision course with Caesar. And then we shall have war."

Cicero went straight from the Senate meeting to find Milo, and told him in blunt terms that he must now abandon his campaign for the consulship. "If you send a message to Pompey before night-fall and announce that you are withdrawing your candidacy in the interests of national unity, you might just head off a prosecution. If you don't, you're finished."

"And if I *am* prosecuted," responded Milo slyly, "will you defend me?"

I had expected Cicero to say it was impossible. Instead he sighed and ran his hand through his hair. "Listen to me, Milo—listen carefully. When I was at the lowest point of my life, six years ago in Thessalonica, you were the only one who offered me hope. There-fore you can rest assured, whatever happens I shan't turn my back on you now. But for pity's sake, don't let it come to that. Write to Pompey today."

Milo promised to think about it, although naturally he did not withdraw. The vaulting ambition that had carried him, in a mere half-dozen years, from ownership of a gladiator school to the brink of the consulship, was hardly likely at this late stage to be bridled by caution and good sense. Besides, his campaign debts were so enormous (some said the amount he owed was seventy million ses-terces) that he was facing exile whatever he did; he gained nothing by giving up now. So he continued with his canvass and Pompey moved ruthlessly to destroy him by setting up an inquiry into the events of the eighteenth and nineteenth of January—including the murder of Clodius, the burning of the Senate house and the attack on the home of Lepidus—under the chairmanship of Domitius Ahenobarbus. The slaves of Milo and Clodius were put to the torture to ascertain the facts, and I feared that some poor wretch, in his desperation, might remember my presence at the scene, which would have been embarrassing to Cicero. But I seem to have been blessed with the sort of personality that nobody notices—the reason perhaps why I have survived to write this account—and nobody mentioned me.

The inquiry led to Milo's trial for murder at the beginning of April and Cicero was required to honour his pledge to defend him. It was the only time I ever saw him prostrated by nerves. Pompey had filled the centre of the city with soldiers to guarantee order. But the effect was the opposite of reassuring. They blockaded every approach to the Forum and guarded the main public buildings. All the shops were closed. An atmosphere of tension and dread lay over the city. Pompey himself came to watch the proceedings and took a seat high up on the steps of the Temple of Saturn, surrounded by troops. Yet despite the show of force, the vast pro-Clodian crowd was allowed to intimidate the court. They jeered both Milo and Cicero whenever they tried to speak and made it difficult for the defence to be heard. All outrage and emotion was on their side—the brutality of the crime, the spectacle of the weeping widow and her fatherless children, and above all perhaps that curious retro-spective sanctity that settles over the reputation of any politician, however worthless, if his career is cut off in its prime.

As chief defence advocate, allowed under the special rules of the court only two hours to speak, Cicero had an almost impossible task. He could hardly pretend that Milo, who had openly boasted of what he had done, was innocent of the crime. Indeed some of Milo's supporters, such as Rufus, thought that Cicero should make a virtue of it and argue that the murder was not a crime at all but a public service. Cicero recoiled from that line of reasoning. "What are you saying? That any man can be condemned to death without trial and summarily executed by his enemies if it suits enough peo-ple? That's mob rule, Rufus—exactly what Clodius believed in—and I refuse to stand up in a Roman court and make such a case."

The only feasible alternative was to argue that the killing was justified on the grounds of self-defence—but that was difficult to reconcile with the evidence that Clodius had been dragged out of the tavern and finished off in cold blood. Still, it was not impossible. I had known Cicero to win from weaker positions. And he wrote a good speech. However, on the morning he was due to deliver it, he woke gripped by a terrible anxiety. At first I took no notice. He was often nervous before a big oration, and suffered from loose bowels and vomiting. But this morning was different. He was not gripped by fear, which he sometimes called "cold strength" and had learned how to harness; rather he was simply in a funk and could not remember a word of what he was supposed to say.

Milo suggested he should go down to the Forum in a closed litter and wait somewhere out of sight, calmly composing himself until it was time for him to speak; and this was what we tried. Cicero, at his request, had been provided with a bodyguard by Pompey for the duration of the trial, and they cordoned off a part of the Grove of Vesta and kept everyone away while the orator reclined beneath the thick embroidered canopy, trying to commit his speech to memory and occasionally leaning out to retch on the sacred earth. But although he could not see the crowd, he could hear it chanting and roaring nearby, and that was almost worse. When the praetor's clerk finally came to fetch us, Cicero's legs were so weak he could barely stand. As we walked into the Forum, the noise was terrific, and the sunlight glinting on the armour and weapons of the soldiers dazzled our eyes.

The Clodians jeered Cicero when he appeared and jeered him all the louder when he tried to speak. His nerves were so obvious he actually confessed them in his opening sentence—"I am afraid, gentlemen of the jury: an unseemly condition in which to begin a speech in defence of the bravest of men, but there it is"— and blamed his fear squarely on the rigged nature of the hearing: "Wherever I look, I look in vain for the familiar environment of the courts and the traditional procedure of the law."

Unfortunately, complaining about the rules of a contest is always a sure sign of a man who knows he is about to lose it, and although Cicero made some effective points—"Suppose, gentle-men, I could induce you to acquit Milo, but only on condition that Clodius comes back to life again: why all those terrified glances?"—a speech is only as good as its delivery. By thirty-eight votes to thirteen the jury found Milo guilty, and he was sent into exile for life. His property was hastily auctioned at knock-down prices to pay his creditors, and Cicero directed Terentia's steward, Philoti-mus, to buy a lot of it anonymously so that it could be disposed of later and the profits handed to Milo's wife, Fausta: she had made it clear she would not be accompanying her husband into exile. A day or two later Milo went off with remarkable cheerfulness to Mas-silia in southern Gaul. His departure was very much in the spirit of a gladiator who knew he would lose eventually and was simply grateful to have lived so long. Cicero tried to make amends by pub-lishing the speech he would have given if his nerves hadn't got the better of him. He sent a copy to Milo, who replied charmingly a few months later that he was glad Cicero hadn't spoken it, *for otherwise I should not be eating such wonderful Massilian mullets.*

SOON AFTER MILO LEFT ROME, POMPEY INVITED CICERO TO DINNER to show there were no hard feelings. Cicero went off grumbling and reeled home afterwards in such a state of amazement that he came and woke me up, for who should have been at the dinner table but the widow of Publius Crassus, the teenaged Cornelia—and Pompey had married her!

Cicero said, "Well, naturally I congratulated him—she's a beau-tiful and accomplished girl, even if she is young enough to be his granddaughter—and then I asked him, by way of conversation, what Caesar had made of the match. He looked at me with great disdain and said that he hadn't even told Caesar: what business was it of Caesar's? He was fifty-three years old and he would marry whomever he pleased!

"I replied, as gently as I could, that perhaps Caesar might take a different view—after all, he had sought a marital alliance and been rebuffed, and the bride's father has not exactly shown himself a friend of Caesar's. To which Pompey replied, 'Oh, don't worry about Scipio, he's entirely friendly. I'm appointing him my consular colleague for the remainder of my term!' Is the man mad, do you suppose? Caesar is going to look at Rome and think that the whole place has been taken over by the aristocratic party, with Pompey at their head." Cicero groaned and closed his eyes; I guessed he had drunk rather a lot. "I told you this would happen. I am Cassandra—doomed to see the future yet destined never to be believed."

Cassandra or not, there was one consequence of Pompey's special consulship that Cicero had not foreseen. To help end electoral corruption, Pompey had decided to reform the laws relating to the fourteen provincial commands. Up to this point, consuls and praetors had always left Rome immediately upon the expiry of their term of office to take up their allotted province; and because of the huge sums that could be extorted from such commands, a practice had arisen of candidates borrowing against their expected earnings in order to fund their election campaigns. Pompey, with amazing hypocrisy considering his own abuse of the system, decided to put a stop to all that. Henceforth, a period of five years would have to elapse between holding office in Rome and taking up a governorship overseas. To fill such positions in the interim it was decreed that every senator of praetorian rank who had never done their turn as governor would have to draw lots for the vacant provinces.

To his horror, Cicero now realised he was in danger of having to do what he had always sworn to avoid: sweating it out in some corner of the empire, administering justice to the natives. He went to see Pompey to plead to be excused. His health was poor, he said. He was getting old. He even suggested that the time he had spent in exile might be counted as his term abroad.

Pompey wouldn't hear of it. Indeed he seemed to take a malicious pleasure in running through all the possible commands that might now fall to Cicero, with their various unique drawbacks—extreme distance from Rome, rebellious tribesmen, ferocious customs, hostile climates, savage wild beasts, impassable roads, incurable local diseases and so forth. Lots to determine who went where were drawn at a special session of the Senate, with Pompey in the chair. Cicero went up and plucked his token from the urn and handed it to Pompey, who read out the result with a smile: "Marcus Tullius draws Cilicia."

Cilicia! Cicero could barely conceal his dismay. This mountainous, primitive homeland of pirates at the extreme eastern edge of the Mediterranean—which included within its administration the island of Cyprus—was about as far away from Rome as it was possible to get. It also shared a border with Syria, and so was within range of the Parthian army, if Cassius was unable to hold them in check. Finally, to cap Cicero's woes, the current governor was Clodius's brother, Appius Clodius Pulcher, who could be relied upon to make his successor's life as difficult as possible.

I knew he would expect me to go with him and I tried desperately to think of excuses why I should stay behind. He had just completed *On the Republic*. I told him that in my view I would be more use to him in Rome, overseeing its publication.

"Nonsense," he said, "Atticus will take care of copying and circulation."

"There's also my health," I continued, "I've never really recovered from that fever I contracted at Arpinum."

"In that case a sea voyage will do you good."

And so it went on. My every objection was met by an answer. He started to become offended. But I had a bad feeling about this expedition. Although he swore we would only be gone a year, I sensed it would be longer. Rome felt strangely impermanent to me. Perhaps it was a consequence of having to pass the burnt-out shell of the Senate house every day, or maybe it was my knowledge of the widening split between Pompey and Caesar. Whatever the reason, I had a superstitious dread that if I left I might never come back, and that even if I did return it would be to a different city.

Eventually Cicero said, "Well, I cannot force you to come— you're a free man now. But I feel you owe me this one last service, and I'll make a bargain with you. When we return, I'll give you the money to buy that farm you've always wanted, and I shan't press you to perform any more duties for me. The rest of your life will be your own."

I could hardly refuse such an offer, and so I tried to ignore my forebodings and set about helping him plan his administration.

As governor of Cilicia, Cicero would have command of a standing army of about fourteen thousand men, with every prospect of having to fight a war. He decided therefore to appoint two legates with military experience. One was his old comrade Caius Pomptinus, the praetor who had helped him round up Catilina's co-conspirators. For the second he turned to his brother, Quintus, who had expressed a strong desire to quit Gaul. At first his service under Caesar had been a great success. He had taken part in the invasion of Britain, and on his return Caesar had placed him in command of a legion that soon afterwards was attacked in its winter camp by a vastly superior force of Gauls. The fighting had been fierce: nine tenths of the Romans had been wounded. But Quintus, although ill and exhausted, had kept a cool head and the legion had survived the siege long enough for Caesar to arrive and relieve them; afterwards he had been singled out for praise by Caesar in his *Commentaries*.

The following summer he was promoted to command of the newly formed Fourteenth Legion. This time, however, he had disobeyed Caesar's orders. Instead of keeping all his men in camp, he had sent out several hundred raw recruits to forage for food. They had been cut off by an invading force of Germans. Caught in the open, they had stood gaping at their commanders, unsure of what to do, and half of them had been massacred when they tried to make a run for it. *All my previous good standing with Caesar has been destroyed,* Quintus wrote sadly to his brother. *He treats me to my face with civility but I detect a certain coldness, and I know he goes behind my back to consult with my junior officers; in short I fear I may never fully regain his trust.* Cicero wrote to Caesar asking if his brother might be allowed to join him in Cilicia; Caesar readily agreed; and two months later Quintus arrived back in Rome.

As far as I am aware, Cicero never uttered a word of reproach to his brother. Nevertheless, something was altered in their relationship. I believe Quintus felt a keen sense of failure. He had hoped to find fame and fortune and independence in Gaul; instead he came back tarnished, out of pocket and more dependent than ever on his famous sibling. His marriage remained bitter. He was still drinking heavily. And his only son, young Quintus, who was now fifteen, had all the charms of that particular age, being sullen, secretive, insolent and duplicitous. Cicero believed the boy needed more of his father's attention and suggested he should accompany us to Cilicia, along with his own son, Marcus. My expectations of our trip, already low, receded further.

When we left Rome at the start of the senatorial recess, we were a huge party. Cicero had been invested with imperium and was obliged to travel with six lictors as well as a great retinue of slaves carrying all our baggage for the voyage abroad. Terentia came part of the way to see her husband off, and so did Tullia, who had just been divorced by Crassipes. She was closer to her father than ever and read him poetry on the journey. Privately he fretted to me about her future: twenty-five years old, no child, no husband . . . We stopped off at Tusculum to say goodbye to Atticus, and Cicero asked him as a favour to keep an eye on Tullia and try to find her a new match while he was away.

"Of course I shall," Atticus replied, "and would you in return do a favour for me? Will you try to make Quintus just a little kinder to my sister? I know Pomponia is a difficult woman, but he has returned from Gaul in a permanent foul temper, and their constant arguments are having a bad effect on their boy."

Cicero agreed, and when we met up with Quintus and his family at Arpinum, he took his brother aside and repeated what Atticus had said. Quintus promised to do his best. But Pomponia, I'm afraid, was quite impossible, and it was not long before the couple were refusing to speak to one another, let alone share a bed, and they parted very coldly.

Relations between Terentia and Cicero were more civil, apart from the one vexed area that had been a source of antagonism between them all their married life—money. In contrast to her husband, Terentia had welcomed his appointment as governor, seeing in it a wonderful opportunity for enrichment. She had even brought her steward, Philotimus, along on the journey south so that he could give Cicero the benefit of his various ideas for skimming off a profit. Cicero kept postponing the conversation and Terentia kept nagging him to have it until at last on their final day together he lost his temper.

"This fixation of yours with making money is really most unseemly."

"This fixation of yours with spending it gives me no choice!"

Cicero paused for a moment to control his irritation and then tried to explain the matter calmly. "You don't seem to understand—a man in my position cannot risk the slightest impropriety. My enemies are just waiting for an opportunity to prosecute me for corruption."

"So you intend to be the only provincial governor in history not to come home richer than he went out?"

"My dear wife, if you ever read a word I wrote, you would know I am just about to publish a treatise on good government. How will that sit with a reputation for thievery in office?"

"Books!" said Terentia with great contempt. "Where is the money in *books*?"

They repaired their quarrel sufficiently to dine together that night, and to humour her Cicero agreed that at some stage in the coming year he would at least listen to Philotimus's business proposals—but only on condition they were legal.

The next morning the family parted, with many tears and much embracing—Cicero and Marcus, who was now fourteen, setting off on horseback together side by side, while Terentia and Tullia stood at the gate of the family farm, waving. I remember that just before the road carried us out of sight I took a final look over my shoulder. Terentia had gone in by then but Tullia was still there watching us, a fragile figure against the majesty of the mountains.

. . .

WE WERE DUE TO EMBARK ON THE FIRST LEG OF OUR VOYAGE TO Cilicia from Brundisium, and it was while we were on the road there, at Venusia, that Cicero received an invitation from Pompey. The great man was taking the winter sun at his villa in Tarentum and suggested that Cicero should come and stay for a couple of days "to discuss the political situation." As Tarentum was only forty miles from Brundisium, and as our route would take us practically past the door, and as Pompey was not a man to whom it was easy to say no, Cicero had little option but to accept.

Once again we found Pompey living in a state of great domestic happiness with a young bride: they seemed almost to be playing at being a married couple. The house was surprisingly modest; as governor of Spain Pompey had a mere fifty legionaries to protect him, and they were billeted on the neighbouring properties. Otherwise he was without executive authority, having given up his consulship amid universal praise for his wisdom. In fact I would say he was at the summit of his popularity. Crowds of locals stood around outside hoping to catch a glimpse of him; once or twice a day he would sally forth to shake hands and pat the heads of infants. He was quite corpulent now, breathless and rather an unhealthy purplish colour. Cornelia fussed over him like a little mother, trying to restrain his appetite at meals and encouraging him to take walks along the seashore, his guards following at a discreet distance. He was idle, somnolent, uxorious. Cicero presented him with a copy of *On the Republic*. He expressed great pleasure but immediately laid it aside and I never saw him open it.

Whenever I look back at this three-day interlude, it seems to stand out in my memory like some sunlit glade in the middle of a vast and darkening forest. Watching the two ageing statesmen throwing a ball for Marcus, or standing with their togas hitched up, skimming stones across the waves, it was impossible to believe that anything sinister was impending—or if it was, that it would amount to much. Pompey exuded absolute confidence.

I was not privy to all that passed between him and Cicero, although Cicero told me most of it afterwards. The political situation in essence was this: that Caesar had completed his conquest of Gaul; that the Gallic leader, Vercingetorix, had surrendered and was in custody; and that the enemy's army was wiped out (the final engagement had been the capture of the hilltop fortress of Uxellodunum along with its garrison of two thousand Gallic fighters, all of whom, on Caesar's orders, according to his *Commentaries,* had had both hands cut off before being sent home, *so that everyone might see what punishment was meted out to those who resisted Rome's rule;* there had been no trouble since).

Given all this, the question now arose of what to do with Caesar. His own preference was to be allowed to stand for a second consulship *in absentia* so that he could enter Rome with legal immunity for all the crimes and misdemeanours he had committed during his first; at the very least he wanted his command extended so that he could remain as ruler of Gaul. His opponents, led by Cato, believed that he should return to Rome and submit himself to the electorate just like any other citizen; and failing that, he should be forced to give up his army, it being intolerable to have a man in control of what was now eleven legions, sitting on the Italian border issuing diktats to the Senate.

"And what is Pompey's view?" I asked.

"Pompey's view varies according to the hour of the day you ask him. In the morning he thinks it entirely proper, as a reward for his achievements, that his good friend Caesar should be permitted to stand for the consulship without entering Rome. After lunch he sighs and wonders why Caesar can't simply come home and canvass face to face like anybody else: after all, that was what he did in Caesar's position, and what was so undignified about that? And then by evening, when—despite the best efforts of the good Lady Cornelia—he is flushed with wine, he starts shouting, 'To hell with bloody Caesar! I'm sick of hearing about Caesar! Let him just try and set one toe in Italy with his bloody legions, and you'll see what I can do—I'll stamp my foot and a hundred thousand men will rise up at my command and come to the defence of the Senate!'"

"And what do you think will happen?"

"My guess is that if I were here I could probably just about persuade him to do the right thing and avoid civil war, which would be the ultimate calamity. My fear," he added, "is that when the vital decisions are being taken, I shall be a thousand miles from Rome."

# IX

———•◦•———

I DO NOT PROPOSE TO DESCRIBE IN ANY DETAIL CICERO'S TIME AS governor of Cilicia. I am sure history will judge it as of minor importance in the scale of things; Cicero judged it minor even at the time.

We reached Athens in the spring and stayed for ten days with Aristus, the principal professor of the Academy, who was at that time the greatest living exponent of the philosophy of Epicurus. Like Atticus, who was also a devoted Epicurean, Aristus took a practical, material view of what makes for a happy life: a healthy diet, moderate exercise, pleasant surroundings, congenial company and the avoidance of stressful situations. Cicero, whose god was Plato and whose life was full of stress, disputed this. He believed that Epicureanism amounted to a kind of antiphilosophy: "You say happiness depends on bodily well-being. But continual physical well-being is beyond our control. If a man is suffering an agonising illness, say, or if he is being tortured, then in your philosophy he cannot be happy."

"Perhaps he cannot be *supremely* happy," conceded Aristus, "but happiness will still be there in some form."

"No, no, he cannot be happy *at all*," insisted Cicero, "because his happiness is entirely contingent on the physical. Whereas the most magnificent and fruitful promise in the entire history of philosophy is the simple maxim: *nothing is good except what is morally good.* From this we can prove that *moral goodness is sufficient by itself to create the happy life.* And from that derives a third maxim: *moral goodness is the only sort of good there is.*"

"Ah, but if I torture you," objected Aristus, with a knowing laugh, "you will be every bit as unhappy as I am."

Cicero, however, was very serious. "No, no, because if I remain morally good—which I am not claiming is easy, by the way, let alone that I have achieved it—then I must remain happy, however great my pain. Even as my torturer falls back in exhaustion there will be something beyond the physical that he cannot reach."

Naturally I am simplifying a long and complicated discussion that lasted several days as we toured the buildings and antiquities of Athens. But this was what it boiled down to, and it was now that Cicero began to conceive of the idea of writing some work of philosophy that would not be a set of high-flown abstractions but rather a practical guide to achieving the good life.

From Athens we sailed down the coast and then hopped from island to island across the Aegean in a fleet of a dozen vessels. The Rhodian boats were large, cumbersome and slow; they pitched and rolled in even moderate seas and were open to the elements. I remember how I shivered in a rainstorm as we passed Delos, that melancholy rock where up to ten thousand slaves are said to be sold in a single day. Everywhere the crowds that turned out to see Cicero were immense; among Romans only Pompey and Caesar, and I suppose just possibly Cato, can have been more famous in the world. At Ephesus our teeming expedition of legates, quaestors, lictors and military tribunes, with all their slaves and baggage, was transferred to a convoy of ox carts and pack mules and we set off along the dusty mountain roads into the interior of Asia Minor.

It was a full fifty-two days after leaving Italy that we reached Laodicea, the first town in the province of Cilicia, where Cicero was immediately required to begin hearing cases. The poverty and exhaustion of the common people, the endless shuffling queues of petitioners in the gloomy basilica and the glaring white-stone forum, the constant moans and groans about customs officials and poll taxes, the petty corruption, the flies, the heat, the dysentery, the sharp stink of goat and sheep dung that seemed always in the air, the bitter-tasting wine and oily spicy food, the small scale of the town and the lack of anything beautiful to look at, or sophisticated to listen to, or savoury to eat—oh, how Cicero hated being stuck in such a place while the fate of the world was being decided back in Italy without him! I had barely unpacked my ink and stylus before he was dictating letters to everyone he could think of in Rome, pleading with them to make sure his term was restricted to a year.

We had not been there long when a dispatch arrived from Cassius reporting that the King of Parthia's son had invaded Syria at the head of such a massive force he had been obliged to withdraw his legions to the fortified city of Antioch. This meant Cicero had to set off immediately to join his own army at the foot of the Taurus mountains, the immense natural barrier separating Cilicia from Syria. Quintus was greatly excited, and for a month there seemed a real possibility that Cicero might have to command the defence of the entire eastern flank of the empire. But then a fresh report came from Cassius: the Parthians had retreated before the impregnable walls of Antioch; he had pursued and defeated them; the king's son was dead and the threat was over.

I am not sure whether Cicero was more relieved or disappointed. However, he still managed to have a war of sorts. Some of the local tribes had taken advantage of the Parthian crisis to rise in revolt against Roman rule. There was one fortress in particular, named Pindessium, where the rebel forces were concentrated, and Cicero laid siege to it.

We lived in an army camp in the mountains for two months, and Quintus was as happy as a schoolboy building ramps and towers, digging moats and bringing up artillery. I found the whole adventure distasteful, and so I think did Cicero, for the rebels stood no chance. Day after day we launched arrows and flaming projectiles into the town, until eventually it surrendered and our legionaries poured into the place to ransack it. Quintus had the leaders executed. The rest were put in chains and led off to the coast to be shipped to Delos and sold into slavery. Cicero watched them go with a gloomy expression. "I suppose if I were a great military man like Caesar I would have all their hands amputated. Isn't that how one brings peace to these people? But I can't say I derive much satisfaction from using all the resources of civilisation to reduce a few barbarian huts to ashes." Still, his men hailed him as imperator in the field, and afterwards he had me write six hundred letters— that is, one to every member of the Senate—requesting that he be awarded a triumph: a tremendous labour for me, working in the primitive conditions of an army camp, that left me prostrate with exhaustion.

CICERO PLACED QUINTUS IN COMMAND OF THE ARMY FOR THE winter and returned to Laodicea. He was rather shocked by the relish with which his brother had crushed the rebellion, and also by his brusque manner with subordinates (*irritable, rude, careless,* as he described him to Atticus); he did not care much for his nephew, either—*a boy with a fine conceit for himself.* Quintus Junior liked to make sure everyone knew who he was—his name alone saw to that—and he treated the locals with great disdain. Still, Cicero tried to do his duty as an affectionate uncle, and at that spring's Festival of Liberalia, in the absence of the boy's father, he presided over the ceremony at which young Quintus became a man, personally helping him to shave his wispy beard and dress in his first toga.

As for his own son, young Marcus gave him cause for concern in a different way. The lad was affable, lazy, fond of sport and somewhat slow on the uptake when it came to his schoolwork. Rather than study Greek and Latin, he liked to hang around the army officers and practise swordplay and javelin throwing. "I love him dearly," Cicero said to me, "and he is certainly a good-hearted fellow, but sometimes I wonder where on earth he comes from— I detect nothing in him of me at all."

Nor was that the end of his family worries. He had left the choice of Tullia's new husband up to her and her mother, having made clear simply that his own preference was for a safe, worthy, respectable young aristocrat such as Tiberius Nero or the son of his old friend Servius Sulpicius. But the women had set their hearts instead on Publius Cornelius Dolabella, a most unsuitable match in Cicero's view. He was a notorious rake, only nineteen—about seven years younger than Tullia—yet remarkably he had already been married once, to a much older woman.

By the time the letter announcing their choice reached him, it was too late for Cicero to intervene: the wedding would have taken place before his answer arrived in Rome—a fact the women must have known. "What is one to do?" he sighed to me. "Well, such is life—let the gods bless what is done. I can understand why Tullia wants it—no doubt he's a handsome, charming type, and if anyone deserves a taste of life at last, it's she. But Terentia! What is *she* thinking of? It sounds as though she's half in love with the fellow herself. I'm not sure I understand her any more."

And here I come to the greatest of all Cicero's personal worries: that something clearly was amiss with Terentia. Recently he had received a reproachful letter from the exiled Milo demanding to know what had happened to all that property of his that Cicero had bought so cheaply at auction: his wife, Fausta, had never received a penny. As it happened, the agent who had acted on Cicero's behalf—Philotimus, Terentia's steward—was still hoping to persuade Cicero to adopt some dubious money-making scheme and was due to visit him in Laodicea.

Cicero received him in my presence and told him bluntly that there was no question of him or any member of his staff or family engaging in any shady business. "So you can save your breath as far as that's concerned and tell me instead what's become of Milo's bankrupt estate. You remember the sale was fixed so you got it all for next to nothing, and then you were supposed to sell it at a profit and give the proceeds to Fausta?"

Philotimus, plumper than ever and already sweating in the summer heat, flushed even redder and started to stammer that he couldn't recall the details precisely: it was more than a year ago; he would have to consult his accounts and they were in Rome.

Cicero threw up his hands. "Come now, man, you must remember. It's not that long ago. We're talking about tens of thousands. What has become of it all?"

But Philotimus would only repeat the same tale over and over: he was very sorry; he couldn't remember; he would need to check.

"I'm beginning to think you've pocketed the money yourself."

Philotimus denied it.

Suddenly Cicero said, "Does my wife know about this?"

At the mention of Terentia, a remarkable change came over Philotimus. He stopped squirming and became completely silent, and no matter how many times Cicero pressed him, he refused to say another word. Eventually Cicero told him to clear off out of his sight. After he had gone he said to me, "Did you note that last piece of impertinence? Talk about defending a lady's honour—it was as if he thought I wasn't fit to utter my own wife's name."

I agreed it was remarkable.

"*Remarkable*—that's one word for it. They were always very close, but ever since I went into exile . . ."

He shook his head and didn't finish the sentence. I made no reply. It did not seem proper to comment. To this day I have no idea whether his suspicions were correct. All I can say is that he was deeply perturbed by the whole affair and wrote at once to Atticus asking him to investigate discreetly: *I can't put all I fear into words.*


A MONTH BEFORE THE END OF HIS OFFICIAL TERM AS GOVERNOR, Cicero, escorted by his lictors, set off back to Rome taking me and the two boys with him and leaving his quaestor in charge of the province.

He knew he could face censure for abandoning his post prematurely and for placing Cilicia in the hands of a first-year senator, but he calculated that with Caesar's governorship of Gaul about to come to an end, most men would have bigger issues on their minds. We travelled via Rhodes, which he wanted to show to Quintus and Marcus. He also desired to visit the tomb of Apollonius Molon, the great tutor of oratory whose lessons almost thirty years before had started him on his political ascent. We found it on a headland looking across the Carpathian Straits. A simple white marble stone bore the orator's name, and beneath it was carved in Greek one of his favourite precepts: *Nothing dries more quickly than a tear.* Cicero stood looking at it for a long time.

Unfortunately the diversion to Rhodes slowed our return considerably. The Etesian winds were unusually strong that summer, blowing in from the north day after day, and they trapped our open boats in harbour for three weeks. During that period the political situation in Rome worsened sharply, and by the time we reached Ephesus there was a sackful of alarming news waiting for Cicero. *The nearer the struggle approaches,* wrote Rufus, *the plainer the danger appears. Pompey is determined not to allow Caesar to be elected consul unless he surrenders his army and provinces; whereas Caesar is persuaded that he cannot survive if he leaves his army. So this is what their love affair, their scandalous union has come to—not covert backbiting, but outright war!*

In Athens, a week later, Cicero found more letters, including ones from both Pompey and Caesar, each complaining about the other and appealing to his loyalty. *As far as I am concerned, he may be consul or he may keep his legions,* wrote Pompey, *but I am certain that he cannot do both; I assume that you agree with my policy and will stand resolutely on my side and on the side of the Senate as you have always done.* And from Caesar: *I fear that Pompey's noble nature has blinded him to the true intentions of those individuals who have always wished me harm; I rely upon you, dear Cicero, to tell him that I cannot be, should not be, and will not be left defenceless.*

The two letters plunged Cicero into a state of acute anxiety. He sat in Aristus's library with both laid on the table before him and looked back and forth from one to the other. *I fancy I see the greatest struggle that history has ever known,* he wrote to Atticus. *There looms ahead a tremendous contest between them. Each counts me as his man. But what am I to do? They will try to draw a statement of my views. You will laugh when I say it, but I wish to heaven I was still back in my province.*

That night I lay shivering despite the Athens heat, my teeth chattering, hallucinating that Cicero was dictating a letter to me, a copy of which had to go to both Pompey and Caesar, assuring each of his support. But a phrase that would please one would infuriate the other, and I spent hour after hour in a panic trying to construct sentences that were utterly neutral. Whenever I thought I had managed it, the words would become disorganised in my head and I would have to start again. It was utter madness yet at the same time it seemed absolutely real, and when morning came I realised in a lucid interval that I had lapsed back into the fever that had afflicted me at Arpinum.

That day we were due to set off again by ship to Corinth. I tried hard to carry on as normal. But I guess I must have looked ghastly and hollow-eyed. Cicero tried to persuade me to eat but I was unable to keep food in my stomach. Although I managed to board the boat unaided, I spent the day's voyage almost comatose, and when we landed at Corinth that evening, apparently I had to be carried off the ship and put to bed.

The question now arose of what should be done with me. I was desperate not to be left behind, and Cicero did not want to abandon me. But he needed to get back to Rome, firstly to do what little was in his power to avert the impending civil war, and secondly to try to lobby for a triumph, of which, unrealistically, he still had slight hopes. He could not afford to waste days in Greece waiting for his secretary to recover. In retrospect I should have stayed in Corinth. Instead we gambled that I would be strong enough to withstand the two-day journey to Patrae, where a ship would be waiting to take us to Italy. It was a foolish decision. I was wrapped in blankets and placed in the back of a carriage and conveyed along the coastal road in great discomfort. When we reached Patrae, I begged them to go on without me. I was sure a long sea voyage would kill me. Cicero was still reluctant, but in the end he agreed. I was put to bed in a villa near the harbour belonging to Lyso, a Greek merchant. Cicero, Marcus and young Quintus gathered around my bed to say goodbye. They shook my hand. Cicero wept. I made some feeble joke about our parting scene resembling the deathbed of Socrates. And then they were gone.

. . .

CICERO WROTE ME A LETTER THE FOLLOWING DAY AND SENT IT BACK with Mario, one of his most trusted slaves.

*I thought I could bear the want of you not too hard, but frankly I find it unendurable. I feel I did wrong to leave you. If after you are able to take nourishment you think you can overtake me, the decision is in your hands. Think it over in that clever head of yours. I miss you but I love you. Loving you I want to see you fit and well; missing you I want to see you as soon as possible. The former therefore must come first. So make it your chief concern to get well. Of your countless services to me this is the one I shall most appreciate.*

He wrote me many such letters during the time I was ill—once he sent three in a single day. Naturally I missed him as much as he missed me. But my health was broken. I could not travel. It was to be eight months before I saw him again, and by then his world, our world, was utterly transformed.

Lyso was an attentive host and brought in his own doctor, a fellow Greek named Asclapo, to treat me. I was purged and sweated and starved and hydrated: all the standard remedies for a tertian fever were attempted when what I really needed was rest. Cicero, however, fretted that Lyso was *a little casual: all Greeks are,* and arranged for me to be moved after a few days to a larger and more peaceful house up the hill, away from the noise of the harbour. It belonged to a childhood friend of his, Manius Curius: *All my hopes of your getting proper treatment and attention are pinned on Curius. He has the kindest of hearts and the truest affection for me. Put yourself entirely in his hands.*

Curius was indeed an amiable, cultured man, a widower, a banker by profession, and he looked after me well. I was given a room with a terrace looking westwards to the sea, and later, when I started to feel strong enough, I would sit outside for an hour in the afternoons watching the merchant ships going in and out of the harbour. Curius was in regular touch with all sorts of contacts in Rome—senators, equestrians, tax farmers, shipowners—and his letters, plus mine, together with the geographical situation of Patrae as the gateway to Greece, meant that we received the political news as quickly as anyone could in that part of the world.

One day around the end of January—this must have been about three months after Cicero's departure—Curius came into my room with a grim expression and asked me whether I was strong enough to take bad news. When I nodded, he said, "Caesar has invaded Italy."

Years afterwards, Cicero used to wonder whether the three weeks we had lost on Rhodes might have made the difference between war and peace. If only, he lamented, he could have reached Rome a month earlier! He was one of the few who was listened to by both sides, and in the short time he was on the outskirts of Rome before the conflict broke out—which was barely a week—he told me he had begun to broker the beginnings of a compromise: Caesar to give up Gaul and all his legions apart from one, and in return to be allowed to stand for the consulship *in absentia*. But by then it was far too late. Pompey was dubious about the deal; the Senate rejected it; and Caesar, he suspected, had already made up his mind to strike, having calculated that he would never be stronger than at that moment: "In short, I was among madmen wild for war."

The moment he heard that Caesar had invaded, he went straight to Pompey's house on the Pincian hill to pledge his support. It was packed with the leaders of the war party—Cato, Ahenobarbus, the consuls Marcellinus and Lentulus: fifteen or twenty men in all. Pompey was enraged, and he was panicking. He was under the misapprehension that Caesar was advancing at full strength, with perhaps fifty thousand troops. In fact, that inveterate gambler had crossed the Rubicon with only a tenth of that number and was relying on the shock effect of his aggression. But Pompey did not yet know that, and so he decreed that the city should be abandoned.

He was ordering every senator to leave Rome. Any who remained behind would be regarded as traitors. When Cicero demurred, arguing that this was a mad policy, Pompey turned on him: "And that includes you, Cicero!" This war would not be decided in Rome, he declared, or even in Italy—that was to play into Caesar's hands. Instead it would be a world war, fought in Spain, Africa, the eastern Mediterranean and especially at sea. He would blockade Italy. He would starve the enemy into submission. Caesar would rule over a charnel house.

*I shuddered at the kind of war intended,* wrote Cicero to Atticus, *savage and vast beyond what men yet envision.* Pompey's personal hostility towards him was also a shock. He left Rome as ordered and withdrew to Formiae and brooded on what course to take. Officially he was placed in charge of sea defences and recruitment in northern Campania; practically he did nothing. Pompey sent him a cold reminder of his duties: *I strongly urge you, in view of your outstanding and unswerving patriotism, to make your way over to us, so that in concert we may bring aid and comfort to our afflicted country.*

Around this time, Cicero wrote to me: I received the letter about three weeks after I learned of the outbreak of war.

*From Cicero to his dear Tiro, greetings.*

*My existence and that of all honest men and the entire commonwealth hangs in the balance, as you may tell from the fact that we have left our homes and the mother city herself to plunder or burning. Swept along by some spirit of folly, forgetting the name he bears and the honours he has won, Caesar seized Ariminium, Pisaurum, Ancona and Arretium. So we abandoned Rome—how wisely or how courageously it is idle to argue. We have reached the point when we cannot survive unless some god or accident comes to our rescue. To add to my vexations, my son-in-law Dolabella is with Caesar.*

*I wanted you to be aware of these facts. Mind you don't let them upset you and hinder your recovery. Since you could not be with me when I most needed your services and loyalty, make sure you do not hurry or be so foolish as to undertake the voyage either as an invalid or in winter.*

I obeyed his instruction and thus I found myself following the collapse of the Roman Republic from my sick room—and in my memory, my illness and the madness being played out in Italy are forever merged in a single fevered nightmare. Pompey and his hastily assembled army headed to Brundisium to embark for Macedonia to begin their world war. Caesar chased after him to stop him. He tried to blockade the harbour. He failed. He watched the sails of Pompey's troopships dwindle into the distance, then turned round and marched back the way he had come, towards Rome. His route along the Via Appia took him past Cicero's door in Formiae.

*Formiae, 29 March*

*From Cicero to his dear Tiro, greetings.*

*So I have seen the madman at last—for the first time in nine years, can one believe it? He appeared quite unchanged. A little harder, leaner, greyer, and more lined perhaps; but I fancy this life of brigandage suits him. Terentia, Tullia and Marcus are with me (they send their love, by the way).*

*What happened was this. All yesterday his legionaries were streaming past our door—a wild-looking lot, but they left us unmolested. We were just settling down to dinner when a commotion at the gate signalled the arrival of a column of mounted men. What an entourage, what an underworld! A grimmer group of desperadoes you have never seen! The man himself—if man he is: one starts to wonder—was alert and audacious and in a hurry. Is he a Roman general or is he Hannibal? "I could not pass so close without stopping for a moment to see you." As if he was a country neighbour! To Terentia and Tullia he was most civil. He refused all hospitality ("I must press on") and we went into my study to talk. We were quite alone. He came straight to the point. He was summoning a meeting of the Senate in four days' time.*

*"On what authority?"*

*"This," he said, and touched his sword. "Come along and work for peace."*

*"At my own discretion?"*

*"Naturally. Who am I to lay down rules for you?"*

*"Well then, I shall say that the Senate should not give its approval if you plan to send your troops to Spain or Greece to fight the armies of the republic. And I shall have much to say in defence of Pompey."*

*At this he protested that these were not the sort of things he wanted said.*

*"So I supposed," I replied, "and that is just why I don't want to be present. Either I must stay away or speak in that strain—and bring up much else besides which I could not possibly suppress if I was there."*

*He became very cold. He said I was in effect passing judgement against him, and that if I was reluctant to come across to him, others would be too. He told me I should think the matter over and let him know. With that he got up to leave. "One last thing," he said. "I should like your counsels, but if I cannot have them I shall take advice wherever I can, and I shall stop at nothing."*

*On that note we parted. I don't doubt our meeting has put him out of humour with me. It is becoming ever clearer that I cannot remain here much longer. I see no end to the mischief.*

I did not know how to reply, and besides, I was frightened that any letter I sent would be intercepted, for Cicero had discovered that he was surrounded by Caesar's spies. The boys' tutor, Dionysius, for example, who had accompanied us to Cilicia, turned out to be an informant. So too, much more shockingly to Cicero, was his own nephew, young Quintus, who sought an interview with Caesar directly after his visit to Formiae and told him that his uncle was planning to defect to Pompey.

Caesar was at that time in Rome. He had pressed ahead with the plan he had outlined to Cicero and had summoned a meeting of the Senate. Hardly anyone attended: senators were abandoning Italy on almost every tide to join Pompey in Macedonia. But by an unbelievable stroke of incompetence, in his eagerness to flee, Pompey had forgotten to empty the treasury in the Temple of Saturn. Caesar went to seize it at the head of a cohort of troops. The tribune L. Caecilius Metellus barred the door and made a speech about the sanctity of the law, to which Caesar replied, "There is a time for laws and a time for arms. If you don't like what is being done, save me your speeches and get out of the way." And when Metellus still refused to move, Caesar said, "Get out of the way or I shall have you killed, and you know, young man, that I dislike saying this more than I would dislike doing it." Metellus moved out of the way very swiftly after that.

Such was the man to whom Quintus betrayed his uncle. The first clue Cicero had about his treachery was a letter he received a few days later from Caesar, on his way now to fight Pompey's forces in Spain.

*En route to Massilia, 16 April*

*Caesar Imperator to Cicero Imperator.*

*I am troubled by certain reports and therefore I feel I ought to write and appeal to you in the name of our mutual goodwill not to take any hasty or imprudent step. You will be committing a grave offence against friendship. To hold aloof from civil quarrels is surely the most fitting course for a good, peace-loving man and a good citizen. Some who favoured that course were prevented from following it by fears for their safety. But you have the witness of my career and the judgement implied in our friendship. Weigh them well, and you will find no safer and no more honourable course than to keep aloof from all conflict.*

Cicero told me afterwards that it was only when he read this letter that he knew for certain that he would have to take ship and join Pompey—"by rowing boat if necessary"—because to submit to such a crude and sinister threat would be intolerable to him. He summoned young Quintus to Formiae and gave him a furious dressing-down. But secretly he felt quite grateful to him, and persuaded his brother not to treat the young man too harshly. "What did he do, after all, except tell the truth about what was in my heart—something I had not had the courage to do when I met Caesar? Then when Caesar offered me a funk hole where I could sit out the rest of the war in safety while other men died for the cause of the republic, my duty suddenly became clear to me."

In strictest confidence he sent me a cryptic message via Atticus and Curius that he was travelling *to that place where you and I were first visited by Milo and his gladiator, and if, when your health permits, you would care to join me there again, nothing would give me greater joy.*

I knew at once that he was referring to Thessalonica, where Pompey's army was now assembling. I had no desire to become involved in the civil war. It sounded highly dangerous to me. On the other hand, I was devoted to Cicero and I supported his decision. For all Pompey's faults, he had shown himself in the end to be willing to obey the law: he had been given supreme power after the murder of Clodius and had then surrendered it; legality was on his side; it was Caesar, not he, who had invaded Italy and destroyed the republic.

My fever had passed. My health was restored. I, too, knew what I had to do. Accordingly, at the end of June, I said farewell to Curius, who had become a good friend, and set off to chance my fortunes in war.

# X

---

I TRAVELLED BY SHIP MOSTLY—EAST ACROSS THE BAY OF CORINTH and north along the Aegean coast. Curius had offered me one of his slaves as a manservant but I preferred to journey alone: having once been another man's property myself, I was uneasy in the role of master. Gazing at that ancient tranquil landscape with its olive groves and goatherds, its temples and fishermen, one would never have guessed at the stupendous events now in train across the world. Only when we rounded a headland and came within sight of the harbour of Thessalonica did everything appear different. The approaches to the port were crammed with hundreds of troop-ships and supply vessels. One could almost have walked dry-footed from one side of the bay to the other. Inside the port, wherever one looked there were signs of war—soldiers, cavalry horses, wagons full of weapons and armour and tents, siege engines—and all that vast concourse of hangers-on who attend a great army mustering to fight.

I had no idea amid this chaos of where to find Cicero, but I remembered a man who might. Epiphanes didn't recognise me at first, perhaps because I was wearing a toga and he had never thought of me as a Roman citizen. But when I reminded him of our past dealings, he cried out and seized my hand and pressed it to his heart. Judging by his jewelled rings and the hennaed slave girl pouting on his couch, he seemed to be prospering nicely from the war, although for my benefit he lamented it loudly. Cicero, he said, was back in the same villa he had occupied almost a decade before. "May the gods bring you a swift victory," he called after me, "but not perhaps before we have done good business together."

How odd it was to make that familiar walk again, to enter that unchanged house, and to find Cicero sitting in the courtyard on the same stone bench, staring into space with the same expression of utter dejection. He jumped up when he saw me, threw wide his arms and clasped me to him. "But you're too thin!" he protested, feeling the boniness of my shoulders and ribs. "You'll become ill again. We must fatten you up!"

He called to the others to come and see who was here, and from various directions came his son, Marcus, now a strapping, floppy-haired sixteen-year-old, wearing the toga of manhood; his nephew, Quintus, slightly sheepish as he must have known his uncle would have told me of his malicious blabbing; and finally Quintus senior, who smiled to see me but whose face quickly lapsed back into melancholy. Apart from young Marcus, who was training for the cavalry and loved spending his time around the soldiers, it was plainly an unhappy household.

"Everything about our strategy is wrong," Cicero complained to me over dinner that evening. "We sit here doing nothing while Caesar rampages across Spain. Far too much notice is being taken of auguries, in my opinion—no doubt birds and entrails have their place in civilian government, but they sit badly with commanding an army. Sometimes I wonder if Pompey is quite the military genius he's cracked up to be."

Cicero being Cicero, he did not restrict such opinions to his own household but voiced them around Thessalonica to whoever would listen, and it was not long before I realised he was regarded as something of a defeatist. Not surprisingly Pompey hardly ever saw him, but then I suppose this may have been because he was away so much training his new legions. Close to two hundred senators with their staffs were crammed into the city by the time I arrived, many of them elderly. They hung around the Temple of Apollo with nothing to do, bickering among themselves. All wars are horrible, but civil wars especially so. Some of Cicero's closest friends, such as young Caelius Rufus, were fighting with Caesar, while his new son-in-law, Dolabella, actually had command of a squadron of Caesar's fleet in the Adriatic. Pompey's first words to Cicero when he arrived had been a curt "Where's your new son-in-law?" To which Cicero had replied, "With your old father-in-law." Pompey had grunted and walked away.

I asked Cicero what Dolabella was like. He rolled his eyes. "An adventurer like all of Caesar's crew; a rogue, a cynic, too full of animal spirits for his own good—I rather like him actually. But oh dear, poor Tullia! What kind of husband has she landed herself with this time? The darling girl gave birth at Cumae prematurely just before I left but the child didn't last out the day. I fear another attempt at motherhood will kill her. And of course the more Dolabella wearies of her and her illnesses—she's older than him—the more desperately she loves him. And still I haven't paid him the second part of her dowry. Six hundred thousand sesterces! But where am I to find such a vast sum when I'm trapped here?"

That summer was even hotter than the one when Cicero was exiled—and now half of Rome was exiled with him. We wilted in the humidity of the teeming city. Sometimes I found it hard not to take a certain grim satisfaction at the sight of so many men who had ignored Cicero's warnings about Caesar—who had been prepared indeed to see Cicero driven from Rome in the interests of a quiet life—and who now found themselves experiencing what it was like to be far from home and facing an uncertain future.

If only Caesar had been stopped earlier! That was the lament upon everyone's lips. But now it was too late and all the momentum of war was with him. At the height of the summer's heat, messengers reached Thessalonica with the news that the Senate's army in Spain had surrendered to Caesar after a campaign of just forty days. The news provoked intense dismay. Not long afterwards the commanders of that defeated army arrived in person: Lucius Afranius, the most loyal of all Pompey's lieutenants, and Marcus Petreius, who fourteen years earlier had defeated Catilina on the field of battle. The Senate-in-exile was flabbergasted at their appearance. Cato rose to ask the question on the minds of them all: "Why are you not dead or prisoners?" Afranius had to explain somewhat shamefacedly that Caesar had pardoned them, and that all the soldiers who had fought for the Senate had been allowed to return to their homes.

"Pardoned you?" raged Cato. "What do you mean, *pardoned* you? Is he now a king? You are the legitimate leaders of a lawful army. He is a renegade. You should have killed yourselves rather than accept a traitor's mercy! What's the use of living when you've lost your honour? Or is the point of your existence now just so that you can piss out of the front and shit out of the back?"

Afranius drew his sword and declared in a trembling voice that no man would ever call him a coward, not even Cato. There might have been serious bloodshed if the two had not been jostled away from one another.

Cicero said to me later that of all the clever strokes that Caesar pulled, perhaps the most brilliant was his policy of clemency. It was, in a curious way, akin to sending home the garrison of Uxellodunum with their hands cut off. These proud men were humbled, neutered; they crept back to their astonished comrades as living emblems of Caesar's power. And by their very presence they lowered morale across the entire army, for how could Pompey persuade his soldiers to fight to the death when they knew that if it came to it they could lay down their arms and return to their families?

Pompey called a council of war to discuss the crisis, consisting of the leaders of the army and of the Senate. Cicero, who was still officially the governor of Cilicia, naturally attended, and was accompanied to the temple by his lictors. He tried to take Quintus in with him but he was barred at the door by Pompey's aide-de-camp, and much to his fury and embarrassment Quintus had to stay outside with me. Among those I watched going in were Afranius, whose conduct in Spain Pompey staunchly defended; Domitius Ahenobarbus, who had managed to escape from Massilia when Caesar besieged it and now saw traitors wherever he looked; Titus Labienus, an old ally of Pompey's who had served as Caesar's second in command in Gaul but had refused to follow his chief across the Rubicon; Marcus Bibulus, Caesar's former consular colleague, now admiral of the Senate's huge fleet of five hundred warships; Cato, who had been promised command of the fleet until Pompey decided it would not be wise to give so fractious a colleague so much power; and Marcus Junius Brutus, who was only thirty-six and Cato's nephew, but whose arrival was said to have given more joy to Pompey than anyone else's, because Pompey had killed Brutus's father back in Sulla's time and there had been a blood feud ever since.

Pompey, according to Cicero, exuded confidence. He had lost weight, had put himself on an exercise regime, and looked a full decade younger than he had in Italy. He dismissed the loss of Spain as inconsequential, a sideshow. "Listen to me, gentlemen; listen to what I have always said: *this war will be won at sea.*" According to Pompey's spies in Brundisium, Caesar had less than half the number of ships that the Senate possessed. It was purely a question of mathematics: Caesar did not have sufficient troop transports to break out of Italy in anything like the strength he would need to confront Pompey's legions; therefore he was trapped. "We have him where we want him, and when we are ready we shall take him. From now on, this war will be fought on my terms and according to my timetable."

IT MUST HAVE BEEN ABOUT THREE MONTHS AFTER THIS, IN THE middle of the night, that we were roused by a furious hammering on the door. We gathered bleary-eyed in the tablinum, where the lictors were waiting with an officer from Pompey's headquarters. Caesar's forces had landed four days earlier on the coast of Illyricum, near Dyrrachium; Pompey had ordered the entire army to begin moving out at dawn to confront them. It would be a march of three hundred miles.

Cicero said, "Is Caesar with his army?"

"So we believe."

Quintus said, "But I thought he was in Spain."

"Indeed he *was* in Spain," replied Cicero drily, "but apparently now he's here. How strange: I seem to remember being categorically assured that such a thing was impossible because he didn't have sufficient ships."

At daybreak we went up to the Egnatian Gate to see if we could discover any more. The ground was vibrating with the weight of the military traffic on the road—a vast column was passing through the town, forty thousand men in all. I was told it stretched for thirty miles, although of course we could only see a fraction of it—the legionaries on foot carrying their heavy packs, the cavalry-men with their javelins glinting, the forest of standards and eagles all bearing the thrilling legend "SPQR" ("The Senate and People of Rome"), trumpeters and cornet players, archers, slingers, artil-lerymen, slaves, cooks, scribes, doctors, carts full of baggage, pack mules laden with tents and tools and food and weapons, horses and oxen dragging crossbows and ballistae.

We joined the column around the middle of the morning, and even I, the least military of men, found it exhilarating; even Cicero for that matter was filled with confidence for once. As for young Marcus, he was in heaven, moving back and forth between our sec-tion and the cavalry. We rode on horseback. The lictors marched in front of us with their laurelled rods. As we tramped across the plain towards the mountains, the road began to climb and I could see far ahead the reddish-brown dust raised by the endless column and the occasional glitter of steel as a helmet or a javelin caught the sun.

At nightfall we reached the first camp, with its ditch and earthen rampart and its spiked palisade. The tents were already pitched, the fires lit; a wonderful scent of cooking rose into the darkening sky. I remember especially the clink of the blacksmiths' hammers in the dusk, the whinnying and movement of the horses in their enclosure, and also the pervading smell of leather from the scores of tents, the largest of which had been set aside for Cicero. It stood at the crossroads in the centre of the camp, close to the standards and to the altar, where Cicero that evening presided over the tra-ditional sacrifice to Mars. He bathed and was anointed, dined well, slept peacefully in the fresh air, and the following morning we set off again.

This pattern was repeated for the next fifteen days as we made our way across the mountains of Macedonia towards the border with Illyricum. Cicero constantly expected to receive a summons to confer with Pompey, but none came. We did not know even where the commander-in-chief was, although occasionally Cicero received dispatches, and from these we pieced together a clearer picture of what was happening. Caesar had landed on the fourth day of January with a force of several legions, perhaps fifteen thousand men in all, and had achieved complete surprise, seizing the port of Apollonia, about thirty miles south of Dyrrachium. But that was just one half of his army. While he stayed with the bridgehead, his troop-ships had set off back to Italy to bring over the second half. (Pompey had never factored into his calculations the audacity of his enemy making two trips.) At this point, however, Caesar's famous luck ran out. Our admiral, Bibulus, had managed to intercept thirty of his transports. These he set on fire and all their crews he burnt alive, and then he deployed his immense fleet to prevent Caesar's navy returning.

As matters stood, therefore, Caesar's position was precarious. He had his back to the sea and was blockaded, with no chance of resupply, with winter coming on, and was about to be confronted by a much larger force.

As we were nearing the end of our march, Cicero received a further dispatch from Pompey:

*Pompey Imperator to Cicero Imperator.*

*I have received a proposal from Caesar that we should hold an immediate peace conference, disband both our armies within three days, renew our old friendship under oath, and return to Italy together. I regard this as proof not of his friendly intentions but of the weakness of his position and of his realisation that he cannot win this war. Accordingly, knowing that you would concur, I have rejected his offer, which I suspect was in any case a trick.*

"Is he right?" I asked him. "Would you have concurred?"

"No," responded Cicero, "and he knows perfectly well I wouldn't. I would do anything to stop this war—which of course is why he never asked for my opinion. I cannot see anything ahead of us except slaughter and ruin."

At the time I thought that Cicero was being unduly defeatist even for him. Pompey deployed his vast army in and around Dyrrachium, and contrary to expectations, he once again settled down to wait. No one in the supreme war council could fault his reasoning: that with every passing day Caesar's position became weaker; that he might eventually be starved into submission without the need for fighting; and that in any case, the best time to attack would be in the spring when the weather was less treacherous.

The Ciceros were billeted in a villa just outside Dyrrachium, built up high on a headland. It was a wild spot, with commanding views of the sea, and I found it odd to think of Caesar encamped only thirty miles away. Sometimes I would lean out over the terrace and crane my neck to the south in the hope that I might see some evidence of his presence, but naturally I never did.

And then at the beginning of April a very remarkable spectacle presented itself. The weather had been calm for several days, but suddenly a storm blew up from the south that howled around our house in its exposed position, the rain whipping down on the roof. Cicero was in the middle of composing a letter to Atticus, who had written from Rome to inform him that Tullia was desperately short of money. Sixty thousand sesterces was missing from the first payment of her dowry, and once again Cicero suspected Philotimus of shady dealing. He had just dictated the words *You tell me she is in want of everything; I beg you not to let this continue* when Marcus came running in and said that a great number of ships were visible out at sea and that he thought a battle might be in progress.

We put on our cloaks and hurried into the garden. And there indeed was a vast fleet of several hundred vessels a mile or more offshore, being tossed up and down in the heavy swell and driven at speed by the wind. It reminded me of our own near-shipwreck when we were crossing to Dyrrachium at the start of Cicero's exile. We watched for an hour until they had all passed out of sight, and then gradually a second flotilla began to appear—making, as it seemed to me, much heavier weather of it, but obviously trying to catch up with the ships that had gone before. We had no idea what it was that we were watching. To whom did these ghostly grey ships belong? Was it actually a battle? If so, was it going well or badly?

The next morning Cicero sent Marcus to Pompey's headquarters, to see what he could discover. The young man returned at dusk in a state of eager anticipation. The army would be breaking camp at dawn. The situation was confused. However, it appeared that the missing half of Caesar's army had sailed over from Italy. They had been unable to make land at Caesar's camp at Apollonia, partly because of our blockade but also because of the storm, which had blown them more than sixty miles north along the coast. Our navy had tried to pursue them, without success. Reportedly, men and materiel were now coming ashore around the port of Lissus. Pompey's intention was to crush them before they could link up with Caesar.

The next morning we rejoined the army and headed north. It was rumoured that the newly arrived general we would be facing was Mark Antony, Caesar's deputy—a report Cicero hoped was true, for he knew Antony: a young man of only thirty-four with a reputation for wildness and indiscipline; Cicero said he was not nearly as formidable a tactician as Caesar. However, when we drew closer to Lissus, where Antony was supposed to be, we found only his abandoned camp, dotted with dozens of smouldering fires where he had burned all the equipment his men could not carry with them. It turned out that he had led them east into the mountains.

We performed an abrupt about-turn and marched back south again. I thought we would return to Dyrrachium. Instead we passed by it in the distance, pressed on further south and after a four-day march took up a new position in a vast camp around the little town of Apsos. And now one began to get a sense of just how brilliant a general Caesar was, for we learned that somehow he *had* linked up with Antony, who had brought his army through the mountain passes, and that although Caesar's combined force was smaller than ours, nevertheless he had retrieved a hopeless position and was now on the offensive. He captured a settlement to our rear and cut us off from Dyrrachium. This was not a fatal disaster—Pompey's navy still commanded the coast, and we could be resupplied by sea across the beaches as long as the weather was not too rough. But one began to experience the uneasy sensation of being hemmed in. Sometimes we could see Caesar's men moving on the distant slopes of the mountains: he had control of the heights above us. And then he began a vast programme of construction—felling trees, building wooden forts, digging trenches and ditches and using the excavated earth to erect ramparts.

Naturally, our commanders tried to interrupt these works, and there were many skirmishes—sometimes four or five in a day. But the labour went on more or less continuously for several months until Caesar had completed a fifteen-mile fortified line that ran all the way round our position in a great loop, from the beaches to the north of our camp to the cliffs to the south. Within this loop we built our own system of trenches facing theirs, with perhaps fifty or a hundred paces of no man's land between the two sides. Siege engines were brought up and the artillerymen would lob rocks and flaming missiles at one another. Raiding parties would creep across the lines at night and slit the throats of the men in the opposing trench. When the wind dropped, we could hear them talking. Often they shouted insults at us; our men yelled back. I remember a constant atmosphere of tension. It began to prey on one's nerves.

Cicero fell ill with dysentery and spent most of his time reading and writing letters in his tent. "Tent" was something of a misnomer. He and the leading senators seemed to vie with one another to see who could make their accommodation the most luxurious. There were carpets, couches, tables, statues and silverware shipped over from Italy on the inside, and walls of turf and leafy bowers outside. They dined with one another and bathed together as if they were still on the Palatine. Cicero became particularly close to Cato's nephew Brutus, who had the tent next door, and who was seldom seen without a book of philosophy in his hand. They would spend hours sitting up talking late into the night. Cicero liked him for his noble nature and his learning but worried that his head was actually crammed too full of philosophy for him to make practical use of it: "I sometimes fear he may have been educated out of his wits."

One of the peculiarities of this style of trench warfare was that one could also have quite friendly contact with the enemy. The ordinary soldiers would periodically meet in the unoccupied middle ground to talk or gamble, although our officers inflicted severe penalties for fraternisation. Letters were lobbed over from one side to the other. Cicero received several messages by sea from Rufus, who was in Rome, and even one from Dolabella, who was with Caesar less than five miles away, and who sent a courier under a flag of truce:

*If you are well I am glad. I myself am well and so is our Tullia. Terentia has been rather out of sorts, but I know for certain that she has now recovered. Otherwise all your domestic affairs are in excellent shape.*

*You see Pompey's situation. Driven out of Italy, Spain lost, he is now, to crown it all, blockaded in his camp—a humiliation which I fancy has never previously befallen a Roman general. One thing I do beg of you: if he does manage to escape from his present dangerous position and takes refuge with his fleet, consult your own best interests and at long last be your own friend rather than anybody else's.*

*My most delightful Cicero, if it turns out that Pompey is driven from this area too and forced to seek yet other regions of the earth, I hope you will retire to Athens or to any peaceful community you please. Any concessions that you need from the commander-in-chief to safeguard your dignity you will obtain with the greatest ease from so kindly a man as Caesar. I trust to your honour and kindness to see that the courier I am sending you is able to return to me and brings a letter from you.*

Cicero's breast could barely contain all the conflicting emotions aroused by reading this extraordinary missive—delight that Tullia was well, outrage at his son-in-law's impudence, guilty relief that Caesar's policy of clemency still extended to him, fear that the letter could fall into the hands of a fanatic like Ahenobarbus who might use it to bring a charge of treason against him...

He scribbled a cautious line to say that he was well and would continue to support the Senate's cause, and then he had the courier escorted back across our lines.

As the weather began to turn hotter, life became more unpleasant. Caesar had a genius for damming springs and diverting water—it was how he had often won sieges in France and Spain, and now he used the same tactic against us. He controlled the rivers and streams coming down from the mountains and his engineers cut them off. The grass turned brown. Water had to be brought in by sea in thousands of amphorae and was rationed. The senators' daily baths were forbidden on Pompey's orders. More importantly, the horses began to fall sick from dehydration and lack of forage. We knew that Caesar's men were in an even worse state—unlike us, they could not be resupplied with food by sea, and both Greece and Macedonia were closed to them. They were reduced to making their daily bread out of roots they grubbed up. But Caesar's battle-hardened veterans were tougher than our men; they showed no sign of weakening.

I am not sure how much longer this could have gone on. But about four months after our arrival in Dyrrachium, there was a breakthrough. Cicero was summoned to one of Pompey's irregular war councils in his vast tent in the centre of the camp, and returned a few hours later looking almost cheerful for once. He told us that two Gallic auxiliaries serving in Caesar's army had been caught stealing from their legionary comrades and sentenced to be flogged to death. Somehow they had managed to escape and come over to our side. They offered information in return for their lives. There was, they said, a weakness in Caesar's fortifications some two hundred paces wide, close to the sea: the outer perimeter appeared sound but there was no secondary line behind it. Pompey warned them they would die the most horrible death if what they had said proved to be false. They swore it was true, but begged him to hurry before the hole was plugged. He saw no reason to disbelieve them, and an attack was fixed for dawn the following day.

All that night our troops moved stealthily into position. Young Marcus, now a cavalry officer, was among them. Cicero fretted sleeplessly about his safety, and at first light he and I, accompanied by his lictors and Quintus, went over to watch the battle. Pompey had brought up a huge force. We could not get close enough to see what was happening. Cicero dismounted and we walked along the beach, the waves lapping at our ankles. Our ships were anchored in a line about a quarter of a mile offshore. Up ahead we could hear the noise of fighting mingling with the roar of the sea. The air was dark with clouds of arrows, occasionally lit up by flaming missiles. There must have been five thousand men on the beach. We were asked by one of the military tribunes not to proceed any further because of the danger, so we sat down under a myrtle tree and had something to eat.

Around midday the legion moved off and we followed it cau-tiously. The wooden fort Caesar's men had built in the dunes was in our hands, and in the flat lands beyond it thousands of men were deploying. It was very hot. Bodies lay everywhere, pierced by arrows and javelins or with horrible gaping wounds. To our right we saw several squadrons of cavalry galloping towards the fighting. Cicero was sure he spotted Marcus among them and we all cheered them loudly, but then Quintus recognised their colours and announced that they were Caesar's. At that point Cicero's lictors hustled him away from the battlefield and we returned to camp.

The battle of Dyrrachium, as it became known, was a great vic-tory. Caesar's line was irretrievably broken and his entire position thrown into danger. Indeed he would have been utterly defeated that very day had it not been for the network of trenches that slowed up our advance and meant we had to dig in for the night. Pompey was hailed as imperator by his men on the field, and when he got back to the camp in his war chariot, attended by his body-guards, he raced around inside the perimeter and up and down the torchlit tented streets, cheered by his legionaries.

The next day, towards the end of the morning, far in the distance in the direction of Caesar's camp, columns of smoke began to rise over the plain. At the same time reports started coming in from all around our front lines that the trenches opposite were empty. Our men ventured out cautiously at first but were soon wandering over the enemy's fortifications, astonished that so many months of labour could be so readily abandoned. But there was no doubt about it: Caesar's legionaries were marching off to the east along the Via Egnatia. We could see the dust. Whatever equipment they could not take was burning behind them. The siege was over.

Pompey summoned a meeting of the Senate-in-exile late in the afternoon to decide what should be done next. Cicero asked me to accompany him and Quintus so that he could have a record of what was decided. The sentries guarding Pompey's tent nodded me through without question and I took up a discreet position, stand-ing at the side, along with the other secretaries and aides-de-camp. There must have been almost a hundred senators present, seated on benches. Pompey, who had been out all day inspecting Cae-sar's positions, arrived after everyone else, and was given a stand-ing ovation, which he acknowledged with a touch of his marshal's baton to the side of his famous quiff.

He reported on the situation of the two armies after the battle. The enemy had lost about a thousand men killed and three hundred taken prisoner. Immediately Labienus proposed that the prisoners should all be executed. "I worry they will infect our own men who guard them with their treasonous thoughts. Besides, they have for-feited the right to life."

Cicero, with a look of distaste, rose to object. "We have achieved a mighty victory. The end of the war is in sight. Isn't now the time to be magnanimous?"

"No," replied Labienus. "An example must be made."

"An example that can only cause Caesar's men to fight with even more determination once they learn the fate that awaits them if they surrender."

"So be it. This tactic of Caesar's of offering clemency is a danger to our fighting spirit." He glanced pointedly at Afranius, who lowered his head. "If we take no prisoners, Caesar will be forced to do the same."

Pompey spoke with a firmness that was designed to settle the matter. "I agree with Labienus. Besides, Caesar's soldiers are traitors who have taken up arms illegally against their own countrymen. That puts them in a different category to our troops. Let's move on."

But Cicero wouldn't let the matter drop. "Wait a moment. Are we fighting for civilised values or are we wild beasts? These men are Romans just like us. I would like it to be recorded that in my view this is a mistake."

"And I would like it to be recorded," said Ahenobarbus, "that it isn't only those who have fought openly on Caesar's side who should be treated as traitors, but all those who have tried to be neutral, or have argued for peace, or had contact with the enemy."

Ahenobarbus was warmly applauded. Cicero's face flushed and he fell silent.

Pompey said, "Well then, that's settled. Now it is my proposal that the entire army, bar let's say fifteen cohorts which I'll leave behind to defend Dyrrachium, should set off in pursuit of Caesar with a view to offering him battle at the first opportunity."

This fateful pronouncement met with loud grunts of approval.

Cicero hesitated, glanced around and then stood up again. "I seem to find myself playing the role of perennial contrarian. Forgive me—but is there not a case for seizing this opportunity and instead of chasing Caesar eastwards, sailing west instead to Italy and regaining control of Rome? That is after all supposed to be the point of this war."

Pompey shook his head. "No, that would be a strategic error. If we return to Italy, there will be nothing to stop Caesar conquering Macedonia and Greece."

"Let him—I'd trade Macedonia and Greece for Italy and Rome any day. Besides, we have an army there under Scipio."

"Scipio can't beat Caesar," retorted Pompey. "Only I can beat Caesar. And this war won't end merely because we're back in Rome. This war will end only when Caesar is dead."

AT THE END OF THE CONFERENCE, CICERO APPROACHED POMPEY and asked for permission to remain behind in Dyrrachium rather than join the army on the campaign. Pompey, plainly irritated by his criticism, looked him up and down with something like contempt, then nodded. "I think that's a good idea." He turned from Cicero as if dismissing him, and began discussing with one of his officers the order in which the legions should depart the next day. Cicero waited for their conversation to end, presumably intending to wish Pompey good fortune. But Pompey was too engrossed in the logistics of the march, or at any rate he pretended to be, and eventually Cicero gave up and left the tent.

As we walked away, Quintus asked him why he didn't want to go with the army.

Cicero said, "This global strategy of Pompey's means we could be stuck out here for years. I can't support it any longer. Nor to be frank can I face another journey through those damned mountains."

"People will say it's because you're afraid."

"Brother, I *am* afraid. So should you be. If we win, there'll be a massacre of good Roman blood—you heard Labienus. And if we lose . . ." He left it at that.

When we got back to his tent, he made a half-hearted attempt to persuade his son not to go either, even though he knew it was hopeless: Marcus had shown much bravery at Dyrrachium and despite his youth had been rewarded with the command of his own cavalry squadron. He was eager for battle. Quintus's son was also determined to fight.

Cicero said, "Well then, go if you must. I admire your spirit. However, I shall stay here."

"But Father," protested Marcus, "men will speak of this great clash of arms for a thousand years."

"I'm too old to fight and too squeamish to watch others doing it. You three are the soldiers in the family." He stroked Marcus's hair and pinched his cheek. "Bring me back Caesar's head on a stick, won't you, my darling boy?" And then he announced that he needed to rest and turned away so that no one could see that he was crying.

Reveille was scheduled for an hour before dawn. Plagued by insomnia it seemed to me that I had barely fallen asleep when the infernal caterwauling of the war horns started. The legion's slaves came in and began dismantling the tent around me. Everything was timed exactly. Outside the sun had yet to show over the ridge. The mountains were still in shadow. But above them loomed a cloudless blood-red sky.

The scouts moved off at dawn, followed half an hour later by a detachment of Bythinian cavalry, and then, a further half-hour after that, Pompey, yawning loudly, surrounded by his staff officers and bodyguards. Our legion had been chosen for the honour of serving as the vanguard on the march and therefore was the next to leave. Cicero stood by the gate, and as his brother and son and nephew passed, he raised his hand and called farewell to each in turn. This time he did not try to conceal his tears. Two hours later, all the tents were down, the refuse fires were burning and the last of the baggage mules was swaying out of the deserted camp.

WITH THE ARMY GONE, WE SET OFF TO RIDE THE THIRTY MILES TO Dyrrachium escorted by Cicero's lictors. Our road took us past

Caesar's old defensive line, and soon we came upon the spot where Labienus had massacred the prisoners. Their throats had been cut and a gang of slaves was burying the corpses in one of the old defensive ditches. The stench of ripening flesh in the summer heat and the sight of the vultures circling overhead are among the many memories of that campaign I would prefer to forget. We spurred our horses and pressed on to Dyrrachium, reaching it before dusk.

We were billeted away from the cliffs this time for safety, in a house within the walls of the city. Command of the garrison should, in principle, have been awarded to Cicero, who was the senior ex-consul and who still possessed imperium as governor of Cilicia. But it was a sign of the mistrust in which he had come to be held that Pompey gave the position instead to Cato, who had never risen higher than praetor. Cicero was not offended. On the contrary, he was glad to escape the responsibility: the troops Pompey had left behind were his least reliable, and Cicero had serious doubts about their loyalty if it came to fighting.

The days dragged by very slowly. Those senators who, like Cicero, had not gone with the army acted as if the war was already won. For example they drew up lists of those who had stayed behind in Rome, and who would be killed on our return, and whose property would be seized to pay for the war; one of the wealthy men they proscribed was Atticus. Then they squabbled over who would get which house. Other senators fought shamelessly over the jobs and titles that would fall vacant with the demise of Caesar and his lieutenants—Spinther I remember was adamant that he should be pontifex maximus. Cicero observed to me, "The one outcome worse than losing this war will be winning it."

As for him, his mind was full of cares and anxieties. Tullia continued to be short of money and the second instalment of her dowry remained unpaid, despite Cicero's instructions to Terentia to sell some of his property. All his old worries about her relationship with Philotimus and their fondness for questionable money-making schemes came crowding back into his mind. He chose to convey his anger and suspicion by writing her infrequent, short and chilly letters in which he did not even address her by name.

But his greatest fears were for Marcus and Quintus, still on the march somewhere with Pompey. Two months had passed since their departure. The Senate's army had pursued Caesar across the mountains to the plain of Thessalonica and had then struck south: that much was known. But where exactly they were now, no one knew, and the further Caesar drew them away from Dyrrachium and the longer the silence went on, the more uneasy the atmosphere in the garrison became.

The commander of the fleet, Caius Coponius, was a clever but highly strung senator who had a strong belief in signs and omens, especially portentous dreams, which he encouraged his men to share with their officers. One day, when there was still no news from Pompey, he came to dine with Cicero. Also at the table were Cato and M. Terentius Varro, the great scholar and poet, who had commanded a legion in Spain and who, like Afranius, had been pardoned by Caesar.

Coponius said, "I had an unsettling encounter just before I set off to come here. You know that immense Rhodian quinquereme, the *Europa*, anchored offshore down there? One of the oarsmen was brought to see me to recount his dream. He claims to have had a vision of a terrible battle on some high Grecian plain, with the blood soaking into the dust and men limbless and groaning, and then this city besieged with all of us fleeing to the ships and looking back and seeing the place in flames."

Normally this was just the sort of gloomy prophecy Cicero liked to laugh at, but not this time. Cato and Varro looked equally pensive. Cato said, "And how did this dream end?"

"For him, very well—he and his comrades will enjoy a swift voyage back to Rhodes, apparently. So I suppose that's hopeful."

Another silence fell over the table. Eventually Cicero said, "Unfortunately, that merely suggests to me that our Rhodian allies will desert us."

The first hints that some terrible disaster had occurred began to emanate from the docks. Several fishermen from the island of Corcyra,* about two days' voyage to the south, claimed to have passed a group of men encamped on a beach on the mainland, who had shouted out that they were survivors from Pompey's army. Another merchant vessel put in the same day with a similar tale— of desperate, starving men crowding the little fishing villages try-ing to find some means of escape from the soldiers they cried out were pursuing them.

Cicero attempted to console himself and others by saying that all wars consisted of rumours that frequently turned out to be false, and that perhaps these phantoms were merely deserters, or the survivors of some skirmish rather than a full-scale battle. But I think he knew in his heart that the gods of war were with Caesar: I believe he had foreseen it all along, which was why he did not go with Pompey.

Confirmation came the next evening, when he received an urgent summons to attend Cato's headquarters. I went with him. There was a terrible atmosphere of panic and despair. The secre-taries were already burning correspondence and account books in the garden to prevent them falling into enemy hands. Inside, Cato, Varro, Coponius and some of the other leading senators were seated in a grim circle around a bearded, filthy man, badly cut about the face. This was the once-proud Titus Labienus, commander of Pompey's cavalry and the man who had slaughtered the prison-ers. He was exhausted, having ridden non-stop for ten days with a few of his men across the mountains. Sometimes he would lose the thread of his story and forget himself, or nod off, or repeat things—occasionally he would break down entirely—so that my notes are incoherent and perhaps it is best if I simply say what we eventually discovered happened.

The battle, which at that time had no name but afterwards came to be called Pharsalus, should never have been lost, according to Labienus, and he spoke bitterly of Pompey's generalship, calling

---

*Corfu

it vastly inferior to Caesar's. (Mind you, others, whose tales we heard later, blamed the defeat partly on Labienus himself.) Pompey occupied the best ground, he had the most troops—his cavalry outnumbered Caesar's by seven to one—and he could choose the timing of the battle. Even so, he had hesitated to engage the enemy. Only after some of the other commanders, notably Ahenobarbus, had openly accused him of cowardice had he drawn up his forces to fight. Labienus said, "That was when I saw his heart wasn't in it. Despite what he said to us, he never felt confident of beating Caesar." And so the two armies had faced one another across a wide plain; and the enemy, at last offered his chance, had attacked.

Caesar had obviously recognised from the start that his cavalry was his greatest weakness and therefore had cunningly stationed some two thousand of his best infantry out of sight behind them. So when Labienus's horsemen had broken the charge of their opponents and gone after them in an attempt to turn Caesar's flank, they suddenly found themselves confronted by a line of advancing legionaries. The cavalrymen's attack broke upon the shields and javelins of these fierce unyielding veterans and they galloped from the field, despite Labienus's attempts to rally them. (All the time he was speaking I was thinking of Marcus: a reckless youth, he, I was sure, would not have been one of those who fled.) With their enemy's cavalry gone, Caesar's men had fallen upon Pompey's unprotected archers and wiped them out. After that, it was a slaughter as Pompey's panicking infantry had proved no match for Caesar's disciplined, hardened troops.

Cato said, "How many men did we lose?"

"I cannot say—thousands."

"And where was Pompey amid all this?"

"When he saw what was happening, he was like a man paralysed. He could barely speak, let alone issue coherent orders. He left the field with his bodyguard and returned to camp. I never saw him after that." Labienus covered his face with his hands; we waited; when he had recovered, he went on: "I'm told he lay down in his tent until Caesar's men broke through the defences and then he got away with a handful of others; he was last seen riding north towards Larissa."

"And Caesar?"

"No one knows. Some say he's gone off with a small detachment in pursuit of Pompey, others that he's at the head of his army and coming this way."

"Coming this way?"

Knowing Caesar's reputation for forced marches and the speed at which his troops could move, Cato proposed that they should evacuate Dyrrachium immediately. He was very cool. To Cicero's surprise, he revealed that he had already discussed precisely this contingency with Pompey, and that it had been decided that in the event of a defeat, all the surviving leadership of the senatorial cause should attempt to make for Corcyra—which, as an island, could be sealed off and defended by the fleet.

By now, rumours of Pompey's defeat were spreading throughout the garrison, and the meeting was interrupted by reports of soldiers refusing to obey orders; there had already been some looting. It was agreed that we should embark the next day. Before we returned to our house, Cicero put his hand on Labienus's shoulder and asked him if he knew what had happened to Marcus or Quintus. Labienus raised his head and looked at him as if he were crazy even to ask the question—the slaughter of thousands seemed to swirl like smoke in those staring, bloodshot eyes. He muttered, "What do I know? I can only tell you that at least I did not see them dead." Then he added, as Cicero turned to go, "You were right—we should have returned to Rome."

# XI

———••••———

AND SO THE PROPHECY OF THE RHODIAN OARSMAN CAME TRUE, AND
the following day we fled from Dyrrachium. The granaries had
been ransacked and I remember how the precious corn was strewn
across the streets and crunched beneath our shoes. The lictors
had to clear a passage for Cicero, striking out with their rods to
get him through the panicking crowds. But when we reached the
dockside, we found it even more impassable than the streets. It
seemed that every captain of a seaworthy craft was being besieged
by offers of money to carry people to safety. I saw the most pitiful
scenes—families with all the belongings they could carry, including their dogs and parrots, attempting to force their way on to
ships; matrons wrenching the rings from their fingers and offering their most precious family heirlooms for a place in a humble
rowing boat; the white doll-like corpse of a baby dropped from the
gangplank by its mother in a fumble of terror and drowned.

The harbour was so clogged with vessels it took hours for the
tender to pick us up and ferry us out to our warship. By then it was
growing dark. The big Rhodian quinquereme had gone: Rhodes, as
Cicero had predicted, had deserted the Senate's cause. Cato came
aboard, followed by the other leaders, and immediately we slipped
anchor—the captain preferring the dangers of a night-time voyage
to the risks of remaining where we were. When we had gone a mile
or two we looked back and saw an immense red glow in the sky;
afterwards we learnt that the mutinying soldiers had set all the
ships in the harbour on fire so that they could not be forced to sail
to Corcyra and continue to fight.

We rowed on throughout the night. The smooth sea and the

rocky coastline were silvered in the moonlight. The only sounds were the splash of the oars and the murmur of men's voices in the darkness. Cicero spent a long time talking alone with Cato. Later he told me that Cato was not merely calm, he was serene. "This is what a lifetime's devotion to stoicism can do for you. As far as he's concerned, he has followed his conscience and is at peace; he is fully resigned to death. He is as dangerous in his way as Caesar and Pompey."

I asked him what he meant. He took his time replying.

"Do you remember what I wrote in my little work on politics? How long ago that seems! 'Just as the purpose of a pilot is to ensure a smooth passage for his ship, and of a doctor to make his patient healthy, so the statesman's objective must be the happiness of his country.' Not once has either Caesar or Pompey conceived of their role in that way. For them, it is all a matter of their personal glory. And so it is with Cato. I tell you, the man is actually quite content simply to have been right, even though this is where his principles have led us—to this fragile vessel drifting alone in the moonlight along a foreign shore."

He was utterly disillusioned with it all—recklessly so, in truth. When we reached Corcyra, we found that beautiful island crowded with refugees from the carnage of Pharsalus. The tales of chaos and incompetence were appalling. Of Pompey, there was no word. If he was alive, he sent no message; if he was dead, no one had seen his body: he had vanished from the earth. In the absence of the commander-in-chief, Cato called a meeting of the Senate in the Temple of Zeus, on its promontory overlooking the sea, to decide the future conduct of the war. That once-numerous assembly was now reduced to about fifty men. Cicero had hoped to be reunited with his son and brother, but they were nowhere to be found. Instead he saw other survivors—Metellus Scipio, Afranius and young Gnaeus, the son of Pompey, who had convinced himself that his father's ruin was entirely the result of treachery. I noticed how he kept glaring at Cicero; I feared he could be dangerous. Cassius was also present. But Ahenobarbus was not—it turned out that he was one of the many senators who had been killed in the battle. Outside, it was hot and dazzling; inside, cool and shadowy. A statue of Zeus, twice the size of a man, looked down with indifference upon the deliberations of these beaten mortals.

Cato began by stating that in Pompey's absence the Senate needed to appoint a new commander-in-chief. "It should go, according to our ancient custom, to the most senior ex-consul among us, and therefore I propose it should be Cicero."

Cicero burst out laughing. All heads turned to look at him.

"Seriously, gentlemen?" responded Cicero with incredulity. "Seriously—after all that has occurred, you think that *I* should assume direction of this catastrophe? If it was my leadership you wanted, you should have listened to my counsel earlier, and then we would not be in our present desperate straits. I refuse this honour absolutely."

It was unwise for him to have spoken so harshly. He was exhausted and overwrought, but then so were they all, and some were also wounded. The cries of protest and disgust were eventually stilled by Cato, who said, "I take it from what Cicero says that he regards our position as hopeless, and that he would sue for peace."

Cicero said, "I would, most certainly. Haven't enough good men died to satisfy your philosophy?"

Scipio said, "We have suffered a reverse but we are not defeated. There are still allies loyal to us all over the world, especially King Juba in Africa."

"So that is what we have sunk to, is it? Fighting alongside Numidian barbarians against our fellow Romans?"

"Nevertheless, we still have seven eagles."

"Seven eagles would be fine if we were fighting *jackdaws*."

"What do you know of fighting," demanded Gnaeus Pompey, "you contemptible old coward?" And with that he drew his sword and lunged at Cicero. I was sure that Cicero was about to die, but with the skill of an expert swordsman Gnaeus checked his thrust at the last moment and left the tip of his blade touching Cicero's throat. "I propose we kill this traitor, and I ask the Senate's permission to do the deed this instant." And he pressed just a fraction harder so that Cicero had to tilt his head right back to avoid having his windpipe pierced.

"Stop, Gnaeus!" cried Cato. "You will bring shame on your father! Cicero is a friend of his—he wouldn't want to see him insulted in this way. Remember where you are and put your sword down."

I doubt whether anyone else could have stopped Gnaeus when his blood was up. For a moment or two the young brute hesitated, but then he withdrew his sword, and swore and stamped back to his place. Cicero straightened and stared directly ahead. A trickle of blood ran down his neck and stained the front of his toga.

Cato said, "Listen to me, gentlemen. You know my views. When our republic was under threat, I believed it was our right and duty to compel every citizen, the lukewarm and the bad included, to support our cause and protect the state. But now the republic is lost . . ." He paused and looked around; no one challenged his assertion. "Now that our republic is lost," he repeated quietly, "even I believe it would be senseless and cruel to compel any individual to share in its ruin. Let those who wish to continue the fight remain here, and we shall discuss our future strategy. Let those who wish to retire from the struggle depart from this assembly now—and let no man do them harm."

At first no one moved. And then very slowly Cicero rose to his feet. He nodded to Cato, whom he knew had saved his life, and then turned and walked out—out of the temple, out of the senatorial cause, out of the war and out of public life.

CICERO FEARED THAT IF HE STAYED ON THE ISLAND HE WOULD BE murdered—if not by Gnaeus then by one of his associates. Accordingly we left that same day. We could not sail back north again in case the coast had fallen into enemy hands. Instead we found ourselves drifting further south, until after several days we arrived in Patrae, the port where I had spent my illness. As soon as the ship docked, Cicero sent word by one of his lictors to his friend Curius to say that we were in the city, and without waiting for a reply, we hired litters and porters to transport us and our baggage to his house.

I believe the lictor must have lost his way, or perhaps he was tempted by the bars of Patrae, for all six lictors in their boredom since our departure from Cilicia had fallen into the habit of drinking heavily. At any rate, we arrived at the villa before our messenger did, only to be told that Curius was away for two days on business, at which point we heard male conversation emanating from the interior. The voices sounded familiar. We glanced at one another, neither of us quite believing what we were hearing, then hurried past the steward and into the tablinum to discover Quintus, Marcus and Quintus Junior seated in a huddle. They turned to stare at us in amazement, and I sensed at once a certain embarrassment. I am fairly certain they must have been speaking ill of us—or rather of Cicero. This awkwardness, I should add, was over in an instant—Cicero never even noticed it—and we fell upon one another and kissed and embraced with the sincerest affection. I was shocked by how haggard they looked. There was something haunted about them, as there had been with the other survivors of Pharsalus, although they tried not to show it.

Quintus said, "This is the most wonderful good fortune! We'd engaged a ship and were planning to set off for Corcyra tomorrow, having heard that the Senate was assembling there. And to think we might have missed you! What happened? Did the conference end earlier than expected?"

Cicero said, "No, the conference is still going on, as far as I know."

"But you're not with them?"

"Let us discuss that later. First let us hear what happened to you."

They took it in turns to tell their story, like runners in a relay race handing on the baton—first the month-long march in pursuit of Caesar's army and the occasional skirmishes along the way, and then at last the great confrontation at Pharsalus. On the eve of the battle Pompey had dreamed that he was in Rome entering the

Temple of Venus the Victorious, and that the people were applauding him as he offered the goddess the spoils of war. He awoke content, thinking this a good omen, but then someone pointed out
that Caesar claimed direct descent from Venus, and immediately he
decided the meaning of the dream was the opposite of what he'd
hoped. "From that moment on," said Quintus, "he seemed resigned
to losing and acted accordingly." The Quinti had been in the second
line and so had avoided the worst of the fighting. Marcus, though,
had been in the middle of the struggle. He reckoned he had killed
at least four of the enemy—one with his javelin, three with his
sword—and had been confident of victory until the cohorts of
Caesar's Tenth Legion had seemed to rise up out of the ground
before them. "Our units lost formation: it was a massacre, Father."
It had taken them the best part of a month, much of it spent living
rough and dodging Caesar's patrols, to escape to the western coast.

"And Pompey?" asked Cicero. "Is there news of him?"

"None," replied Quintus, "but I believe I can guess where he
went: east, to Lesbos. That's where he sent Cornelia to await news
of his victory. In defeat I'm certain he would have gone to her for
consolation—you know what he's like with his wives. Caesar must
have guessed the same. He's after him like a bounty hunter in pursuit of a runaway slave. My money is on Caesar in that particular
race. And if he catches him, or kills him, what do you think that
will mean for the war?"

Cicero said, "Oh, the war will go on, it seems, whatever
happens—but it will continue without me," and then he told them
what had happened at Corcyra. I am sure he did not mean to sound
flippant. It was simply that he was happy to have found his family
alive, and naturally that light-hearted mood coloured his remarks.
But as he repeated, with some satisfaction, his quip about eagles
and jackdaws, and mocked the very idea that he should take command of 'this losing cause,' and derided the bone-headedness of
Gnaeus Pompey—"He makes even his father look intelligent"—
I could see Quintus's jaw beginning to work back and forth in irritation; even Marcus's expression was clenched with disapproval.

"So that's it, then?" said Quintus in a cold, flat voice. "As far as this family is concerned, it's over?"

"Do you disagree?"

"I feel I should have been consulted."

"How could I consult you? You weren't there."

"No, I wasn't. How could I have been? I was fighting in the war you encouraged me to join, and then I was trying to save my life, along with those of your son and your nephew!"

Too late Cicero saw how casually he had spoken. "My dear brother, I assure you, your welfare—the welfare of all of you—has ever been uppermost in my mind."

"Spare me your casuistry, Marcus. Nothing is ever uppermost in your mind except yourself. *Your* honour, *your* career, *your* interests—so that while other men go off to die, you sit behind with the elderly and the womenfolk, polishing your speeches and your pointless witticisms!"

"Please, Quintus—you are in danger of saying things you will regret."

"My only regret is that I didn't say them years ago. So let me say them now, and you will do me the courtesy of sitting there and listening to *me* for once! My whole life has been lived as nothing more than an appendix to yours—I am no more important to you than poor Tiro here, whose health has been broken in your service; less important, actually, as I don't have his skills as a note-taker. When I went out to Asia as governor, you tricked me into staying for two years rather than one, so that you could have access to my funds to pay off your debts. During your exile I almost died fighting Clodius in the streets of Rome, and my reward when you came home was to be packed off again, to Sardinia, to appease Pompey. And now here I am, thanks largely to you, on the losing side in a civil war, when it would have been perfectly honourable for me to have stood side by side with Caesar, who gave me command of a legion in Gaul . . ."

There was more in this vein. Cicero endured it without comment or movement, apart from the occasional clenching and unclenching of his hands on the armrests of his chair. Marcus looked on, white with shock. Young Quintus smirked and nodded. As for me, I yearned to leave but couldn't: some force seemed to have pinned my feet to the spot.

Quintus worked himself up into such a pitch of fury that by the end he was breathless, his chest heaving as if he had shifted some heavy physical load. "Your action in abandoning the Senate's cause without consulting me or considering my interests is the final selfish blow. Remember, my position wasn't exquisitely ambiguous like yours: I *fought* at Pharsalus—I am a marked man. So I have no choice: I shall have to try to find Caesar, wherever he is, and plead for his pardon, and believe me, when I see him, I shall have something to tell him about *you*."

With that he stalked out of the room, followed by his son; and then, after a short hesitation, Marcus left too. In the shocking silence that ensued, Cicero continued to sit immobile. Eventually I asked if there was anything I could fetch him, and when still he made no response, I wondered if he might have suffered a seizure. Then I heard footsteps. It was Marcus returning. He knelt beside the chair.

"I have said goodbye to them, Father. I will stay with you."

Wordless for once, Cicero grasped his hand, and I withdrew to let them talk.

CICERO TOOK TO HIS BED AND REMAINED IN HIS ROOM FOR THE next few days. He refused to see a doctor—"My heart is broken and no Greek quack can fix that"—and kept his door locked. I hoped that Quintus would return and the quarrel might be repaired, but he had meant what he said and had left the city. When Curius got back from his business trip, I explained what had happened as discreetly as I could, and he agreed with me and Marcus that the best course was for us to charter a ship and sail back to Italy while the weather was still fair. Such, then, was the grotesque paradox we had reached: that Cicero was likely to be safer in a country under

Caesar's control than he would be in Greece, where armed bands belonging to the republican cause were only too eager to strike down men perceived as traitors.

As soon as his depression had lifted sufficiently for him to contemplate the future, Cicero approved this plan—"I'd rather die in Italy than here"—and when there was a decent southeasterly wind we embarked. The voyage was good, and after four days at sea we saw on the horizon the great lighthouse at Brundisium. It was a blessed sight. Cicero had been away from the mother country for a year and a half, I for more than three years.

Fearful of his reception, Cicero remained in his cabin below decks while I went ashore with Marcus to find somewhere for us to stay. The best we could manage for that first night was a noisy inn near the waterfront, and we decided that the safest course would be for Cicero to come ashore at dusk wearing an ordinary toga belonging to Marcus rather than one of his own with the purple stripe of a senator. An additional complication was the presence, like the chorus in a tragedy, of his six lictors—for absurdly, although he was entirely powerless, he still technically possessed imperium as governor of Cilicia, and was reluctant even now to break the law by sending them away; nor would they leave him until they had been paid. So they too had to be disguised and their fasces wrapped in sacking and rooms hired for them.

Cicero found this procedure so humiliating that after a sleepless night he resolved the next day to announce his presence to whoever was the most senior representative of Caesar in the town and accept whatever fate was decreed for him. He had me search through his correspondence for Dolabella's letter guaranteeing his safety—*Any concessions that you need from the commander-in-chief to safeguard your dignity you will obtain with the greatest ease from so kindly a man as Caesar*—and I made sure I had it with me when I went to the military headquarters.

The new commander of the region turned out to be Publius Vatinius, widely known as the ugliest man in Rome, and an old opponent of Cicero's—indeed it was Vatinius, as tribune, who had first proposed the law awarding Caesar both the provinces of Gaul and an army for five years. He had fought with his old chief at the battle of Dyrrachium and returned to take control of the whole of southern Italy. But by a great stroke of good fortune Cicero had made up his quarrel with Vatinius at Caesar's request several years before and had defended him in a prosecution for bribery. As soon as he learned of my arrival, I was shown straight into his presence and he greeted me most affably.

Dear gods, he *was* ugly! His eyes were crossed, and his face and neck were covered in scrofulous growths the colour of birthmarks. But what did his looks matter? He barely even glanced at Dolabella's letter before assuring me that it was an honour to welcome Cicero back to Italy, that he would protect his dignity as he was sure Caesar would wish, and that he would arrange for suitable accommodation to be provided while he awaited instructions from Rome.

The latter phrase sounded ominous. "May I ask who will issue these instructions?"

"Well indeed—that is a good question. We are still sorting out our administration. Caesar has been appointed dictator for a year by the Senate—*our* Senate, that is," he added with a wink, "but he is still away chasing your former commander-in-chief, and so in his absence, power is vested in the Master of Horse."

"And who is that?"

"Mark Antony."

My spirits sank further.

That same day Vatinius sent a platoon of legionaries to escort us with our baggage to a house in a quiet district of the town. Cicero was carried all the way in a closed litter so that his presence remained a secret.

It was a small villa, old, with thick walls and tiny windows. A sentry was posted outside. To begin with, Cicero was simply relieved to be back in Italy. Only gradually did he realise that he was in fact under house arrest. It was not so much that he was physically prevented from leaving the villa—he did not venture beyond the gate, so we never discovered what orders the guards had been given. Rather, Vatinius implied, when he came to check how Cicero was settling in, it would be dangerous for him to leave, and, worse, disrespectful towards Caesar's hospitality. For the first time we tasted life under a dictatorship: there were no freedoms any more; no magistrates, no courts; one existed at the whim of the ruler.

Cicero wrote to Mark Antony asking permission to return to Rome. But he did so without much hope. Although he and Antony had always been polite to one another, there was a long-standing enmity between them, born of the fact that Antony's stepfather, P. Lentulus Sura, had been one of the five co-conspirators of Catilina that Cicero had had executed. Therefore it was no surprise when Antony refused Cicero's request. Cicero's fate, he said, was a matter for Caesar, and until Caesar made a ruling, he must stay in Brundisium.

I would say that the months that followed were the worst of Cicero's life—worse even than his first exile in Thessalonica. At least then there had still been a republic to fight for, there was honour in his struggle, and his family was united; now these supports had gone, and all was death, dishonour and discord. And so much death! So many old friends gone! One could almost smell it in the air. We had only been in Brundisium a few days when we were visited by C. Matius Calvena, a wealthy member of the equestrian order and a close associate of Caesar, who told us that both Milo and Caelius Rufus had died trying to stir up trouble together in Campania—Milo, at the head of a ragamuffin army of his old gladiators, had been killed in battle by one of Caesar's lieutenants; Rufus had been put to death on the spot by some Spanish and Gallic horsemen he had been trying to bribe. The death of Rufus at the age of only thirty-four was a particular blow to Cicero, and he wept when he heard of it—which was more than he did when he learned of the fate of Pompey.

Vatinius brought us the news of that himself, his hideous features especially composed for the occasion into a simulacrum of grief.

Cicero said, "Is there any doubt?"

"None whatever—I have a dispatch here from Caesar: he has seen his severed head."

Cicero blanched and sat down, and I pictured that massive head with its thick crest of hair and that bull neck: it must have taken some effort to hack it off, I thought, and been quite a sight for Caesar to behold.

"Caesar wept when he was shown it," Vatinius added, as if he had seen into my mind.

Cicero said, "When did this happen?"

"Two months ago."

Vatinius read aloud from Caesar's account. It transpired that Pompey had done exactly as Quintus had predicted: he had fled from Pharsalus to Lesbos to seek solace with Cornelia; his youngest son, Sextus, was also with her. Together they had embarked in a trireme and sailed to Egypt, in the hope of persuading the Pharaoh to join his cause. He had anchored off the coast at Pelusium and sent word of his arrival. But the Egyptians had heard of the disaster at Pharsalus and preferred to side with the winner. Rather than merely send Pompey away, they saw an opportunity to gain credit with Caesar by taking care of his enemy for him. Pompey was invited ashore for talks. A tender was sent to fetch him, containing Achillas, general of the Egyptian army, and several senior Roman officers who had served under Pompey and now commanded the Roman forces protecting the Pharaoh.

Despite the entreaties of his wife and son, Pompey had boarded the tender. The assassins had waited until he was stepping ashore and then one of them, the military tribune Lucius Septimius, had run him through from behind with his sword. Achillas then drew his dagger and stabbed him, as did a second Roman officer, Salvius.

*"Caesar wishes it to be known that Pompey met his death bravely. According to witnesses, he drew his toga over his face with both hands and fell down upon the sand. He did not beg or plead but only groaned a little as they finished him off. The cries of Cornelia, who watched the murder, could be heard from the shore.*

*"Caesar was only three days behind Pompey. When he arrived in Alexandria he was shown the head and Pompey's signet ring on which is engraved a lion holding a sword in its paws; he encloses it with this letter as proof of the story. The body having already been burnt where it fell, Caesar has given orders for the ashes to be sent to Pompey's widow."*

Vatinius rolled up the letter and handed it to his aide.

"My condolences," he said, and saluted. "He was a fine soldier."

"But not fine enough," said Cicero, after Vatinius had gone.

Later he wrote to Atticus:

*As to Pompey's end I never had any doubt, for all rulers and peoples had become so thoroughly persuaded of the hopelessness of his case that wherever he went I expected this to happen. I cannot but grieve for his fate. I knew him for a man of good character, clean life and serious principle.*

That was all he had to say. He never wept over the loss, and thereafter I barely heard him mention Pompey again.

TERENTIA DID NOT OFFER TO VISIT CICERO AND HE DID NOT ASK TO see her; on the contrary: *There is no reason for you to leave home at present,* he wrote to her. *It is a long, unsafe journey, and I do not see what good you can do if you come.* He sat by the fire that winter and brooded on the state of his family. His brother and nephew were still in Greece and writing and speaking about him in the most poisonous terms: Vatinius and Atticus both showed him copies of their letters. His wife, whom he had no desire to meet, was refusing to send him any money to pay for his living expenses; when finally he arranged for Atticus to advance him some cash via a local banker, he discovered that she had deducted two thirds of it for her own use. His son was out all hours drinking with the local soldiers and refusing to attend to his studies: he yearned for war and often did not trouble to hide his contempt for his father's situation.

But mostly Cicero brooded on his daughter.

He learned from Atticus that Dolabella, who had returned to Rome as tribune of the plebs, now ignored Tullia entirely. He had left the marital home and was having affairs all over the city, most notoriously with Antonia, the wife of Mark Antony (an infidelity that enraged Antony, even though he lived quite openly with his own mistress, Volumnia Cytheris, a nude actress; later he divorced Antonia and married Fulvia, the widow of Clodius). Dolabella gave Tullia no money for her upkeep, and Terentia—despite Cicero's repeated pleas—was refusing to pay off her creditors, saying it was her husband's responsibility. Cicero blamed himself entirely for the wreckage of his public and private lives. *My ruin is my own work,* he wrote to Atticus. *Nothing in my adversity is due to chance. I am to blame for it all. Worse than the rest of my afflictions put together, however, is that I shall leave that poor girl despoiled of her father, of her inheritance, of all that was supposed to be hers . . .*

In the spring, with still no word from Caesar who was said to be in Egypt with his latest paramour, Queen Cleopatra, Cicero received a letter from Tullia announcing her intention of joining him in Brundisium. He was alarmed that she should undertake such an arduous expedition alone. But it was too late for him to stop her—she had made sure she was already on the road before he learned of her intentions—and I shall never forget his horror when at last she arrived, after a month of travelling, attended only by a maid and one elderly male slave.

"My darling girl, don't tell me this is the extent of your entou- rage . . . How could your mother have allowed it? You might have been robbed, or worse."

"There's no point in worrying about it now, Father. I'm here safe and well, aren't I? And to see you again is worth any risk or dis- comfort."

The journey showed the strength of the spirit that burned within that fragile frame, and soon her presence was brightening the entire household. Rooms shut up for the winter began to be cleaned and redecorated. Flowers appeared. The food improved. Even young Marcus tried to be civilised in her company. But more important than these domestic improvements was the revival in Cicero's spirits. Tullia was a clever young woman: if she had been born a man, she would have made a good advocate. She read poetry and philosophy and—what was harder—understood them well enough to hold her own in a discussion with her father. She did not complain, but made light of her troubles. *I believe her like on earth has never been seen,* Cicero wrote to Atticus.

The more he came to admire her, the less he could forgive Terentia for the way she had treated her. Occasionally he would mutter to me, "What kind of mother allows her daughter to travel hundreds of miles without an escort, or stands by and allows her to be humiliated by tradesmen whose bills she cannot pay?" One night when we were having dinner he asked Tullia straight out what she thought could explain Terentia's behaviour.

Tullia answered simply, "Money."

"But that's ridiculous. Money—it's so demeaning."

"She's got it into her head that Caesar will need to raise a huge sum to pay for the costs of the war, and the only way he'll get it is by confiscating the property of his opponents—you chief among them."

"And for that reason she lets you live in penury? Where's the logic in that?"

Tullia hesitated before replying. "Father, the last thing I want to do is to add to your anxieties. That's why until this moment I've said nothing. But now that you seem stronger, I think you ought to know why I wanted to come, and why Mother wanted to stop me. She and Philotimus have been plundering your estate for months—perhaps years. Not just the rent from your properties, but your houses themselves. You'd barely recognise some of them any more—they've been almost entirely stripped."

Cicero's first reaction was disbelief. "It can't be true. Why? How could she do such a thing?"

"I can only tell you what she said to me: 'He may sink into ruin because of his own folly but I shan't let him take me with him.'"

Tullia paused and added quietly, "If you want the truth, I believe she's been taking back her dowry."

And now Cicero began to grasp the situation. "You mean she's divorcing me?"

"I don't think she's fully decided yet. But I believe she's taking precautions in case it comes to that and you no longer have the means of repaying her yourself." She leaned across the table and grasped his hand. "Try not to be too angry with her, Father. Money is her only means of independence. She still has very strong feelings for you, I know it."

Cicero, unable to control his emotions, left the table and went out into the garden.

OF ALL THE DISASTERS AND BETRAYALS THAT HAD STRUCK HIM OVER recent years, this was the worst. It completed the collapse of his fortunes. He was numbed by it. What made it harder was that Tullia begged him to say nothing about it until such time as he could confront Terentia face to face, otherwise her mother would know it was she who was his informant. The notion of a meeting seemed a remote prospect. And then, out of the blue, just as the heat of the summer was starting to become uncomfortable, a letter arrived from Caesar.

> *Caesar Dictator to Cicero Imperator.*
>
> *I have received various messages from your brother complaining of dishonesty on your part towards me and insisting that but for your influence he would never have taken up arms against me. I have sent these letters to Balbus to pass on to you. You may do with them as you wish. I have pardoned him, and his son. They may live where they please. But I have no desire to renew relations with him. His behaviour towards you confirms a certain low opinion I had begun to form of him in Gaul.*
>
> *I am travelling ahead of my army and will return to Italy*

*earlier than expected next month, landing at Tarentum, when I*
*hope it will be possible for us to meet to settle matters regarding*
*your own future once and for all.*

Tullia was greatly excited when she read this: she called it "a handsome letter." But Cicero was secretly thrown into confusion. He had hoped he would be allowed to make his way back quietly to Rome, without fuss. He viewed the prospect of actually meeting Caesar with dread. The Dictator would doubtless be friendly enough, even if the gang around him were rough and insolent. However, no amount of politeness could disguise the basic truth: that he would be begging for his life from a conqueror who had usurped the constitution. Meanwhile fresh reports were coming in almost every day from Africa, where Cato was raising a huge new army to continue to uphold the republican cause.

He put on a cheerful face for Tullia's sake, only to collapse into agonies of conscience once she had gone to bed. "You know that I have always tried to steer the right course by asking myself how history would judge my actions. Well, in this instance I can be certain of the verdict. History will say that Cicero wasn't with Cato and the good cause because in the end Cicero was a coward. Oh, I have made such a mess of it all, Tiro! I actually believe Terentia is quite right to salvage what she can from the wreckage and divorce me."

Soon afterwards Vatinius brought the news that Caesar had landed at Tarentum and wished to see Cicero the day after tomorrow.

Cicero said, "Where exactly are we to go?"

"He is staying in Pompey's old villa by the sea. Do you know it?"

Cicero nodded. No doubt he was recalling his last visit, when he and Pompey had skimmed stones across the waves. "I know it."

Vatinius insisted on providing a military escort, even though Cicero said that he would prefer to travel without ostentation: "No, I'm afraid that's out of the question: the countryside is too dangerous. I hope we will meet again soon in happier circumstances. Good luck with Caesar. You will find him gracious, I'm sure."

Afterwards, as I was showing him out, Vatinius said, "He doesn't seem very happy."

"He feels his humiliation keenly. The fact that he will have to bow the knee in his old chief's former home will only add to his discomfort."

"I might let Caesar know that."

We set off the next morning—ten cavalrymen in the vanguard, followed by the six lictors; Cicero, Tullia and me in a carriage; Marcus on horseback; a baggage train of pack mules and servants; and finally another ten cavalry bringing up the rear. The Calabrian plain was flat and dusty. We saw almost no one apart from the occasional shepherd or olive farmer, and I realised that of course our escort wasn't for our protection at all, but to make sure Cicero didn't escape. We stayed overnight at a house reserved for us in Uria and continued the following day until around the middle of the afternoon, when we were only two or three miles from Tarentum, and then we saw a long column of horsemen in the distance, coming towards us.

In the rising heat and dust they seemed mere watery apparitions. It wasn't until they were only a few hundred paces away that I recognised by the red crests on their helmets and the standards in their midst that they were soldiers. Our column halted, and the officer in charge dismounted and hurried back to tell Cicero that the oncoming cavalry was carrying Caesar's personal standard. They were his praetorian guard and the Dictator was with them.

Cicero said, "Dear gods, is he planning to have me done in by the roadside, do you suppose?" Then, seeing Tullia's horrified expression, he added, "That was a joke, child. If he'd wanted me dead it would have happened long ago. Well, let's get it over with. You'd better come, Tiro. It will make a scene in your book."

He clambered out of the carriage and called to Marcus to join us.

Caesar's column had drawn up about a hundred paces away and deployed across the road as if for battle. It was huge: there must have been four or five hundred men. We walked towards them.

Cicero was between Marcus and me. At first I couldn't make out which of them was Caesar. But then a tall man swung himself out of his saddle, took off his helmet and gave it to an aide, and began to advance towards us, stroking his thin hair flat across his head.

How unreal it felt to watch the approach of this titan who had so dominated everyone's thoughts for so many years—who had conquered countries and upended lives and sent thousands of soldiers marching hither and thither and had smashed the ancient republic to fragments as if it were nothing more substantial than a chipped antique vase that had gone out of fashion—to watch him, and to find him, in the end ... just an ordinary breathing mortal! He walked in short strides with great rapidity—there was something curiously birdlike about him, I always thought: that narrow avian skull, those glittering watchful dark eyes. He stopped just in front of us. We stopped too. I was close enough to see the red indentations that his helmet had made in his surprisingly soft pale skin.

He looked Cicero up and down and said in his rasping voice, "Entirely unscathed, I am glad to see—exactly as I would have expected! I have a bone to pick with you," he said, jabbing a finger at me, and for a moment I felt my insides turn to liquid. "You assured me ten years ago that your master was at death's door. I told you then he would outlive me."

Cicero said, "I'm glad to hear of your prediction, Caesar, if only because you are the one man in a position to make sure it comes true."

Caesar threw back his head and laughed. "Ah yes, I've missed you! Now look here—do you see how I've come out of the town to meet you, to show you my respect? Let's walk in the direction you're headed and talk a little."

And so they strolled on together for perhaps half a mile towards Tarentum, Caesar's troops parting to allow them through. A few bodyguards walked behind them, one leading Caesar's horse. Marcus and I followed. I could not hear what was said, but observed that Caesar occasionally took Cicero's arm while gesturing with his other hand. Afterwards Cicero said that their conversation was friendly enough, and he roughly summarised it for me as follows:

CAESAR: "So what is it you would like to do?"

CICERO: "To return to Rome, if you'll permit it."

CAESAR: "And can you promise you will cause me no trouble?"

CICERO: "I swear it."

CAESAR: "What will you do there? I'm not sure I want you making speeches in the Senate, and the law courts are all closed."

CICERO: "Oh, I'm finished in politics, I know that. I shall retire from public life."

CAESAR: "And do what?"

CICERO: "I thought I might write philosophy."

CAESAR: "Excellent. I approve of statesmen who write philosophy. It means they have given up all hope of power. You may go to Rome. Will you teach the subject as well as write it? If so, I might send you a couple of my more promising men for instruction."

CICERO: "Aren't you worried I might corrupt them?"

CAESAR: "Nothing worries me when it comes to you. Do you have any other favours to ask?"

CICERO: "Well, I would like to be relieved of these lictors."

CAESAR: "It's done."

CICERO: "Doesn't it require a vote of the Senate?"

CAESAR: "I am the vote of the Senate."

CICERO: "Ah! So I take it you have no intention of restoring the republic . . . ?"

CAESAR: "One cannot rebuild using rotten timber."

CICERO: "Tell me—did you always aim at this outcome: a dictatorship?"

CAESAR: "Never! I sought only the respect due to my rank and achievements. For the rest, one merely adapts to circumstances as they arise."

CICERO: "I wonder sometimes, if I had come out to Gaul as your legate—as you were kind enough once to suggest—whether all of this might have been averted."

CAESAR: "That, my dear Cicero, we shall never know."

"He was perfectly amiable," recalled Cicero. "He allowed no glimpse of those monstrous depths. I saw only the calm and glittering surface."

At the end of their talk, Caesar shook Cicero's hand. Then he mounted his horse and galloped away in the direction of Pompey's villa. His action took his praetorian guard by surprise. They set off quickly after him, and the rest of us, Cicero included, had to scramble into the ditch to avoid being trampled.

Their hooves threw up the most tremendous cloud of dust. We choked and coughed, and when they had thundered past, we climbed back up on to the road to clean ourselves off. For a while we stood watching until Caesar and his followers had dissolved into the haze of heat, and then we began our journey back to Rome.

Part Two

# Redux

47 BC–43 BC

*Defendi rem publicam adulescens; non deseram senex.*

I defended the republic in my youth; I will not
desert it in old age.

      —Cicero, Second Philippic, 44 BC

# XII

———•◆•———

THIS TIME NO CROWDS TURNED OUT TO CHEER CICERO ON HIS WAY home. With so many men away at war, the fields we passed looked untended, the towns dilapidated and half empty. People stared at us sullenly; either that or they turned away.

Venusia was our first stop. From there Cicero dictated a chilly message to Terentia:

*I think I shall go to Tusculum. Kindly see that everything is ready.*
*I may have a number of people with me and shall probably make*
*a fairly long stay there. If there is no tub in the bathroom, get one*
*put in; likewise whatever else is necessary for health and subsistence.*
*Goodbye.*

There was no term of endearment, no expression of eager anticipation, not even an invitation to her to meet him. I knew then he had made up his mind to divorce her, whatever she might have decided.

We broke our journey for two nights at Cumae. The villa was shuttered; most of the slaves had been sold. Cicero moved through the stuffy, unventilated rooms and tried to remember what items were missing—a citrus-wood table from the dining room, a bust of Minerva that had been in the tablinum, an ivory stool from his library. He stood in Terentia's bedroom and contemplated the bare shelves and alcoves. It was to be the same story in Formiae; she had taken all her personal belongings—clothes, combs, perfumes, fans, parasols—and he said, "I feel like a ghost revisiting the scenes of my life."

At Tusculum she was waiting for us. We knew she was inside because one of her maids was looking out for us by the gate.

I recoiled at the prospect of another terrible scene, like the one between Cicero and his brother. In the event, she was gentler than I had ever known her. I suppose it was the effect of seeing her son again after such a long and anxious separation—he was certainly the person she ran to first and she clutched him to her tightly; it was the only time in thirty years I saw her cry. Next she embraced Tullia and finally she turned to her husband. Cicero told me later that he felt all his bitterness drain away the moment she came towards him, for he saw that she had aged. Her face was creased with worry; her hair flecked grey; her once proud back was slightly stooped. "Only at that moment did I realise how much she must have suffered, living in Caesar's Rome and being married to me. I cannot say I felt love for her any more, but I did feel great pity and affection and sadness, and I resolved there and then to make no mention of money or property—it was all done with, as far as I was concerned." They clung to one another like strangers who had survived a shipwreck, then parted, and as far as I know they never embraced again for the remainder of their lives.

TERENTIA RETURNED TO ROME THE FOLLOWING MORNING, divorced. Some regard it as a threat to public morality that a marriage, however long its duration, may be broken so easily, without any form of ceremony or legal document. But such is the ancient freedom, and at least on this occasion the desire to end the partnership was mutual. Naturally I was not present for their private talk. Cicero said it was amicable: "We had been apart too much; amid the vast upheaval of public events our old shared private interests were gone." It was agreed that Terentia would live in the house in Rome until she moved into a property of her own. In the meantime, Cicero would remain in Tusculum. Marcus chose to go back to the city with his mother; Tullia—whose faithless husband,

Dolabella, was about to sail to Africa with Caesar to fight Cato—stayed with her father.

If one of the miseries of being human is that happiness can be snatched away at any moment, one of the joys is that it may be restored equally unexpectedly. Cicero had long relished the tranquillity and clear air of his house in the Frascati hills; now he could enjoy it uninterrupted, and in the company of his beloved daughter. As it was to become his principal residence from now on, I shall describe the place in more detail. There was an upper gymnasium that led to his library and which he called the Lyceum in honour of Aristotle: this was where he walked in the mornings, composed his letters and talked with his visitors, and where in the old days he had practised his speeches. From here one could see the pale undulation of the seven hills of Rome, fifteen miles in the distance. But because what went on there was now entirely beyond his control, he no longer had to fret about it and was free to concentrate on his books—in that sense paradoxically dictatorship had liberated him. Below this terrace was a garden with shady walks like Plato's, in whose memory he called it his Academy. Both these areas, Lyceum and Academy, were adorned with beautiful Greek statues in marble and bronze, of which Cicero's favourite was the Hermathena, a Janus-like bust of Hermes and Athena staring in opposite directions, given to him by Atticus. From the various fountains came the soft music of trickling water, and that combined with the birdsong and the scent of the flowers created an atmosphere of Elysian tranquillity. Otherwise the hillside was quiet because most of the senatorial owners of the neighbouring villas were either fled or dead.

It was here that Cicero lived with Tullia for the whole of the next year, apart from occasional excursions to Rome. Afterwards he regarded this interlude as the most contented period of his life, as well as his most creative, for he made good on his undertaking to Caesar to confine his activity to writing. And such was the force of his energy, no longer dispersed into the law and politics but channelled solely into literary creation, that he produced in one year as many books on philosophy and rhetoric as most scholars might in a lifetime, turning them out one after another without pause. His objective was to put into Latin a summary of all the main arguments of Greek philosophy. His method of composition was extremely rapid. He would rise with the dawn and go straight to his library, where he would consult whatever texts he needed and scrawl notes—he had poor handwriting: I was one of the few who could decipher it—and then when I joined him an hour or two later he would stroll around the Lyceum dictating. Often he would leave me to look up quotations, or even to write whole passages according to the scheme he had laid out; usually he did not bother to correct them, as I had learned very well how to imitate his style.

The first work he completed that year was a history of oratory, which he named *Brutus* after Marcus Junius Brutus and dedicated to him. He had not seen his young friend since their tents stood side by side in the army camp at Dyrrachium. Even to choose such a subject as oratory was provocative, given that the art was no longer much valued in a country where the elections, the Senate and the law courts were under the control of the Dictator:

> I have reason to grieve that I entered on the road of life so late that the night which has fallen upon the republic has overtaken me before my journey was ended. But I grieve more deeply when I look on you, Brutus, whose youthful career, faring in triumph amidst the general applause, has been thwarted by the onset of a malign fortune.

*A malign fortune . . .* I was surprised at the risk Cicero was willing to run in publishing such passages, especially considering that Brutus was now an important member of Caesar's administration. Having pardoned him after Pharsalus, the Dictator had recently appointed him governor of Nearer Gaul, even though Brutus had never been praetor let alone consul. People said it was because he was the son of Caesar's old mistress Servilia, and that the promotion was meant as a favour to her, but Cicero dismissed such talk: "Caesar never does anything out of sentiment. He has given him the job in part no doubt because he is talented, but mostly because he is Cato's nephew and this is a good way for Caesar to divide his enemies."

Brutus, who along with a certain lofty idealism also had a good share of his uncle's perversity and stiffness, did not like the work named in his honour, nor a companion volume, *Orator*, which Cicero wrote not long afterwards and also dedicated to him. He sent a letter from Gaul to say that Cicero's speaking style had been fine in its day but was too high-flown both for good taste and for the modern age—too full of tricks and jokes and funny voices: what was needed was absolute flat, emotionless sincerity. I considered it typical of Brutus's conceit that he should presume to lecture the greatest orator of the age on how to speak in public, but Cicero always respected Brutus for his honesty and refused to take offence.

These were oddly happy, I would almost say carefree, days. The old Lucullus property next door, which had long stood empty, was sold, and the new occupant turned out to be Aulus Hirtius, the immaculate young aide to Caesar whom I had met in Gaul all those years ago. He was now praetor, though the law courts met so rarely he was mostly at home, where he lived with his elder sister. One morning he came round to invite Cicero to dinner. He was a noted gourmet and had grown quite plump on such delicacies as swan and peacock. He was still in his thirties, like nearly all Caesar's inner circle, with impeccable manners and exquisite literary taste. He was said to have written many of Caesar's *Commentaries*, which Cicero had gone out of his way to praise in *Brutus* (*they are like nude figures, upright and beautiful, stripped of all ornament of style as if they had removed a garment,* he dictated to me, before adding, not for publication, "yes, and as characterless as stick figures drawn in the sand by an infant"). Cicero saw no reason not to accept Hirtius's hospitality. He went round that evening accompanied by Tullia, and so began an unlikely country friendship; often I was invited too.

One day Cicero asked if he could give Hirtius anything in return for all these splendid dinners he was enjoying, and Hirtius replied yes, as a matter of fact, he could: that Caesar had urged him, if he ever got the chance, to study philosophy and rhetoric "at the feet of the Master" and that he would appreciate some instruction. Cicero agreed and started to give Hirtius lessons in declamation, similar to those he had received as a young man from Apollonius Molon. The lessons took place in the Academy beside the water clock, where Cicero taught him how to memorise a speech, to breathe, project his voice and use his hands and arms to make gestures that would better convey his meaning. Hirtius boasted about his new skills to his friend Gaius Vibius Pansa, another young officer from Caesar's Gallic staff, who was scheduled to replace Brutus as governor of Nearer Gaul at the end of the year. As a result, Pansa too became a regular visitor to Cicero's villa that year and he also learned how to speak better in public.

A third pupil in this informal school was Cassius Longinus, the battle-hardened survivor of Crassus's expedition to Parthia and the former ruler of Syria, whom Cicero had last seen at the war conference on the island of Corcyra. Like Brutus, to whose sister he was married, he had surrendered to Caesar and been pardoned; now he was impatiently awaiting a senior appointment. I always found him hard company, taciturn and ambitious, and Cicero didn't much care for his philosophy either, which was extreme Epicureanism: he picked at his food, never touched wine and exercised fanatically. He once confided to Cicero that the greatest regret of his life was accepting his pardon from Caesar: that it ate away at his soul from the start and that six months after his surrender he attempted to kill Caesar when the Dictator was returning from Egypt after the death of Pompey. He would have succeeded, too, if only Caesar had moored for the night on the same side of the Cydnus river as Cassius's triremes; instead he had unexpectedly chosen the opposite bank, and by then it was too late at night and he was too far away for Cassius to reach him. Even Cicero, who was not easily shocked, was alarmed by his indiscretion and advised him not to repeat it, and certainly not to do so under his roof in case Hirtius and Pansa got to hear of it.

Finally I must mention a fourth visitor, and he in many ways was the least likely of the lot, for this was Dolabella, Tullia's errant husband. She believed he was in Africa, campaigning with Caesar against Cato and Scipio, but at the beginning of spring Hirtius received a report that the campaign was finished and that Caesar had just won a great victory. Hirtius cut short his lesson and hastened back to Rome, and a few days later, first thing in the morning, a messenger brought Cicero a letter:

> From Dolabella to his dear father-in-law, Cicero.
>
> I have the honour to inform you that Caesar has beaten the enemy and that Cato is dead by his own hand. I arrived in Rome this morning to give a report to the Senate. I called at my house and was told that Tullia is with you. May I have your permission to come out to Tusculum and see the two people who are dearest to me in the world?

"Shock after shock after shock," observed Cicero. "The republic beaten, Cato dead and now my son-in-law asks to see his wife." He stared bleakly over the countryside towards the distant hills of Rome, blue in the early spring light. "The world will not be the same place without Cato in it."

He sent a slave to fetch Tullia, and when she came, he showed her the letter. She had spoken so often of Dolabella's cruelty towards her that I assumed, as did Cicero, that she would insist she didn't want to see him. Instead she said it was up to her father and that she didn't much care either way.

Cicero said, "Well, if that is really how you feel, then perhaps I shall let him come—if only so that I can tell him what I think of the way he's treated you."

Tullia said quickly, "No, Father, I beg you, please don't do that.

He's too proud to submit to a scolding, and besides, I have only myself to blame—everyone warned me what he was like before I married him."

Cicero was uncertain what to do, but in the end, his desire to hear at first hand what had happened to Cato overcame his distaste at having such a scoundrel under his roof—a scoundrel not just as a husband, incidentally, but as a rabble-rousing politician in the mould of Catilina and Clodius, who favoured the cancellation of all debts. He asked me if I would go to Rome at once with an invitation for Dolabella. Just before I left, Tullia took me aside and asked if she could have her husband's letter. Naturally I gave it to her; only afterwards did I discover she had none of her own and wanted it as a keepsake.

By midday I was in Rome—a full five years after I had last set foot in the city. In the fervid dreams of my exile I had pictured wide streets, and fine temples and porticoes clothed in marble and gold, all filled with elegant, cultured citizens. I found instead filth, smoke, rutted muddy roads much narrower than I remembered them, unrepaired buildings and limbless, disfigured veterans begging in the Forum. The Senate building was still a blackened shell. The places in front of the temples where the law courts used to meet were deserted. I was amazed at the general emptiness. When a census was taken later that year, the population was found to be less than half what it had been before the civil war.

I thought I might find Dolabella attending the Senate, but no one seemed to know where it was or even if it was in session these days. In the end I went to the address on the Palatine that Tullia had given me, which was where she said she had last lived with her husband, and there I found Dolabella in the company of an elegant, expensively dressed woman who I later discovered was Metella, daughter of Clodia. She behaved as if she was the mistress of the house, ordering refreshment for me and a chair to be brought, and I saw at a glance the hopelessness of Tullia's situation.

As for Dolabella, he was striking for three attributes: the fierce handsomeness of his features, the obvious strength of his physique, and the shortness of his stature. (Cicero once joked, "Who has tied my son-in-law to that sword?") This pocket Adonis, for whom I had long tended an intense dislike because of the way he treated Tullia, even though I had never met him, read Cicero's invitation and declared that he would return with me immediately. He said, "My father-in-law writes here that this message is brought to me by his trusted friend Tiro. Would that be the Tiro who created the famous shorthand system? Then I am delighted to meet you! My wife has always talked of you most fondly, as a kind of second father to her. May I shake your hand?" And such was the charm of the rogue that I felt my hostility immediately begin to wilt.

He asked Metella to send his slaves after him with his luggage, and then joined me in the carriage for the journey to Tusculum. Most of the way he slept. By the time we reached the villa, the slaves were preparing to serve dinner, and Cicero ordered an extra place to be set. Dolabella made straight for Tullia's couch and reclined with his head in her lap. After a while I noticed she began to stroke his hair.

It was a fair spring evening with the nightingales calling to one another, and the incongruity between the charm of the setting and the horror of the story Dolabella unfolded made it all the more unsettling. First there was the battle itself, named Thapsus, at which Scipio had commanded the republican force of seventy thousand men in alliance with King Juba of the Numidians. They had used a shock force of elephant cavalry to try to break Caesar's line, but volleys of arrows and flaming missiles from the ballistae had caused the wretched beasts to panic, turn and trample their own infantry. Thereafter it was the same story as at Pharsalus: the republican formations had broken on the iron discipline of Caesar's legionaries, only this time Caesar had decreed there would be no prisoners taken: all ten thousand who surrendered were massacred.

"And Cato?" asked Cicero.

"Cato was not present at the battle but was three days' journey away, commanding the garrison at Utica. Caesar went there straight away. I rode with him at the head of the army. He wanted very much to capture Cato alive so that he could pardon him."

"A wasted mission, I could have told you that: Cato would never have accepted a pardon from Caesar."

"Caesar was sure he would. But you are right, as always: Cato killed himself the night before we arrived."

"How did he do it?"

Dolabella pulled a face. "I'll tell you if you really want to know, but it's not a fit subject for a woman's ears."

Tullia said firmly, "I'm quite strong enough, thank you."

"Even so, I think it would be better if you withdrew."

"I shall certainly do no such thing!"

"And what does your father say about that?"

"Tullia is stronger than she looks," said Cicero, adding pointedly, "She has had to be."

"Well, you asked for it. According to Cato's slaves, when he learned that Caesar would arrive the next day, Cato bathed and dined, discussed Plato with his companions, and retired to his room. Then when he was alone he took his sword and slashed himself just here." Dolabella reached up and drew a finger under Tullia's breastbone. "All his guts spilled out."

Cicero, squeamish as ever, winced, but Tullia said, "That's not so bad."

"Ah," said Dolabella, "but that's not the end of the story. He failed to make the wound fatal and the sword slipped out of his bloodied hand. His attendants heard his groans and rushed in. They summoned a doctor. The doctor arrived and pushed his intestines back in to the cavity and sewed up the wound. I might add that Cato was entirely conscious throughout. He promised he would not make another attempt, and his staff believed him, although as a precaution they took his sword away. As soon as they had gone, he tore the wound open with his fingers and dragged his intestines out again. That killed him."

.   .   .

THE DEATH OF CATO HAD A POWERFUL EFFECT ON CICERO. AS THE lurid details became more widely known, there were those who said it was proof that Cato was insane; certainly this was Hirtius's view. Cicero disagreed. "He could have had an easier death. He could have thrown himself from a building, or opened his veins in a warm bath, or taken poison. Instead he chose that particular method— exposing his entrails like a human sacrifice—to demonstrate the strength of his will and his contempt for Caesar. In philosophical terms it was a good death: the death of a man who feared nothing. Indeed I would go so far as to say he died happy. Neither Caesar, nor any man, nor anything in the world could touch him."

The effect on Brutus and Cassius—both of whom were related to Cato, the one by blood and the other by marriage—was if any-thing even stronger. Brutus wrote from Gaul to ask if Cicero would compose a eulogy of his uncle. His letter arrived at the same time as Cicero learned that he had been named in Cato's will as one of the guardians of his son. Like the others who had accepted Caesar's pardon, Cicero found the suicide of Cato shaming. So he ignored the risk of offending the Dictator, complied with Brutus's request, and dictated a short work, *Cato,* in little more than a week.

> Sinewy in thought and person; indifferent to what men said of him; scornful of glory, titles and decorations, and even more of those who sought them; defender of laws and freedoms; vigilant in the public interest; contemptuous of tyrants, their vulgarities and presumptions; stubborn, infuriating, harsh, dogmatic; a dreamer, a fanatic, a mystic, a soldier; willing at the last to tear the very organs from his stomach rather than submit to a conqueror—only the Roman Republic could have bred such a man as Cato, and only in the Roman Republic did such a man as Cato desire to live.

Around this time Caesar returned from Africa, and soon after-wards, at the height of summer, he staged finally four separate triumphs on successive days to commemorate his victories in

Gaul, the Black Sea, Africa and on the Nile—such an epic of self-glorification as even Rome had never seen. Cicero moved back into his house on the Palatine in order to attend—not that he wanted to: *In civil war,* as he wrote to his old friend Sulpicius, *victory is always insolent.* There were five wild-beast hunts, a mock battle in the Circus Maximus that included elephants, a naval battle in a lake dug out near the Tiber, stage plays in every quarter of the city, athletics on the Field of Mars, chariot races, games in honour of the memory of the Dictator's daughter Julia, a banquet for the entire city at which meat from the sacrifices was served, a distribution of money, a distribution of bread, endless parades of soldiers and treasure and prisoners coiling through the streets—that noble leader of the Gauls, Vercingetorix, after six years of imprisonment, was garrotted in the Carcer—and day after day we could hear the vulgar chanting of the legionaries even from the terrace:

> *Home we bring our bald whoremonger,*
> *Romans, lock your wives away!*
> *All the bags of gold you lent him*
> *Went his Gallic tarts to pay!*

Yet despite their bombast, or perhaps because of it, Cato's reproachful ghost seemed to haunt even these proceedings. When a float went by during the Africa triumph depicting him tearing out his entrails, the crowd let out a loud groan. It was said that Cato's death had a particular religious meaning: that he had done it to bring down the wrath of the gods on Caesar's head. When that same day the axle on the Dictator's triumphal chariot broke and he was pitched to the ground, it was held to be a sign of divine displeasure, and Caesar took the crowd's disquiet seriously enough to lay on the most extraordinary spectacle of all: at night, with forty elephants on either side of him ridden by men holding flaming torches, he mounted the slope of the Capitol on his knees to atone to Jupiter for his impiety.

.  .  .

JUST AS SOME PARTICULARLY FAITHFUL DOGS ARE SAID TO LIE BY the graves of their masters, unable to accept that they are dead, so there were those in Rome who clung to the hope that the old republic might yet twitch back into life. Even Cicero fell briefly victim to this delusion. After the triumphs were over, he decided to attend a meeting of the Senate. He had no intention of speaking. He went partly for old times' sake and partly because he knew that Caesar had appointed several hundred new senators and he was curious to see what they looked like.

"It was a chamber full of strangers," he said to me afterwards, "a few of them actually foreign, many not elected—and yet somehow it was still a Senate for all that." It met on the Field of Mars, in the same room within Pompey's theatre complex where it had assembled in emergency session after the old Senate house was burned down. Caesar had even allowed the large marble statue of Pompey to remain in its original position, and the image of the Dictator presiding from the dais with Pompey's statue behind him gave Cicero hope for the future. The issue for debate was whether the ex-consul, M. Marcellus, one of the most intransigent of Caesar's opponents, who had gone into exile after Pharsalus and was living on Lesbos, might be allowed to return to Rome. His brother Caius—the magistrate who had sanctioned my manumission—led the appeals for clemency, and he was just finishing his speech when a bird seemed to appear from nowhere, fluttered over the senators' heads and swooped out of the door. Caesar's father-in-law, L. Calpurnius Piso, immediately got up and declared it to be an omen: the gods were saying that Marcellus too should be given the freedom to fly home. Then the whole Senate, Cicero included, rose as one and approached Caesar to appeal for clemency; Caius Marcellus and Piso actually fell to their knees at his feet.

Caesar gestured at them to return to their seats. He said, "The man for whom you all plead has heaped more deadly insults upon me than any other person living. And yet I am touched by your entreaties and the omen seems to me especially propitious. There is no need for me to place my dignity above the unanimous desire of this house: I have lived long enough for nature or for glory. Therefore let Marcellus come home and dwell in peace in the city of his distinguished ancestors."

This was received with loud applause, and several of the senators sitting around Cicero urged him to rise and make some expression of gratitude on behalf of them all. The scene so affected Cicero that he forgot his vow never to speak in Caesar's illegitimate Senate and did as they asked, lauding the Dictator to his face in the most extravagant terms: "You seem to have vanquished Victory herself, now that you have surrendered to the vanquished all that Victory had gained. Truly you are invincible!"

Suddenly it seemed possible to him that Caesar might rule as "first among equals" rather than as a tyrant. *I thought I saw some semblance of reviving constitutional freedom,* he wrote to Sulpicius. The next month he pleaded for the pardon of another exile, Quintus Ligarius—a senator almost as detestable to Caesar as Marcellus—and again Caesar listened and gave judgement in favour of clemency.

But the notion that this amounted to a restoration of the republic was an illusion. A few days afterwards, the Dictator had to leave Rome in a hurry in order to return to Spain and deal with an uprising led by Pompey's sons, Gnaeus and Sextus. Hirtius told Cicero that the Dictator was in a rage. Many of the rebels were men he had pardoned on condition they did not take up arms again; now they had betrayed his forgiving nature. There would be no further acts of clemency, Hirtius warned: no more gracious gestures. For his own sake Cicero would be well advised to stay away from the Senate, keep his head down and stick to philosophy: "This time it will be a fight to the death."

TULLIA WAS PREGNANT AGAIN BY DOLABELLA—THE RESULT, SHE told me, of her husband's visit to Tusculum. At first she was delighted by the discovery, believing it would save her marriage. Dolabella seemed happy too. But when she returned to Rome with Cicero to attend Caesar's four triumphs, and when she went to the house she shared with Dolabella intending to surprise him, she discovered Metella asleep in her bed. It was a terrible shock and to this day I feel the most profound guilt that I failed to warn her of what I had seen when I went there earlier.

She asked my advice and I urged her to divorce Dolabella without delay. The baby was due in four months. If she was still married when she gave birth, he would be entitled under the law to take the child; however if she were divorced, the situation would be much more complicated. Dolabella would have to take her to court to prove paternity, and at the very least, thanks to her father, she would have the best legal counsel available. She talked to Cicero and he agreed: the baby would be his sole grandchild and he had no intention of seeing it taken away from his daughter and entrusted to the care of Dolabella and the daughter of Clodia.

Accordingly, on the morning that Dolabella was due to leave with Caesar for the war in Spain, Tullia went to his house, accompanied by Cicero, and informed him that the marriage was over but that she wished to look after the baby. Cicero told me Dolabella's reaction: "The scoundrel merely shrugged, wished her well with the child, and said that of course it must remain with its mother. Then he drew me aside to say that there was no way at the moment that he could repay her dowry and he hoped this would not affect our relations! What could I say? I can hardly afford to make an enemy of one of Caesar's closest lieutenants, and besides, I still can't bring myself entirely to dislike him."

He was anguished and blamed himself for allowing the mess to develop. "I should have insisted that she divorce him the moment I heard of the way he was carrying on. Now what is she to do? An abandoned mother of thirty-one with a weak constitution and no dowry is hardly the most marriageable of prospects."

If there was any marrying to be done, he realised grimly, the person who would have to do it would be him. Nothing could have suited him less. He liked his new bachelor existence, preferred living with his books to the prospect of living with a wife. He was now sixty, and although he still cut a handsome figure, sexual desire—never a strong part of his character even in his youth—was waning. It is true that he flirted more as he got older. He liked dinner parties where pretty young women were present—he even once attended the same table as Mark Antony's mistress, the nude actress Volumnia Cytheris, a thing he would never have countenanced in the past. But murmured compliments on a dining couch and the occasional love poem sent round by a messenger the next morning were as far as things went.

Unfortunately, he now needed to marry to raise some money. Terentia's clandestine recovery of her dowry had crippled his finances; he knew Dolabella would never repay him; and although he had plenty of properties—including two new ones, at Astura on the coast near Antium and at Puteoli on the Bay of Naples—he could barely afford to run them. You might ask, "Well, why did he not sell some of them?" But that was never Cicero's way. His motto was always "Income adjusts to meet expenditure, not the other way round." Now that his income could no longer be expanded by legal practice the only realistic alternative was once again to take a rich wife.

It is a sordid story. But I swore at the outset to tell the truth, and I shall do so. Three potential brides were available. One was Hirtia, the elder sister of Hirtius. Her brother was immensely rich from his time in Gaul, and to get this tiresome woman off his hands he was prepared to offer her to Cicero with a dowry of two million sesterces. But as Cicero put it in a letter to Atticus, she was *quite remarkably ugly,* and it struck him as absurd that the cost of keeping his beautiful houses should be to install in them a hideous wife.

Then there was Pompeia, the daughter of Pompey. She had been the wife of Faustus Sulla, the owner of Aristotle's manuscripts, recently killed fighting for the Senate's cause in Africa. But if he married her, that would make Gnaeus—the man who had threatened to kill him at Corcyra—his brother-in-law. It was unthinkable. Besides, she bore a strong facial resemblance to her father. "Can you imagine," he said to me with a shudder, "waking up beside Pompey every morning?"

That left the least suitable match of all. Publilia was only fif-teen years old. Her father, M. Publilius, a wealthy equestrian friend of Atticus, had died leaving his estate in trust for his daughter until she married. The principal trustee was Cicero. It was Atticus's idea—"an elegant solution," he called it—that Cicero should marry Publilia and so gain access to her fortune. There was nothing illegal about this. The girl's mother and uncle were all for it, flattered by the prospect of forming a connection with such a distinguished man. And Publilia herself, when Cicero hesitantly broached the subject, declared that she would be honoured to be his wife.

"Are you sure?" he asked her. "I am forty-five years older than you—old enough to be your grandfather. Do you not find that . . . unnatural?"

She stared at him quite frankly. "No."

After she had gone, Cicero said, "Well, she seems to be tell-ing the truth. I wouldn't dream of it if she was repulsed by the very thought of me." He sighed heavily and shook his head. "I suppose I had better go through with it. But people will be very disapproving."

I could not help remarking, "It isn't *people* you have to worry about."

"What are you referring to?"

"Well, Tullia, of course," I replied, amazed that he hadn't consid-ered her. "How do you think she is going to feel?"

He squinted at me in genuine puzzlement. "Why would Tullia be opposed? I'm doing this for her benefit as much as mine."

"Well," I said mildly, "I think you'll find she *will* mind."

And she did. Cicero said that when he told her of his intention she fainted, and for an hour or two he feared for her health and that of the baby. When she recovered, she wanted to know how he could possibly think of such a thing. Was she really expected to call this child her stepmother? Were they to live under the same roof? He was dismayed by the strength of her reaction. However, it was too late for him to back out. He had already borrowed from the moneylenders on the expectation of his new wife's fortune. Neither of his children attended the wedding breakfast: Tullia moved to live with her mother for the final stages of her pregnancy, while Marcus asked his father for permission to go out and fight in Spain as part of Caesar's army. Cicero managed to persuade him that such an action would be dishonourable to his former comrades, and instead he went to Athens on a very generous allowance to try to have some philosophy dinned into his thick skull.

I did attend the wedding, which took place in the bride's house. The only other guests from the groom's side were Atticus and his wife, Pilia—who was herself, of course, thirty years her husband's junior but who seemed quite matronly beside the slender figure of Publilia. The bride, dressed all in white, with her hair pinned up and wearing the sacred belt, looked like an exquisite doll. Perhaps some men could have carried the whole thing off—Pompey I am sure would have been entirely at ease—but Cicero was so obviously uncomfortable that when he came to recite the simple vow ("Where you are Gaia, I am Gaius"), he got the names the wrong way round, an ill omen.

After a long celebratory banquet the wedding party walked to Cicero's house in the fading daylight. He had hoped to keep the marriage secret and almost scuttled through the streets, avoiding the gaze of passers-by, gripping his wife's hand firmly and seeming to drag her along. But a wedding procession always attracts attention, and his face was too famous for anonymity, so that by the time we reached the Palatine we must have been trailing a crowd of fifty or more. At least that number of applauding clients was waiting outside the house to throw flowers over the happy couple. I had worried that Cicero might injure his back if he tried to carry his bride over the threshold, but he hoisted her easily and swept her into the house, hissing at me over his shoulder to close the door behind us, quick. She went straight upstairs to Terentia's old suite of rooms, where her maids had already unpacked her belongings, to prepare for her wedding night. Cicero tried to persuade me to stay up a little longer and take some wine with him, but I pleaded exhaustion and left him to it.

THE MARRIAGE WAS A DISASTER FROM THE START. CICERO HAD NO idea how to treat his young wife. It was as if a friend's child had come to stay. Sometimes he played the role of kindly uncle, delighting in her playing of the lyre or congratulating her on her embroidery. On other occasions he was her exasperated tutor, appalled at her ignorance of history and literature. But mostly he tried to keep out of her way. Once he confided to me that the only workable basis for such a relationship would have been lust, and that he simply did not feel. Poor Publilia—the more her famous husband ignored her, the more she clung to him, and the more irritated he became.

Finally Cicero went to see Tullia to plead with her to move back in with him. She could have the baby at his house, he said—the birth was imminent—and he would send Publilia away, or rather he would get Atticus to send her away for him, as he found the situation too upsetting to deal with. Tullia, who was distressed to see her father in such a state, agreed, and the long-suffering Atticus duly found himself having to visit Publilia's mother and uncle to explain why the young woman would have to return home after less than a month of married life. He held out the hope that once the baby was born the couple might be able to resume their relationship, but for now Tullia's wishes took priority. They had little option but to agree.

It was January when Tullia moved back into the house. She was brought to the door in a litter and had to be helped inside. I recall a cold winter's day, everything very clear and bright and sharp. She moved with difficulty. Cicero fussed around her, telling the porter to close the door, ordering more wood for the fire, worrying that she would catch a chill. She said that she would like to go to her room to lie down. Cicero sent for a doctor to examine her. He came out soon afterwards and reported that she was in labour. Terentia was fetched, along with a midwife and her attendants, and they all disappeared into Tullia's room.

The screams of pain that rang through the house did not sound like Tullia at all. They did not sound like any human being in fact. They were guttural, primordial—all trace of personality obliterated by pain. I wondered how they fitted in to Cicero's philosophical scheme. Could happiness remotely be associated with such agony? Presumably it could. But he was unable to bear the shrieks and howls and went out into the garden, walking around and around it, for hour after hour, oblivious to the cold. Eventually there was silence and he came back in again. He looked at me. We waited. A long time seemed to pass, and then there were footsteps and Terentia appeared. Her face was drawn and pale but her voice was triumphant.

"It's a boy," she said, "a healthy boy—and she is well."

SHE WAS WELL. THAT WAS ALL THAT MATTERED TO CICERO. THE BOY was robust and was named Publius Lentulus, after his father's adopted patronymic. But Tullia could not feed the infant and the task was assigned to a wet nurse, and as the days passed following the trauma of the birth, she did not seem to get any stronger. Because it was so cold in Rome that winter, there was a lot of smoke, and the racket from the Forum disturbed her sleep. It was decided that she and Cicero should go back to Tusculum, scene of their happy year together, where she could recuperate in the tranquillity of the Frascati hills while he and I pressed on with his philosophical writings. We took a doctor with us. The baby travelled with his nurse, plus a whole retinue of slaves to look after him.

Tullia found the journey difficult. She was breathless and flushed with fever, although her eyes were wide and calm and she said she felt contented: not ill, just tired. When we reached the villa, the doctor insisted she go straight to bed. Afterwards he took me to one side and said that he was fairly certain now that she was suffering from the final stages of consumption and she would not last the night: should he inform her father, or would it be better if I did it?

I said that I would do it. After I had composed myself, I found Cicero in his library. He had taken down some books but had made no attempt to unroll them. He was sitting, staring straight ahead at nothing. He didn't even turn to look at me. He said, "She's dying, isn't she?"

"I'm afraid she is."

"Does she know it?"

"The doctor hasn't told her, but I think she's too clever not to realise, don't you?"

He nodded. "That was why she was so keen to come here, where her memories are happiest. This is where she wants to die." He rubbed his eyes. "I think I shall go and sit with her now."

I waited in the Lyceum and watched the sun sink behind the hills of Rome. Some hours later, when it was entirely dark, one of her maids came to fetch me, and conducted me by candlelight to Tullia's room. She was unconscious, lying in bed with her hair unpinned and spread across her pillow. Cicero sat on one side, holding her hand. On her other side, her baby lay asleep. Her breathing was very shallow and rapid. There were people in the room—her maids, the baby's nurse, the doctor—but they were in the shadows and I have no memory of their faces.

Cicero saw me and beckoned me closer. I leaned over and kissed her damp forehead, then retreated to join the others in the semi-darkness. Soon afterwards her breathing began to slow. The intervals between each breath became longer, and I kept imagining she must have died, but then she would take another gasp of air. The end when it came was different and unmistakable—a long sigh, accompanied by a slight tremor along the length of her body, and then a profound stillness as she passed into eternity.

# XIII

———•—•———

THE FUNERAL WAS IN ROME. ONLY ONE GOOD THING CAME OUT OF it: Cicero's brother, Quintus, from whom he had been estranged ever since that terrible scene in Patrae, came round to offer his condolences the moment we got back, and the two men sat beside the coffin, wordless, holding hands. As a mark of their reconciliation, Cicero asked Quintus to deliver the eulogy: he doubted he would be able to get through it himself.

That apart, it was one of the most melancholy occasions I have ever witnessed—the long procession out on to the Esquiline Field in the freezing winter dusk; the wail of the musicians' dirges mingled with the cawing of the crows in the sacred grove of Libitina; the small enshrouded figure lying on its bier; the racked face of Terentia, like Niobe's seemingly turned to stone by grief; Atticus supporting Cicero as he put the torch to the pyre; and finally the great sheet of flame that suddenly shot up, illuminating us all in its scorching red glow, our rigid expressions set like masks in a Greek tragedy.

The following day, Publilia turned up on the doorstep with her mother and uncle, sulky that she had not been invited to the funeral and determined to move back into the house. She made a little speech that had obviously been written out for her and that she had memorised: "Husband, I know that your daughter found my presence difficult, but now that this impediment has been removed, I hope that we can resume our married life together and that I may help you to forget your grief."

But Cicero didn't want to forget his grief. He wished to be enveloped by it, consumed by it. Without telling Publilia where he was going, he fled the house that same day, carrying the urn containing Tullia's ashes. He moved in to Atticus's place on the Quirinal, where he locked himself away in the library for days on end, seeing no one and compiling a great handbook of all that has ever been written by the philosophers and poets on how to cope with grief and dying. He called it his *Consolation.* He told me that while he worked, he could hear Atticus's five-year-old daughter playing in her nursery next door, exactly as Tullia had done when he was a young advocate: "The sound was as sharp to my heart as a red-hot needle; that kept me at my task."

When Publilia discovered where he was, she began to pester Atticus for admittance, so Cicero fled again, to the newest and most isolated of all his properties—a villa on the tiny island of Astura, at the mouth of a river, only a hundred yards or so from the shore of the Bay of Antium. The island was entirely deserted and covered with trees and groves, cut into shady walks. In this lonely place he shunned all human company. Early in the day he would hide himself away in the thick, thorny wood, with nothing to disturb his meditations but the cries of the birds, and would not emerge till evening. *What is the soul?* he asks in his *Consolation. It is not moist or airy or fiery or compounded of the earth. There is nothing in these elements that accounts for the power of memory, mind or thought, that recalls the past, foresees the future or comprehends the present. Rather the soul must be counted as a fifth element—divine and therefore eternal.*

I remained in Rome and handled all his affairs—financial, domestic, literary and even marital, as now it fell to me to fend off the hapless Publilia and her relatives by pretending I had no idea where he was. As the weeks passed, his absence became increasingly difficult to explain, not just to his wife but to his clients and friends, and I was aware that his reputation was suffering, it being considered unmanly to surrender to grief so completely. Many letters of condolence arrived, including a line from Caesar in Spain, and these I forwarded to Cicero.

Eventually Publilia discovered his hiding place and wrote to him announcing her intention of visiting him in the company of her mother. To escape such a fraught confrontation, he abandoned the island, ashes in hand, and finally nerved himself to write a letter to his wife setting out his desire for a divorce. No doubt it was cowardly of him not to do it face to face. But he felt that her lack of sympathy over Tullia's death had made their ill-conceived relationship entirely untenable. He left Atticus to sort out the financial details, which entailed selling one of his houses, and then he invited me to join him in Tusculum, saying he had a project he wished to discuss.

By the time I arrived, it was the middle of May. I had not seen him for more than three months. He was seated in his Academy reading when he heard my approach, and turned to look at me with a sad smile. His appearance shocked me. He was much gaunter, especially around the neck. His hair was greyer, longer and unkempt. But the real change was beneath the surface. There was a kind of resignation about him. It showed in the slowness of his movements and the gentleness of his manner—as if he had been broken and remade.

Over dinner I asked him if he had found it painful to return to a place where he had spent so much time with Tullia.

He replied: "I dreaded the prospect of coming, naturally, but when I arrived it was not so bad. One deals with grief, I have come to believe, either by never thinking of it or by thinking of it all the time. I chose the latter path, and here at least I am surrounded by memories of her, and her ashes are interred in the garden. Friends have been very kind, especially those who have suffered similar losses. Did you see the letter Sulpicius wrote me?"

He passed it to me over the table:

*I want to tell you of something which has brought me no slight comfort, in the hope that perhaps it may have some power to lighten your sorrow too. As I was on my way back from Asia, sailing from Aegina towards Megara, I began to gaze at the landscape around me. There behind me was Aegina, in front of me Megara, to the right Piraeus, to the left Corinth; once flourishing towns, now lying low in ruins before one's eyes. I began to think to myself:*

*"Ah! How can we manikins wax indignant if one of us dies or is killed, ephemeral creatures as we are, when the corpses of so many towns lie abandoned in a single spot? Check yourself, Servius, and remember that you were born a mortal man." That thought, I do assure you, strengthened me not a little. Can you really be so greatly moved by the loss of one poor little woman's frail spirit? If her end had not come now, she must none the less have died in a few years' time, for she was mortal.*

"I never thought Sulpicius could be so eloquent," I remarked.

"Nor I. You see how all of us poor creatures strive to make sense of death, even dry old jurists such as him? It's given me an idea. Suppose we were to compose a work of philosophy that helped relieve men of their fear of death."

"That would be an achievement."

"The *Consolation* seeks to reconcile us to the deaths of those we love. Now let us try to reconcile ourselves to our own deaths. If we were to succeed—well, tell me, what could bring humanity greater relief from terror than that?"

I had no answer. His proposition was irresistible. I was curious to see how he would manage it. And so was born what is now known as the *Tusculan Disputations,* upon which we started work the following day. From the outset, Cicero conceived it as five books:

1. On the fear of death
2. On the endurance of pain
3. On the alleviation of distress
4. On the remaining disorders of the soul
5. On the sufficiency of virtue for a happy life

Once again we assumed our old routine of composition. Like his hero Demosthenes, who hated to be beaten to the dawn by a diligent workman, Cicero would rise in the darkness and read in his library by lamplight until the day had broken; later in the morning he would describe to me what was in his mind and I would probe his logic with questions; in the afternoon while he napped I would write up my shorthand notes into a draft, which he would then correct; we would discuss and revise the day's work over dinner in the evening, and finally before retiring we would decide the topics for the following morning.

The summer days were long and our progress swift, mostly because Cicero decided to cast the work in the form of a dialogue between a philosopher and a student. Usually I played the student and he was the philosopher, but occasionally it was the other way round. These *Disputations* of ours are still widely available, so it is unnecessary, I hope, for me to describe them in detail. They are the summation of all that Cicero had come to believe after the battering of recent years: namely, that the soul possesses a divine animation different to the body's and therefore is eternal; that even if the soul is not eternal and ahead of us lies only oblivion, such a state is not to be feared as there will be no sensation and therefore no pain or misery (*the dead are not wretched, the living are wretched*); that we should think about death constantly and so acclimatise ourselves to its inevitable arrival (*the whole life of a philosopher, as Socrates said, is a preparation for death*); and that if we are determined enough, we can teach ourselves to scorn death and pain, just as professional fighters do:

> What even average gladiator has ever uttered a groan or changed expression? Which has ever disgraced himself after a fall by drawing in his neck when ordered to suffer the fatal stroke? Such is the force of training, practice and habit. Shall a gladiator be capable of this while a man who is born to fame proves so weak in his soul that he cannot strengthen it by systematic preparation?

In the fifth book, Cicero offered his practical prescriptions. A human being can only train for death by leading a life that is morally good; that is—to desire nothing too much; to be content with what one has; to be entirely self-sufficient within oneself, so that whatever one loses, one will still be able to carry on regardless; to do none harm; to realise that it is better to suffer an injury than to inflict one; to accept that life is a loan given by Nature without a due date and that repayment may be demanded at any time; that the most tragic character in the world is a tyrant who has broken all these precepts.

Such were the lessons Cicero had learned and desired to impart to the world in the sixty-second summer of his life.

ABOUT A MONTH AFTER WE STARTED WORK ON THE *DISPUTATIONS*, in the middle of June, Dolabella came to visit. He was on his way back to Rome from Spain, where he had once again been fighting alongside Caesar. The Dictator had been victorious; the remnants of Pompey's forces were smashed. But Dolabella had been wounded in the battle of Munda. There was a slash from his ear to his collar-bone and he walked with a limp: his horse had been killed beneath him by a javelin, throwing him to the ground and rolling on him. Still, he was as full of animal spirits as ever. He wanted particularly to see his son, who was living with Cicero at this time, and also to pay his respects at the place where Tullia's ashes were buried.

Baby Lentulus at four months old was a large and rosy speci-men, as healthy-looking as his mother had been frail. It was almost as if he had sucked all the life out of her, and I am sure that was the reason why I never saw Cicero hold him or pay him much attention—he could not quite forgive him for being alive when she was dead. Dolabella took the baby from the nurse and turned him around and examined him as if he were a vase, before announc-ing that he would like to take him back to Rome. Cicero did not object. "I have made provision for him in my will. If you wish to discuss his upbringing, come and see me any time."

They strolled together to view the spot where Tullia's ashes were resting, beside her favourite fountain in a sunny spot in the Academy. Cicero told me later that Dolabella knelt and placed some flowers on the grave, and wept. "When I saw his tears I ceased to feel angry with him. As she always said, she knew the type of man she was marrying. And if her first husband was more of a school friend to her than anything, and her second just a convenient way of escaping her mother, at least her third was someone she loved passionately, and I am glad she experienced that before she died."

Over dinner Dolabella, who was unable to recline because of his wound but had to eat sitting up in a chair like a barbarian, described the campaign in Spain, and confided to us that it had been a near-disaster: that at one point the army's line had broken and Caesar himself had been obliged to dismount, seize a shield and rally his fleeing legionaries. "He said to us when it was over, 'Today for the first time I fought for my life.' We killed thirty thousand of the enemy, no prisoners taken. Gnaeus Pompey's head was stuck on a pole and publicly displayed on Caesar's orders. It was grim work, I can tell you, and I fear you and your friends will not find him as amenable as before when he gets home."

"As long as he leaves me alone to write my books, he'll get no trouble from me."

"My dear Cicero, you of all men have no need to worry. Caesar loves you. He always says that you and he are the last two left."

Late in the summer Caesar returned to Italy, and all the ambitious men in Rome flocked to welcome him. Cicero and I stayed in the country, working. We finished the *Disputations* and Cicero sent it to Atticus so that his team of slaves could copy it and distribute it—he particularly asked for one to be sent to Caesar—and then he began composing two new treatises, *On the Nature of the Gods* and *On Divination.* Occasionally the barbs of grief still pierced him and he would withdraw for hours into some remote part of the grounds. But increasingly he was contented: "What a lot of trouble one avoids if one refuses to have anything to do with the common herd! To have no job, to devote one's time to literature, is the most wonderful thing in the world."

Even in Tusculum, however, we were aware, as if it were a storm in the distance, of the Dictator's return. Dolabella had spoken correctly. The Caesar who came back from Spain was different from the Caesar who had gone out. It was not simply his intolerance of dissent; it was as if his grasp on reality, once so terrifyingly secure, had at last begun to loosen. First he circulated a riposte to Cicero's eulogy of Cato, which he called his *Anti-Cato,* full of vulgar gibes that Cato was a drunkard and a crank. As nearly every Roman had at least a grudging respect for Cato, and most revered him, the pettiness of the pamphlet did the Dictator's reputation far more harm than it did Cato's. ("What is this restless desire of his to dominate everyone?" Cicero wondered aloud when he read it. "That requires him to trample even on the dust of the dead?") Then there was his decision to hold yet another triumph, this time to celebrate his victory in Spain: it seemed to most people that the annihilation of thousands of fellow Romans, including the son of Pompey, was not a thing to glory in. There was also his continuing infatuation with Cleopatra: it was bad enough that he installed her in a grand house with a park beside the Tiber, but when he had a golden statue of his foreign mistress erected in the Temple of Venus, he offended the pious and the patriotic alike. He even had himself declared a god— "the Divine Julius"—with his own priesthood, temple and images, and like a god began to interfere in all aspects of daily life: restricting overseas travel for senators and banning elaborate meals and luxurious goods—to the extent of stationing spies in the marketplaces who would burst into citizens' homes in the middle of dinner to search, confiscate and arrest.

Finally, as if his ambition had not caused enough bloodshed in recent years, he announced that in the spring he would be off to war again at the head of an immense army of thirty-six legions, to eliminate Parthia first of all, in revenge for the death of Crassus, and then to wheel around the far side of the Black Sea in a vast swathe of conquest that would encompass Hyrcania, the Caspian Sea and the Caucasus, Scythia, all the countries bordering on Germany and finally Germany itself, before returning to Italy by way of Gaul. He would be away three years. Over none of this did the Senate have any say. Like the men who built the pyramids for the pharaohs, they were mere slaves to their master's grand design.

In December, Cicero proposed that we should transfer our labours to a warmer climate. A wealthy client of his on the Bay of Naples, M. Cluvius, had died recently, leaving him a substantial property at Puteoli, and it was to this that we headed, taking a week over the journey and arriving on the eve of Saturnalia. The villa was large and luxurious, built on the seashore, and even more beautiful than Cicero's nearby house at Cumae. The estate came with a substantial portfolio of commercial properties located inside the town and a farm just outside it. Cicero was as delighted as a child with his new possession, and the moment we arrived he took off his shoes, hoisted his toga and walked down the beach to the sea to bathe his feet.

The following morning, after he had handed out Saturnalian gifts to all the slaves, he called me into his study and gave me a handsome sandalwood box. I assumed that the box was my present, but when I thanked him, he told me to open it. Inside I found the deeds to the farm near Puteoli. It had been transferred to my name. I was as stunned by the gesture as I had been on the day he granted me my freedom.

He said, "My dear old friend, I wish it were more and I wish I could have given it to you sooner. But here it is at last, that farm you always wanted—and may it bring you as much joy and comfort as you have brought to me over the years."

EVEN THOUGH IT WAS A HOLIDAY, CICERO WORKED. HE HAD NO family anymore with whom to celebrate—dead, divorced and scattered as they were—and I suppose that writing eased his loneliness. Not that he was melancholy. He had started a new work, a philosophical investigation of old age, and he was enjoying it (*O wretched indeed is that old man who has not learned in the course of his long life that death should be held of no account*). But he insisted that I, at any rate, should have the day off, and so I went for a walk along the beach, turning over in my mind the extraordinary fact that I was now a man of property—a farmer indeed. It felt like the end of one part of my life and the start of another, a portent that my work with Cicero was almost done and that we would soon part.

All along that stretch of coast one encounters large villas looking west across the bay towards the promontory of Misenum. The property next door to Cicero's was owned by L. Marcius Philippus, a former consul a few years younger than Cicero, who had been awkwardly placed during the civil war, given that he was Cato's father-in-law and yet was also married to Caesar's closest living relative, his niece Atia. He had been granted permission by both sides to keep out of the conflict, and had sat it out down here—a cautious neutrality that perfectly suited his nervous temperament.

Now, as I drew closer to the boundary of his estate, I saw that the beach was blocked off by soldiers who were preventing people passing in front of the house. For a moment I wondered what was happening, and when at last I worked it out, I turned and hurried back to tell Cicero—only to find that he had already received a message:

*Caesar Dictator to M. Cicero.*
*Greetings.*
*I am in Campania inspecting my veterans and shall be spending part of Saturnalia with my niece Atia at the villa of L. Philippus. If it is convenient, my party and I could visit you on the third day of the festival. Please let my officer know.*

I asked, "How did you reply?"

"How else does one reply to a god? I said yes, of course."

He pretended to be put-upon, but I could tell that secretly he was flattered, although when he enquired as to the size of Caesar's entourage, which he would also have to feed, and was told it consisted of two thousand men, he had second thoughts. His entire household were obliged to postpone their holiday, and for the remainder of that day and the whole of the next made frantic preparations, emptying the food markets of Puteoli and borrowing couches and tables from neighbouring villas. A camp was pitched in the field behind the house and sentries were posted. We were given a list of twenty men who were to dine in the house itself, headed by Caesar and including Philippus, L. Cornelius Galba and C. Oppius—these last two Caesar's closest associates—and a dozen officers whose names I have forgotten. It was organised like a military manoeuvre, according to a strict timetable. Cicero was informed that Caesar would be working with his secretaries in Philippus's house until shortly after noon, that he would then take an hour's vigorous exercise along the seashore, and would appreciate it if a bath could be provided for his use before dinner. As to the menu, the Dictator was following a course of emetics and so would have an appetite equal to whatever was provided, but he would particularly appreciate oysters and quail if they were available.

By this time Cicero was heartily wishing he had never agreed to the visit: "Where am I to find quail in December? Does he think I am Lucullus?" Nevertheless, he was determined, as he put it, "to show Caesar that we know how to live," and took pains to provide the finest of everything, from scented oils for the bathroom to Falernian wine for the table. Then, just before the Dictator was due to walk through the door, the ever-anxious Philippus hurried round with the news that M. Mamurra, Caesar's chief engineer— the man who had built the bridge across the Rhine, among many other amazing feats—had died of apoplexy. For a moment it looked as if the occasion might be ruined. But when Caesar swept in, red-faced from the exertion of his walk, and Cicero broke the news to him, his expression did not even flicker.

"That's too bad for him. Which way is my bath?"

No further mention was made of Mamurra—and yet, as Cicero observed, he must have been one of Caesar's closest comrades for more than a decade. Oddly, that brief insight into the coldness of Caesar's character is the thing I remember most clearly of his visit, for I was soon distracted by the house being full of noisy men, spread between three dining rooms, and naturally I was not at the same table as the Dictator. In my room they were all soldiers— a rough crowd, polite enough to begin with but soon drunk, and there was a lot of trooping in and out between courses to vomit on the beach. All the talk was of Parthia and the forthcoming campaign. Afterwards I asked Cicero what had passed between him and Caesar.

He said, "It was really surprisingly pleasant. We avoided politics and talked mostly of literature. He said that he had just read our *Disputations* and was full of compliments—'Except,' he said, 'I have to tell you that I am the living refutation of your principal proposition.' 'And what is that?' 'You claim that one can only conquer one's fear of death by living a good life. Well, according to your definition I have hardly done that, and yet I have no fear of dying. What is your answer?' To which I replied that for a man with no fear of dying, he certainly travelled with a large bodyguard."

"Did he laugh?"

"No he did not! He turned very serious, as if I had insulted him, and said that as the head of state he had a responsibility to take proper precautions, that if anything happened to him there would be chaos, but this didn't mean that he was afraid to die—far from it. So I probed a little further into the subject and asked why it was that he was so unafraid: did he believe the soul was eternal, or did he think we all die with our bodies?"

"And what was his reply?"

"He said that he didn't know about anyone else, but that obviously *he* wouldn't die along with his body because *he* was a god. I looked to see if he was joking but I'm not sure that he was. At that moment, I tell you honestly, I ceased to envy him all his power and glory. It has driven him mad."

The only time I saw Caesar again that night was when he left. He emerged from the principal dining room, leaning on Cicero and laughing at some remark he had just made. He appeared slightly flushed with wine, which was rare for him as he usually drank in moderation, if at all. His soldiers formed into lines as an honour guard and he lurched off into the night supported by Philippus and followed by his officers.

The next morning Cicero wrote an account of the visit to Atticus: *Strange that so onerous a guest should leave a memory not disagreeable. But once is enough. He is not the kind of person to whom one says, "Do drop round the next time you are in the neighbourhood."*

As far as I know, that was the last time Cicero and Caesar ever spoke to one another.

ON THE EVE OF OUR RETURN TO ROME, I RODE OVER TO LOOK AT MY farm. It was difficult to find, almost invisible from the coastal road, at the end of a long track leading up into the hills: an ancient, ivy-covered building commanding a wonderful panorama of the island of Capri. There was an olive grove and a small vineyard surrounded by low dry-stone walls. Goats and sheep grazed in the fields and on the nearby slopes; the tinkle of their neck bells rang soft as wind chimes; otherwise the place was entirely silent.

The farmstead was modest but fully appointed: a courtyard with portico, barns containing an olive press and stalls and feed racks, a fish pond, a vegetable and herb garden, a dovecote, chickens, a sundial. Beside the wooden gate a shaded terrace with fig trees faced out to sea. Inside, up a stone staircase, beneath the terra-cotta roof, was a large, dry, raftered room where I could keep my books and write: I asked the overseer to have some shelves built. Six slaves maintained the place and I was glad to see that all appeared healthy, unfettered and well fed. The overseer and his wife lived on the premises and had a child; they could read and write. Forget Rome and its empire: this was more than world enough for me. I should have stayed and told Cicero that he would have to return to the city on his own—I knew it even at the time. But that would have been poor thanks for his generosity, and besides, there were still books he wanted to finish and my assistance was needed. So I bade farewell to my little household, undertook to return to them as soon as I could, and rode back down the hill.

. . .

THE SPARTAN STATESMAN LYCURGUS, SEVEN HUNDRED YEARS AGO, IS said to have observed:

*When falls on man the anger of the gods,*
*First from his mind they banish understanding.*

Such was to be the fate of Caesar. I am sure Cicero was correct: he *had* gone mad. His success had made him vain, and his vanity had devoured his reason.

It was around this time—"since the days of the week are all taken," as Cicero joked—that he had the seventh month of the year retitled "July" in his honour. He had already declared himself a god and decreed that his statue should be carried in a special chariot during religious processions. Now his name was added to those of Jove and the Penates of Rome in every official oath. He was granted the title Dictator for Life. He styled himself Emperor and Father of the Nation. He presided over the Senate from a golden throne. He wore a special purple and gold toga. To the statues of the seven ancient kings of Rome that stood on the Capitol, he added an eighth—himself—and his image was introduced on the coinage— another prerogative of royalty.

Nobody spoke now of the revival of constitutional freedom— it was surely only a matter of time before he was declared monarch. At the Lupercalian festival in February, watched by a crowd in the Forum, Mark Antony actually placed a crown upon his head, whether mockingly or as a serious gesture none could say; but it was placed there, and the people resented it. On the statue of Brutus—the distant forefather of our contemporary Brutus—who had driven out the kings of Rome and established the consulship, graffito appeared: *If only you were alive now!* And on Caesar's statue someone scrawled:

*Brutus was elected consul*
*When he sent the kings away;*

*Caesar sent the consuls packing,*
*Caesar is our king today.*

He was scheduled to leave Rome at the start of his campaign of world conquest on the eighteenth day of March. Before he left, it was necessary for him to decree the results of all the elections for the next three years. A list was published. Mark Antony was to be consul for the remainder of the year alongside Dolabella; they would be succeeded by Hirtius and Pansa; Decimus Brutus (whom I shall henceforth call Decimus, to distinguish him from his kinsman) and L. Munatius Plancus would take over the year after that. Brutus himself was to be urban praetor and thereafter governor of Macedonia; Cassius was to be praetor and then governor of Syria; and so on. There were hundreds of names; it was drawn up like an order of battle.

The moment he saw it, Cicero shook his head in amazement at the sheer hubris of it: "Julius the god seems to have forgotten what Julius the politician never would: that every time you fill an appointment, you make one man grateful and ten resentful." On the eve of Caesar's departure, Rome was full of angry, disappointed senators. For example, Cassius, already insulted not to be chosen for the Parthian campaign, was offended that the less-experienced Brutus should be given a praetorship superior to his. But the greatest resentment was Mark Antony's at the prospect of sharing the consulship with Dolabella, a man whom he had never forgiven for committing adultery with his wife, and to whom he felt greatly superior; in fact such was his jealousy, he was actually using his powers as an augur to block the nomination on the grounds that it was ill-omened. A meeting of the Senate was summoned in Pompey's portico for the fifteenth, three days before Caesar's departure, to settle the issue once and for all. The rumour was that the Dictator would also demand to be granted the title of king at the same session.

Cicero had avoided the Senate as much as possible. He could not bear to look upon it. "Do you know that some of these upstarts from Gaul and Spain that Caesar has put into the place can't even speak Latin?" He felt old and out of touch. His eyesight was poor. Nevertheless, he decided to attend on the Ides—and not merely to attend, but to speak for once, on behalf of Dolabella and against Mark Antony, whom he regarded as another tyrant in the making. He suggested that I should accompany him, as in the old days, "if only to see what the Divine Julius has done to our republic of mere mortals."

We set off two hours after dawn, in a pair of litters. It was a public holiday. A gladiator fight was scheduled for later in the day and the streets around Pompey's theatre, where the contest was to be held, were already packed with spectators. Lepidus, whom Caesar shrewdly judged weak enough to be a suitable deputy and therefore was the new Master of Horse, had a legion stationed on Tiber Island, ready to embark for Spain, of which he was to be governor; many of his men were heading for a final visit to the games.

Inside the portico, a troop of about a hundred gladiators belonging to Decimus, the governor of Nearer Gaul, practised their lunges and feints in the shadow of the bare plane trees, watched by their owner and a crowd of aficionados. Decimus had been one of the Dictator's most brilliant lieutenants in Gaul, and Caesar was said to treat him almost as a son. But he was not widely known in the city and I had hardly ever seen him. He was stocky and broad-shouldered: he could have been a gladiator himself. I remember wondering why he needed so many pairs of fighters for what were only minor games. Around the covered walkways several of the praetors, including Cassius and Brutus, had set up their tribunals, conveniently closer to the Senate than the Forum, and were hearing cases. Cicero leaned out of his litter and asked the porters to set us down in a sunny spot so that we could have some spring warmth. They did as ordered, and while he reclined on his cushions and read through his speech, I enjoyed the sensation of the sun upon my face.

Presently, through half-closed eyes, I saw Caesar's golden throne being carried through the portico and into the Senate chamber.

I pointed it out to Cicero. He rolled up his speech. A couple of slaves helped him to his feet and we joined the throng of senators queuing to go in. There must have been three hundred men at least. Once I could have named almost every member of that noble order, and identified his tribe and family, and told you his particular interests. But the Senate that I knew had bled to death on the battlefields of Pharsalus, Thapsus and Munda.

We filed into the chamber. In contrast to the old Senate house it was light and airy, in the modern style, with a central aisle of black-and-white mosaic tiles. On either side rose three wide, shallow steps, along which the benches were arranged in tiers, facing one another. At the far end, on its dais, stood Caesar's throne beside the statue of Pompey, upon the head of which some subversive hand had placed a laurel wreath. One of Caesar's slaves kept jumping up, trying to knock it off, but much to the amusement of the watching senators he couldn't quite reach it. Eventually he fetched a stool and climbed up to remove the offending symbol and was rewarded with mocking applause. Cicero shook his head and rolled his eyes at such levity and went off to find his place. I stayed by the door with the other spectators.

After that, a long time passed—I should say at least an hour. Eventually Caesar's four attendants came back in from the portico, walked up the aisle to the throne, hoisted it on to their shoulders with difficulty (for it was made of solid gold) and carried it out again. A groan of exasperation went round the chamber. Many senators stood to stretch their legs; some left. Nobody seemed to know what was happening. Cicero strolled down the aisle. He said to me, "I don't much want to deliver this speech in any case. I think I'll go home. Will you find out if the session is definitely cancelled?"

I went out into the portico. The gladiators were still there, but Decimus had gone. Brutus and Cassius had given up listening to their petitioners and were talking together. I knew both men well enough to approach them—Brutus the noble philosopher, still youthful-looking at forty; Cassius the same age, but grizzled, harder. About a dozen other senators were hanging round them, listening—the Casca brothers, Tillius Cimber, Minucius Basilus and Gaius Trebonius, who had been designated by Caesar to be governor of Asia; I also remember Quintus Ligarius, the exile whom Cicero had persuaded the Dictator to allow home, and Marcus Rubrius Ruga, an old soldier who had also been pardoned and had never got over it. They fell silent and turned to look at me as I approached. I said, "Forgive me for disturbing you, gentlemen, but Cicero would like to know what's happening."

The senators looked sideways at one another. Cassius said suspiciously, "What does he mean by 'what's happening'?"

Puzzled, I replied, "Why, he simply wants to know if there will be a meeting."

Brutus said, "The omens are unpropitious, therefore Caesar is refusing to leave his house. Decimus has gone to try to persuade him to come. Tell Cicero to be patient."

"I'll tell him, but I think he wants to go home."

Cassius said firmly, "Then persuade him to stay."

It struck me as odd, but I went and relayed the remark to Cicero. He shrugged. "Very well, let's give it a little longer."

He returned to his seat and looked at his speech again. Senators came up and spoke to him and drifted away. He showed Dolabella what he was planning to say. Another long wait ensued. But eventually, after a further hour, Caesar's throne was carried back in and placed upon the dais. Clearly Decimus had persuaded him to come after all. Those senators who had been standing around talking resumed their places, and an air of expectation settled over the chamber.

I heard cheering outside. Turning, I saw through the open door that a crowd was streaming into the portico. In the middle of the throng, like battle standards, I could see the fasces of Caesar's twenty-four lictors, and swaying above their heads the golden canopy of the Dictator's litter. I was surprised there was no military bodyguard. Only later did I learn that Caesar had recently dismissed all those hundreds of soldiers he used to travel around with, saying, "It is better to die once by treachery than live always in fear of it." I have often wondered if his conversation with Cicero three months earlier had anything to do with this piece of bravado. At any rate, the litter was carried across the open space and set down outside the Senate, and when his lictors helped him out of it, the crowd was able to get very close to him. They thrust petitions into his hands, which he passed immediately to an aide. He was dressed in the special purple toga embroidered with gold that he alone was permitted by the Senate to wear. He certainly looked like a king; all that was missing was the crown. And yet I could see at once that he was uneasy. He had a habit, like a bird of prey, of cocking his head this way and that, and looking about him, as if searching for some slight stirring in the undergrowth. At the sight of the open door to the chamber, he seemed to draw back. But Decimus took him by the hand, and I suppose the momentum of the occasion must also have propelled him forwards: certainly he would have lost face if he had turned round and returned home; there were already rumours that he was ill.

His lictors cleared a path for him and in he came. He passed within three feet of me, so close I could smell the sweet and spicy scent of the oils and unguents with which he had been anointed after his bath. Decimus slipped in after him. Mark Antony was just behind Decimus, also on his way in, but Trebonius suddenly intercepted him and drew him aside.

The Senate stood. In the silence Caesar walked down the central aisle, frowning and pensive, twirling a stylus in his right hand. A couple of scribes followed him, carrying document boxes. Cicero was in the front row, reserved for ex-consuls. Caesar did not acknowledge him, or anyone else. He was glancing back and forth, up and down, flicking that stylus between his fingers. He mounted the dais, turned to face the senators, gestured to them to be seated and lowered himself into his throne.

Immediately various figures rose and approached him offering petitions. This was normal practice now that the debates themselves no longer mattered: they had become instead rare opportunities to give the Dictator something in person. The first to reach him—

from the left, both his hands stretched out in supplication—was Tillius Cimber. He was known to be seeking a pardon for his brother, who was in exile. But instead of lifting the hem of Caesar's toga to kiss it, he suddenly grabbed the folds of fabric around Caesar's neck and yanked so hard on the thick material that Caesar was pulled sideways, effectively pinioned and unable to move. He shouted angrily, but his voice was half strangled so I couldn't quite make it out. It sounded something like, "But this is violence!" A moment later, one of the Casca brothers, Publius, strode towards him from the other side and jammed a dagger into Caesar's exposed neck. I couldn't believe what I was seeing: it was unreal—a play, a dream.

"Casca, you villain, what are you doing?" Despite his fifty-five years, the Dictator was still a strong man. Somehow he grabbed the blade of Casca's dagger with his left hand—he must have torn his fingers to shreds—squirmed free of Cimber's grasp, then swung round and stabbed Casca in the arm with his stylus. Casca cried in Greek, "Help me, brother!" and an instant later his brother Gaius knifed Caesar in the ribs. The Dictator's gasp of shock echoed round the chamber. He dropped to his knees. More than twenty toga-clad figures were now stepping up on to the dais and surrounding him. Decimus ran past me to join in. There was a frenzy of stabbing. Senators rose in their places to see what was happening. People have often asked me why none of these hundreds of men, whose fortunes Caesar had made and whose careers he had advanced, attempted to go to his aid. I cannot answer except to say that it was all so fast, so violent and so unexpected, one's senses were stupefied.

I could no longer see Caesar through the ring of his assailants. I was told afterwards by Cicero, who was closer than I, that by some superhuman effort he briefly regained his feet and tried to break away. But such was the force, the desperate haste and the closeness of the attack that escape was impossible. His assailants even wounded one another. Cassius knifed Brutus in the hand. Minucius Basilus stabbed Rubrius in the thigh. It is said that the Dictator's last words were a bitter reproach to Decimus, who had tricked him into coming: "Even you?" Perhaps it is true. I wonder, though, how much speech he was capable of by then. Afterwards the doctors counted twenty-three stab wounds on his body.

Their business done, the assassins drew back from what a moment before had been the beating heart of the empire and was now a punctured skein of flesh. Their hands were gloved in blood. Their gory daggers were held aloft. They shouted a few slogans: "Liberty!" "Peace!" "The republic!" Brutus even called out "Long live Cicero!" Then they ran down the aisle and out into the portico, their eyes staring wildly in their excitement, their togas spattered like butchers' aprons.

The moment they had gone, it was as if a spell had been broken. Pandemonium erupted. Senators clambered over the benches and even over one another in their panic to get away. I was almost trampled in the rush. But I was determined not to leave without Cicero. I ducked and twisted my way through the oncoming press of bodies until I reached him. He was still seated, staring at Caesar's body, which lay entirely unattended—his slaves having fled—sprawled on its back, its feet pointed towards the base of Pompey's statue, its head lolling over the edge of the dais, facing the door.

I told Cicero we needed to leave, but he did not seem to hear me. He was staring at the corpse, transfixed. He murmured, "No one dares go near him, look."

One of the Dictator's shoes had come off; his bare depilated legs were exposed where his toga had ridden up his thighs; his imperial purple was ragged and bloodied; there was a slash across his cheek that exposed the pale bone; his dark eyes seemed to stare, outraged, upside down, at the emptying chamber; blood ran from his wound diagonally across his forehead and dripped on to the white marble.

All those details I see today as clearly as I saw them forty years ago, and for an instant there flashed into my mind the prophecy of the sibyl: that Rome would be ruled by three, then two, then one, and finally by none. It took an effort for me to drag my gaze away, to seize Cicero by the arm and pull him to his feet. Finally, like a sleepwalker, he allowed himself to be led from the scene, and together we made our way out into the daylight.

# XIV

THE PORTICO WAS IN CHAOS. THE ASSASSINS HAD GONE, ESCORTED
by Decimus's gladiators. No one knew their destination. People
were rushing to and fro trying to find out what had happened. The
Dictator's lictors had thrown away their symbols of authority and
made a run for it. The remaining senators were also leaving as fast
as they could; a few had even stripped off their togas to disguise
their rank and were trying to infiltrate themselves into the crowd.
Meanwhile, at the far end of the portico, some of the audience from
the gladiator fights in the adjacent theatre had heard the commotion and were pouring in to see what was going on.

I sensed that Cicero was in mortal danger. Even though he'd
known nothing in advance of the conspiracy, Brutus had called out
his name; everyone had heard it. He was an obvious target for vengeance. Caesar's loyalists might even assume he was the assassins'
leader. Blood would demand blood.

I said, "We have to get you away from here."

To my relief, he nodded, still too stunned to argue. Our porters had fled, abandoning their litters. We had to hurry out of the
portico on foot. Meanwhile the games continued oblivious. From
Pompey's theatre welled the roar of applause as the gladiators
fought. One would never have guessed what had just occurred, and
the more distance we put between ourselves and the portico, the
more normal things seemed, so that by the time we reached the
Carmenta Gate and entered the city it appeared to be a perfectly
ordinary holiday and the assassination felt as if it had been a lurid
dream.

Nevertheless, invisible to us, along the back streets and through the markets, conveyed on running feet and in panicky whispers, the news was travelling faster than we could—so that somehow, by the time we reached the house on the Palatine, it had overtaken us, and Cicero's brother Quintus and Atticus were already arriving from separate directions with garbled versions of what had happened. They did not know much. There had been an attack in the Senate, was all they had heard: Caesar was hurt.

"Caesar is dead," said Cicero, and described what we had just seen. It seemed even more fantastical in recollection than it had at the time. Both men were at first disbelieving and then overjoyed that the Dictator was slain. Atticus, normally so urbane, even performed a little skipping dance.

Quintus said, "And you truly had no idea this was coming?"

"None," replied Cicero. "They must have kept it from me deliberately. I ought to be offended, but to be honest I'm relieved to have been spared the anxiety. It demanded far more nerve than I could ever have mustered. To have come to the Senate with a concealed blade, to have waited all that time, to have held one's nerve, to have risked massacre by Caesar's supporters, and finally to have looked the tyrant in the eye and plunged in the dagger—I don't mind confessing I could never have done it."

Quintus said, "I could!"

Cicero laughed. "Well, you're more used to blood than I am."

"And yet do none of you feel any sorrow for Caesar, simply as a man?" I asked. "After all," I said to Cicero, "it's only three months since you were laughing with him over dinner."

Cicero looked at me with incredulity. "I'm amazed that you should ask me that. I imagine I feel as you must have felt on the day you received your freedom. Whether Caesar was a kind master or a cruel one is neither here nor there—master he was, and slaves was what he made us. And now we have been liberated. So let's have no talk of sorrow."

He sent out a secretary to see if he could discover the whereabouts of Brutus and the other conspirators. The man came back soon afterwards and reported that they were said to be occupying the upper ground of the Capitol.

Cicero said, "I must go at once and offer my support."

"Is that wise?" I asked. "As things stand, you bear no responsibility for the killing. But if you go and show your solidarity with them in public, Caesar's supporters may not see much difference between you and Cassius and Brutus."

"Let them. I intend to thank the men who've given me back my liberty."

The others agreed and we set off at once, all four of us, with a few slaves for protection—along the slope of the Palatine, down the steps into the valley and across the road of Jugarius to the foot of the Tarpeian Rock. The air was eerily still and torpid with an approaching storm; the thoroughfare, normally busy with ox carts, was deserted apart from a few people wandering in the direction of the Forum. Their expressions were stunned, bewildered, fearful. And certainly if one sought for portents one had only to glance up at the sky. Massy dense black clouds seemed to be pressing down upon the roofs of the temples, and as we began to climb the steep flight of steps there was a flash and a crack of thunder. The rain was cold and heavy. The stones became slippery. We had to pause halfway to recover our breath. Beside us a stream ran over the green mossy rock and turned into a waterfall; below us I could see the curve of the Tiber, the city walls, the Field of Mars. I realised then how shrewd a piece of military planning it had been to retire straight from the scene of the assassination to the Capitol: its sheer cliffs made it a naturally impregnable fortress.

We pressed on until we came to the gate at the summit, which was guarded by gladiators, fearsome-looking characters from Nearer Gaul. With them was one of Decimus's officers. He recognised Cicero and ordered the men to admit us, then he conducted us himself into the walled compound, past the chained dogs that guarded the place at night, and into the Temple of Jupiter, where at least a hundred men were gathered, sheltering in the gloom from the rain.

As Cicero entered he was greeted with applause and he went round shaking hands with all of the assassins apart from Brutus, whose hand was bandaged because of the wound Cassius had accidentally inflicted on him. They had changed out of their bloodied clothes into freshly laundered togas, and their demeanour was sober, even grim, with nothing left of the euphoria that had immediately followed the killing. I was amazed to see how many of Caesar's closest followers had rushed to join them: L. Cornelius Cinna, for example, the brother of Caesar's first wife and uncle of Julia—Caesar had recently made him praetor, yet here he was with his ex-brother-in-law's murderers. And here too was Dolabella—the ever-faithless Dolabella—who had raised not a finger to defend Caesar in the Senate chamber, and who now had his arm round the shoulder of Decimus, the man who had lured their old chief to his doom. He came over to join in the conversation that Cicero was having with Brutus and Cassius.

Brutus said, "So you approve of what we have done?"

"Approve? It's the greatest deed in the history of the republic! But tell me," asked Cicero, with a glance around the sombre interior, "why are you all cooped up here out of sight like criminals? Why aren't you down in the Forum rallying the people to your cause?"

"We are patriots, not demagogues. Our aim was to remove the tyrant, nothing more."

Cicero stared at him in surprise. "But then who is running the country?"

Brutus said, "At the moment, no one. The next step is to establish a new government."

"Shouldn't you simply declare yourselves to be the government?"

"That would be illegal. We didn't pull down a tyrant in order to set ourselves up as tyrants in his place."

"Well then summon the Senate here now, to this temple—you have the power as praetors—and let the Senate declare a state of emergency until elections can be held. That would be entirely legal."

"We think it would be more constitutional if Mark Antony, as consul, summoned the Senate."

"Mark Antony?" Cicero's surprise was turning to alarm. "You mustn't let him anywhere near this business. He has all of Caesar's worst qualities and none of his best." He appealed to Cassius to back him up.

Cassius said, "I agree with you. In my view we should have killed him at the same time as we killed Caesar. But Brutus wouldn't tolerate it. Therefore Trebonius delayed him on his way in to the chamber, so that he could get away."

"And where is he now?"

"Presumably in his house."

"That I would doubt, knowing him," said Dolabella. "He will be busy in the city."

Throughout these exchanges I had noticed Decimus talking to a couple of his gladiators. Now he hurried across, his expression grim. He said, "There's a report that Lepidus is moving his legion off Tiber Island."

Cassius said, "We'll be able to see for ourselves from here."

We went outside and followed Cassius and Decimus around the side of the great temple to the raised paved area to the north that gives a view for miles over the Field of Mars and beyond. And there was no doubt of it: the legionaries were marching across the bridge and forming up on the riverbank nearest the city.

Brutus betrayed his anxiety by a constant tapping of his foot. He said, "I sent a messenger to Lepidus hours ago but he hasn't returned an answer."

Cassius pointed. "That's his answer."

Cicero said, "Brutus, I implore you—I implore you all—go down to the Forum and tell the people what you've done and why you've done it. Fire them with the spirit of the old republic. Otherwise Lepidus will trap you up here and Antony will take control of the city."

Even Brutus could now see the wisdom of this, and so a procession of the conspirators—or assassins, or freedom fighters, or liberators: no one ever could agree exactly what to call them—descended the twisting road that led from the summit of the Capitol around behind the Temple of Saturn and down into the Forum. At Cicero's suggestion they left their bodyguard of gladiators behind: "It will make the best possible impression of our sincerity if we walk alone and unarmed; besides, if there is trouble, we can retreat quickly enough."

It had stopped raining. Three or four hundred citizens had gathered in the Forum and were standing around listlessly among the puddles, apparently waiting for something to happen. They saw us coming when we were still quite a long way off, and moved towards us. I had no idea how they would react. Caesar had always been a great favourite of the mob, although latterly even they had come to weary of his kingly ways—to dread his looming wars and to pine for the old days of elections when they had to be courted by the dozens of candidates with flattery and bribes. Would they applaud us or try to tear us apart? In the event they did neither. The crowd watched in absolute silence as we entered the Forum and then parted to let us pass. The praetors—Brutus, Cassius and Cinna—went up on to the rostra to address them, while the rest of us, including Cicero, stood at the side to watch.

Brutus spoke first, and although I can remember his sombre opening line—"As my noble ancestor Junius Brutus drove the tyrant-king Tarquin from the city, so today have I rid us of the tyrant-dictator Caesar"—the rest of it I have forgotten. That was the problem. He had obviously laboured hard over it for days, and no doubt as an essay on the wickedness of despotism it read well. But as Cicero had long tried to convince him, a speech is a performance, not a philosophical discourse: it must appeal to the emotions more than to the intellect. A fiery oration at that moment might have transformed the situation—might have inspired the crowd to defend the Forum and their liberty from the soldiers who even now were massing on the Field of Mars. But Brutus gave them a lecture that was three parts history to one part political theory. I could hear Cicero beside me muttering under his breath. It did not help that while he was speaking, Brutus's wound began to bleed beneath its bandage; one was distracted from what he was saying by that gory reminder of what he had done.

After what felt like a long time, Brutus ended to applause best described as thoughtful. Cassius spoke next, and not badly either, for he had taken lessons in oratory from Cicero in Tusculum. But he was a professional soldier who had spent little time in Rome: he was respected but he was not much known, let alone loved. He received less applause even than Brutus. The disaster, however, was Cinna. He was an orator of the old-fashioned, melodramatic school, and tried to inject some passion into proceedings by tearing off his praetorian robe and hurling it from the rostra, denouncing it as the gift of a despot that he was ashamed to be seen wearing. The hypocrisy was too much to bear. Someone yelled out, "You didn't say that yesterday!" The remark was cheered, which emboldened another heckler to shout: "You'd have been nothing without Caesar, you old has-been!" In the chorus of jeering, Cinna's voice was lost—and the meeting with it.

Cicero said, "Now this is a fiasco."

"You are the orator," said Decimus. "Will you say something to retrieve the situation?" and to my horror I saw that Cicero was tempted. But at that moment Decimus was handed a new report that Lepidus's legion appeared to be moving towards the city. He beckoned urgently to the praetors to come down off the rostra, and with as much confidence as we could muster, which was little, we all trooped back up to the Capitol.


IT WAS TYPICAL OF BRUTUS'S OTHER-WORLDLINESS THAT HE SHOULD have believed right up until the last moment that Lepidus would never dare to break the law by bringing an army across the sacred boundary and into Rome. After all, he assured Cicero, he knew the Master of Horse extremely well: Lepidus was married to his sister Junia Secunda (just as Cassius was married to his half-sister Junia Tertia).

"Believe me, he's a patrician through and through. He won't do anything illegal. I have always found him an absolute stickler for dignity and protocol."

And at first it seemed he might be right, as the legion, after crossing the bridge and moving towards the city walls, halted on the Field of Mars and pitched camp about half a mile away. Then soon after nightfall, we heard the plaintive notes of the war horns. They set the dogs barking in the walled compound of the temple and sent us hurrying out to see what was going on. Heavy cloud obscured the moon and stars but the distant lights of the legion's campfires shone clearly in the darkness. Even as we watched, the fires seemed to splinter and rearrange themselves into snakes of fire.

Cassius said, "They are marching with torches."

A line of light began wavering along the road towards the Carmenta Gate. Presently on the moist night air we heard the faint tramp of the legionaries' boots. The gate was almost directly beneath us, obscured from sight by outcrops of rock. Lepidus's vanguard found it locked and hammered for admittance and cried out to the porter. But I guess he must have run away. There was a long interval when nothing happened. Then a battering ram was brought up. A series of heavy thuds was followed by the noise of splintering wood. Men cheered. Leaning over the parapet, we watched the legionaries with their torches slip quickly through the ruptured gate, deploy around the base of the Capitol and fan out across the Forum to secure the main public buildings.

Cassius said, "Will they attack us tonight, do you think?"

"Why should they," replied Decimus bitterly, "when they can take us at their leisure in the daylight?" The anger in his tone suggested he held the others responsible, that he regarded himself as having fallen in among fools. "Your brother-in-law, Brutus, has proved more ambitious and more daring than you led me to believe."

Brutus, his foot tapping ceaselessly, did not respond.

Dolabella said, "I agree, a night attack would be too hazardous. Tomorrow is when they'll make their move."

Now Cicero spoke up. "The question is surely whether Lepidus is acting in alliance with Antony or not. If he is, then our position is frankly hopeless. If he isn't, then I doubt Antony will want him to have the sole glory of wiping out Caesar's assassins. That, gentlemen, I fear, is our best hope."

Cicero was now obliged to take his chances with the rest: it would have been far too risky to attempt to leave—not in darkness, with the place surrounded by potentially hostile soldiers and with Antony at large in the city. So there was nothing for it except to settle down for the night. It was to our advantage that the summit of the Capitol can only be approached in four ways: by the Moneta Steps to the north-east, the Hundred Steps to the south-west (the route we had climbed that afternoon) and by the two routes that lead up from the Forum—one a flight of stairs, the other a steep road. Decimus strengthened the guard of gladiators at the top of each and then we all retreated to the Temple of Jupiter.

I cannot say we got much rest. The temple was damp and chilly, the benches hard, the memory of the day's events too vivid. The dim light from the lamps and candles played upon the stern faces of the gods; from the shadows of the roof the wooden eagles looked down with disdain. Cicero talked for a while with Quintus and Atticus—quietly, so as not to be overheard. He couldn't believe how ill-thought-out the assassination had been. "Was ever a deed carried through with such manly resolution and yet such childish judgement? If only they *had* brought me into their confidence! I could at least have told them that if you are going to kill the devil, there's no point in leaving his apprentice alive. And how could they have neglected Lepidus and his legion? Or let an entire day go by with no attempt to seize control of the government?"

The edge of frustration in his voice, if not the words themselves, must have carried to Brutus and Cassius, who were sitting nearby, and I saw them look across at Cicero and frown. He noticed them too. He lapsed into silence and sat propped up against a pillar, huddled in his toga, doubtless brooding on what had been done, what hadn't, and what might be done yet.

With the dawn it became possible to see the main event that had occurred overnight. Lepidus had moved perhaps a thousand men into the city. The smoke from their cooking fires rose over the Forum. A further three thousand or so remained encamped on the Field of Mars.

Cassius, Brutus and Decimus convened a meeting to discuss what should be done. Cicero's proposal of the previous day, that they should summon the Senate to the Capitol, had plainly been overtaken by events. Instead it was decided that a delegation of ex-consuls, none of whom had been party to the assassination, should go to the house of Mark Antony and ask him formally, as consul, to convene the Senate. Servius Sulpicius, C. Marcellus and L. Aemilius Paullus, the brother of Lepidus, all volunteered to go, but Cicero refused to join them, arguing that the group would do better to approach Lepidus directly: "I don't trust Antony. Besides, any agreement reached with him will only have to be approved by Lepidus, who at the moment is the man with the power, so why not deal with him and cut out Antony altogether?" But Brutus's argu-ment that Antony had legal if not military authority carried the day, and in the middle of the morning the former consuls set off, preceded by an attendant carrying a white flag of truce.

We could do nothing now except wait and watch developments in the Forum—literally so, for if one was willing to scramble down to the roof of the public records office, one had a clear view of pro-ceedings. The entire space was packed with soldiers and civilians listening to speeches from the rostra. They crammed the steps of the temples and clung to the pillars; more still were pressing to enter from the Via Sacra and the Argiletum, which were backed up as far as the eye could see. Unfortunately we were too far away to be able to hear what was being said. Around noon, a figure in full military uniform and the red cloak of a general began to address the crowd and spoke for well over an hour, receiving prolonged applause: that, I was told, was Lepidus. Not long afterwards, another soldier—his Herculean swagger and his thick black hair and beard identifying him unmistakably as Mark Antony—also appeared on the platform. Again, I could not hear his words, but it was significant simply that he was there at all, and I hastened back to tell Cicero that Lepidus and Antony were now apparently in alliance.

The tension on the Capitol by this time was acute. We had had little to eat all day. Nobody had slept much. Brutus and Cassius expected an attack at any time. Our fate was out of our hands. Yet Cicero was oddly serene. He felt himself to be on the right side, he told me, and would take the consequences.

Just as the sun was starting to go down over the Tiber, the delegation of ex-consuls returned. Sulpicius spoke for them all: "Antony has agreed to call a meeting of the Senate tomorrow at the first hour in the Temple of Tellus."

Joy greeted the first part of his statement, groans the second, for the temple was right across town, on the Esquiline, very close to Antony's house. Cassius said at once, "That's a trap, to lure us out of our strong position. They'll kill us for sure."

Cicero said, "You may be right. But you could all stay here and I could go. I doubt they'd kill me. And if they did—well, what does it matter? I'm old, and there could be no better death than in defence of freedom."

His words lifted our hearts. They reminded us why we were here. It was agreed on the spot that while the actual assassins would remain on the Capitol, Cicero would lead a delegation to speak on their behalf in the Senate. It was also decided that rather than spend another night in the temple, he and all the others who were not actually part of the original conspiracy would return to their homes to rest before the debate. Accordingly, after an emotional farewell, and under the flag of truce, we set off down the Hundred Steps into the gathering twilight. At the foot of the stairs, Lepidus's soldiers had erected a checkpoint. They demanded Cicero go forward and show himself. Fortunately he was recognised, and after he had vouched for the rest of us, we were all allowed to go through.

·  ·  ·

CICERO WORKED ON HIS SPEECH LATE INTO THE NIGHT. BEFORE I went to bed he asked if I would accompany him to the Senate the next day and take it down in shorthand. He thought it might be his last oration and he wanted it recorded for posterity: a summation of all he had come to believe about liberty and the republic, the healing role of the statesman and the moral justification for murdering a tyrant. I cannot say I relished the assignment but of course I could not refuse.

Of all the hundreds of debates Cicero had attended over the past thirty years none promised to be tenser than this one. It was scheduled to begin at dawn, which meant that we had to leave the house in darkness and pass through the shuttered streets— a nerve-racking business in itself. It was held in a temple that had never before served as a meeting place for the Senate, surrounded by soldiers—and not just those of Lepidus but many of Caesar's roughest veterans, who on hearing the news of their old chief's murder had armed themselves and come to the city to protect their rights and take revenge on his killers. And finally when we had run the gauntlet of pleas and imprecations and entered the temple, it proved so cramped that men who hated and distrusted one another were nonetheless packed into close proximity so that one sensed that the slightest ill-judged remark might turn the thing into a bloodbath.

And yet from the moment Antony rose to speak it became clear that the debate would be different from Cicero's expectation. Antony was not yet forty—handsome, swarthy, his wrestler's physique fashioned by nature for armour rather than a toga. Yet his voice was rich and educated, his delivery compelling. "Fathers of the nation," he declared, "what is done is done and I profoundly wish it were not so, because Caesar was my dearest friend. But I love my country more even than I loved Caesar, if such a thing is possible, and we must be guided by what is best for the commonwealth. Last night I was with Caesar's widow, and amid her tears and anguish that gracious lady Calpurnia spoke as follows: 'Tell the Senate,' she said, 'that in the agony of my grief I wish for two things only: that my husband be given a funeral appropriate to the honours he won in life, and that there be no further bloodshed.'"

This drew a loud, deep-throated growl of approval, and to my surprise I realised the mood was more for compromise than revenge.

"Brutus, Cassius and Decimus," continued Antony, "are patriots just as we are, men from the most distinguished families in the state. We can salute the nobility of their aim even as we may despise the brutality of their method. In my view enough blood has been shed over these past five years. Accordingly I propose that we show the same clemency towards his assassins that was the mark of Caesar's statecraft—that in the interests of civic peace we pardon them, guarantee their safety, and invite them to come down from the Capitol and join us in our deliberations."

It was a commanding performance, but then of course Antony's grandfather was regarded by many, including Cicero, as one of Rome's greatest orators, so perhaps the gift was in his blood. At any rate he set a tone of high-minded moderation—so much so that Cicero, who spoke next, was entirely wrong-footed and could do little except praise him for his wisdom and magnanimity. The only point with which he took issue was Antony's use of the word "clemency":

"Clemency in my view means a pardon, and a pardon implies a crime. The murder of the Dictator was many things but it was not a crime. I would prefer a different term. Do you remember the story of Thrasybulus, who more than three centuries ago overthrew the Thirty Despots of Athens? Afterwards he instituted what was called an amnesty for his opponents—a concept taken from their Greek word *amnesia,* meaning "forgetfulness." That is what is needed here—a great national act not of forgiveness but of forgetfulness, that we may begin our republic anew freed from the enmities of the past, in friendship and in peace."

Cicero received the same applause as Antony and a motion was immediately proposed by Dolabella offering amnesty to all those who had taken part in the assassination and urging them to come to the Senate. Only Lepidus was opposed: not I am sure out of principle—Lepidus was never a man for principles—so much as because he saw his chance of glory slipping away. The motion passed and a messenger was dispatched to the Capitol. During the recess while this was being done, Cicero came to the door to talk to me. When I congratulated him on his speech, he said, "I arrived expecting to be torn to pieces and instead I find myself drowning in honey. What is Antony's game, do you suppose?"

"Perhaps there isn't one. Perhaps he is sincere."

Cicero shook his head. "No, he has some plan, but he's keeping it well hidden. Certainly he's more cunning than I gave him credit for."

When the session resumed, it soon became not so much a debate as a negotiation. First Antony warned that when the news of the assassination reached the provinces, particularly Gaul, it might lead to widespread rebellion against Roman rule: "In the interests of maintaining strong government in a time of emergency, I propose that all the laws promulgated by Caesar, and all appointments of consuls, praetors and governors made before the Ides of March should be confirmed by the Senate."

Then Cicero rose. "Including your own appointment, of course?"

Antony replied, with a first hint of menace, "Yes, obviously including my own—unless, that is, you object?"

"And including Dolabella's, as your fellow consul? That was Caesar's wish as well, as I recall, until you blocked it by your auguries."

I glanced across the temple to Dolabella, suddenly leaning forward in his place.

This was obviously a bitter draught for Antony to swallow—but swallow it he did. "Yes, in the interests of unity, if that is the will of the Senate—including Dolabella's."

Cicero pressed on. "And you confirm therefore that both Brutus and Cassius will continue as praetors, and afterwards will be the governors of Nearer Gaul and Syria, and that Decimus will in the meantime take control of Nearer Gaul, with the two legions already allotted to him?"

"Yes, yes and yes." There were whistles of surprise, some groans and some applause. "And now," continued Antony, "will your side agree: all acts and appointments issued before Caesar's death are to be confirmed by the Senate?"

Later Cicero said to me that before he rose to make his answer, he tried to imagine what Cato would have done. "And of course he would have said that if Caesar's rule was illegal, it followed that his laws were illegal too and we should have new elections. But then I looked out of the door and saw the soldiers and asked myself how we could possibly have elections in these circumstances—there would be a bloodbath."

Slowly Cicero got to his feet. "I cannot speak for Brutus, Cassius and Decimus, but speaking for myself, since it is to the advantage of the state, and on condition that what goes for one goes for all—yes, I agree that the Dictator's appointments should be allowed to stand."

"I cannot regret it," he told me afterwards, "because I could have done nothing else."

THE SENATE CONTINUED ITS DELIBERATIONS FOR THE WHOLE OF that day. Antony and Lepidus also laid a motion calling for Caesar's grants to his soldiers to be ratified by the Senate, and in view of the hundreds of veterans waiting outside, Cicero could hardly dare to oppose that either. In return Antony proposed abolishing forever the title and functions of dictator; it passed without protest. About an hour before sunset, after issuing various edicts to the provincial governors, the Senate adjourned and walked through the smoke and squalor of the Subura to the Forum, where Antony and Lepidus gave an account to the waiting crowd of what had just been agreed. The news was greeted with relief and acclamation, and this sight of Senate and people in civic harmony was almost enough to make one imagine the old republic had been restored. Antony even invited Cicero up onto the rostra, the first time the ageing statesman had appeared there since he had addressed the people after his return from exile. For a moment he was too emotional to speak.

"People of Rome," he said at last, gesturing to quiet the ovation, "after the agony and violence not just of the last few days but of the last few years, let past grievances and bitterness be set aside." Just at that moment a shaft of sunlight pierced the clouds, gilding the bronze roof of Jupiter's temple on the Capitol, where the white togas of the conspirators were plainly visible. "Behold the sun of Liberty," cried Cicero, seizing the moment, "shining once again over the Roman Forum! Let it warm us—let it warm the whole of humanity—with the beneficence of its healing rays."

Shortly afterwards Brutus and Cassius sent a message down to Antony that in view of what had been decided at the Senate, they were willing to leave their stronghold, but only on condition that he and Lepidus sent hostages to remain on the Capitol overnight as a guarantee of their safety. When Antony went up on to the rostra and read this aloud, there were cheers. He said, "As a token of my good faith, I am willing to pledge to them my own son—a lad of barely three, who the gods know I love more than any living thing. Lepidus," he said, holding out his hand to the Master of Horse who was standing next to him, "will you do the same with your son?"

Lepidus had little choice but to agree, and so the two boys—one a toddler, the other in his teens—were collected from their homes and taken with their attendants up on to the Capitol. As dusk fell, Brutus and Cassius appeared, descending the steps without an escort. Yet again the crowd roared its pleasure, especially when they shook hands with Antony and Lepidus, and accepted a public invitation to dine with them as a symbol of reconciliation. Cicero was also invited but he declined. Utterly exhausted by his efforts over the past two days, he went home to sleep.

AT DAWN THE FOLLOWING DAY THE SENATE MET AGAIN IN THE temple of Tellus; and once again I went with Cicero.

It was astonishing to enter and see Brutus and Cassius sitting a few feet away from Antony and Lepidus and even from Caesar's father-in-law, L. Calpurnius Piso. There were far fewer soldiers hanging around the door and the atmosphere was tolerant, indeed notable for a certain dark humour. For example when Antony rose to open the session he welcomed back Cassius in particular and said that he hoped this time he wasn't carrying a concealed dagger, to which Cassius replied that he wasn't, but would certainly bring a large one if ever Antony tried to set himself up as a tyrant. Everyone laughed.

Various items of business were transacted. Cicero proposed a motion thanking Antony for his statesmanship as consul, which had averted a civil war; it passed unanimously. Antony then proposed a complementary motion thanking Brutus and Cassius for their part in preserving the peace; that too was accepted without objection. Finally Piso rose to express his thanks to Antony for providing guards to protect his daughter Calpurnia and all Caesar's property on the night of the assassination.

He went on: "It remains for us now to decide what to do with Caesar's body and with Caesar's will. As regards the body, it has been brought back from the Field of Mars to the residence of the chief priest, has been anointed and awaits cremation. As regards the will, I must tell the house that Caesar made a new one six months ago, on the Ides of September, at his villa near Lavicum, and sealed and deposited it with the Chief Vestal. No one knows its contents. In the spirit of openness and trust that has now been established, I move that both these things—the funeral and the reading of the will—should be conducted in public."

Antony spoke strongly in favour of the proposal. The only senator who rose to object was Cassius. "This seems to me a dangerous course. Remember what happened the last time there was a public funeral for a murdered leader—when Clodius's followers burned down the Senate house? Just as we've established a fragile peace, it would be insanity to put it at risk."

Antony said, "From what I've heard, Clodius's funeral was allowed to get out of hand by some who might have known better." He paused for laughter: everyone knew he was now married to Clodius's widow, Fulvia. "As consul, I shall preside over Caesar's funeral, and I can assure you order will be maintained."

Cassius indicated by an angry gesture that he was still opposed. For a moment the truce threatened to break. Then Brutus rose. He said, "Caesar's veterans who are in the city will not understand it if their commander-in-chief is denied a public funeral. Besides, what sort of message will it send to the Gauls, already said to be contemplating rebellion, if we dump the body of their conqueror in the Tiber? I share Cassius's unease, but in truth we have no alternative. Therefore in the interests of concord and amity I support the proposal."

Cicero said nothing and the motion carried.

THE READING OF CAESAR'S WILL TOOK PLACE THE FOLLOWING DAY, a little way up the hill in Antony's house. Cicero knew the place well. It had been Pompey's main residence before he moved out to his palace overlooking the Field of Mars. Antony, in charge of auctioning the confiscated assets of Caesar's opponents, had sold it to himself at a knockdown price. It was not much changed. The famous battering rams of the pirate triremes, trophies of Pompey's great naval victories, were still set into the outside walls. Inside, the elaborate decoration had scarcely been touched since the old man's day.

Cicero found it unsettling to be back—the more so when he was confronted by the scowling face of the villa's new mistress, Fulvia. She had hated him when she was married to Clodius, and now that she was married to Antony she hated him all over again—and made no attempt to hide it. The moment she saw him, she ostentatiously turned her back and began talking to someone else.

"What a shameless pair of grave-robbers," Cicero whispered to me, "and how typical of that harpy to be here. Why *is* she, in fact? Even the widow isn't here. What business of Fulvia's is the reading of Caesar's will?"

But that was Fulvia. More than any other woman in Rome—

more even than Servilia, Caesar's old mistress, who at least had the grace to operate behind the scenes—Fulvia loved meddling in politics. And watching her move from visitor to visitor, ushering them towards the room where the will was to be read, I felt a sudden sense of unease: what if hers was the brain behind Antony's skilful policy of reconciliation? That would put it in a very different light.

Piso stood on a low table so that everyone could see him, and with Antony on one side and the Chief Vestal on the other, and with all the most prominent men of the republic listening in the audience, he first displayed the wax seal to show that it had not been tampered with, then broke it open and started to read.

To begin with, its meaning buried in legal jargon, the will seemed entirely innocuous. Caesar left his whole estate to any son that might be born to him after the drawing up of the document. However, in the absence of such a son, his wealth passed to the three male descendants of his late sister: that is to Lucius Pinarius, Quintus Pedius and Gaius Octavius, to be divided in the proportions one eighth each to Pinarius and Pedius and three quarters to Octavius, whom he now adopted as his son, henceforth to be known as Gaius Julius Caesar Octavianus ...

Piso stopped reading and frowned, as if he was not sure what he had just announced. *An adopted son?* Cicero glanced at me, screwed up his eyes in an effort at memory and mouthed, "Octavius?" Antony meanwhile looked as if he had been struck in the face. Unlike Cicero, he knew at once who Octavius was—the eighteen-year-old son of Caesar's niece Atia—and for him it must have been a bitter disappointment as well as a total surprise: I am sure he must have hoped to be named as the Dictator's main heir. Instead, he was merely mentioned as an heir in the second degree—that is, one who would inherit only if the first heirs died or turned down their legacy—an honour he shared with Decimus, one of the assassins! In addition, Caesar bequeathed every citizen of Rome the sum of three hundred sesterces in cash, and decreed that his estate beside the Tiber should become a public park.

The meeting broke up into puzzled groups, and afterwards,

walking home, Cicero was full of foreboding. "That will is a Pandora's box—a posthumous poisoned gift to the world that lets loose all manner of evils amongst us." He was thinking not so much of the unknown Octavius, or Octavian as he was now restyled, who promised to be a short-lived irrelevance (he was not even in the country but was in Illyricum); it was the mention of Decimus combined with the gifts to the people that troubled him.

All through the remainder of that day and throughout the next, preparations went on in the Forum for Caesar's funeral. Cicero watched them from his terrace. A golden tabernacle, built to resemble the Temple of Venus the Victorious, was erected on the rostra for the body to lie in. Barriers were put up to control the crowds. Actors and musicians rehearsed. Hundreds more of Caesar's veterans began to appear on the streets, carrying their weapons: some had travelled a hundred miles to attend. Atticus came round and remonstrated with Cicero for having allowed such a spectacle to go ahead: "You and Brutus and the others have all gone mad."

"It's easy for you to say that," replied Cicero, "but how was it to be prevented? We control neither the city nor the Senate. The crucial mistakes were made not *after* the assassination but *before* it—a child should have foreseen the consequences of simply removing Caesar and leaving it at that. And now we have the Dictator's will to contend with."

Brutus and Cassius sent messages to say that they intended to remain indoors throughout the day of the funeral: they had hired guards and advised Cicero to do the same. Decimus with his gladiators had barricaded his house and turned it into a fortress. Cicero, however, refused to take such precautions, although he prudently decided not to show himself in public. He suggested instead that I might attend the funeral and report back to him.

I did not mind going. No one would recognise me. Besides, I wanted to see it. I could not help feeling a certain secret regard for Caesar, who over the years had always been civil to me. Accordingly I went down into the Forum before dawn (this was now five days after the assassination—it was hard, amid the rush of events, to keep track of time). The centre of the city was already packed with thousands, women as well as men—not so much the polite citizenry but mostly old soldiers, the urban poor, many slaves, and a large contingent of Jews, who revered Caesar for allowing them to rebuild the walls of Jerusalem. I managed to work my way around the vast crowd to the corner of the Via Sacra, where the cortège would pass, and a few hours after daybreak I saw in the distance the procession start to leave the official residence of the chief priest.

It paraded right in front of me, and I was amazed by the planning that had gone into it: Antony and I am sure Fulvia had left out nothing that might be relied upon to inflame the emotions. First came the musicians, playing their haunting plangent dirges; then dancers dressed as spirits from the Underworld, who ran up shrieking to the front of the crowd striking poses of grief and horror; then came household slaves and freedmen carrying busts of Caesar; then not one but five actors went marching past representing each of Caesar's triumphs, wearing masks of the Dictator fashioned from beeswax that were so incredibly lifelike one felt he had risen from the dead five-fold in all his glory; then, carried on an open litter, came a life-size model of the corpse, naked except for a loincloth, with each of the stab wounds, including that to his face, depicted as deep red gashes in the white wax flesh—this caused the spectators to gasp and cry and some of the women to swoon; then came the body itself, lying on an ivory couch, carried on the shoulders of senators and soldiers and shrouded from view by covers of purple and gold, followed by Caesar's widow Calpurnia and niece Atia, veiled in black and holding on to one another, accompanied by their relatives; and finally came Antony and Piso, Dolabella, Hirtius, Pansa, Balbus, Oppius, and all the leading supporters of Caesar.

After the cortège had passed, there was a strange hiatus while the body was taken to the steps behind the rostra. Neither before nor afterwards did I ever hear such a profound silence in the centre of Rome in the middle of the day. During this ominous lull the leading mourners were filing on to the platform, and when at last the corpse appeared, Caesar's veterans began banging their swords against their shields as they must have done on the battlefield— a terrific, warlike, intimidating din. The body was placed carefully into the golden tabernacle; Antony stepped forward to deliver the eulogy, and held up his hand for silence.

"We come to bid farewell to no tyrant!" he declared, his power ful voice ringing round the temples and statues. "We come to bid farewell to a great man foully murdered in a consecrated place by those he had pardoned and promoted!"

He had assured the Senate he would speak with moderation. He broke that assurance with his opening words, and for the next hour he worked the vast assembly, already aroused by the spectacle of the procession, to a pitch of grief and fury. He flung out his arms. He sank almost to his knees. He beat his breast. He pointed to the heavens. He recited Caesar's achievements. He told them of Caesar's will—the gift to every citizen, the public park, the bitter irony of his honouring of Decimus. "And yet this Decimus, who was like a son to him—and Brutus and Cassius and Cinna and the rest— these men swore an oath—they made a sacred promise—to serve Caesar faithfully and to protect him! The Senate has given them amnesty, but by Jupiter what revenge I should like to take if pru dence did not restrain me!" In short he used every trick of oratory that the austere Brutus had rejected. And then came his—or was it Fulvia's?—masterstroke. He summoned up on to the platform one of the actors wearing Caesar's lifelike mask, who in a rasping voice declaimed to the crowd that famous speech from Pacuvius's tragedy *The Trial for Arms:*

> *That ever I, unhappy man, should save*
> *Wretches, who thus have brought me to the grave!*

The impersonation was uncannily good. It was like a message from the Underworld. And then, to groans of horror, the manikin of Caesar's corpse was raised by some mechanical contraption and rotated full circle so that all the wounds were shown.

From that point onwards Caesar's funeral followed the pattern of Clodius's. The body was supposed to be burned on a pyre already prepared on the Field of Mars. But as it was being borne down from the rostra, angry voices cried out that it should instead be cremated in Pompey's Senate chamber, where the crime was committed, or on the Capitol, where the conspirators had taken refuge. Then the crowd, with some collective impulse, changed its mind and decided that it should be burned on the spot. Antony did nothing to stop any of this but looked on indulgently as once again the bookshops of the Argiletum were ransacked and the benches of the law courts were dragged into the centre of the Forum and stacked in a pile. Caesar's bier was set upon the bonfire and torched. The actors and dancers and musicians pulled off their robes and masks and threw them into the flames. The crowd followed suit. They tore at their own clothes in their hysteria and these along with everything else flammable went flying on to the fire. When the mob started running through the streets carrying torches, looking for the houses of the assassins, I finally lost my nerve and headed back to the Palatine. On my way I passed poor Helvius Cinna, the poet and tribune, who had been mistaken by the mob for his namesake the praetor Cornelius Cinna, whom Antony had mentioned in his speech. He was being dragged away screaming with a noose around his neck, and afterwards his head was paraded around the Forum on a pole.

When I staggered back into the house and told Cicero what had happened, he put his face in his hands. All that night the sounds of destruction went on and the sky was lit up by the houses that had been set on fire. The following day Antony sent a message to Decimus warning that the lives of the assassins could no longer be protected and urging them to withdraw from Rome. Cicero advised them to do as Antony suggested: they would be more useful to the cause alive than dead. Decimus went to Nearer Gaul to try to take control of his allotted province. Trebonius travelled by a circuitous route to Asia to do the same. Brutus and Cassius retreated to the coast at Antium. Cicero headed south.

# XV

———•◦•———

HE WAS FINISHED WITH POLITICS, HE SAID. HE WAS FINISHED WITH Italy. He would go to Greece. He would stay with his son in Athens. He would write philosophy.

We packed up most of the books he needed from his libraries in Rome and Tusculum and set off with a large entourage, including two secretaries, a chef, a doctor and six bodyguards. The weather had been unseasonably cold and wet ever since the assassination, which of course was taken as yet another sign of the gods' displeasure at Caesar's murder. My strongest memory of those days spent travelling is of Cicero in his carriage composing philosophy with a blanket over his knees while the rain drummed continuously on the thin wooden roof. We stayed one night with Matius Calvena, the equestrian, who was in despair over the future of the nation: "If a man of Caesar's genius could find no way out, who will find one now?" But apart from him, in contrast to the scenes in Rome, we found no one who was not glad to see the back of the Dictator. "Unfortunately," as Cicero observed, "none of them has control of a legion."

He sought refuge in his work, and by the time we reached Puteoli on the Ides of April, he had completed one entire book—*On Auguries*—half of another—*On Fate*—and had begun a third—*On Glory*—three examples of his genius that will live for as long as men are still capable of reading. And no sooner had he got out of his carriage and stretched his legs along the seashore than he began sketching the outline of a fourth, *On Friendship* (*With the single exception of wisdom, I am inclined to regard it as the greatest of all the gifts the gods have bestowed upon mankind*), which he planned to dedicate to Atticus. The physical world might have become a hostile and dangerous place for him, but in his mind he lived in freedom and tranquillity.

Antony had dismissed the Senate until the first day of June, and gradually the great villas around the Bay of Naples began to fill with the leading men of Rome. Most of the new arrivals, like Hirtius and Pansa, were still in a state of shock at Caesar's death. The pair were supposed to take over as consuls at the end of the year, and as part of their preparation they asked Cicero if he would give them further lessons in oratory. He didn't much want to—it was a distraction from his writing, and he found their doleful talk about Caesar irritating—but in the end he was too easy-going to refuse. He took them on to the beach to learn elocution as Demosthenes had done, by speaking clearly through a mouth full of pebbles, and to learn voice projection by delivering their speeches into the crashing waves. Over the dinner table they were full of stories of Antony's high-handedness: of how he had tricked Calpurnia on the night of the assassination into giving him custody of her late husband's private papers as well as his fortune; of how he now pretended these documents contained various edicts that had the force of law, whereas in fact he had forged them in return for enormous bribes.

Cicero said, "So he has his hands on all the money? But I thought three quarters of Caesar's fortune was supposed to go to this boy Octavian?"

Hirtius rolled his eyes. "He'll be lucky!"

Pansa added, "He'll have to come and get it first, and I wouldn't give much for his chances."

Two days after this exchange, I was sheltering from the rain in the portico, reading the elder Cato's treatise on agriculture, when the steward came up to me to announce that L. Cornelius Balbus had arrived to see Cicero.

"Then tell the master he's here."

"But I'm not sure that I should—he gave me strict instructions that he was not to be disturbed, no matter who came to call."

I sighed and laid aside my book: Balbus was one man who would have to be seen. He was the Spaniard who had handled Caesar's business affairs in Rome. He was well known to Cicero, who had once defended him in the courts against an attempt to strip him of his citizenship. He was now in his middle fifties and owned a huge villa nearby. I found him waiting in the tablinum with a toga-clad youth I took at first to be his son or grandson, except when I looked more closely I saw that he couldn't be, for Balbus was swarthy whereas this boy had damp blond hair badly cut in a basin style; he was also rather short and slender, pretty-faced but with a pasty complexion pitted by acne.

"Ah, Tiro," cried Balbus, "will you kindly drag Cicero away from his books? Just tell him I have brought Caesar's adopted son to see him—Gaius Julius Caesar Octavianus—that ought to do it."

And the young man smiled shyly at me, showing gapped uneven teeth.

Naturally Cicero came at once, overwhelmed by curiosity to meet this exotic creature, seemingly dropped into the tumult of Roman politics from the sky. Balbus introduced the young man, who bowed and said, "It is one of the greatest honours of my life to meet you. I have read all your speeches and works of philosophy. I have dreamed of this moment for years." His voice was pleasant: soft and well educated.

Cicero fairly preened at the compliment. "You are very kind to say it. Now please tell me, before we go further: what am I to call you?"

"In public I insist on Caesar. To my friends and family I am Octavian."

"Well, since at my age I would find another Caesar hard to get used to, perhaps it could be Octavian for me as well, if I may?"

The young man bowed again. "I would be honoured."

And so began two days of unexpectedly friendly exchanges. It turned out that Octavian was staying next door with his mother Atia and his stepfather Philippus, and he wandered back and forth quite freely between the two houses. Often he appeared on his own, even though he had brought an entourage of friends and soldiers over with him from Illyricum, and more had joined him at Naples. He and Cicero would talk in the villa or walk along the seashore together in the intervals between showers. Watching them, I was reminded of a line in Cicero's treatise on old age: *just as I approve of the young man in whom there is a touch of age, so I approve of the old man in whom there is some flavour of youth . . .* Oddly enough, it was Octavian who sometimes seemed the older of the two: serious, polite, deferential, shrewd; it was Cicero who made the jokes and skimmed the stones across the sea. He told me that Octavian had no small talk. All he wanted was political advice. The fact that Cicero was publicly aligned with his adopted father's killers appeared to be neither here nor there as far as he was concerned. How soon should he go to Rome? How should he handle Antony? What should he say to Caesar's veterans, many of whom were hanging around the house? How was civil war to be avoided?

Cicero was impressed: "I can understand entirely what Caesar saw in him—he has a certain coolness rare in one of his years. He might make a great statesman one day, if only he can survive long enough." The men around him were a different matter. These included a couple of Caesar's old army commanders, with the hard, dead eyes of professional killers; and some arrogant young companions, two in particular: Marcus Vipsanius Agrippa, not yet twenty but already bloodied by war, taciturn and faintly menacing even in repose; and Gaius Cilnius Maecenas, a little older, effeminate, giggling, cynical. *"Those,"* said Cicero, "I do not care for *at all.*"

On only one occasion did I have an opportunity to observe Octavian closely for any length of time. That was on the final day of his stay, when he came to dinner with his mother and stepfather, along with Agrippa and Maecenas; Cicero also invited Hirtius and Pansa; I made up the nine. I noticed how the young man never touched his wine, how quiet he was, how his pale grey eyes flicked from one speaker to another and how intently he listened, as if he was trying to commit everything they said to memory. Atia, who looked as if she might have been the model for a statue commemorating the ideal Roman matron, was far too proper to voice a political opinion in public. Philippus, however, who certainly did drink, became increasingly voluble, and towards the end of the evening announced, "Well, if anyone wants to know *my* opinion, I think Octavian should renounce this inheritance."

Maecenas whispered to me, "*Does* anyone want to know his opinion?" and he bit on his napkin to stifle his laughter.

Octavian said mildly, "And what leads you to that opinion, Father?"

"Well, if I may speak frankly, my boy, you can *call* yourself Caesar all you like but that doesn't *make* you Caesar, and the closer you get to Rome the greater the danger will be. Do you really think Antony is just going to hand over all these millions? And why would Caesar's veterans follow you rather than Antony, who commanded a wing at Pharsalus? Caesar's name is just a target on your back. You'll be killed before you've gone fifty miles."

Hirtius and Pansa nodded in agreement.

Agrippa said quietly, "No, we can get him to Rome safely enough."

Octavian turned to Cicero. "And what do you think?"

Cicero dabbed carefully at his mouth with his napkin before replying. "Just four months ago your adopted father was dining precisely where you are now and assuring me he had no fear of death. The truth is, all our lives hang by a thread. There is no safety anywhere, and no one can predict what will happen. When I was your age, I dreamed only of glory. What I wouldn't have given to be in your place now!"

"So you would go to Rome?"

"I would."

"And do what?"

"Stand for election."

Philippus said, "But he's only eighteen. He's not even old enough to vote."

Cicero continued: "As it happens, there's a vacancy for a tribune: Cinna was killed by the mob at Caesar's funeral—they got the wrong man, poor devil. You should propose yourself to fill his place."

Octavian said, "But surely Antony would never allow it?"

Cicero replied, "That doesn't matter. Such a move would show your determination to continue Caesar's policy of championing the people: the plebs will love it. And when Antony opposes you—as he must—he'll be seen as opposing them."

Octavian nodded slowly. "That's not a bad idea. Perhaps you should come with me?"

Cicero laughed. "No, I'm retiring to Greece to study philosophy."

"That's a pity."

After the dinner, when the guests were preparing to leave, I overheard Octavian say to Cicero, "I meant what I said. I would value your wisdom."

Cicero shook his head. "I fear my loyalties lie in the other direction, with those who struck down your adopted father. But if ever there was a possibility of your reconciling with them—well then, in such circumstances, in the interests of the state, I would do all I could to help you."

"I'm not opposed to reconciliation. It's my legacy I want, not vengeance."

"Can I tell them that?"

"Of course. That's why I said it. Goodbye. I shall write to you."

They shook hands. Octavian stepped out into the road. It was a spring evening, not yet entirely dark, no longer raining either but with moisture still in the air. To my surprise, standing silently in the blue gloom across the street were more than a hundred soldiers. When they saw Octavian they set up the same din I had heard at Caesar's funeral, banging their swords against their shields in acclamation: it turned out these were some of the Dictator's veterans from the Gallic wars, settled nearby on Campanian land. Octavian went over with Agrippa to talk to them. Cicero watched for a moment, then ducked back inside to avoid being seen.

When the door was shut I asked, "Why did you urge him to go

to Rome? Surely the last thing you want is to encourage another Caesar?"

"If he goes to Rome he'll cause problems for Antony. He'll split their faction."

"And if his adventure succeeds?"

"It won't. Philippus is right. He's a nice boy, and I hope he survives, but he's no Caesar—you only have to look at him."

Nevertheless, he was sufficiently intrigued by Octavian's prospects to postpone his departure for Athens. Instead he conceived a vague idea of attending the Senate meeting Antony had summoned for the first of June. But when we arrived in Tusculum towards the end of May, everyone advised him not to go. Varro sent a letter warning that there would be murder. Hirtius agreed. He said, "Even I'm not going, and no one's ever accused *me* of disloyalty to Caesar. But there are too many old soldiers in the streets too quick to draw their swords—look what happened to Cinna."

Octavian, meanwhile, had arrived in the city unscathed and sent Cicero a letter:

*From G. Julius Caesar Octavianus to M. Tullius Cicero, greetings.*

*I wanted you to know that yesterday Antony finally agreed to see me at his house: the one that used to be Pompey's. He kept me waiting for more than an hour—a silly tactic that I believe shows his weakness rather than mine. I began by thanking him for looking after my adopted father's property on my behalf, invited him to take from it whatever trinkets he desired as keepsakes, but asked him to hand over the rest to me at once. I told him I needed the money to make an immediate cash disbursement to three hundred thousand citizens in accordance with my father's will. The rest of my expenses I asked to be met by a loan from the public treasury. I also told him of my intention to stand for the vacant tribunate and asked him for evidence of the various edicts he claims to have discovered in my father's papers.*

*He replied with great indignation that Caesar had not been king and had not bequeathed me control of the state; that accordingly*

*he did not have to give an account of his public acts to me; that*
*as far as the money went, my father's effects were not as great as*
*all that, and that he had left the public treasury bankrupt so there*
*was nothing to be got from there either; as for the tribunate, my*
*candidacy would be illegal and was out of the question.*

*He thinks because I am young he can intimidate me. He is*
*wrong. We parted on bad terms. Among the people, however, and*
*among my father's soldiers my reception has been as warm as*
*Antony's was cold.*

Cicero was delighted at the enmity between Antony and Octavian and showed the letter to several people: "You see how the cub tweaks the old lion's tail?" He asked me to go to Rome on his behalf on the first of June and report back what happened in the Senate meeting.

I found Rome, as everyone had warned us, teeming with soldiers, mostly Caesar's veterans whom Antony had summoned to the city to serve as his private army. They stood around on the street corners in sullen, hungry groups, intimidating anyone who looked as though they might be wealthy. As a result, the Senate was very thinly attended, and there was no one brave enough to oppose Antony's most audacious proposal: that Decimus should be removed from the governorship of Nearer Gaul and that he, Antony, should be awarded both of the Gallic provinces, together with command of their legions, for the next five years—exactly the same concentration of power that had set Caesar on the road to the dictatorship. As if this were not enough, he also announced that he had summoned home the three legions based in Macedonia that Caesar had planned to use in the Parthian campaign and placed these under his own command as well. Dolabella did not object, as might have been expected, because he was to receive Syria, also for five years; Lepidus was bought off with Caesar's old position of pontifex maximus. Finally, as this arrangement left Brutus and Cassius without their anticipated provinces, he arranged for them to be offered instead a couple of Pompey's old corn commissionerships—

one in Asia, the other in Sicily; they would have no power at all; it was a humiliation; so much for reconciliation.

The bills were approved by the half-empty Senate and Antony took them to the Forum the next day to be voted on by the people. The inclement weather continued. There was even a thunderstorm halfway through the proceedings—such a terrible omen that the assembly should have been dismissed at once. But Antony was an augur: he claimed to have seen no lightning and ruled that the vote could go ahead, and by dusk he had what he wanted. There was no sign of Octavian. As I turned to leave the assembly I saw Fulvia watching from a litter. She was soaked from the rain but did not seem to notice, so engrossed was she in her husband's apotheosis. I made a mental note to myself to warn Cicero that a woman who hitherto had been nothing more than a nuisance to him had just become a far more dangerous enemy.

The following morning I went to see Dolabella. He took me to the nursery and showed me Cicero's grandson, the infant Lentulus, who had just learnt to take a few wobbling steps. It was now more than fifteen months since Tullia's death, yet still Dolabella had not repaid her dowry. At Cicero's request I began to broach the subject ("Do it politely, mind you: I can't afford to antagonise him"), but Dolabella cut me off at once.

"It's out of the question, I'm afraid. You can give him this instead in full and final settlement. It's worth far more than money." And he threw across the table an imposing legal document with black ribbons and a red seal. "I've made him my legate in Syria. Don't worry, tell him—he doesn't have to *do* anything. But it means he can leave the country honourably and gives him immunity for the next five years. My advice, tell him, is that he should get out as soon as he can. Things are worsening by the day and we can't be held responsible for his safety."

I took the message back to Tusculum and relayed it verbatim to Cicero, who was sitting in the garden beside Tullia's grave. He studied the warrant for his legateship. "So this little piece of paper has cost me a million sesterces? Does he really imagine that waving this in the face of some illiterate half-drunk legionary would deter him from sticking his sword in my throat?" He had already heard what had happened at the Senate and in the public assembly, but wanted me to recite my precis of the speeches. At the end he said, "So there was no opposition?"

"None."

"Did you see Octavian at all?"

"No."

"No—of course not—why would you? Antony has the money, the legions and the consulship. Octavian has nothing but a borrowed name. As for us, we daren't even show our faces in Rome." He slumped against the wall in despair. "I tell you something, Tiro, between you and me—I'm starting to wish the Ides of March had never happened."

There was to be a family conference with Brutus and Cassius on the seventh day of June in Antium to decide their next steps: he had been invited and he asked me to accompany him.

We set off early, descending the hills just as the sun came up, and crossed the marshy land in the direction of the coast. The mist was rising. I remember the croaking of the bullfrogs, the cries of the gulls; Cicero barely spoke. Just before midday we reached Brutus's villa. It was a fine old place built right on the shoreline with steps cut into the rocks leading down to the sea. The gate was blocked by a strong guard of gladiators; others patrolled the grounds; more were visible walking on the beach—I guess there must have been a hundred armed men in all. Brutus was waiting with the others in a loggia filled with Greek statuary. He looked strained—the familiar nervous tapping of his foot was more pronounced than ever. He told us he had not left the house for two months—amazing considering he was urban praetor and not supposed to be out of Rome for more than ten days a year. At the head of the table sat his mother, Servilia; also present were his wife, Porcia, and his sister Tertia, who was married to Cassius. Finally there was M. Favonius, the former praetor known as Cato's Ape on account of his closeness to Brutus's uncle. Tertia announced that Cassius was on his way.

Cicero suggested I might fill in the time while we waited by giving a detailed account of the recent debates in the Senate and the public assembly, whereupon Servilia, who had ignored me up to that point, turned her fierce eye upon me and said, "Oh, so this is your famous *spy*?"

She was a female Caesar—that is the best way I can describe her: quick-brained, handsome, haughty, bone-hard. The Dictator had presented her with lavish gifts, including estates confiscated from his enemies and huge jewels picked up on his conquests, yet when her son arranged his murder and she was given the news, her eyes stayed as dry as the gemstones he had given her. In this too she was like Caesar. Cicero was slightly awed by her.

I stammered my way through the transcript of my notes, all the while conscious of Servilia's stare, and at the end she said with great contempt, "A grain commissionership in Asia! It was for this that Caesar was assassinated—so that my son could become a corn merchant?"

"Even so," said Cicero, "I think he should take it. It's better than nothing—certainly better than staying here."

Brutus said, "I agree with you on your last point at least. I can't stay hidden from view any longer. I'm losing respect with every day that passes. But Asia? No, what I really need to do is go to Rome and do what the urban praetor always does at this time of year—stage the Games of Apollo and show myself to the Roman people." His sensitive face was full of anguish.

"You can't go to Rome," replied Cicero. "It's far too dangerous. Listen, the rest of us are more or less expendable, but not you, Brutus—your name and your honour make you the great rallying point of freedom. My advice is to take this commission, do some honourable public work far away from Italy in safety, and await more favourable events. Things will change: in politics they always do."

At that moment Cassius arrived and Servilia asked Cicero to repeat what he'd just said. But whereas adversity had reduced Brutus to a state of noble suffering, it had put Cassius in a rage, and he started pounding on the table: "I did not survive the massacre at Carrhae and save Syria from the Parthians in order to be made a grain collector in Sicily! It's an insult."

Cicero said, "Well then, what will you do?"

"Leave Italy. Go abroad. Go to Greece."

"Greece," observed Cicero, "will soon be rather crowded, whereas first of all Sicily is safe, second you'll be doing your duty like a good constitutionalist, and third and above all you'll be closer to Italy to exploit opportunities when they arise. You must be our great military commander."

"What sort of opportunities?"

"Well, for example, Octavian could yet cause all sorts of trouble for Antony."

"Octavian? That's one of your jokes! He's far more likely to come after us than he is to pursue a quarrel with Antony."

"Not at all—I saw the boy when he was on the Bay of Naples, and he's not as ill-disposed towards us as you might think. 'It's my legacy I want, not vengeance'—those were his very words. His real enemy is Antony."

"Then Antony will crush him."

"But Antony has to crush Decimus first, and that's when the war will start—when Antony tries to take Nearer Gaul away from him."

"Decimus," said Cassius bitterly, "is the man who has let us down more than any other. Just think what we could have done with those two legions of his if he'd brought them south in March! But it's too late now: Antony's Macedonian legions will outnumber him two to one."

The mention of Decimus was like the breaking of a dam. Denunciations flowed from everyone round the table, Favonius especially, who maintained he should have warned them he was mentioned in Caesar's will: "That did more to turn the people against us than anything else."

Cicero listened in growing dismay. He intervened to say that there was no point in weeping over past errors, but couldn't resist adding, "Besides, if it's mistakes you're talking about, never mind

Decimus—the seeds of our present plight were sown when you failed to call a meeting of the Senate, failed to rally the people to our cause, and failed to seize control of the republic."

"Well upon my word!" exclaimed Servilia. "I never heard anything like it—to be accused of a lack of resolution by you of all people!"

Cicero glowered at her and immediately fell silent, his cheeks burning either with fury or embarrassment, and not long after that the meeting ended. My notes record only two conclusions. Brutus and Cassius agreed grudgingly at least to consider accepting their grain commissionerships, but only after Servilia announced in her grandest manner that she would arrange for the wording of the Senate resolution to be couched in more flattering terms. And Brutus reluctantly conceded that it was impossible for him to go to Rome and that his praetorian games would have to be staged in his absence. Apart from that the conference was a failure, with nothing decided. As Cicero explained to Atticus in a letter dictated on the way home, it was now a case of "every man for himself": *I found the ship going to pieces, or rather its scattered fragments. No plan, no thought, no method. Hence, though I had no doubts before, I am now all the more determined to escape from here, and as soon as I possibly can.*

The die was cast. He would go to Greece.

AS FOR ME, I WAS ALMOST SIXTY AND HAD PRIVATELY RESOLVED that the time had come for me to leave Cicero's service and live what remained of my life alone. I knew from the way he talked that he wasn't expecting us to part company. He assumed we would share a villa in Athens and write philosophy together until one or other of us died of old age. But I could not face leaving Italy again. My health was not good. And love him as I did, I was tired of being a mere appendage to his brain.

I dreaded having to tell him and kept postponing the fateful moment. He undertook a kind of farewell progress south through Italy, saying goodbye to all his properties and reliving old memo-

ries, until eventually we reached Puteoli at the beginning of July—
or Quintilis, as he still defiantly insisted on calling it. He had one
last villa he wished to visit, along the Bay of Naples in Pompeii,
and he decided he would leave on the first leg of his journey abroad
from there, hugging the coast down to Sicily and boarding a merchant ship in Syracuse (he judged it too dangerous to sail from
Brundisium, as the Macedonian legions were due to start arriving
any day). To convey all his books, his property and household staff,
I hired three ten-oared boats. He took his mind off the voyage,
which he dreaded, by trying to decide what literary composition
we should undertake while at sea. He was working on three treatises simultaneously, moving between them as his reading and his
inclination took him: *On Friendship*, *On Duties* and *On Virtues*. With
these he would complete his great scheme of absorbing Greek philosophy into Latin and of turning it in the process from a set of
abstractions into principles for living.

He said, "I wonder if this would be a good opportunity for us
to write our version of Aristotle's *Topics*? Let's face it: what could
be more useful in this time of chaos than to teach men how to use
dialectics to construct reasoned arguments? It could be in the form
of a dialogue, like the *Disputations*—you playing one part and I the
other. What do you think?"

"My friend," I replied hesitantly, "if I may call you that, I have
wanted for some time to speak to you but have not been sure how
to do it."

"This sounds ominous! You'd better go on. Are you ill again?"

"No, but I need to tell you I have decided not to accompany you
to Greece."

"Ah." He stared at me for what felt like a very long time, his jaw
moving slightly as it often did when he was trying to find the right
word. Finally he said, "Where will you go instead?"

"To the farm you so kindly gave me."

His voice was very quiet: "I see, and when would you want to
do that?"

"At any time convenient to you."

"The sooner the better?"

"I don't mind when it is."

"Tomorrow?"

"It can be tomorrow if you like. But that is not necessary. I don't want to inconvenience you."

"Tomorrow then." And with that he turned back to his Aristotle.

I hesitated. "Would it be all right if I borrowed young Eros from the stables and the little carriage, to transport my belongings?"

Without looking up he replied, "Of course. Take whatever you need."

I left him alone and spent the remainder of the day and the evening packing my belongings and carrying them out into the courtyard. He did not appear for dinner. The next morning there was still no sign of him. Young Quintus, who was hoping for a place on Brutus's staff and staying with us while his uncle tried to fix an introduction, said that he had gone off very early to visit Lucullus's old house on the island of Nesis. He put a consoling hand on my shoulder. "He asked me to tell you goodbye."

"He didn't say more than that? Just goodbye?"

"You know how he is."

"I know how he is. Would you please tell him I'll come back in a day or two to say a proper farewell?"

I felt quite sick, but determined. I had made up my mind. Eros drove me to the farm. It was not far, only two or three miles, but the distance seemed much greater as I moved from one world to another.

The overseer and his wife had not been expecting me so soon but nonetheless seemed pleased to see me. One of the slaves was called from the barn to carry my luggage into the farmhouse. The boxes containing my books and documents went straight upstairs into the raftered room I had selected earlier as the site for my little library. It was shuttered and cool. Shelves had been put up as I requested—rough and rustic, but I didn't care—and I set about unpacking at once. There is a wonderful line in one of Cicero's letters to Atticus in which he describes moving into a property and says: *I have put out my books and now my house has a soul.* That was how I felt as I emptied my boxes. And then to my surprise in one of them I discovered the original manuscript of *On Friendship*. Puzzled, I unrolled it, thinking I must have brought it with me by mistake. But when I saw that Cicero had copied out at the top of the roll in his shaking hand a quotation from the text, on the importance of having friends, I realised it was a parting gift:

> If a man ascended into heaven and gazed upon the whole workings of the universe and the beauty of the stars, the marvellous sight would give him no joy if he had to keep it to himself. And yet, if only there had been someone to describe the spectacle to, it would have filled him with delight. Nature abhors solitude.

I ALLOWED TWO DAYS TO PASS BEFORE I RETURNED TO THE VILLA IN Puteoli to say my proper goodbye: I needed to be sure I was strong enough in my resolve not to be persuaded out of it. But the steward told me Cicero had already left for Pompeii and I returned at once to the farm. From my terrace I had a sweeping view of the entire bay, and often I found myself standing there peering into the immense blueness, which ran from the misty outline of Capri right round to the promontory at Misenum, wondering if any of the myriad ships I could see was his. But then gradually I became caught up in the routine of the farm. It was almost time to harvest the vines and the olives, and despite my creaking knees and my soft scholar's hands, I donned a tunic and a wide-brimmed straw hat and worked outside with the rest, rising with the light and going to bed when it faded, too exhausted to think. Gradually the pattern of my former life began to fade from my mind, like a carpet left out in the sun. Or so I thought.

I had no cause to leave my property save one: the place had no bath. A good bath was the thing I missed most, apart from Cicero's conversation. I couldn't bear to wash myself only in the cold water from the mountain spring. Accordingly I commissioned the construction of a bathhouse in one of the barns. But that couldn't be done until after the harvest, and so I took to riding off every two or three days to use one of the public baths that are found everywhere along that stretch of coast. I tried many different establishments—in Puteoli itself, in Bauli and in Baiae—until I decided Baiae had the best, on account of the natural hot sulphurous water for which the area is famous. The clientele was sophisticated and included the freedmen of senators who had villas nearby; some of whom I knew. Without even meaning to, I began to pick up the latest gossip from Rome.

Brutus's games had passed off well, I discovered: no expense spared, even though the praetor himself was not present. Brutus had amassed hundreds of wild beasts for the occasion and, desperate for popular acclaim, he gave orders that every last one of them should be used up in fights and hunts. There were also musical performances and plays, including *Tereus,* a tragedy by Accius that contained copious references to the crimes of tyrants: apparently it received knowing applause. But unfortunately for Brutus, his games, although generous, were quickly overshadowed by an even more lavish set that Octavian gave immediately afterwards in honour of Caesar. It was the time of the famous comet, the hairy star that rose every day an hour before noon—we could see it even in the brilliantly sunny skies of Campania—and Octavian claimed it was nothing less than Caesar ascending into heaven. Caesar's veterans were greatly taken with this notion, I was told, and young Octavian's fame and reputation began to soar with the comet.

Not long after this I was lying one afternoon in a hot pool on a terrace overlooking the sea when some men joined me who I soon gathered by their talk were on the staff of Calpurnius Piso. He had a veritable palace about twenty miles away at Herculaneum and I suppose they must have decided to break their journey from Rome and complete their travelling the next day. I didn't consciously eavesdrop but I had my eyes closed and they may have thought I was sleeping. At any rate, I quickly pieced together the sensational intelligence that Piso, the father of Caesar's widow, had made an outspoken attack on Antony in the Senate, accusing him of theft, forgery and treason, of aiming at a new dictatorship and of setting the nation on the road to a second civil war. When one of them said, "Aye, and there's not another man in Rome with the courage to say it, now that our so-called liberators are all either hiding or have fled abroad," I thought with a pang of Cicero, who would have hated to know that he had been supplanted as an upholder of liberty by Piso, of all people.

I waited until they'd moved on before I climbed out of the pool. I remember I thought I would have a massage while I pondered what I'd just heard. I was moving towards the shaded area where the tables were set out when a woman appeared carrying a pile of freshly laundered towels. I cannot say I recognised her at once—it must have been fifteen years since I had last set eyes on her—but a few paces after we had passed one another I stopped and looked round. She had done the same. I recognised her then all right. It was the slave girl Agathe whose freedom I had bought before I went into exile with Cicero.

THIS IS CICERO'S STORY, NOT MINE; IT IS CERTAINLY NOT AGATHE'S. Nevertheless, our three lives were entwined, and before I resume the main part of my story I believe she deserves some mention.

I had met her when she was seventeen and a slave in the bath chambers of Lucullus's great villa in Misenum. She and her parents, by then dead, had been seized as slaves in Greece and brought to Italy as part of Lucullus's war booty. Her beauty, her gentleness and her plight all moved me. When I saw her next she was in Rome, one of six household slaves produced as witnesses at the trial of Clodius to support Lucullus's contention that Clodius, his former brother-in-law, had committed incest and adultery in Misenum with his ex-wife. After that I glimpsed her just once more, when Cicero visited Lucullus before going into exile. She seemed to me by then to be broken in spirit and half dead. Having some small savings put aside, on the night we fled Rome I gave the money to Atticus so that he could purchase her from Lucullus on my behalf and set her free. I had kept an eye out for her in Rome over the years but had never seen her.

She was thirty-six, still beautiful to me, although I could tell from her lined face and raw-boned hands that she still had to work hard. She seemed embarrassed and kept brushing back loose strands of grey hair with the back of her wrist. After a few awkward pleasantries there was a difficult silence and I found myself saying, "Forgive me, I am keeping you from your work—you will be in trouble with the owner."

"There will be no trouble on that score," she replied, laughing for the first time. "I *am* the owner."

After that we began to talk more freely. She told me she had tried to find me when she was freed, but of course by then I was in Thessalonica. Eventually she had come back to the Bay of Naples: it was the place she knew best and it reminded her of Greece. Because of her experience in the household of Lucullus, she had found plentiful work as an overseer in the local hot baths. After ten years some wealthy clients, merchants in Puteoli, had set her up in this place, and now it belonged to her. "But all this is because of you. How can I ever begin to thank you for your kindness?"

*Live the good life,* Cicero had said: *learn that virtue is the sole prerequisite for happiness.* As we sat on a bench in the sunshine, I felt I had proof of that particular piece of his philosophy, at least.


MY SOJOURN ON THE FARM LASTED FORTY DAYS.

On the forty-first, the eve of the Festival of Vulcan, I was working in the vineyard in the late afternoon when one of the slaves called out to me and pointed down the track. A carriage, accompanied by twenty men on horseback, was bouncing over the ruts, throwing up so much dust in the shafts of summer sunshine, it looked as if it was travelling on golden clouds. It drew up outside the villa and from it descended Cicero. I suppose I had always known in my heart that he would come looking for me. I was fated never to escape. As I walked towards him, I snatched off my straw hat and swore to myself that on no account would I be persuaded to return with him to Rome. Beneath my breath I whispered, "I will not listen ... I will not listen ... I will not listen ..."

I could see at once from the swing of his shoulders as he wheeled round to greet me that he was in tremendous spirits. Gone was the drooping dejection of recent times. He put his hands on his hips and roared with laughter at my appearance. "I leave you alone for a month and see what happens! You have turned into the elder Cato's ghost!"

I arranged for his entourage to be given refreshment while we went on to the shaded terrace and drank some of last year's wine, which he pronounced to be not bad at all. "What a view!" he exclaimed. "What a place to live out one's declining years! Your own wine, your own olives ..."

"Yes," I replied carefully, "it suits me very well. I shan't be going far. And your plans? What happened to Greece?"

"Ah well, I got as far as Sicily, whereupon the southerly winds got up and kept blowing us back into harbour and I began to wonder if the gods weren't trying to tell me something. Then, while we were stuck in Regium waiting for better weather, I heard about this extraordinary attack on Antony made by Piso. You must have heard the commotion even here. After that, letters came from Brutus and Cassius saying that Antony was definitely starting to weaken— they were to be offered provinces after all, and he had written to them saying he hoped they would soon be able to come to Rome. He has summoned the Senate for a meeting on the first of September and Brutus has sent a letter to all former consuls and praetors asking them to attend.

"So I said to myself: am I really going to run away at this of all moments, while there's still a chance? Will I go down in history as a coward? I tell you, Tiro, suddenly it was as if a thick mist that had enshrouded me for months had cleared and I saw my duty absolutely. I turned right around and sailed back the way I had come.

As it happened, Brutus was at Velia, preparing to set sail, and he practically went down on his knees to thank me. He's been given Crete as his province; Cassius has Cyrene."

I could not help pointing out that these were hardly adequate compensation for Macedonia and Syria, which was what they had been allotted.

"Of course not," replied Cicero, "which is why they're resolved to ignore Antony and his wretched illegal edicts and go straight to their original provinces. After all, Brutus has followers in Macedonia, and Cassius was the hero of Syria. They will raise legions and fight for the republic against the usurper. A whole new spirit has infused us—a flame pure white and sublime."

"And you will go to Rome?"

"Yes, for the meeting of the Senate in nine days' time."

"Then it sounds to me as though you have the most dangerous assignment of the three."

He waved his hand dismissively. "So what is the worst that can happen? I'll die. Very well: I'm past sixty; I've run my race. And at least this will be a good death—which as you know is the supreme objective of the good life." He leaned forwards. "Tell me: do I seem happy to you?"

"You do," I conceded.

"That's because I realised when I was stuck in Regium that finally I have conquered my fear of death. Philosophy—our work together—has accomplished that for me. Oh, I know that you and Atticus won't believe me. You'll think that underneath I'm still the same timid creature I always was. But it's true."

"And presumably you expect me to come with you?"

"No, not at all—the opposite! You have your farm and your literary studies. I don't want you to expose yourself to any more risk. But our earlier parting was not what it should have been, and I couldn't pass your gate without remedying that." He stood and opened his arms wide. "Goodbye, my old friend. Words are inadequate to express my gratitude. I hope we meet again."

He clasped me to him so firmly and for so long that I could feel the strong and steady beating of his heart. Then he pulled away, and with a final wave he walked towards his carriage and his body-guards.

I watched him go, his familiar gestures: the straightening of his shoulders, the adjustment of the folds of his tunic, the unthinking way he offered his hand to be helped into his carriage. I glanced around at my vines and my olive trees, my goats and my chickens, my dry-stone walls, my sheep. Suddenly it seemed a small world—a very small world.

I called after him: "Wait!"

# XVI

IF CICERO HAD PLEADED WITH ME TO RETURN WITH HIM TO ROME, I probably would have refused. It was his willingness to set off without me on the last great adventure of his life that piqued my pride and sent me chasing after him. Of course my change of heart did not surprise him. He knew me far too well. He merely nodded and told me to gather what I required for the journey, and to be quick about it: "We need to make good progress before nightfall."

I called my little household together in the courtyard and wished them luck with the harvest. I told them I would come back as soon as possible. They knew nothing of politics or Cicero. Their expressions were bewildered. They lined up to watch me leave. Just before the place disappeared from view, I turned to wave, but they had already returned to the fields.

It took us eight days to reach Rome, and every mile of the journey was fraught with peril, despite the guards that had been provided for Cicero by Brutus, and always the threat was the same: Caesar's old soldiers, who had sworn oaths to hunt down those responsible for the assassination. The fact that Cicero had known nothing of it beforehand did not concern them: he had defended it afterwards, and that was enough to render him guilty in their eyes. Our route took us across the fertile plains that had been given to Caesar's veterans to farm, and at least twice—once when we passed through the town of Aquinum and then soon afterwards at Fregellae—we were warned of ambushes up ahead and had to halt and wait until the road was secured.

We saw burnt-out villas, scorched fields, slaughtered livestock; even once a body hanging from a tree with a placard reading "Traitor" round its neck. Caesar's demobbed legionaries roamed Italy in small bands as if they were back in Gaul, and we heard many stories of looting, rape and atrocities. Whenever Cicero was recognised by the ordinary citizens, they flocked to him, kissed his hands and clothes and pleaded with him to deliver them from terror. Nowhere was the common population's devotion more evident than when we reached the gates of Rome on the day before the Senate was due to meet. His welcome was even warmer than when he returned from exile. There were so many deputations, petitions, greetings, handshakes and sacrifices of thanks to the gods that it took him nearly all day to cross the city to his house.

In terms of reputation and renown I guess he was now the pre-eminent figure in the state. All his great rivals and contemporaries—Pompey, Caesar, Cato, Crassus, Clodius—had died violent deaths. "They are not cheering me as an individual so much as the memory of the republic," he said to me when finally we got inside. "I don't flatter myself—I'm merely the last left standing. And of course demonstrating in support of me is a safe way of protesting against Antony. I wonder what *he* makes of today's outpouring. He must want to *crush* me."

One by one the leaders of the opposition to Antony in the Senate trooped up the slope to pay their respects. There were not many but I must mention two in particular. The first was P. Servilius Vatia Isauricus, the son of the old consul who had recently died aged ninety: he had been a strong supporter of Caesar and had only just returned from governing Asia—a difficult and arrogant man, he was deeply envious of Antony's dominant position in the state. The second opponent of Antony I have already mentioned: Lucius Calpurnius Piso, the father of Caesar's widow, who had been the first to raise his voice against the new regime. He was a sallow, stooping, hairy-faced old man with very bad teeth who had been consul at the time Cicero went into exile: for years he and Cicero had hated one another, but now they both hated Antony even more, and so in politics at least that made them friends. There were others present, but this was the pair who mattered most and they were of one voice in warning Cicero to stay away from the Senate the next day.

"Antony has laid a trap for you," said Piso. "He plans to propose a resolution tomorrow calling for fresh honours in memory of Caesar."

"Fresh honours!" cried Cicero. "The man is already a god. What other honours does he need?"

"The motion will state that every public festival of thanksgiving should henceforth include a sacrifice in honour of Caesar. Antony will demand to know your opinion. The meeting will be surrounded by Caesar's veterans. If you support the proposal, your return to public life will be destroyed before it even starts—all the crowds who cheered you today will jeer you as a turncoat. If you oppose it, you will never reach home alive."

"But if I refuse to attend I'll look like a coward, and what sort of leadership is that?"

Isauricus said, "Send word that you're too exhausted from your journey. You're getting on in years. People will understand."

"None of us is going," added Piso, "despite his summons. We'll show him up as a tyrant whom no one will obey. He'll look like a fool."

This was not the heroic return to public life that Cicero had planned, and he was reluctant to hide away at home. Still, he saw the wisdom of what they were saying and the following day he sent a message to Antony pleading tiredness as his excuse for not attending the session. Antony's response was to fly into a rage. According to Servius Sulpicius, who gave Cicero a full report, in front of the Senate he threatened to send a team of workmen and soldiers round to Cicero's house to tear down his door and drag him to the meeting. He was only deterred from such extreme action when Dolabella pointed out that Piso, Isauricus and a few others had also stayed away: he could hardly round up all of them. The debate went ahead and Antony's proposal to honour Caesar was passed, but only under duress.

Cicero was outraged when he heard what Antony had said. He

insisted he would go to the Senate the next day and make a speech, regardless of the risk: "I haven't returned to Rome in order to cower under my blankets!" Messages went back and forth between him and the others, and in the end they agreed to attend together, reasoning that Antony wouldn't dare to massacre them all. The following morning, shielded by bodyguards, they walked down in a phalanx from the Palatine—Cicero, Piso, Isauricus, Servius Sulpicius and Vibius Pansa (Hirtius could not join them because he really was ill)—all the way through the cheering crowds to the Temple of Concordia on the far side of the Forum, where the Senate was due to meet. Dolabella was waiting on the steps with his curule chair. He came over to Cicero and announced that Antony was sick and that he would be presiding in his place.

Cicero laughed. "So much illness going around at the moment— the entire state seems to be ailing! One might almost imagine that Antony shares the common characteristic of all bullies: eager to dish out punishment, unable to take it."

Dolabella replied coldly: "I trust you won't say anything today that will put our friendship in jeopardy: I've reconciled with Antony and any attack on him I'd regard as an attack on myself. Also I'd remind you that I did give you that legateship on my staff in Syria."

"Yes, although actually I'd prefer the return of my dear Tullia's dowry, if you don't mind. And as far as Syria is concerned—well, my young friend, I should make haste to get there, or Cassius might be in Antioch before you."

Dolabella glared at him. "I see you have abandoned your usual affability. Very well, but be careful, old man. The game is getting rougher."

He stalked away. Cicero watched him go with satisfaction. "I have wanted to say that for a long time." He was like Caesar, I thought, sending his horse to the rear before a battle: he would either win where he stood or die.

The Temple of Concordia was the place where Cicero had convened the Senate as consul all those years before, in order to debate the punishment of the Catiline conspirators; from here he had led them to their deaths in the Carcer. I had not set foot in it since and I felt the oppressive presence of many ghosts. But Cicero seemed immune to such memories. He sat on the front bench between Piso and Isauricus and waited patiently for Dolabella to call him—which he did, as late in the proceedings as he could and with insulting offhandedness.

Cicero started quietly, as was his way: "Before I begin to speak on public affairs, I will make a brief complaint of the wrong done to me yesterday by Antony. Why was I so bitterly denounced? What subject is so urgent that sick men should be carried to this chamber? Was Hannibal at the gates? Who ever heard of a senator being threatened with having his house attacked because he failed to appear to discuss a public thanksgiving?

"And in any case, do you think I would have supported his proposal if I had been here? I say: if a thanksgiving is to be given to a dead man, let it be given to the elder Brutus, who delivered the state from the despotism of kings and who nearly five hundred years later has left descendants prepared to show similar virtue to achieve a similar end!"

There was a gasp. Men's voices are supposed to weaken as they age; but not Cicero's on that day.

"I am not afraid to speak out. I am not afraid of death. I am grieved that senators who have achieved the rank of consul did not support Lucius Piso in June, when he condemned all the abuses now widespread in the state. Not one single ex-consul seconded him by his voice—no, not even by a look. What is the meaning of this slavery? I say these men have fallen short of what their rank requires!"

He put his hands on his hips and glared around him. Most senators could not meet his eye.

"In March I accepted that the acts of Caesar should be recognised as legal, not because I agreed with them—who could do that?—but for the sake of reconciliation and public harmony. Yet any act that Antony disagrees with, such as that which limits provincial commands to two years, has been repealed, while other decrees of the Dictator have been miraculously discovered and posted after his death, so that criminals have been brought back from exile—by a dead man. Citizenship has been given to whole tribes and provinces—by a dead man. Taxes have been imposed—by a dead man.

"I wish Mark Antony were here to explain himself—but apparently he is unwell: a privilege he did not grant me yesterday. I hear he is angry with me. Well, I will make him an offer—a fair one. If I say anything against his life and character, let him declare himself my most bitter enemy. Let him keep an armed guard if he really feels he needs it for his own protection. But don't let that guard threaten those who express their own free opinions on behalf of the state. What can be fairer than that?"

For the first time his words drew murmurs of agreement.

"Gentlemen, I have already reaped the reward of my return simply by making these few remarks. Whatever happens to me, I have kept faith with my beliefs. If I can speak again here safely, I shall. If I can't, then I shall hold myself ready in case the state should call me. I have lived long enough for years and for fame. Whatever time remains to me will not be mine, but will be devoted to the service of our commonwealth."

Cicero sat to a low rumble of approval and some stamping of feet. The men around him clapped him on the shoulder.

When the session ended, Dolabella swept out with his lictors, no doubt heading straight to Antony's house to tell him what had happened, while Cicero and I went home.

FOR THE NEXT TWO WEEKS THE SENATE DID NOT MEET AND CICERO stayed barricaded in his house on the Palatine. He recruited more guards, bought a ferocious new watchdog, and fortified the villa with iron shutters and doors. Atticus lent him some scribes, and these I set to work making copies of his defiant speech to the Senate, which he sent to everyone he could think of—to Brutus in

Macedonia, to Cassius en route to Syria, to Decimus in Nearer Gaul, to the two military commanders in Further Gaul, Lepidus and L. Munatius Plancus, and to many others. He called it, half seriously and half in self-mockery, his Philippic, after the famous series of orations Demosthenes had delivered in opposition to the Macedonian tyrant Philip II. A copy must have reached Antony: at any rate, he made known his intention to reply in the Senate, which he summoned to meet on the nineteenth day of September.

There was never any question of Cicero attending in person: being unafraid of death was one thing, committing suicide another. Instead he asked if I would go and make a record of what Antony said. I agreed, reasoning that my natural anonymity would pro-tect me.

The moment I entered the Forum, I thanked the gods that Cicero had stayed away, for Antony had filled every corner with his private army. He had even stationed a squadron of Iturean archers on the steps of the Temple of Concordia—wild-looking tribesmen from the borders of Syria, notorious for their savagery. They watched as each senator entered the temple, occasionally fitting arrows into their bows and pretending to take aim.

I managed to squeeze in at the back and take out my stylus and tablet just as Antony arrived. In addition to Pompey's house in Rome, he had also commandeered Metellus Scipio's estate at Tibur, and it was there that he was said to have composed his speech. He looked badly hungover as he passed me, and when he reached the dais, he leaned forward and vomited a thick stream into the aisle. This drew laughter and applause from his supporters: he was notorious for being sick in public. Behind me his slaves locked and barred the door. It was against all custom to take the Senate hostage in this manner, and clearly intended to intimidate.

As to his harangue against Cicero, it was in essence a continu-ation of his vomit. He spewed forth years of swallowed bile. He gestured around the temple and reminded senators that it was in this very building that Cicero had arranged for the illegal execution of five Roman citizens, among them P. Lentulus Sura, Antony's own stepfather, whose body Cicero had refused to return to his family for a decent burial. He accused Cicero ("this bloodstained butcher who lets others do his killing") of having masterminded the assassination of Caesar, just as he had the murder of Clodius. He maintained that it was Cicero who had artfully poisoned the relations between Pompey and Caesar that had led to civil war. I knew the charges were all lies, but also that they would be damaging, as would the more personal accusations he made—that Cicero was a physical and moral coward, vain and boastful and above all a hypocrite, forever twisting this way and that to keep in with all factions, so that even his own brother and nephew deserted him and denounced him to Caesar. He quoted from a private letter Cicero had sent him when he was trapped in Brundisium: *I shall always, without hesitation and with my whole heart, do anything that I can to accord with your wishes and interests.* The temple rang with laughter. He even dragged up Cicero's divorce from Terentia and his subsequent marriage to Publilia: "With what trembling, debauched and covetous fingers did this lofty philosopher undress his fifteen-year-old bride on her wedding night, and how feebly did he perform his husbandly duties—so much so that the poor child fled from him in horror soon afterwards and his own daughter preferred to die rather than live with the shame."

It was all horribly effective, and when the door was unlocked and we were released into the light, I dreaded having to return to Cicero and read it back to him. However, he insisted on hearing it word for word. Whenever I tried to miss out a passage or a phrase, he spotted it at once and made me go back and put it in. At the end he looked quite crumpled. "Well, that's politics," he said, and tried to shrug it off. But I could tell he was shaken. He knew he would have to retaliate in kind or retire humiliated. Trying to do so in person in the Senate, controlled as it was by Antony and Dolabella, would be too dangerous. Therefore his counter-charge would have to be made in writing, and once it was published there could be no going back. Against such a wild man as Antony, it was a duel to the death.

Early in October, Antony left Rome for Brundisium, in order to secure the loyalty of the legions he had brought over from Macedonia, and which were now bivouacked just outside the town. With Antony gone, Cicero also decided to retire from Rome for a few weeks and devote himself to composing his riposte, which he was already calling his Second Philippic. He headed off to the Bay of Naples and left me behind to look after his interests.

It was a melancholy season. As always in late autumn, the skies above Rome were darkened by countless thousands of starlings arriving from the north, and their chattering shrieks seemed to warn of some imminent calamity. They would nestle in the trees beside the Tiber only to rise in huge black flags that would unfurl overhead and sweep back and forth as if in panic. The days became chilly; the nights longer; winter approached and with it the certainty of war. Octavian was in Campania, very close to where Cicero was staying, recruiting troops in Casilinum and Calatia from among Caesar's veterans. Antony was trying to bribe the soldiers in Brundisium. Decimus had raised a new legion in Nearer Gaul. Lepidus and Plancus were waiting with their forces beyond the Alps. Brutus and Cassius had hoisted their standards in Macedonia and in Syria. That made a total of seven armies, formed or forming. It was merely a question of who would strike first.

In the event, that honour, if honour is the word, fell to Octavian. He had mustered the best part of a legion by promising the veterans a staggering bounty of two thousand sesterces a head—Balbus had guaranteed the money—and now he wrote to Cicero begging his advice. Cicero sent the sensational news to me to pass on to Atticus.

*His object is plain: war with Antony and himself as commander-in-chief. So it looks to me as though in a few days' time we shall be in arms. But who are we to follow? Consider his name; consider his age. He wanted my advice as to whether he should proceed to Rome with three thousand veterans or hold Capua and block Antony's route or go to join the three Macedonian legions now marching along the Adriatic coast, which he hopes to have on his side. They*

*refused to take a bounty from Antony, so he says, booed him
savagely, and left him standing as he tried to harangue them. In
short, he proffers himself as our leader and expects me to back him
up. For my part I have recommended him to go to Rome. I imagine
he will have the city rabble behind him, and the honest men too if
he convinces them of his sincerity.*

Octavian followed Cicero's recommendation and entered Rome
on the tenth day of November. His soldiers occupied the Forum.
I watched as they deployed across the centre of the city, securing
the temples and the public buildings. They remained in position
throughout that night and the whole of the following day while
Octavian set up his headquarters in Balbus's house and tried to
arrange a meeting of the Senate. But the senior magistrates were
all gone: Antony was trying to win over the Macedonian legions;
Dolabella had left for Syria; half the praetors, including Brutus and
Cassius, had fled Italy—the city was leaderless. I could see why
Octavian was pleading with Cicero to join him on his adventure,
writing to him once and sometimes twice a day: Cicero alone might
have had the moral authority to rally the Senate. But he had no
intention of putting himself under the command of a mere boy
leading an armed insurrection with precarious chances of success;
prudently he stayed away.

In my role as Cicero's eyes and ears in Rome, I went down to
the Forum on the twelfth to hear Octavian speak. By this time he
had abandoned his attempts to summon the Senate and instead
had persuaded a sympathetic tribune, Ti. Cannutius, to convene a
public assembly. He stood on the rostra under a grey sky waiting to
be called—slender as a reed, blond, pale, nervous; it was, as I wrote
to Cicero, "a scene both ridiculous and yet oddly compelling, like
an episode from a legend." He was not a bad speaker, either, once
he got started, and Cicero was delighted by his denunciation of
Antony ("this forger of decrees, this subverter of laws, this thief
of rightful inheritances, this traitor who is even now seeking to
make war upon the entire state ..."). But he was less pleased when I

reported how Octavian had pointed to the statue of Caesar that had been set up on the rostra and praised him as "the greatest Roman of all time, whose murder I shall avenge and whose hopes in me I swear to you by all the gods I shall fulfil." With that he came down from the platform to loud applause and soon afterwards left the city, taking his soldiers with him, alarmed at reports that Antony was approaching with a much larger force.

Events now moved with great rapidity. Antony halted his army—which included Caesar's famous Fifth Legion, "the Larks"— a mere twelve miles from Rome at Tibur and entered the city with a bodyguard of a thousand men. He summoned the Senate for the twenty-fourth and let it be known that he expected them to declare Octavian a public enemy. Failure to attend would be regarded as condoning Octavian's treason and punishable by death. Antony's army was ready to move into the city if his will was thwarted. Rome was gripped by the certainty of a massacre.

The twenty-fourth arrived, the Senate met—but Antony himself did not appear. One of the Macedonian legions that had booed him, the Martian, encamped sixty miles away at Alba Fucens, had suddenly declared itself for Octavian, in return for a bounty five times the size of that Antony had offered them. He raced off to try to win them back, but they mocked him openly for his stinginess. He returned to Rome, summoning the Senate for the twenty-eighth, this time to meet in an emergency session at night. Never before in living memory had the Senate gathered in darkness: it was contrary to all custom and the sacred laws. When I went down to the Forum intending to make my report for Cicero, I found it full of legionaries drawn up in the torchlight. The sight was so sinister I lost my nerve and did not dare to enter the temple, but instead stood around with the crowd outside. I saw Antony arrive, hotfoot from Alba Fucens, accompanied by his brother Lucius, an even wilder-looking character than him, who had fought as a gladiator in Asia and slit a friend's throat. And I was still there an hour later to see them both leave in a hurry. Never will I forget the rolling-eyed look of panic on Antony's face as he rushed down the temple steps. He had just been told that another legion, the Fourth, had followed the example of the Martian and had also declared for Octavian. Now he was the one who risked being outnumbered. Antony fled the city that same night and went to Tibur to rally his army and raise fresh recruits.

WHILE ALL THIS WAS GOING ON, CICERO FINISHED HIS SO-CALLED Second Philippic and sent it to me with instructions to borrow twenty scribes from Atticus and ensure it was copied and circulated as soon as possible. It took the form of a long speech—had it been delivered, it would have lasted a good two hours—and therefore rather than set each man to work making a single copy, I divided the roll into twenty parts and shared the pieces between them. In this way, once their completed sections were glued together, we were able to turn out four or five copies a day. These we sent to friends and allies with a request that they either make copies themselves or at least hold meetings at which the speech could be read aloud.

News of it soon spread. On the day after Antony withdrew from the city, it was posted in the Forum. Everyone wanted to read it, not least because it was filled with the most venomous gossip, for example that Antony had been a homosexual prostitute in his youth and was always falling down drunk and had kept a nude actress as his mistress. But I ascribe its phenomenal popularity more to the fact that it was also full of detailed information no one had dared disclose before—that Antony had stolen seven hundred million sesterces from the Temple of Ops and had used part of it to pay off personal debts of forty million; that he and Fulvia had forged Caesar's decrees to extort ten million sesterces from the king of Galatia; that the pair had seized jewels, furniture, villas, farms and cash and had divided it all up among themselves and their entourage of actors, gladiators, soothsayers and quacks.

On the ninth day of December, Cicero finally returned to Rome. I had not been expecting him. I heard the watchdog barking and went out into the passage to discover the master of the house standing there with Atticus. He had been away for nearly two months and looked to be in exceptionally good health and spirits. Without even taking off his cloak and hat he handed me a letter he had received the previous day from Octavian:

*I have read your new Philippic and think it quite magnificent—worthy of Demosthenes himself. I only wish I could see the face of our latter-day Philip when he reads it. I learn he has decided against attacking me here, no doubt nervous that his men would refuse to take the field against Caesar's son, and instead is marching his army rapidly to Nearer Gaul with the intention of wresting that province from your friend Decimus.*

*My dear Cicero, you must agree my position is stronger than we ever could have dreamed of when we met at your house in Puteoli. I am here now in Etruria seeking fresh recruits. They are flocking to me. And yet as ever I am in sore need of your wise advice. Can we not contrive a meeting? There is no man in all the world I would sooner speak with.*

"Well," said Cicero with a grin, "what do you think?"

I replied, "It's very gratifying."

"Gratifying? Come now—use your imagination! It's more than that! I've been thinking about it ever since I got it."

After a slave had helped him out of his outdoor clothes, he beckoned me and Atticus to follow him into his study and asked me to close the door.

"Here is the situation as I see it. Were it not for Octavian, Antony would have taken Rome and our cause would be finished by now. But fear of Octavian forced the wolf to drop his prey at the last moment and now he's slinking north to devour Nearer Gaul instead. If he defeats Decimus this winter and takes the province—which he probably will—he will have the financial base and the forces to return to Rome in the spring and finish us off. All that stands between us and him is Octavian."

Atticus said sceptically, "You really think Octavian has raised an army in order to defend what's left of the republic?"

"No, but equally is it in his interests to allow Antony to take control of Rome? Of course not. Antony at this juncture is his real enemy—the one who has stolen his inheritance and denies his claims. If I can persuade Octavian to see that, we may yet save ourselves from disaster."

"Possibly—but only to deliver the republic from the clutches of one tyrant into those of another; and a tyrant who calls himself Caesar at that."

"Oh, I don't know if the lad is a tyrant—I think I may be able to use my influence to keep him on the side of virtue, at least until Antony is disposed of."

"His letter certainly seems to suggest he would listen to you," I said.

"Exactly. Believe me, Atticus, I could show you thirty such letters if I could be bothered to find them, going all the way back to April. Why is he so eager for my counsel? The truth is the boy lacks a father figure—his natural father is dead; his stepfather is a goose; and his adopted father has left him the greatest legacy in history but no guidance on how to gain hold of it. Somehow I seem to have stepped into the paternal role, which is a blessing—not so much for me as for the republic."

Atticus said, "So what are you going to do?"

"I shall go and see him."

"In Etruria, in the middle of winter, at your age? It's a hundred miles away. You must be mad."

I said, "But you can hardly expect Octavian to come to Rome."

Cicero waved away these objections. "Then we'll meet halfway. That villa you bought the other year, Atticus, on Lake Volsinii— that would suit the purpose admirably. Is it occupied?"

"No, but I can't vouch for its comfort."

"That doesn't matter. Tiro, draft a letter from me to Octavian proposing a meeting in Volsinii as soon as he can manage it."

Atticus said, "But what about the Senate? What about the

consuls-designate? You have no power to negotiate on behalf of the republic with anyone, let alone with a man at the head of a rebel army."

"Nobody is wielding power in the republic any more. That's the point. It's lying in the dust waiting for whoever dares to pick it up. Why shouldn't I be the one to seize it?"

Atticus had no answer to that and Cicero's invitation went off to Octavian within the hour. After three days of anxious waiting Cicero received his reply: *Nothing would give me greater pleasure than to see you again. I shall meet you in Volsinii on the sixteenth as you propose unless I hear that that has become inconvenient. I suggest we keep our rendezvous secret.*

TO ENSURE THAT NO ONE WOULD GUESS WHAT HE WAS UP TO, Cicero insisted we leave in the darkness long before dawn on the morning of the fourteenth of December. I had to bribe the sentries to open the Fontinalian Gate especially for us.

We knew we would be venturing into lawless country, full of roaming bands of armed men, and so we travelled in a closed carriage escorted by a large retinue of guards and attendants. Once across the Mulvian Bridge we turned left along the bank of the Tiber and joined the Via Cassia, a road I had never travelled before. By noon we were climbing into hilly country. Atticus had promised me spectacular views. But the dismal weather Italy had endured ever since Caesar's assassination continued to curse us, and the distant peaks of the pine-covered mountains were draped in mist. For the entire two days we were on the road it barely seemed to get light.

Cicero's earlier ebullience had faded. He was uncharacteristically quiet, conscious no doubt that the future of the republic might depend on the coming meeting. On the afternoon of the second day, as we reached the edge of the great lake and our destination came into view, he began to complain of feeling cold. He shivered and blew on his hands, but when I tried to cover his knees with a blanket, he threw it off like an irritable child and said that although he might be ancient, he was not an invalid.

Atticus had bought his property as an investment and had only visited it once; still, he never forgot a thing when it came to money and he quickly remembered where to find it. Large and dilapidated— parts of it dated back to Etruscan times—the villa stood just outside the city walls of Volsinii, right on the edge of the water. The iron gates were open. Drifts of dead leaves had rotted in the damp court- yard; black lichen and moss covered the terracotta roofs. Only a thin curl of smoke rising from the chimney gave any sign it was inhab- ited. We assumed from the deserted grounds that Octavian had not yet arrived. But as we descended from the carriage, the steward hur- ried forward and said that a young man was waiting inside.

He was sitting in the tablinum with his friend Agrippa and he rose as we entered. I looked to see if the spectacular change in his fortunes was reflected at all in his manner or person, but he seemed exactly as before: quiet, modest, watchful, with the same unstylish haircut and youthful acne. He had come without any escort, he said, apart from two chariot drivers, who had taken their teams to be fed and watered in the town. ("No one knows what I look like, so I prefer not to draw attention to myself; it is better to hide in plain sight, don't you think?") He clasped hands very warmly with Cicero. After the introductions were over, Cicero said, "I thought Tiro here could make a note of anything we agree on and then we could each have a copy."

Octavian said, "So you're empowered to negotiate?"

"No, but it would be useful to have something to show to the leaders of the Senate."

"Personally, if you don't mind, I would prefer it if nothing were written down. That way we can talk more freely."

There is therefore no verbatim record of their conference, although I wrote up an account immediately afterwards for Cice- ro's personal use. First Octavian gave a summary of the military situation as he understood it. He had, or would have shortly, four legions at his disposal: the veterans from Campania, the levies he was raising in Etruria, the Martian and the Fourth. Antony had three legions, including the Larks, but also another entirely inexperienced, and was closing in on Decimus, whom he understood from his agents had retreated to the city of Mutina, where he was slaughtering and salting cattle and preparing for a long siege. Cicero said that the Senate had eleven legions in Further Gaul: seven under Lepidus and four under Plancus.

Octavian said, "Yes, but they are the wrong side of the Alps and are needed to hold down Gaul. Besides, we both know the commanders are not necessarily reliable, especially Lepidus."

"I shan't argue with you," said Cicero. "The position boils down to this: you have the soldiers but no legitimacy; we have the legitimacy but no soldiers. What we do both have, however, is a common enemy—Antony. And it seems to me that somewhere in that mixture must be the basis for an agreement."

Agrippa said, "An agreement you've just told us you have no authority to make."

"Young man, take it from me, if you want to make a deal with the Senate, I am your best hope. And let me tell you something else—it will be no easy task to convince them, even for me. There'll be plenty who'll say, 'We didn't get rid of one Caesar to ally ourselves with another.'"

"Yes," retorted Agrippa, "and plenty on our side who'll say, 'Why should we fight to protect the men who murdered Caesar? This is just a trick to buy us off until they're strong enough to destroy us.'"

Cicero slammed his hands on the armrests of his chair. "If that is how you feel, then this has been a wasted journey."

He made as if to rise, but Octavian leaned across and pressed down on his shoulder. "Not so fast, my dear friend. No need to take offence. I agree with your analysis. My sole objective is to defeat Antony, and I would much prefer to do that with the legal authority of the Senate."

Cicero said, "Let us be clear: you would prefer it even if—and this is what it *would* mean—you have to go to the rescue of Decimus, the very man who lured your adopted father to his death?"

Octavian fixed him with his cold grey eyes. "I have no problem with that."

From then on, there was no doubt in my mind that Cicero and Octavian would make a deal. Even Agrippa seemed to relax a little. It was agreed that Cicero would propose in the Senate that Octavian, despite his age, be given imperium and the legal authority to wage war against Antony. In return, Octavian would place himself under the command of the consuls. What might happen in the longer term, after Antony was destroyed, was left vague. Nothing was written down.

Cicero said, "You will be able to tell if I have fulfilled my side of my bargain by reading my speeches—which I shall send you—and in the resolutions passed by the Senate. And I shall know from the movements of your legions if you are fulfilling yours."

Octavian said, "You need have no doubts on that score."

Atticus went off to find the steward and came back with a jug of Tuscan wine and five silver cups which he filled and handed round. Cicero felt moved to make a speech. "On this day youth and experience, arms and the toga, have come together in solemn compact to rescue the commonwealth. Let us go forth from this place, each man to his station, resolved to do his duty to the republic."

"To the republic," said Octavian, and raised his cup.

"To the republic!" we all echoed, and drank.

Octavian and Agrippa politely refused to stay the night: they explained that they needed to reach their nearby camp before darkness as the next day was Saturnalia and Octavian was expected to distribute gifts to his men. After much mutual backslapping and protestations of undying affection, Cicero and Octavian said goodbye to one another. The young man's parting phrase I still remember: "Your speeches and my swords will make an unbeatable alliance." When they had gone, Cicero went out on to the terrace and walked around in the rain to calm his nerves while I out of habit cleared away the wine cups. Octavian, I noticed, had not touched a drop.

# XVII

———•———

CICERO HAD NOT EXPECTED TO HAVE TO ADDRESS THE SENATE UNTIL the first day of January, when Hirtius and Pansa were due to take over as consuls. But on our return we discovered the tribunes had summoned an emergency meeting to be held in two days' time to discuss the looming war between Antony and Decimus. Cicero decided that the sooner he made good on his promise to Octavian the better. Accordingly he went down to the Temple of Concordia early in the morning to show his intention of speaking. As usual I went with him and stood at the door to record his remarks.

Once word spread that Cicero was in his place, people began pouring into the Forum. Senators who might not otherwise have attended also decided they had better come to hear what he had to say. Within an hour the benches were packed. Among those who changed his plans was the consul-designate, Hirtius. He rose from his sickbed for the first time in weeks, and his appearance when he walked into the temple drew gasps. The plump young gourmet who had helped write Caesar's *Commentaries* and who used to entertain Cicero to dinners of swan and peacock had shrivelled to barely more than a skeleton. I believe he was suffering from what Hippocrates, the father of Greek medicine, calls a *carcino;* he had a scar on his neck where a growth had been recently removed.

The tribune who presided over the session was Appuleius, a friend of Cicero. He began by reading out an edict issued by Decimus denying Antony permission to enter Nearer Gaul, reiterating his determination to keep the province loyal to the Senate and confirming that he had moved his forces into Mutina. That was the town where I had delivered Cicero's letter to Caesar all those years before, and I recalled its stout walls and heavy gates: much would depend on whether it could hold out against a long siege by Antony's superior forces. When he had finished reading, Appuleius said, "Within days—perhaps even already—the republic will be gripped once more by civil war. The question is: what are we to do? I call on Cicero to give us his opinion."

Hundreds of men leaned forwards in anticipation as Cicero rose.

"This meeting, honourable gentlemen, comes not a moment too soon in my opinion. An iniquitous war against our hearths and altars, our lives and fortunes, is no longer just being prepared but is actually being waged by a profligate and wanton man. It is no good our waiting for the first day of January before we act. Antony does not wait. He's already attacking the eminent and remarkable Decimus. And from Nearer Gaul he threatens to descend on us in Rome. Indeed, he would have done so before now had it not been for a young man—or almost rather a boy, but one of incredible and near-godlike intelligence and courage—who raised an army and saved the state."

He paused to allow his words to register. Senators turned to their neighbours to check they had heard correctly. The temple became a hubbub of surprise mingled with some notes of indignation and gasps of excitement. Did he just say the boy had saved the state? It was a while before Cicero could continue.

"Yes, this is my belief, gentlemen, this is my judgement: had not a single youth stood up to that madman, this commonwealth would have utterly perished. On him today—and we are here today, free to express our views, only because of him—on him we must confer the authority to defend the republic, not as something merely undertaken by him, but as a charge *entrusted to him by us.*"

There were a few cries of "No!" and "He's bought you!" from Antony's supporters but these were drowned by applause from the rest of the Senate. Cicero pointed to the door. "Do you not see the packed Forum and how the Roman people are encouraged to hope for the recovery of their liberty? That now, after a long interval, when they see us assembled here in such numbers, they hope we have met together as free men?"

Thus opened what became known as the Third Philippic. It turned Roman politics on its axis. It lavished praise on Octavian, or Caesar, as Cicero now called him for the first time. ("Who is more chaste than this young man? Who more modest? What brighter example have we among youth of old-world purity?") It pointed the way to a strategy that might yet lead to the salvation of the republic. ("The immortal gods have given us these safeguards— for the city, Caesar; Decimus for Gaul.") But perhaps even more important, for tired and careworn hearts, after months and years of supine acquiescence, it fired the Senate with fighting spirit.

"Today for the first time after a long interval we set our feet in possession of liberty. It is to glory and to liberty we were born. And if the final episode in the long history of our republic has arrived, then let us at the least behave like champion gladiators: they meet death honourably; let us see to it that we too—who stand foremost of all nations on the earth—fall with dignity rather than serve with ignominy."

Such was the effect that when Cicero sat down a large part of the Senate immediately stood and rushed to crowd around him with their congratulations. It was clear that for the time being he had carried all before him. At Cicero's behest a motion was proposed thanking Decimus for his defence of Nearer Gaul, praising Octavian for his "help, courage and judgement," and promising him future honours as soon as the consuls-elect convened the Senate in the new year. It passed overwhelmingly. Then, most unusually, the tribunes invited Cicero rather than a serving magistrate to go out into the Forum and report to the people on what the Senate had decided.

He had told us before he went to meet Octavian that power in Rome was lying in the dust merely waiting for someone to pick it up. That was what he did that day. He climbed on to the rostra, watched by the Senate, and turned to face all those thousands of citizens. "Your incredible numbers, Romans," he bellowed at them, "and the size—the greatest I can ever remember—of this assembly, inspire me to defend the republic and give me the hope of re-establishing it!

"I can tell you that Gaius Caesar, who has protected and is protecting the state and your liberty, has just been thanked by the Senate!" A great swell of applause arose from the crowd. "I commend," shouted Cicero, struggling to make his voice heard, "I commend you, Romans, for greeting with the warmest applause the name of a most noble young man. Divine and immortal honours are due for his divine and immortal services!

"You are fighting, Romans, against an enemy with whom no peace terms are possible. Antony is not just a guilty and villainous man. He is a monstrous and savage animal. The issue is not on what terms we shall live, but whether we shall live at all, or perish in torture and ignominy!

"As for me, I shall spare no efforts on your behalf. We have today, for the first time after a long interval, with my counsel and at my instance, been fired by the hope of liberty!"

With that he took a pace backward to signal that his speech was over, the crowd roared and stamped their feet in approval, and the last and most glorious phase of Cicero's public career began.


FROM MY SHORTHAND NOTES I MADE A TRANSCRIPT OF BOTH speeches, and once again a team of scribes worked in relays to make copies. These were variously posted up in the Forum and dispatched to Brutus, Cassius, Decimus and the other prominent men in the republican cause. Naturally they were also sent to Octavian, who read them at once and replied within a week:

*From G. Caesar to his friend and mentor M. Cicero.*
   *Greetings!*
   *I enjoyed your latest Philippics very much. "Chaste . . .*
*modest . . . purity . . . godlike intelligence"—my ears are burning!*

*Seriously, don't lay it on too thick, mon vieux, as I can only be
a disappointment! I would love one day to talk to you about the
finer points of oratory—I know how much I could learn from you,
on this as on other matters. And so—onwards! As soon as I hear
word from you that my army has been made legal and I have the
necessary authority to wage war, I shall move my legions north to
attack Antony.*

All men now waited anxiously for the next meeting of the Senate, due to be held on the first day of January. Cicero fretted that they were wasting precious time: "It is the most important rule in politics always to keep things moving." He went to see Hirtius and Pansa and urged them to bring the session forward; they refused, saying they did not have the legal authority. Still, he believed he had their confidence and that the three of them would present a united front. But when the new year dawned, and the sacrifices had been conducted on the Capitol in accordance with tradition, and the Senate retired to the Temple of Jupiter to debate the state of the nation, he received a nasty shock. Both Pansa, who presided and made the opening speech, and Hirtius, who spoke next, expressed the hope that, grave though the situation was, it might still be possible to find a peaceful solution with Antony. This was not at all what Cicero wanted to hear.

As the senior ex-consul, he had expected to be called next and rose accordingly. But instead Pansa ignored him in favour of his father-in-law, Quintus Calenus, an old supporter of Clodius and a crony of Antony, who had never been elected consul but had only been appointed to the office by the Dictator. He was a stocky, burly figure, built like a blacksmith, and no great speaker, but he was blunt and heard with respect.

"This crisis," he said, "has been made out by the learned and distinguished Cicero to be a war between the republic on the one side and Mark Antony on the other. That's not correct, gentlemen. It's a war between three different parties: Antony, who was made governor of Nearer Gaul by a vote of this house and by the people;

Decimus, who refuses to surrender his command; and a boy who has raised a private army and is out for all he can get. Of the three, I know and personally favour Antony. Perhaps as a compromise we should offer him the governorship of Further Gaul instead? But if that's too much for the rest of you, I propose we should at the very least stay neutral."

When he sat, Cicero stood again. But again Pansa ignored him and called Lucius Piso, Caesar's ex-father-in-law, whom Cicero had also naturally counted as an ally. Instead Piso made a long speech, the gist of it being that he had always regarded Antony as a danger to the state, and still did, but having lived through the last civil war, he had no desire to live through another and believed the Senate should make one last attempt at peace by sending a delegation to Antony to offer him terms. "I propose that he should submit himself to the will of the Senate and people, abandon his siege of Mutina and withdraw his army to the Italian side of the Rubicon but no closer to Rome than two hundred miles. If he does that, then even at this late stage war may be averted. But if he does not, and war does come, at least the world will have no doubt who bears the blame."

When Piso had finished, Cicero did not even bother to stand, but sat with his chin sunk on his chest, glowering at the floor. The next speaker was his other supposed ally, P. Servilius Vatia Isauricus, who delivered himself of a great many platitudes and spoke bitterly of Antony, but even more bitterly of Octavian. He was a relative by marriage of Brutus and Cassius and raised a question that was in many minds: "Ever since he arrived in Italy Octavian has made the most violent speeches, swearing to avenge his so-called father by bringing his killers to justice. In so doing he threatens the safety of some of the most illustrious men in the state. Have they been consulted about the honours now being contemplated for Caesar's adopted son? What guarantees do we have that if we proceed to make this ambitious and immature would-be warlord the 'sword and shield of the Senate'—as the noble Cicero suggests—he won't turn round and use his sword against *us*?"

These five speeches, coming after the ceremonial opening, took up all of the short January day, and Cicero returned home with his prepared oration undelivered. "Peace!" He spat out the word. Always in the past he had been an advocate of peace; no longer. He jutted his chin in belligerence as he complained bitterly of the consuls: "What a pair of spineless mediocrities. All those hours I spent teaching them how to speak properly! And to what end? I would have been better employed teaching them how to think straight." As for Calenus, Piso and Isauricus, they were "addle-headed appeasers," "faint hearts," "political monstrosities"—after a time I stopped making a note of his insults. He retired to his study to rewrite his speech and the next morning sallied forth for the second day of the debate like a warship in full battle array.

From the moment the session began he was on his feet, and stayed there, signalling that he expected to be called next and would not take no for an answer. Behind him his supporters chanted his name, and eventually Pansa had no option but to indicate by his gestures that Cicero had the floor.

"Nothing, gentlemen," Cicero began, "has ever seemed longer to me in coming than the beginning of this new year and with it this meeting of the Senate. We have waited—but those who wage war against the state have not. Does Mark Antony desire peace? Then let him lay down his arms. Let him ask for peace. Let him appeal to our mercy. But to send envoys to a man on whom thirteen days ago you passed the heaviest and severest judgement is beyond a joke and is—if I must give my real opinion—madness!"

One by one, like the impact of missiles thrown by some mighty ballista, Cicero demolished the arguments of his opponents. Antony did not have any legal title to be governor of Nearer Gaul: his law was pushed through an invalid assembly in a thunderstorm. He was a forger. He was a thief. He was a traitor. To give him the province of Further Gaul would be to give him access to "the sinews of war: unlimited money"—the idea was absurd. "And it is to this man, great heavens, that we are pleased to send envoys? He will never obey anybody's envoys! I know the fellow's madness and arrogance. But time meanwhile will be wasted. The preparations for war will cool—they have already been dragged out by slowness and delay. If we had acted sooner we should not now be having a war at all. Every evil is easily crushed at birth; allow it to become established and it always gathers strength.

"So I propose, gentlemen, that we should send no envoys. I say instead that a state of emergency should be declared, that the courts should be shut, that military dress should be worn, that recruitment should be started, that exemptions from military service should be suspended throughout Rome and the whole of Italy, and that Antony be declared a public enemy . . ."

A spontaneous roar of applause and stamping feet drowned out the remainder of his sentence but he carried on speaking through it:

". . . if we do all that, he will feel that he has begun a war against the state. He will experience the energy and strength of a Senate with one mind. He says this is a war of parties. What parties? This war has not been stirred up by any parties but by him alone!

"And now I come to Gaius Caesar, upon whom my friend Isauricus heaped such scorn and suspicion. Yet if he had not lived, who of us could have been alive now? What god presented to the Roman people this heaven-sent boy? By his protection the tyranny of Antony was thwarted. Let us therefore give Caesar the necessary command, without which no military affairs can be administered, no army held together, no war waged. Let him be pro-praetor with the maximum power of a regular appointment.

"On him our hope of liberty rests. I know this young man. Nothing is dearer to him than the republic, nothing more important than your authority, nothing more desirable than the opinion of good men, nothing sweeter than genuine glory. I shall even venture to give you my word, gentlemen—to you and to the Roman people: I promise, I undertake, I solemnly pledge that Gaius Caesar will always be such a citizen as he is today, the citizen that we all most earnestly wish and pray that he should be."

That speech, and in particular that guarantee, changed everything. I believe it can truly be asserted—and it is a rare boast for any oration—that if Cicero had not delivered his Fifth Philippic, then history would have been different, for opinion in the Senate was almost evenly divided, and until he spoke, the debate was running Antony's way. Now his words stemmed the tide and the votes started to flow back in favour of war. Indeed, Cicero might have won on every point if a tribune named Salvius had not interposed his veto, prolonging the debate into a fourth day, and giving Antony's wife, Fulvia, the chance to appear at the door of the temple to plead for moderation. She was accompanied by her infant son—the one who had been sent up to the Capitol as a hostage—and by Antony's elderly mother, Julia, who was a cousin of Julius Caesar and greatly admired for her noble bearing. They were all dressed in black and made a most affecting spectacle, three generations walking down the aisle of the Senate with their hands clasped in supplication. Every senator was aware that if Antony was to be named a public enemy, all his property would be seized and they would be thrown out on to the streets.

"Spare us this humiliation," cried out Fulvia, "we beseech you!"

The vote to declare Antony an enemy of the state was duly lost, while the motion to send a delegation of envoys to make him a final peace offer was carried. The rest, however, was all for Cicero: Octavian's army was recognised as legitimate and incorporated with Decimus's under the standard of the Senate; Octavian was made a senator, despite his youth, and also awarded a pro-praetorship with power of imperium; as a nod to the future, the age requirement for the consulship was lowered by ten years (although it would still be another thirteen before Octavian was eligible to stand); the loyalty of Plancus and Lepidus was bought, the one being confirmed as consul for the following year, the other being honoured by a gilded equestrian statue on the rostra; and the raising of new armies and the imposition of a state of military preparedness in Rome and all across Italy was ordered to begin immediately.

Once again the tribunes asked Cicero, rather than the consuls, to convey the Senate's decisions to the thousands gathered in the

Forum. When he told them that peace envoys were to be sent to Antony, a collective groan went up. Cicero made a soothing gesture with his hands. "I gather, Romans, that this course is also repudiated by you, as it was by me, and with good reason. But I urge you to be patient. What I did earlier in the Senate I will do before you now. I predict that Mark Antony will ignore the envoys, devastate the land, besiege Mutina and raise more troops. And I am not afraid that when he hears what I have said, he will change his plans and obey the Senate in order to refute me: he is too far gone for that. We shall lose some precious time, but never fear: we shall have victory in the end. Other nations can endure slavery, but the most prized possession of the Roman people is liberty."

THE PEACE DELEGATION LEFT THE NEXT DAY FROM THE FORUM. Cicero went with an ill grace to see them off. The chosen envoys were three ex-consuls: Lucius Piso, who had come up with the idea in the first place and so could hardly refuse to take part; Marcus Philippus, Octavian's stepfather, whose participation Cicero called "disgusting and scandalous"; and Cicero's old friend Servius Sulpicius, who was in such poor health that Cicero begged him to reconsider: "It's two hundred and fifty miles in midwinter, through snow and wolves and bandits, and with only the amenities of an army camp at the end of it. For pity's sake, my dear Servius, use your illness as an excuse and let them find someone else."

"You forget I was at Pompey's side at Pharsalus. I stood and watched the slaughter of the best men in the state. My last service to the republic will be to try to stop that happening again."

"Your instincts are as noble as ever, but your hold on reality is poor. Antony will laugh in your face. All that your suffering will accomplish is to help prolong the war."

Servius looked at him sadly. "What happened to my old friend who hated soldiering and loved his books? I rather miss him. I certainly preferred him to this rabble-rouser who stirs up the crowd for blood."

With that he climbed stiffly into his litter and was borne away with the others to begin the long journey.

Preparations for war now slowed to a half-hearted pace, as Cicero had warned they would, while Romans awaited the outcome of the peace mission. Although levies took place across Italy to recruit four new legions, there was no great sense of urgency now that the immediate threat seemed to have been lifted. In the meantime, the only legions the Senate could draw on were the two encamped near Rome that had declared for Octavian—the Martian and the Fourth—and after receiving permission from Octavian, these agreed to march north to relieve Decimus under the command of one of the consuls. Lots for the office had to be drawn in accordance with the law, and by a cruel jest of the gods it went to the sick man, Hirtius. Watching this ghostly figure in his red cloak painfully ascend the steps of the Capitol, perform the traditional sacrifice of a white bull to Jupiter and then ride off to war filled Cicero with foreboding.

IT WAS TO BE ALMOST A MONTH BEFORE THE CITY'S HERALD announced that the returning peace envoys were approaching the city. Pansa summoned the Senate to hear their report that same day. Only two of them came into the temple—Piso and Philippus. Piso stood and in a grave voice announced that the gallant Servius had no sooner reached Antony's headquarters than he had died of exhaustion. Because of the distance involved, and the slowness of winter travel, it had been necessary to cremate him on the spot rather than bring the body home.

"I have to tell you, gentlemen, that we found that Antony has surrounded Mutina with a very powerful system of siege works, and throughout our time in his camp he continued to pound the town with missiles. He refused to allow us safe passage through his lines to talk to Decimus. As to the terms you had empowered us to offer him, he rejected them in favour of terms of his own." Piso produced a letter and began to read. "He will give up his claim to the governorship of Nearer Gaul but only if he is compensated by the award instead of Further Gaul for five years together with the command of Decimus's army, raising his total strength to six legions. He demands that all the decrees he has issued in Caesar's name should be declared legal; that there should be no further investigation into the disappearance of the state's treasury from the Temple of Ops; that his followers should be given an amnesty; and finally that his soldiers should be paid what they are owed and also awarded land."

Piso rolled up the document and tucked it into his sleeve. "We have done our best, gentlemen. I am disappointed, I will not hide it. I fear this house must recognise that a state of war exists between the republic and Mark Antony."

Cicero got to his feet, but yet again Pansa called his father-in-law, Calenus, to speak first. He said: "I deplore the use of the word 'war.' On the contrary, I believe we have here, gentlemen, the basis for an honourable peace. It was my suggestion, first made in this Senate, that Antony should be offered Further Gaul, and I am glad that he has accepted it. Our main points are all met. Decimus remains as governor. The people of Mutina are spared any further misery. Roman does not take up arms against Roman. I can see by the way he shakes his head that Cicero does not like what I am saying. He is an angry man. But more than that, I venture to say that he is an angry *old* man. Let me remind him that it will not be men of our age who die in this new war. It will be his son, and my son, and yours, gentlemen—and yours, and yours, and yours. I say let us have a truce with Antony and reconcile our differences peacefully as our gallant colleagues Piso, Philippus and the lamented Servius have shown us how to do."

Calenus's speech was warmly received. It was clear that Antony still had his supporters in the Senate, including his legate, the diminutive Cotyla, or "Half-Pint," whom he had sent south to report on the mood in Rome. As Pansa called speaker after speaker—including Antony's uncle, Lucius Caesar, who said he felt duty-bound to defend his nephew—Cotyla ostentatiously made notes of their remarks, presumably so that he could report them back to his master. It had an oddly unnerving effect, and at the end of the day, a majority of the house, including Pansa, voted to remove the word "war" from the motion and declare instead that the country was in a state of "tumult."

Pansa did not call Cicero until the following morning. But once again this worked to Cicero's advantage. Not only did he rise in an atmosphere of intense expectation; he was able to attack the arguments of the previous speakers. He started with Lucius Caesar: "He excuses his vote because of his family connections. He is an uncle. Fair enough. But are the rest of you uncles too?"

And once he had his audience laughing—once he had softened the ground, so to speak—he proceeded to pulverise them with a cataract of invective and derision. "Decimus is being attacked— there is no war. Mutina is being besieged—not even this is war. Gaul is being laid waste—what could be more peaceful? Gentlemen, this is a war such as has never been seen before! We are defending the temples of the immortal gods, our walls, our homes, and the birthrights of the Roman people, the altars, hearths and tombs of our ancestors; we are defending our laws, law courts, liberty, wives, children, fatherland. On the other side, Mark Antony fights to wreck all this and plunder the state.

"At this point my brave and energetic friend Calenus reminds me of the advantages of peace. But I ask you, Calenus: what do you mean? Do you call slavery peace? Heavy fighting is in progress. We have sent three leading members of the Senate to intervene. These Antony has repudiated with contempt. Yet you remain his most constant defender!

"With what dishonour did yesterday dawn upon us! 'Oh, but what if he were to make a truce?' A truce? In the presence, before the very eyes of the envoys he pounded Mutina with his engines. He showed them his works and his siege train. Not for a moment, although the envoys were there, did the siege find a breathing space. Envoys to this man? Peace with this man?

"I will say it with grief rather than with insult: we are deserted—

deserted, gentlemen—by our leaders. What concessions have we not made to Cotyla, the envoy of Mark Antony? Though by rights the gates of this city should have been closed to him, yet this temple was open. He came into the Senate. He entered in his notebooks your votes and everything you said. Even those who had filled the highest offices were currying favour with him to the disgrace of their dignity. Ye immortal gods! Where is the ancient spirit of our ancestors? Let Cotyla return to his general but on condition that he never returns to Rome."

The Senate sat stunned. They had not been shamed in such a fashion since Cato's day. At the end, Cicero laid a fresh motion: that those fighting with Antony would be given until the Ides of March to lay down their arms; after that, any who continued in his army, or who went to join him, would be regarded as traitors. The proposal passed overwhelmingly. There was to be no truce, no peace, no deal; Cicero had his war.

A DAY OR TWO AFTER THE FIRST ANNIVERSARY OF CAESAR'S assassination—an occasion that passed without notice apart from the laying of flowers on his tomb—Pansa followed his colleague Hirtius into battle. The consul rode off from the Field of Mars at the head of an army of four legions: almost twenty thousand men scoured from every corner of Italy. Cicero watched with the rest of the Senate as they paraded past. As a military force it was less impressive than it sounded. Most were the rawest of recruits— farmers, ostlers, bakers and laundrymen who could barely even march in time. Their real power was symbolic. The republic was in arms against the usurper Antony.

With both consuls gone, the most senior magistrate left behind in the city was the urban praetor, Marcus Cornutus—a soldier picked by Caesar for his loyalty and discretion. He now found himself required to preside over the Senate even though he had minimal experience of politics. He soon placed himself entirely in the hands of Cicero, who thus, at the age of sixty-three, became the effective ruler of Rome for the first time since his consulship twenty years before. It was to Cicero that all the imperial governors addressed their reports. It was he who decided when the Senate should meet. It was he who made the main appointments. His was the house that was packed all day with petitioners.

He sent an amused account of his *redux* to Octavian:

> *I do not think I boast when I say that nothing can happen in this city these days without my approval. Indeed it is actually better than a consulship because no one knows where my power begins or ends; therefore rather than run the risk of offending me, everyone consults me on everything. Actually it is even better, come to think of it, than a dictatorship, because nobody holds me to blame when things go wrong! It is proof that one should never mistake the baubles of office for actual power—another piece of avuncular advice for your glittering future, my boy, from your devoted old friend and mentor.*

Octavian wrote back at the end of March to report that he was doing as he had promised: his army of nearly ten thousand men was striking camp just south of Bononia, beside the Via Aemilia, and moving off to join the armies of Hirtius and Pansa in relieving the siege of Mutina:

> *I am placing myself under the command of the consuls. We are expecting a great battle with Antony within the next two weeks. I promise that I shall endeavour to perform as valiantly in the field as you have in the Senate. What was it that the Spartan warriors said? "I shall return either with my shield, or on it."*

Around this time, word began to reach Cicero of events in the east. From Brutus in Macedonia he learned that Dolabella—heading for Syria at the head of a small force—had reached as far as Smyrna on the eastern shores of the Aegean, where he had encountered the governor of Asia, Trebonius. Trebonius had treated him civilly enough and even allowed him to proceed on his way. But that night Dolabella had secretly turned back, entered the city, seized Trebonius while he was asleep, and subjected him to two days and nights of intensive torture, using whips, the rack and hot irons, to force him to disclose the whereabouts of his treasury. After that, on Dolabella's orders, his neck was broken. His head was cut off and Dolabella's soldiers kicked it back and forth through the streets until it was completely crushed, while his body was mutilated and placed on public display. "Thus dies the first of the assassins who murdered Caesar," Dolabella was said to have declared. "The first—but he will not be the last."

Trebonius's remains were shipped to Rome and subjected to a post-mortem examination to confirm the manner of his death before being passed to his family for cremation. His grisly fate had a salutary effect on Cicero and the other leaders of the republic. They knew now what to expect if they fell into the hands of their enemies, especially when Antony issued an open letter to the consuls pledging his loyalty to Dolabella and expressing his delight at Trebonius's fate: *That a criminal has paid the penalty is a matter for rejoicing.* Cicero read the letter out loud in the Senate: it strengthened men's determination not to compromise. Dolabella was declared a public enemy. It was a particular shock to Cicero that his former son-in-law should have exhibited such cruelty. He lamented to me afterwards: "To think that such a monster stayed under my roof and shared a bed with my poor dear daughter; to think that I actually *liked* the man ... Who knows what animals lurk within the people who are close to us?"

The nervous strain under which he lived during those early days of April, while waiting for word from Mutina, was indescribable. First there would be good news. After months without contact, Cassius at last wrote to say that he was taking complete control of Syria: that all sides—Caesareans, republicans and the last remaining Pompeians—were flocking to him and that he had under his command a united army of no fewer than eleven legions. *I want you to know that you and your friends at the Senate are not without powerful support, so you can defend the state in the best interests of hope and cour-age.* Brutus also was meeting with success and had raised a further five legions, some twenty-five thousand men, in Macedonia. Young Marcus was with him, recruiting and training cavalry: *Your son earns my approval by his energy, endurance, hard work and unselfish spirit, in fact by every kind of service.*

But then would come more ominous dispatches. Decimus was in desperate straits after more than four months trapped in Mu-tina. He could only communicate with the outside world by carrier pigeon, and the few birds that got through brought news of star-vation, disease and low morale. Lepidus meanwhile was moving his legions closer to the scene of the impending battle with An-tony, and he urged Cicero and the Senate to consider a fresh offer of peace talks. Cicero was so incensed by this weak and arrogant man's presumption that he dictated to me a letter that went off that same night:

> *Cicero to Lepidus.*
> *I rejoice at your desire to make peace among citizens but only if you can separate that peace from slavery. Otherwise you should understand that all men of sense have taken a resolution to prefer death to servitude. You will act more wisely in my judgement if you meddle no further in this affair, which is not acceptable either to the Senate or the people, or to any honest man.*

Cicero was under no illusions. The city and the Senate still har-boured hundreds of Antony's supporters. If Decimus surrendered, or if the armies of Hirtius, Pansa and Octavian were defeated, he knew he would be the first to be seized and murdered. As a safety precaution he ordered home two of the three legions stationed in Africa to defend Rome. But they would not arrive until the middle of the summer.

It was on the twentieth day of April that the crisis finally broke. Early that morning, Cornutus, the urban praetor, hurried up the hill. With him was a messenger who had been dispatched by Pansa six days earlier. Cornutus's expression was grim. "Tell Cicero," he said to the messenger, "what you've just told me."

In a trembling voice the messenger said, "Vibius Pansa regrets to report a catastrophic defeat. He and his army were surprised by the forces of Mark Antony at the settlement of Forum Gallorum. The lack of experience of our men was immediately evident. The line broke and there was a general slaughter. The consul managed to escape but is himself wounded."

Cicero's face turned grey. "And Hirtius and Caesar? Any news of them?"

Cornutus said, "None. Pansa was on his way to their camp but was attacked before he could join them."

Cicero groaned.

Cornutus said, "Should I summon a meeting of the Senate?"

"Dear gods, no!" To the messenger Cicero said, "Tell me the truth—does anyone else in Rome yet know about this?"

The messenger bowed his head. "I went first to the consul's home. His father-in-law was there."

"Calenus!"

Cornutus said grimly, "He knows it all, unfortunately. He's in the Portico of Pompey at this very moment, on the exact spot where Caesar was struck down. He's telling anyone who'll listen that we're paying the price for an impious killing. He accuses you of planning to seize power as dictator. I believe he's gathering quite a crowd."

I said to Cicero, "We ought to get you out of Rome."

Cicero shook his head emphatically. "No, no. *They're* the traitors, not I. Damn them, I'll not run away. Find Appuleius," he ordered the urban praetor briskly, as if he were his head steward. "Tell him to call a public assembly and then to come and fetch me. I'll speak to the people. I need to steady their nerves. They must be reminded that there's always bad news in war. And you," he said to the messenger, "had better not breathe a word of this to another soul, do you understand, or I'll have you put in chains."

I never admired Cicero more than I did that day, when he stared ruin in the face. He went into his study to compose an oration, while I, from the terrace, watched the Forum begin to fill with citizens. Panic has its own pattern. I had learned to recognise it over the years. Men run from one speaker to another. Groups form and dissolve. Sometimes the public space clears entirely. It is like a cloud of dust drifting and whirling before the onset of a storm.

Appuleius came toiling up the hill as requested and I took him in to see Cicero. He reported that the current rumour going round was that Cicero was to be presented with the fasces of a dictator. It was a trick, of course—a provocation that would be the pretext for his murder. The Antonians would then ape the tactics of Brutus and Cassius and seize the Capitol and try to hold it until Antony arrived in the city to relieve them.

Cicero asked Appuleius, "Will you be able to guarantee my security if I come down to address the people?"

"I can't give an absolute guarantee, but we can try."

"Send as big an escort as you can. Allow me one hour to get myself ready."

The tribune went away, and to my astonishment Cicero then announced that he would have a bath and be shaved, and change into a fresh set of clothes. "Make sure you write all this down," he said to me. "It will make a good end for your book."

He went off with his body slaves, and by the time he came back an hour later, Appuleius had assembled a strong force out in the street, consisting mostly of gladiators along with his fellow tribunes and their attendants. Cicero braced his shoulders, the door was opened, and he was just about to cross the threshold when the lictors of the urban praetor came hurrying up the road, clearing a path for Cornutus. He was holding a dispatch. His face was wet with tears. Too out of breath and emotional to speak, he thrust the dispatch into Cicero's hands.

*From Hirtius to Cornutus. Before Mutina.*
*I send you this in haste. Thanks be to the gods, we have this*
*day retrieved an earlier disaster and won a great victory over the*

enemy. *What was lost at noon has been recouped at sunset. I led out twenty cohorts of the Fourth Legion to relieve Pansa and fell upon Antony's men when they were celebrating prematurely. We have captured two eagles and sixty standards. Antony and the remnants of his army have retreated to his camp, where they are trapped. Now it is his turn to taste what it is like to be besieged. He has lost the greater part of his veteran troops; he has only cavalry. His position is hopeless. Mutina is saved. Pansa is wounded but should recover. Long live the Senate and the people of Rome. Tell Cicero.*

# XVIII

————•◦•————

WHAT FOLLOWED WAS THE GREATEST DAY OF CICERO'S LIFE—MORE
hard-won than his victory over Verres, more exhilarating than his
election to the consulship, more joyful than his defeat of Catilina,
more historic than his return from exile. All those triumphs dwin-
dled to nothing in comparison to the salvation of the republic.

*That day I reaped the richest of rewards for my many days of labour and
sleepless nights,* wrote Cicero to Brutus. *The whole population of Rome
thronged to my house and escorted me up to the Capitol, then set me on the
Speakers' Platform amid tumultuous applause.*

The moment was all the sweeter for having been preceded by
such bitter despair. "This is your victory!" he shouted from the rostra to the thousands in the Forum. "No," they called back, "it is *your*
victory!" The following day in the Senate he proposed that Pansa,
Hirtius and Octavian should be honoured by an unprecedented
fifty days of public thanksgiving, and a monument erected to the
fallen: "Brief is the life given us by nature; but the memory of a life
nobly sacrificed is everlasting." None of his enemies dared oppose
him: either they stayed away from the session or voted tamely as he
asked. Every time he stepped out of doors he was cheered. He was
at his zenith. All he needed now was the final official confirmation
that Antony was dead.

A week later came a dispatch from Octavian:

*From G. Caesar to his friend Cicero.*
   *I am scribbling this by lamplight in my camp on the evening
of the twenty-first. I wanted to be the first to tell you that we*

*have won a second great victory over the enemy. For a week, my legions, in close alliance with those of the gallant Hirtius, probed the defences of Antony's camp for weaknesses. Last night we found a suitable place and this morning we attacked. The fighting was bloody and obstinate, the slaughter great. I was in the midst of it. My standard-bearer was killed beside me. I shouldered the eagle and carried it. This rallied our men. Decimus, seeing that the decisive moment had arrived, at last led his forces out of Mutina and joined the battle. The greater part of Antony's army was destroyed. The villain himself, with his cavalry, has fled, and judging by the direction of his flight he means to cross the Alps.*

*So much is wonderful. But now I must tell you the hard part. Hirtius, despite his failing health, advanced with great spirit into the very heart of the enemy camp and had reached Antony's own tent when he was struck down by a fatal sword thrust to his neck. I have retrieved his body and will return it to Rome, where I am sure you will see that he receives the honours due to a brave consul. I shall write again when I can. Perhaps you will tell his sister.*

When he had finished reading, Cicero passed me the letter, then clenched his fists together and raised his eyes to heaven. "I thank the gods I have been allowed to see this moment."

"Though it is a pity about Hirtius," I added. I was thinking of all those dinners under the stars in Tusculum.

"True—I am very sorry for his sake. Still: how much better to die swiftly and gloriously in battle rather than lingeringly and squalidly on a sickbed. This war has been waiting for a hero. I shall make it my business to put Hirtius on the vacant plinth."

He took Octavian's letter with him to the Senate that morning, intending to read it aloud, to deliver "the eulogy to end all eulogies" and to propose a state funeral for Hirtius. It was a measure of his buoyant spirits that he could take the loss of a consul so lightly. On the steps of the Temple of Concordia he met the urban praetor, who was also just arriving. Senators were streaming in to take their places. The auspices were being taken. Cornutus was grinning. He said, "I surmise by your expression that you too have heard the news of Antony's final defeat?"

"I am in raptures. Now we must make sure the villain doesn't escape."

"Oh, take it from an old soldier—we have more than enough men to cut him off. A pity, though, that it cost us the life of a consul."

"Indeed—a wretched business." Side by side the two men began to climb the steps towards the entrance. Cicero said, "I thought I would deliver a eulogy, if that is all right by you."

"Of course, although Calenus has already asked me if *he* might say something."

"Calenus! What business is it of his?"

Cornutus stopped and turned to Cicero. He looked surprised. "Well, because Pansa was his son-in-law . . ."

"What are you talking about? You've got it the wrong way round. Pansa isn't dead; it's Hirtius who has died."

"No, no. It's Pansa, I assure you. I received a message from Decimus last night. Look." And he gave the dispatch to Cicero. "He says that once the siege was lifted, he set off directly for Bononia to consult with Pansa on how they should best pursue Antony, only to discover that he had succumbed to the wounds he received in the first battle."

Cicero refused to believe it. Only when he read Decimus's letter did he have to concede there was no doubt. "But Hirtius is dead as well—killed while storming Antony's camp. I have a letter here from young Caesar confirming that he has taken custody of the body."

"*Both* consuls are dead?"

"It's unimaginable." Cicero appeared so dazed by the news, I thought he might topple backwards down the steps. "In the entire existence of the republic, only eight consuls have died during their year in office. Eight—in nearly five hundred years! And now we lose two in the same week!"

Some of the passing senators had stopped to look at them. Conscious that they were being overheard, Cicero drew Cornutus to one side and spoke to him in a quiet, urgent voice. "This is a dark moment, but we must live through it. Nothing can be allowed to impede our pursuit and destruction of Antony. That is the alpha and omega of our policy. There are plenty of our colleagues who will try to exploit this tragedy to create mischief."

"Yes, but who will command our forces in the absence of the consuls?"

Cicero made a sound that was something between a groan and a sigh and put his hand to his brow. What a mess this made of all his careful planning, of all his delicate balancing of power! "Well, I suppose there's no alternative. It will have to be Decimus. He's the senior in age and experience, and he's the governor of Nearer Gaul."

"What about Octavian?"

"Leave Octavian to me. But we will need to vote him the most extraordinary thanks and honours if we're to keep him in our camp."

"Is it wise to make him up to be so mighty? One day he'll turn on us, I'm sure of it."

"Perhaps he will. But we can deal with him later. He can be raised, praised and erased."

It was the sort of cynical remark Cicero often made for effect: a play on words; a knowing joke, nothing more. Cornutus said, "Very good, I must remember that—*raised, praised, erased.*" Then the two discussed how best to break the news to the Senate, what motions should be proposed and how the votes should be taken, and after that they proceeded into the temple.

"The nation has sustained a triumph and a tragedy in the same breath," Cicero told the silent Senate. "A mortal danger has been lifted but only at a mortal price. The news has just been received that we have won a second and decisive victory at Mutina. Antony is in flight with his few remaining followers, to where we do not know—to the north, to the mountains, to the gates of hell itself for all we care!" (My notes record cheers at this point.) "But gentlemen,

I have to tell you: Hirtius is dead. Pansa is dead." (Gasps, cries, pro-tests.) "The gods demanded a sacrifice in expiation for our weakness and our folly over recent months and years, and our two gallant consuls have paid it in full measure. In due course their earthly remains will be returned to the city. We will lay them to rest with solemn honours. We will build a great monument to their valour that men will gaze upon for a thousand years. But we will honour them best by finishing the task they so nearly completed and extir-pating Antony once and for all. (Applause.)

"I propose that in the light of the loss of our consuls at Mutina, and mindful of the need to prosecute the war to its end, Decimus Junius Albinus be appointed commander-in-chief of the Senate's armies in the field and that Gaius Julius Caesar Octavianus should be his deputy in all matters; and that in recognition of their bril-liant generalship, heroism and success, the name of Decimus Junius Albinus should be added to the Roman calendar to mark his birth-day for eternity, and that Gaius Julius Caesar Octavianus should be awarded the honour of an ovation as soon as it is convenient for him to come to Rome to receive it."

The ensuing debate was full of mischief. As Cicero wrote to Bru-tus, *That day I realised that gratitude has considerably fewer votes in the Senate than spite.* Isauricus, as jealous of Octavian as he had been of Antony, objected to the idea of awarding him an ovation, which would allow him to parade with his legions through Rome. In the end Cicero was only able to carry his proposal by agreeing to give Decimus the even greater honour of a triumph. A commission of ten men was set up to settle the remuneration, in cash and land, of all the soldiers: the idea was to draw them away from Octavian, reduce their bounty and put them on the payroll of the Senate. To add insult to this injury, neither Octavian nor Decimus was invited to join the commission. Calenus, dressed in mourning, also demanded that his son-in-law's doctor, Glyco, be arrested and examined under torture if necessary to determine whether Pansa's death was murder: "Remember we were assured to begin with that his injuries were not serious, but now we can see that certain persons stand to gain greatly by his removal"—an obvious reference to Octavian.

All in all it was a bad day's work, and Cicero had to sit down that night and explain to Octavian what had happened.

*I am sending you by the same courier the resolutions that have today been agreed by the Senate. I hope you will accept the logic of our placing you and your soldiers under the command of Decimus, just as you were previously subordinate to the consuls. The Commission of Ten is a bit of nonsense I shall try to have rescinded: give me time. You should have been there, my dear friend, to hear the encomia! The rafters rang with praise of your daring and loyalty, and I am glad to say that you will be the youngest commander in the history of the republic to be granted the distinction of an ovation. Press on with your pursuit of Antony, and keep that place in your heart for me that I keep in mine for you.*

After that there was silence.

FOR A LONG TIME CICERO HEARD NOTHING FROM THE THEATRE OF operations. That was not surprising. It was remote, inhospitable country. He comforted himself by imagining Antony with his lonely band of followers struggling along the inaccessible narrow mountain passes while Decimus raced to try to cut him off. It was not until the thirteenth day of May that news arrived from Decimus—and then, as is often the way with these things, not one but three dispatches arrived all at once. I took them straight to Cicero in his study; he opened the document case greedily and read them aloud in order. The first was dated the twenty-ninth of April and put Cicero on his guard at once: *I shall try to ensure that Antony is unable to maintain himself in Italy. I shall be after him immediately.*

"Immediately?" said Cicero, checking again the date at the head of the letter. "What is he talking about? He's already writing eight days after Antony fled Mutina ..."

The next dispatch was written a week later, when Decimus was finally on the march:

*The reasons, my dear Cicero, why I was unable to pursue Antony at once are these. I had no cavalry, no pack animals. I did not know of Hirtius's death. I did not trust Caesar until I had met and talked to him. So the first day passed. Early on the next I had a message from Pansa summoning me to Bononia. As I was on my way, I received the report of his death. I hastened back to my own apology for an army. It is most sadly reduced and in very bad shape through lack of all the necessities. Antony got two days' start of me and made far longer marches as the pursued than I as the pursuer, for he went helter-skelter, while I moved in regular order. Wherever he went he opened up the slave barracks and carried off the men, stopping nowhere until he reached Vada. He seems to have made up a pretty sizeable body. He may go to Lepidus.*

*If Caesar had listened to me and crossed the Apennines I should have put Antony in so tight a corner that he would have been finished by lack of supplies rather than cold steel. But there is no giving orders to Caesar, nor by Caesar to his army—both very bad things. What alarms me is how this situation can be straightened out. I cannot any longer feed my men.*

The third letter was written a day after the second and dispatched from the foothills of the Alps: *Antony is on the march. He is going to Lepidus. Please look to future action in Rome. You will counter the world's malice towards me if you can.*

"He has let him get away," said Cicero, resting his head in his hand and reading the letters through again. "*He has let him get away!* And now he says that Octavian can't or won't obey him as commander-in-chief. Well, this is a pretty mess!"

He wrote a letter at once for the courier to take back to Decimus:

*From what you write, the flames of war, so far from having been extinguished, seem to be blazing higher. We understood that Antony*

*had fled in despair with a few unarmed and demoralised followers.*
*If in fact his condition is such that a clash with him will be a*
*dangerous matter, I do not regard him as having fled from Mutina*
*at all but as having shifted the war to another theatre.*

The next day, the funeral cortège of Hirtius and Pansa reached
Rome, escorted by an honour guard of cavalry sent by Octavian.
It passed through the streets to the Forum at dusk, watched by
hushed and sombre crowds. At the base of the rostra the Senate, all
in black togas, waited by torchlight to receive it. Cornutus gave a
eulogy that Cicero had written for him, and then the vast assembly walked behind the biers to the Field of Mars, where the pyres
had been prepared. As a mark of patriotic respect the undertakers,
actors and musicians refused to take any payment; Cicero joked
that when an undertaker won't take your money, you know you
are a hero. But beneath his public show of bravado, in private he
was profoundly troubled. As the torches were put to the base of the
pyres, and the flames shot up, Cicero's face in the firelight looked
old and hollowed with worry.

Almost as worrying as the fact that Antony had escaped was
that Octavian either would not or could not obey Decimus's order.
Cicero wrote to him, pleading with him to abide by the Senate's
edict and place himself and his legions under the governor's command: *Let any differences be sorted out after victory has been attained;*
*believe me, the surest way to achieve the highest honour in the state will be to*
*play the fullest part now in destroying its greatest enemy.* Ominously, he
received no reply.

Then Decimus wrote again:

*Labeo Segulius tells me that he has been with Octavian and that a*
*good deal of talk about you took place. Octavian to be sure made*
*no complaints about you, he says, except for a remark which he*
*attributed to you: "The young man should be raised, praised and*
*erased." He added that he had no intention of letting himself be*
*erased. As for the veterans, they are grumbling viciously about you*

*and you are in danger from them. They mean to terrorise you and*
*replace you with the young man.*

I had long warned Cicero that his fondness for making puns and
amusing asides would one day land him in trouble. But he couldn't
help himself. He had always enjoyed a reputation as a caustic wit,
and as he grew older he had only to open his mouth and people
would flock around him, eager to laugh. The attention flattered him
and served to inspire him to make ever more cutting remarks. His
dry observations were quickly repeated; sometimes phrases were
attributed to him he had never even uttered: indeed, I have compiled a whole book of these apocrypha. Caesar used to delight in his
barbs, even when he was himself the target—for example, when as
dictator he changed the calendar and someone enquired whether
the Dog Star would still rise on the same date, Cicero replied, "It
will do as it is told." Caesar was said to have roared with laughter.
But his adopted son, whatever his other merits, was deficient when
it came to a sense of humour, and for once Cicero took my advice
and wrote a letter of apology.

*I gather that confounded fool Segulius is going round telling all and*
*sundry about some joke I am supposed to have made, and that now*
*word of it has reached your ears. I cannot remember making the*
*remark but I shall not disown it, for it sounds the sort of thing I might*
*have said—lightly delivered, meant for the moment, not fit to be*
*examined as a serious statement of policy. I know I do not need to tell*
*you how fond I am of you, how zealously I guard your interests, how*
*determined I am that you should play the leading part in our affairs*
*in the years to come; but if I have caused offence, I am truly sorry.*

His letter drew this response:

*From G. Caesar to Cicero.*
*My feelings for you are unchanged. No apology is needed,*
*although if it pleases you to make one, naturally I accept it.*

*Unfortunately my supporters are not so easy-going. They warn
me every day that I am a fool to put my faith in you and in the
Senate. Your unguarded remark was catnip to them. Really—that
Senate edict! How could I have been expected to place myself under
the command of the man who lured my father to his death? My
relations with Decimus are civil but we never can be friends, and
my men, who are my father's veterans, will never follow him. There
is only one circumstance, they say, that would make them fight
for the Senate without reservation: if I am made consul. Is that
impossible? Both consulships are vacant after all, and if I can be
pro-praetor at nineteen, why not consul?*

This letter made Cicero blanch. He wrote back at once to say
that, divinely inspired though Octavian was, the Senate would
never agree to a man not yet even twenty becoming consul. Octavian replied equally swiftly:

*My youth, it seems, is not an impediment to my leading an army
on the field of battle but it is to my becoming consul. If age is the
only issue, could I not have as a consular colleague someone who is
as old as I am young, and whose political wisdom and experience
would make up for my lack of it?*

Cicero showed the letter to Atticus. "What do you make of this?
Is he suggesting what I think he is?"

"I'm sure that's what he's implying. Would you do it?"

"I can't pretend the honour would be meaningless to me—very
few men have been consul twice; that would mean immortal glory,
and I'm doing the job in all but name in any case. But the price!
We've already had to confront one Caesar with an army at his back
demanding an illegal consulship, and we ended up fighting a war
to try to stop him. Do we now have to confront another, and this
time tamely surrender to him? How would it look to the Senate,
and to Brutus and Cassius? Who is planting these ideas in the
young man's head?"

"Perhaps he doesn't need anyone to plant them there," Atticus replied. "Perhaps they arise quite spontaneously."

Cicero made no reply. The possibility did not bear contemplating.

TWO WEEKS LATER, CICERO RECEIVED A LETTER FROM LEPIDUS, who was encamped with his seven legions at Pons Argenteus in southern Gaul. After he had read it, he leaned forwards and rested his head on his desk. With one hand he pushed the letter towards me.

*We have long been friends but I have no doubt that in the present violent and unexpected political crisis my enemies have brought you false and unworthy reports about me, designed to give your patriotic heart no small disquiet. I have one earnest request to make of you, dear Cicero. If previously my life and endeavour, my diligence and good faith in the conduct of public affairs have to your knowledge been worthy of the name I bear, I beg you to expect equal or greater things in time to come, as your kindness places me further and further in your debt.*

"I don't understand," I said. "Why are you so upset?"

Cicero sighed and sat up straight. To my alarm I saw that he had tears in his eyes. "Because it means he intends to join forces with Antony and is providing himself with an alibi in advance. His duplicity is so clumsy it's almost endearing."

He was right of course. On that very day, the thirtieth of May, when Cicero was receiving Lepidus's false assurances, Antony himself—long-haired and bearded after almost forty days on the run—was arriving on the riverbank opposite Lepidus's camp. He waded chest-deep through the water wearing a dark cloak, went up to the palisade and began talking to the legionaries. Many recognised him from the Gallic and the civil wars; they flocked to hear him. The next day he brought all his forces over the river and Lepidus's men welcomed them with outstretched arms. They tore down their fortifications and let Antony stroll unarmed into the camp. He treated Lepidus with the greatest respect, called him by the title "Father" and insisted that if he joined his cause he would retain the rank and honours of a general. The soldiers cheered. Lepidus agreed.

Or that at least was the story they cooked up together. Cicero was sure they had been partners from the start and that their rendezvous had been arranged in advance. It simply made Lepidus seem less of the traitor he was if he could pretend he had bowed to *force majeure*.

It took nine days for Lepidus's dispatch announcing this shattering turn of events to reach the Senate, although panicky rumours ran ahead of his messenger. Cornutus read it out in the Temple of Concordia:

I call on gods and men to witness how my heart and mind have ever been disposed towards the commonwealth and freedom. Of this I should shortly have given you proof, had not Fortune wrested the decision out of my hands. My entire army, faithful to its inveterate tendency to conserve Roman lives and the general peace, has mutinied; and, truth to tell has compelled me to join them. I beg and implore you, do not treat the compassion shown by myself and my army in a conflict between fellow countrymen as a crime.

When the urban praetor finished reading, there was a great collective sigh, a groan almost, as if the whole chamber had been holding its breath in the hope that the rumours would turn out not to be true. Cornutus gestured to Cicero to open the debate. In the ensuing silence as Cicero rose to his feet one could feel an almost childlike yearning for reassurance. But Cicero had none to offer.

"This news from Gaul, which we have long suspected and dreaded, comes as no surprise, gentlemen. The only shock is the impudence of Lepidus in taking us all to be idiots. He begs us, he implores us, he entreats us—this creature! No, not even that: these bitter, squalid dregs of a noble line that merely assume the form of a human being!—he begs us not to regard his treachery as a crime. The cowardice of the fellow! I would have more respect for him if he came right out and told the truth: that he sees an opportunity to further his monstrous ambitions and has found a fellow thief to be his partner in crime. I propose that he be declared a public enemy forthwith and that all his property and estates be confiscated to help us pay for the fresh legions we shall require to replace those he has stolen from the state."

This drew loud applause.

"But it will take us a while to raise new forces, and in the meantime we must face the salutary fact that our strategic situation is perilous in the extreme. If the fires of rebellion in Gaul spread to Plancus's four legions—and I fear we must brace ourselves for that possibility—we may have the best part of sixty thousand men ranged against us."

Cicero had decided beforehand that he would not try to disguise the extent of the crisis. Silence gave way to murmurs of alarm.

"We should not despair," he continued, "not least because we have that number of soldiers ourselves, assembled by the noble and gallant Brutus and Cassius—but they are in Macedonia; they are in Syria; they are in Greece; they are not in Italy. We also have one legion of new recruits in Latium, and the two African legions that are even now at sea and on their way home to defend the capital. And then there are the armies of Decimus and Caesar—although the one is enfeebled and the other truculent.

"We have every chance, in other words. But there is no time to be lost.

"I propose that this Senate orders Brutus and Cassius immediately to send back to Italy sufficient forces to enable us to defend Rome; that we intensify our levies to raise new legions; and that we impose an emergency tax on property of one per cent to enable us to purchase arms and equipment. If we do all of this, and if we draw strength from the spirit of our ancestors and the justice of our cause, it remains my confident belief that liberty will triumph in the end."

He delivered his closing remarks with all his usual force and vigour. But when he sat down, there was scant applause. The dreadful stench of likely defeat hung in the air, as acrid as burning pitch.

Isauricus rose next. Hitherto this haughty and ambitious patrician had been the staunchest senatorial opponent of the presumptuous Octavian. He had denounced his elevation to a special praetorship; he had even tried to deny him the relatively modest honour of an ovation. But now he delivered a paean of praise to the young Caesar that amazed everyone. "If Rome is to be defended against Antony's ambitions, backed up now by the forces of Lepidus, then I have come to believe that Caesar is the man upon whom we must chiefly rely. His is the name that can conjure armies from thin air and make them march and fight. His is the shrewdness that can bring us peace. As a symbol of my faith in him, I have to tell you, gentlemen, that I have lately offered him the hand of my daughter in marriage, and I am gratified to be able to tell you he has accepted."

Cicero twitched suddenly in his seat as if he had been caught by some invisible hook. But Isauricus hadn't finished yet: "To bind this excellent young man to our cause still further, and to encourage his men to fight against Mark Antony, I propose the following motion: that in view of the grave military situation created by the treachery of Lepidus, and mindful of the service he has already rendered to the republic, the constitution be so amended that Gaius Julius Caesar Octavianus may be permitted to stand for the office of consul *in absentia*."

Afterwards Cicero cursed himself for not having seen this coming. It was obvious, once one stopped to think about it, that if Octavian could not persuade Cicero to stand for the consulship as his partner, then he would ask someone else. But occasionally even the shrewdest statesman misses the obvious, and now Cicero found himself in an awkward spot. He had to assume that Octavian had already done a deal with his putative father-in-law. Should he accept it with good grace or should he oppose it? He had no time to think. All around him the benches were abuzz with speculation. Isauricus was sitting with his arms folded, looking very pleased with the sensation he had created. Cornutus called upon Cicero to respond to the proposition.

He stood slowly, adjusting his toga, glancing around, clearing his throat—all his familiar delaying tactics to purchase some time to think. "May I first of all congratulate the noble Isauricus on the excellent family connection he has just announced? I know the young man to be honourable, moderate, modest, sober, patriotic, valiant in war and of calm good judgement—everything in short that a son-in-law should be. He has had no stronger advocate in this Senate than I. His future career in the republic is both glittering and assured. He will be consul, I am sure. But whether he should be consul when he is not yet twenty and solely because he has an army is a different matter.

"Gentlemen, we embarked upon this war with Antony for a principle: the principle that no man—however gifted, however powerful, however ambitious for glory—should be above the law. Whenever in the course of my thirty years in the service of the state we have yielded to temptation and ignored the law, often for what seemed at the time to be good reasons, we have slipped a little further toward the precipice. I helped to pass the special legislation that gave Pompey unprecedented powers to fight the war against the pirates. The war was a great success. But the most lasting consequence was not the defeat of the pirates: it was to create the precedent that enabled Caesar to rule Gaul for almost a decade and to grow too mighty for the state to contain him.

"I do not say that the younger Caesar is like the elder. But I do say that if we make him consul, and in effect give him control of all our forces, then we will betray the very principle for which we fight: the principle that drew me back to Rome when I was on the point of sailing to Greece—that the Roman Republic, with its division of powers, its annual free elections for every magistracy, its law courts and its juries, its balance between Senate and people, its liberty of speech and thought, is mankind's noblest creation, and I would sooner lie choking in my own blood upon the ground than betray the principle on which all this stands—that is, first and last and always, the rule of law."

His remarks elicited warm applause and entirely set the course of the debate—so much so that Isauricus, with icy formality and a glare at Cicero, later withdrew his proposal and it was never voted upon.

I ASKED CICERO IF HE INTENDED TO WRITE TO OCTAVIAN TO EXPLAIN his stand. He shook his head. "My reasons are in my speech and he will have it in his hands soon enough—my enemies will see to that."

In the days that followed he was as busy as he had ever been—writing to Brutus and Cassius to urge them to come to the aid of the tottering republic (*the commonwealth is in the gravest peril because of the criminal folly of M. Lepidus*), overseeing the tax inspectors as they set about raising revenue, touring the blacksmiths' yards to cajole them into making more weapons, inspecting the newly raised legion with Cornutus, who had been appointed military defender of Rome. But he knew the cause was hopeless, especially when he saw Fulvia being carried openly in a litter across the Forum, accompanied by a large entourage.

"I thought we were rid of that shrew, at least," he complained over dinner, "yet here she is, still in Rome and flaunting herself around, even though her husband has at last been declared a public enemy. Is it any wonder we're in such desperate straits? How is it possible, when all her property is supposed to have been seized?"

There was a pause and then Atticus said quietly, "I lent her some money."

"You?" Cicero leaned across the table and peered at him as if he were some mysterious stranger. "Why on earth would you do that?"

"I felt sorry for her."

"No you didn't. You wanted to put Antony under an obligation to you. It's insurance. You think we're going to lose."

Atticus did not deny it, and Cicero left the table.

AT THE END OF THAT WRETCHED MONTH, "JULY," REPORTS REACHED the Senate that Octavian's army had struck camp in Nearer Gaul, crossed the Rubicon, and was marching on Rome. Even though he had been half expecting it, the news still struck Cicero as a tremendous blow. He had given his word to the Roman people that if "the heaven-sent boy" was given imperium, he would be a model citizen. *Every imaginable evil chance has dogged us in this war,* he lamented to Brutus. *As I write, I am in great distress, because it hardly looks as though I can make good my promises in respect to the young man, boy almost, for whom I went bail to the republic.* It was then he asked me if I thought he was honour-bound to kill himself, and for the first time I saw that he was not saying it for effect. I replied that I did not think it had come to that yet.

"Perhaps not, but I must be ready. I don't want these veterans of Caesar's torturing me to death as they did Trebonius. The question is how to do it. I'm not sure I could face a blade—do you think posterity will reckon the less of me if I choose Socrates's method and take hemlock instead?"

"I am sure not."

He asked me to acquire some of the poison on his behalf and I went to see his doctor that same day, who gave me a small jar. He did not ask why I wanted it; I suppose he knew. Despite the wax seal, I could smell its rank odour, like mouse droppings. "It's made from the seeds," he explained, "the most poisonous part of the plant, which I have crushed into a powder. The smallest dose, no more than a pinch, swallowed with water, should do the trick."

"How long does it take to work?"

"Three hours or thereabouts."

"Is it painful?"

"It induces slow suffocation—what do you think?"

I put the jar into a box in my room, and placed the box inside a locked chest, as if by hiding it away, death itself could be postponed.

The next day, gangs of Octavian's legionaries began to appear in the Forum. He had sent four hundred on ahead of his main army, with the aim of intimidating the Senate into granting him the consulship. Whenever they saw a senator, they surrounded him and jostled him and showed him their swords, although they never actually drew their weapons. Cornutus, as an old soldier, refused to be threatened. Determined to visit Cicero on the Palatine, the urban praetor pushed and shoved them back until they let him through. But he advised Cicero that on no account should he venture out himself unless he had a strong escort: "They hold you as much responsible for Caesar's death as they do Decimus or Brutus."

"If only I *had* been responsible! Then we would have taken care of Antony at the same time and we wouldn't be in the mess we are today."

"Well, here is some better news for you: the African legions arrived last night, and we didn't lose a single ship. Eight thousand men and a thousand cavalry are disembarking at Ostia even as I speak. That should be enough to hold off Octavian, at least until Brutus and Cassius send us help."

"But are they loyal?"

"So their commanders assure me."

"Then bring them here as quickly as possible."

The legions were only a day's march from Rome. As they approached the city, Octavian's men slipped away into the surrounding countryside. When the vanguard reached the salt warehouses, Cornutus ordered the column to parade through the Trigemina Gate and across the Forum Boarium in full view of the crowds in order to steady civilian morale. Then they took up position on the Janiculum. From these strategic heights they controlled the western approaches to Rome and could deploy rapidly to block any invading force. Cornutus asked Cicero if he would come out and inspire the men with a rousing speech. Cicero agreed, and he was carried out of the city gates in a litter accompanied by fifty legionaries on foot. I rode on a mule.

It was a hot, muggy day without a tremor of wind. We crossed the River Tiber over the Sublician Bridge and traipsed along a road of dried mud through the shanty towns that have for as long as I can remember filled the flat plain of the Vaticanum. It was notoriously malarial in the summer, and swarming with hostile insects. Cicero's litter had the protection of a mosquito net but I did not, and the insects whined in my ears. The whole place stank of human filth. Children, pot-bellied with hunger, watched us listlessly from the doorways of tumbling shacks, while all around them, disregarded and pecking away at the rubbish, were hundreds of the crows that nest in the nearby sacred grove. We passed through the gates of the Janiculum and went up the hill. The place was teeming with soldiers. They had pitched their tents wherever they could find some space.

On the flatter ground at the top of the slope Cornutus had drawn up four cohorts—almost two thousand men. They stood in lines in the heat. The light on their helmets dazzled as brightly as the sun, and I had to shield my eyes. When Cicero stepped out of his litter there was absolute silence. Cornutus conducted him to a low platform beside an altar. A sheep was sacrificed. Its guts were pulled out and examined by the haruspices and declared propitious: "There is no doubt of ultimate victory." The crows circled overhead. A priest read a prayer. Then Cicero spoke.

I cannot remember exactly what he said. All the usual words were there—liberty, ancestors, hearths and altars, laws and temples—but for once I listened without hearing. I was looking at the faces of the legionaries. They were sunburnt, lean, impassive. Some were chewing mastic. I saw the scene through their eyes. They had been recruited by Caesar to fight against King Juba and the army of Cato. They had slaughtered thousands and had been stuck in Africa ever since. They had travelled hundreds of miles crammed together in boats. They had been force-marched for a day. Now they were lined up in the heat in Rome and an old man was talking at them about liberty, ancestors, hearths and altars—and it meant nothing.

Cicero finished speaking. There was silence. Cornutus ordered them to give three cheers. The silence continued. Cicero stepped off the platform and got back into his litter and we returned down the hill, past the saucer-eyed starving children.

CORNUTUS CAME TO SEE CICERO THE FOLLOWING MORNING AND told him that the African legions had mutinied overnight. It seemed that Octavian's men had crept back from the countryside in the darkness, infiltrated the camps and promised the soldiers twice as much money as the Senate could afford to pay them. Meanwhile Octavian's main army was reported to be moving south along the Via Flaminia and was barely a day's march away.

"What will you do now?" Cicero asked him.

"Kill myself," came the reply, and he did, that same evening, pressing the tip of his sword to his stomach and falling upon it heavily rather than surrender.

He was an honourable man and deserves to be remembered, not least because he was the only member of the Senate who took that course. When Octavian was close to the city, most of the leading patricians went out to meet him on the road to escort him into Rome. Cicero sat in his study with the shutters closed. The air was so close it was hard to breathe. I looked in from time to time but he did not seem to have moved. His noble head, staring straight ahead and silhouetted against the faint light from the window, was like a marble bust in a deserted temple. Finally he noticed me and asked where Octavian had set up his headquarters.

I replied that he had moved into the home of his mother and stepfather on the Quirinal.

"Perhaps you could send a message to Philippus and ask him what he suggests I should do."

I did as he requested and the courier returned with a scrawled reply that Cicero ought to go and talk to Octavian: "You will find him, I am sure, as I did, disposed to mercy."

Wearily Cicero got to his feet. The big house, usually thronged with visitors, was empty. It felt as if no one had lived in it for a long time. In the late summer afternoon sun the silent public rooms glowed as if made of gold and amber.

We went together, in a pair of litters accompanied by a small escort, to the house of Philippus. Sentries guarded the street and the front door but they must have been given orders to let Cicero through, for they parted at once. As we crossed the threshold, Isauricus was just leaving. I had expected him, as Octavian's future father-in-law, to give Cicero a smile of condescension or of triumph; instead he scowled at him and hurried past us.

Through the heavy open door we could see Octavian standing in a corner of the tablinum dictating a letter to a secretary. He beckoned to us to enter. He seemed in no hurry to finish. He was wearing a simple military tunic. His body armour, helmet and sword lay scattered on a couch where he had flung them. He looked like a young recruit. Finally he ended his dictation and sent the secretary away.

He scrutinised Cicero in an amused way that reminded me of his adopted father. "You are the last of my friends to greet me."

"Well, I imagined you would be busy."

"Ah, is that it?" Octavian laughed, revealing those terrible teeth of his. "I was presuming that you disapproved of my actions."

Cicero shrugged. "The world is as it is. I have given up the habit of approving and disapproving. What's the point? Men do as they please, whatever I think."

"So what is it you want to do? Do you want to be consul?"

For the merest fraction of a moment Cicero's face seemed to flood with pleasure and relief, but then he understood that Octavian was joking and immediately the light went out of it again. He grunted, "Now you're toying with me."

"I am. Forgive me. My colleague as consul will be Quintus

Pedius, an obscure relative of mine of whom you will never have heard, which is the whole point of him."

"So not Isauricus?"

"No. There seems to have been some misunderstanding there. I shan't be marrying his daughter either. I shall spend some time here settling matters and then I must go and confront Antony and Lepidus. You can leave Rome too if you like."

"I can?"

"Yes, you can leave Rome. You can write philosophy. You can go anywhere you please in Italy. However, you cannot return to Rome in my absence, nor can you attend the Senate. You cannot write your memoirs or anything political. You cannot leave the country and go to Brutus or Cassius. Is that acceptable? Will you give me your word? I can assure you my men would not be so generous."

Cicero bowed his head. "It is generous. It is acceptable. I give you my word. Thank you."

"In return I will guarantee your safety, in recognition of our past friendship." He picked up a letter to signal that the audience was at an end. "One last thing," he said as Cicero turned to leave. "It makes no difference, but I would like to know: was it a joke, or would you really have erased me?"

"I believe I would have done exactly the same as you are doing now," replied Cicero.

# XIX

———•—•—•———

AFTER THAT, HE SEEMED TO BECOME AN OLD MAN VERY SUDDENLY. He retired to Tusculum the next day and immediately started complaining about his eyesight. He refused to write or even read: he said it gave him a headache. He took no solace from his garden. He visited no one and no one visited him, apart from his brother. They would sit together for hours on a bench in the Lyceum, mostly in silence. The only subject Quintus could tempt him to discuss was the distant past—their shared memories of childhood and of growing up in Arpinum—and for the first time I heard Cicero talk at length about his father and mother. It was unnerving to see him, of all men, so disconnected from the world. Throughout his life he had demanded to know the latest news from Rome. Now, when I told him what I had heard was happening—that Octavius had set up a special court to try the assassins of Caesar, or even that he had left the city at the head of an army of eleven legions to fight Antony—he made no comment, save that he preferred not even to think about it. A few more weeks of this, I thought to myself, and he will die.

People often ask me why he did not try to run away. After all, Octavian did not yet have any firm control of the country. The weather was still clement. The ports were not watched. Cicero could have slipped out of Italy to join his son in Macedonia: I am sure Brutus would have been only too pleased to offer him sanctuary. But the truth was he lacked the will to do anything so decisive. "I am finished with running," he sighed to me. He couldn't even summon the energy to go down to the Bay of Naples. Besides, Octavian had guaranteed his safety.

I guess it must have been about a month after our retreat to Tusculum that he sought me out one morning and told me he would like to review his old letters: "This constant talk with Quintus about my early years has stirred the sediment of my memory." I had preserved them all, however fragmentary, incoming and outgoing, over more than three decades, and had sorted them by correspondent and arranged them on rolls chronologically. I carried the cylinders into his library and he lay on the couch while one of his secretaries read them out. It was all there, an entire life, from his early struggles to gain election to the Senate, through the hundreds of legal cases he took to make his name famous and which culminated in the epic prosecution of Verres, his election to aedile and then to praetor and finally to consul, his struggles with Catilina and Clodius, his exile and return, his relations with Caesar and Pompey and Cato, the civil war, the assassination, his return to power, Tullia and Terentia ...

For more than a week he relived his life, and at the end he had recovered something of his old self. "What an adventure it has been," he mused, stretching out on the couch. "It has all come back to me, the good and the bad, the noble and the base. I truly believe I can say, without being immodest, that these letters add up to the most complete record of an historical era ever assembled by a leading statesman. And what an era! No one else saw so much, and wrote about it while it was still fresh. This is history composed without any benefit of hindsight. Can you think of anything to compare with it?"

"It will be of immense interest a thousand years from now," I said, trying to encourage his new good mood.

"Oh, it's more than merely of interest! It's the case for my defence. I may have lost the past and lost the present, but I wonder if with this I might not yet win the future."

Some of the letters showed him in a bad light—vain, duplicitous, greedy, wrong-headed—and I expected him to weed out the most egregious examples and order me to destroy them. But when I asked him which letters he wished me to discard, he replied, "We must keep them all. I can't present myself to posterity as some improbable paragon—no one will believe it. If this archive is to have the necessary authenticity, I must stand before the muse of history as naked as a Greek statue. Let future generations mock me for my follies and pretensions however much they like—the important thing is that they will have to read me, and in that will lie my victory."

Of all the sayings associated with Cicero, the most famous and characteristic is: "While there is life there is hope." He still had life—or the semblance of it, at least; and now he had the faintest gleam of hope.

Beginning that day, he concentrated what remained of his strength on the task of ensuring his papers survived. Atticus eventually agreed to help, on condition he was allowed to retrieve every letter he had ever written to Cicero. Cicero rather despised him for his caution but in the end agreed: "If he wants to be a mere shadow in history, that's his lookout." With some reluctance I returned the correspondence I had carefully assembled over so many years and watched as Atticus lit a brazier and—not trusting the task to a servant—burnt with his own hand all the rolls on which his letters had been preserved. Then he put his scribes to work. Three complete sets of the collected letters were produced. Cicero kept one, Atticus another and I the third. I sent mine down to my farm along with locked boxes containing all my shorthand notes recording thousands of meetings, speeches, conversations, witticisms and barbed remarks, as well as the dictated drafts of his books. I told the overseer that it all should be hidden in one of the barns and that if anything happened to me he should give it to Agathe Licinia, the freedwoman who owned the baths of Venus Libertina at Baiae. Quite what she would do with it, I was not sure, but I sensed that I could trust her above all people in the world.

At the end of November, Cicero asked me if I would go back to Rome to make sure the last of his papers had been removed from his study, and to carry out a final general inspection. The house was being sold on his behalf by Atticus, and much of the furniture had already gone. It was the start of winter. The morning was chilly, the light gloomy. I wandered between the empty rooms as if I were an invisible spirit, and in my imagination I re-peopled them. I saw the tablinum once again filled with statesmen discussing the future of the republic, heard Tullia's laughter in the dining room, saw Cicero bent over his books of philosophy in the library attempting to explain why fear of death was illogical . . . My eyes were blurred with tears; my heart ached.

Suddenly a dog began to howl—so loudly and frantically that my bittersweet fantasies vanished in an instant. I stopped to listen. Our old dog had gone. This had to be a neighbour's. It was a most piteous wailing and it set off others. I went out on to the terrace. The sky was dark with swirls of starlings, and all across Rome dogs were howling like wolves. Indeed it was later said that at this very moment a wolf was seen darting across the Forum; that statues sweated blood and a newly born baby spoke. I heard the sound of running feet and looking down saw a group of men whooping with delight, racing towards the rostra and tossing to one another what I thought at first was a football but then realised was a human head. A woman started screaming in the street. Without thinking what I was doing I went out to see who it was and found the wife of our elderly neighbour, Caesetius Rufus, crawling on her knees in the gutter, while behind her the trunk of a corpse gushed blood from its neck across the threshold. Her steward, who I knew quite well, was running hopelessly to and fro. Panicking, I grabbed his arm and shook him until he told me what had happened—Octavian, Antony and Lepidus had joined forces and had published a list of hundreds of senators and equestrians who were to be killed and their fortunes seized. There was a bounty of a hundred thousand sesterces for each head that was brought to them. Both of the Cicero brothers were named on the list, and Atticus.

"That cannot be true," I assured him. "We have a solemn promise."

"It's true," he cried. "I've seen it."

I ran back to the house, where the few remaining slaves were gathered, frightened, in the atrium. "Everyone must scatter," I told them. "If they catch us they will torture us to try to make us reveal the whereabouts of the master. If it comes to it, say he is in Puteoli." I scribbled out a message to Cicero: *You and Quintus and Atticus are proscribed—Octavian has betrayed you—the death squads are looking for you—make at once for your house on the island—I will find you a boat.* I gave it to the ostler and told him to take it by his fastest horse to Cicero in Tusculum. Then I went to the stables and found my carriage and driver and ordered him to set off for Astura.

Even as we clattered down the hill, gangs of men armed with knives and staves were running up on to the Palatine, where the richest human pickings would be found, and I banged my head against the side of the carriage in my anguish that Cicero hadn't made good his escape from Italy while he had the chance.

I made that unfortunate driver whip his poor pair of horses until their flanks bled so that we could arrive in Astura before nightfall. We found the boatman in his hut, and even though the sea was beginning to get up and the light was dim, he rowed us the hundred yards over to the little island where Cicero's villa stood secluded in the trees. It had not been visited by him for months, and the slaves were amazed to see me, and not a little resentful at having to light fires and heat the rooms. I lay down on my damp mattress and listened to the wind buffeting around the roof and rustling the trees. As the waves crashed against the rocky shore and the house creaked, I was full of terror, imagining that every sound might be the arrival of Cicero's murderers. If I had brought that jar of hemlock, I almost think I might have taken it.

The next morning the weather was calmer, although when I walked through the trees and contemplated the huge expanse of grey sea with the lines of white waves running in to the shore, I felt utterly desolate. I wondered if this was a foolish plan and that we would do better to make directly for Brundisium, which at least was on the right side of Italy for a voyage east. But of course news of the proscriptions and the vast bounty for a severed head would race ahead of us, and nowhere would be safe. Cicero would never reach the harbour alive.

I sent my driver off in the direction of Tusculum with a second letter for Cicero, saying that I had arrived "on the island"—I kept it vague in case the message fell into the wrong hands—and urging him to make all speed. Then I asked the boatman to go to Antium to see if he could charter a vessel to carry us down the coast. He looked at me as if I were mad to make such a request in winter, when the weather was so treacherous, but after some grumbling he went away, and came back the following day to say that he had procured a ten-oared boat with a sail that would be with us as soon as they could row the seven miles from Antium. After that there was really nothing I could do except wait.

THE WOODED ISLET OF ASTURA WAS THE PLACE WHERE CICERO HAD gone to ground after Tullia had died. He had found the absolute silence, except for the sounds of Nature, soothing; I found the opposite: they jangled my nerves, especially as day after day passed when nothing happened. I kept a regular lookout, but it wasn't until late in the afternoon on the fifth day that there was a sudden eruption of activity on the shoreline. Two litters arrived through the trees accompanied by a retinue of slaves. The boatman rowed me over to take a look, and as we drew closer, I saw that on the beach stood Cicero and Quintus. When I hurried over the sand to greet them, I was shocked by their appearance. Neither had changed his clothes or shaved; both were red-eyed from crying. A light rain was falling. Drenched, they looked like a pair of indigent old men. Quintus, if anything, was in a worse state than Cicero. After a sorrowful greeting, he took one look at the boat I had hired, pulled up on to the beach, and announced he would not set foot in it for a moment.

He turned to Cicero. "My dear brother, this is hopeless. I don't know why I've let you drag me here, except that all my life I have done what you have told me. Look at us! Old men, we're in failing health. The weather is poor. We have no money. We would be better off following Atticus's example."

I asked, "Where is Atticus?"

Cicero said, "He's gone into hiding in Rome." He started to cry. He made no attempt to disguise it. And then, as quickly as he had started, he stopped and continued speaking as if nothing had happened. "No, I'm sorry, Quintus, I can't live in someone's cellar, trembling every time there's a knock at the door. Tiro's plan is as good as any. Let's see how far we can get."

Quintus said, "Then I'm afraid that we must part, and I shall pray to meet you again—if not in this life then the next."

They fell into one another's arms and clung to each other tightly, then Quintus broke away. He embraced me. None of those watching the scene could restrain their tears. Certainly I was overcome by the sadness of it all. After that, Quintus climbed back into his litter and was borne away up the track and into the trees.

It was too late for us to set off that day, and so we were rowed over to the villa. While Cicero dried himself at the fire, he explained that he had lingered for two days in Tusculum, unable to believe that Octavian had betrayed him, sure that there must have been some mistake. This much he had discovered: that Octavian had met Antony and Lepidus in Bononia, on an island in the middle of the river—just the three of them, with a couple of secretaries: they had left their bodyguards behind and had searched one another for concealed weapons—and that over the next three days, working from dawn till dusk, they had divided up the carcass of the republic between them, and to pay their armies had compiled a death list of two thousand wealthy men, including two hundred senators, whose property would be seized. "I am told by Atticus, who heard it from the consul Pedius, that each of the criminals, as a token of good faith, was required to mark for death someone who was precious to them. Thus Antony gave up his uncle, Lucius Caesar, even though he spoke in his defence in the Senate; Lepidus yielded his brother, Aemilius Paullus; and Octavian offered me—Antony insisted, although Pedius maintained the boy had been reluctant to agree."

"Do you believe it?"

"Not particularly. I have looked into those pale grey soulless eyes of his once too often. He is no more affected by the death of a man than he is by the death of a fly." He let out a sigh that seemed to shake his entire body. "Oh Tiro, I am so tired! To think that I, of all people, have been outwitted at the last by a young man who has barely started to shave! Do you have that poison I asked you to get?"

"It's in Tusculum."

"Well then, I can only pray to the immortal gods to allow me to die tonight in my sleep."

But he did not die. He woke depressed, and the next morning, when we were standing on the little quay waiting for the sailors to pick us up, he suddenly announced that he would not leave after all. Then when the boat came within earshot, one of the sailors shouted up to us that he had just seen a unit of legionaries on the road from Antium, heading in our direction, led by a military trib-une. That immediately shook Cicero out of his lethargy. He held out his hand and the sailors helped him down into the boat.

Our voyage quickly began to repeat the pattern of our first flight into exile. It was as if Mother Italy could not bear to allow her favourite son to leave her. We had gone about three miles, hugging close to the shore, when the grey sky began to fill with immense black clouds rolling in from the horizon. A wind got up, stirring the sea into steep waves, and our little boat seemed to rise almost to the perpendicular, only to crash down again, bow first, and saturate us with salt water. If anything, it was worse than before, because this time there was no shelter. Cicero and I sat huddled in hooded cloaks while the men tried to row us crosswise into the oncoming waves. The hull began to fill and the vessel became dangerously low. We all had to help bail, even Cicero, frantically scooping up the freezing water with our hands and tipping it over the side to stop ourselves sinking. Our limbs and faces were numb. We swallowed salt. The rain blinded us. Eventually, after rowing bravely for many hours, the sailors were exhausted, and told us they needed to rest. We rounded a rocky promontory and headed towards a cove, rowing as close to the beach as we could before we all had to jump out and wade ashore. Cicero sank in almost to his waist and four of the sailors had to carry him on to the land. They laid him down and went back to help their crewmates with the boat, hauling it right up on to the beach. They laid it on its side and propped it up using branches cut from the nearby myrtle trees, and with the sail and the mast they built a makeshift shelter. They even managed to light a fire, although the wood was wet, and the wind blew the smoke this way and that, choking us and making our eyes smart.

Darkness soon came, and Cicero, who had not uttered a word of complaint, appeared to sleep. Thus ended the fifth day of December.

I woke at dawn on the sixth after a fitful night to find calmer skies. My bones were chilled, my damp clothes stiff with salt and sand. I stood with difficulty and looked about me. Everyone was still asleep, except for Cicero. He had gone.

I looked up and down the beach and peered out to sea, then turned to scan the trees. There was a small gap, which turned out to lead to a path, and I set off, calling his name. At the top of the path was a road. Cicero was lurching along it. I called to him again but he ignored me. He was making slow and unsteady progress in the direction from which we had come. I caught him up and fell in beside him and spoke to him with a calmness I did not feel.

"We need to get back in the boat," I said. "The slaves in the house may have told the legionaries where we are headed. They may not be far behind us. Where are you going?"

"To Rome." He did not look at me but kept on walking.

"To do what?"

"To kill myself on Octavian's doorstep. He will die of shame."

"He won't," I said, and caught his arm, "because he has no shame, and the soldiers will torture you to death like they did Trebonius."

He glanced at me and stopped walking. "Do you think so?"

"I know it." I took him by the arm and tugged him gently. He did not resist but lowered his head and allowed me to lead him like a child back through the trees to the beach.

HOW MELANCHOLY IT IS TO RELIVE ALL OF THIS! BUT I HAVE NO choice if I am to fulfil my promise to him and tell the story of his life.

We put him back on to the boat and launched it once more into the waves. The day was grey and vast, as at the dawn of time. We rowed on for many hours, assisted by a breeze that filled the sail, and by the end of the afternoon had covered, by my reckoning, a further twenty-five miles or thereabouts. We passed the famous Temple of Apollo that stands a little above the sea on the headland at Caieta, and Cicero, who had been slumped, staring vacantly towards the shore, suddenly recognised it, sat up straight and said, "We are nearly at Formiae. I have a house here."

"I know you do."

"Let us put in here for the night."

"It's too risky. You're well known to have a villa at Formiae."

"I don't care about that," replied Cicero with something of his old firmness. "I want to sleep in my own bed."

And so we rowed towards the shore and tied up at the jetty that was built out into the sea a little way from the villa. As we moored, a great flock of crows rose cawing from the nearby trees as if in warning, and I asked Cicero at least to allow me to make sure his enemies weren't lying in wait for him before he disembarked. He agreed, and I set off up the familiar path through the trees, accompanied by a couple of the sailors. The path led us to the Via Appia. By now it was almost dusk. The road was empty. I walked about fifty paces to where Cicero's villa stood behind a pair of iron gates. I went up the drive and knocked firmly on the oak door, and after a short interval and a great noise of bolts drawn back, the porter appeared. He was startled to see me. I looked past his shoulder and asked if any strangers had come looking for the master. He assured me they had not. He was a good-hearted, simple fellow. I had known him for years, and I believed him.

I said, "In that case, send four slaves with a litter down to the jetty to pick up the master and bring him to the villa, and meanwhile have a hot bath drawn for him and fresh clothes and food prepared, for he is in a poor state."

I also sent two other slaves with fast horses to keep a lookout along the Via Appia for this mysterious and ominous detachment of legionaries that seemed to be on our trail.

Cicero was carried into the villa, and the gate and door were locked behind him.

I saw little of him after that. As soon as he had had his bath, he took a little food and wine in his room and then retired to sleep.

I slept myself—and very deeply, despite my anxieties, for such was my exhaustion—and the following morning had to be roughly woken by one of the slaves I had stationed along the Via Appia. He was out of breath and frightened. A force of thirty legionaries on foot, with a centurion and a tribune on horseback, was marching towards the house from the north-west. They were less than half an hour away.

I ran to wake Cicero. He had the covers up to his chin and refused to stir, but I tore them off him anyway.

"They are coming for you," I said, bending over him. "They're almost here. We have to move."

He smiled at me, and laid his hand on my cheek. "Let them come, old friend. I am not afraid."

I pleaded with him: "For my sake, if not for yours—for the sake of your friends and for Marcus—please *move*!"

I think it was the mention of Marcus that did it. He sighed. "Very well, then. But it is quite pointless."

I withdrew to let him dress and ran around issuing orders— a litter to be ready immediately, the boat prepared to sail with the sailors at their oars, the gate and the door to be locked the moment we were out of the villa, the household slaves to vacate the premises and hide wherever they could.

In my imagination I could hear the steady tramp of the legionaries' boots becoming louder and louder . . .

At length—far too great a length!—Cicero appeared looking
as immaculate as if he were on his way to address the Senate. He
walked through the villa saying goodbye to everyone. They were
all in tears. He took a last look around as if saying farewell to the
building and all his beloved possessions, and then climbed into
the litter, closed the curtains so that no one could see his face,
and we set off out of the gate. But instead of the slaves all making
a run for it, they seized such weapons as they could find—rakes,
brooms, pokers, kitchen knives—and insisted on coming with us,
forming a homely rustic phalanx around the litter. We went the
short distance along the road and turned down the path into the
woods. Through the trees I could glimpse the sea shining in
the morning sun. Escape seemed close. But then, at the bottom of
the path, just before it opened out on to the beach, a dozen legionaries appeared.

The slaves at the front of our little procession cried out in alarm,
and those carrying the litter scrambled to turn it round. It swayed
dangerously and Cicero was almost pitched to the ground. We
struggled back the way we had come, only to discover that more
soldiers were above us, blocking access to the road.

We were trapped, outnumbered, doomed. Nevertheless, we
determined to make a fight. The slaves set the litter down and surrounded it. Cicero drew back the curtain to see what was going
on. He saw the soldiers advancing rapidly towards us and shouted
to me: "No one is to fight!" Then to the slaves he said: "Everyone
lay down your weapons! I am honoured by your devotion, but the
only blood that needs to be shed here is mine."

The legionaries had their swords drawn. The military tribune
leading them was a hirsute, swarthy-looking brute. Beneath the
ridge of his helmet his eyebrows merged together to form a continuous thick black line. He called out, "Marcus Tullius Cicero, I
have a warrant for your execution."

Cicero, still lying in his litter, his chin in his hand, looked him up and down very calmly. "I know you," he said, "I'm sure of it. What's your name?"

The military tribune, plainly taken aback, said, "My name, if you must know it, is Caius Popillius Laenas, and yes, we do know one another: not that it will save you."

"Popillius," murmured Cicero, "that's it," and then he turned to me. "Do you remember this man, Tiro? He was our client—that fifteen-year-old who murdered his father, right at the beginning of my career. He'd have been condemned to death for parricide if I hadn't got him off—on condition he went into the army." He laughed. "This is a kind of justice, I suppose."

I looked at Popillius and indeed I did remember him.

Popillius said, "That's enough talk. The verdict of the Constitutional Commission is that the death sentence should be carried out immediately." He gestured to his soldiers to drag Cicero from his litter.

"Wait," said Cicero, "leave me where I am. I have it in mind to die this way," and he propped himself up on his elbows like a defeated gladiator, threw back his head and offered his throat to the sky.

"If that's what you want," said Popillius. He turned to his centurion. "Let's get it over with."

The centurion took up his position. He braced his legs. He swung his sword. The blade flashed, and in that instant for Cicero the mystery that had plagued him all his life was solved, and liberty was extinguished from the earth.

AFTERWARDS THEY CUT OFF HIS HEAD AND HANDS AND PUT THEM in a sack. They made us sit down and watch them while they did it. Then they marched away. I was told that Antony was so delighted with these extra trophies that he gave Popillius a bonus of a million sesterces. It is also said that Fulvia pierced Cicero's tongue with a needle. I do not know. What is certainly true is that on Antony's orders the head that had delivered the Philippics and the hands that had written them were nailed up on the rostra, as a warning to others who might think of opposing the Triumvirate, and they stayed there for many years, until finally they rotted and fell away.

After the killers had gone, we carried Cicero's body down to the beach and built a pyre, and at dusk we burned it. Then I made my way south to my farm on the Bay of Naples.

Little by little I learned more of what had happened.

Quintus was soon afterwards captured with his son and put to death.

Atticus emerged from hiding and was pardoned by Antony because of the help he had given Fulvia.

And much, much later, Antony committed suicide together with his mistress Cleopatra after Octavian defeated them in battle. The boy is now the Emperor Augustus.

But I have written enough.

Many years have passed since the episodes I have recounted. At first I thought I would never recover from Cicero's death. But time wipes out everything, even grief. Indeed, I would go so far as to say that grief is almost entirely a question of perspective. For the first few years I used to sigh and think, "Well, he would still be in his sixties now," and then a decade later, with surprise, "My goodness, he would be seventy-five," but nowadays I think, "Well, he would be long since dead in any case, so what does it matter how he died in comparison with how he lived?"

My work is done. My book is finished. Soon I will die too.

In the summer evenings I sit on the terrace with Agathe, my wife. She sews while I look at the stars. Always at such moments I think of Scipio's dream of where dead statesmen dwell in *On the Republic*:

I gazed in every direction and all appeared wonderfully beautiful. There were stars which we never see from earth, and they were all larger than we have ever imagined. The starry spheres were much greater than the earth; indeed the earth itself seemed to me so small that I was scornful of our empire, which covers only a single point, as it were, upon its surface.

"If only you will look on high," the old statesman tells Scipio, "and contemplate this eternal home and resting place, you will no longer bother with the gossip of the common herd or put your trust in human reward for your exploits. Nor will any man's reputation endure very long, for what men say dies with them and is blotted out with the forgetfulness of posterity."

All that will remain of us is what is written down.

# GLOSSARY

aedile an elected official, four of whom were chosen annually to serve a one-year term, responsible for the running of the city of Rome: law and order, public buildings, business regulations, etc.

auspices supernatural signs, especially flights of birds and light-ningflashes, interpreted by the augurs; if ruled unfavourable no public business could be transacted

Carcer Rome's prison, situated on the boundary of the Forum and the Capitol, between the Temple of Concord and the Senate house

century the unit in which the Roman people cast their votes on the Field of Mars at election time for consul and praetor; the system was weighted to favour the wealthier classes of society

chief priest see pontifex maximus

comitium the circular area in the Forum, approximately 300 feet across, bounded by the Senate house and the rostra, traditionally the place where laws were voted on by the people, and where many of the courts had their tribunals

consul the senior magistrate of the Roman Republic, two of whom were elected annually, usually in July, to assume office in the following January, taking it in turns to preside over the Senate each month

**curule chair** a backless chair with low arms, often made of ivory, possessed by a magistrate with imperium, particularly consuls and praetors

**dictator** a magistrate given absolute power by the Senate over civil and military affairs, usually in a time of national emergency

**equestrian order** the second most senior order in Roman society after the Senate, the "Order of Knights" had its own officials and privileges, and was entitled to one-third of the places on a jury; often its members were richer than members of the Senate, but declined to pursue a public career

**Gaul** divided into two provinces: **Nearer Gaul**, extending from the River Rubicon in northern Italy to the Alps, and **Further Gaul**, the lands beyond the Alps roughly corresponding to the modern French regions of Provence and Languedoc

**haruspices** the religious officials who inspected the entrails after a sacrifice in order to determine whether the omens were good or bad

**imperator** the title granted to a military commander on active service by his soldiers after a victory; it was necessary to be hailed imperator in order to qualify for a triumph

**imperium** the power to command, granted by the state to an individual, usually a consul, praetor or provincial governor

**legate** a deputy or delegate

**legion** the largest formation in the Roman army, at full strength consisting of approximately 5,000 men

**lictor** an attendant who carried the fasces—a bundle of birch rods tied together with a strip of red leather—that symbolised a magistrate's imperium; consuls were accompanied by twelve lictors, who served as their bodyguards, praetors by six; the senior lictor, who stood closest to the magistrate, was known as the proximate lictor

**manumission** the emancipation of a slave

**Order of Knights** see **equestrian order**

**pontifex maximus** the chief priest of the Roman state religion, the head of the fifteen-member College of Priests, entitled to an official residence on the Via Sacra

**praetor** the second most senior magistrate in the Roman Republic, eight of whom were elected annually, usually in July, to take office the following January, and who drew lots to determine which of the various courts—treason, embezzlement, corruption, serious crime, etc.—they would preside over; see also **urban praetor**

**prosecutions** as there was no public prosecution system in the Roman Republic, all criminal charges, from embezzlement to treason and murder, had to be brought by private individuals

**public assemblies** the supreme authority and legislature of the Roman people was the people themselves, whether constituted by **tribe** (the *comitia tributa,* which voted on laws, declared war and peace, and elected the tribunes) or by **century** (the *comitia centuriata,* which elected the senior magistrates)

**quaestor** a junior magistrate, twenty of whom were elected each year, and who thereby gained the right of entry to the Senate; it was necessary for a candidate for the quaestorship to be over thirty and to show wealth of one million sesterces

**rostra** a long, curved platform in the Forum, about twelve feet high, surmounted by heroic statues, from which the Roman people were addressed by magistrates and advocates; its name derived from the beaks (*rostra*) of captured enemy warships set into its sides

**Senate** *not* the legislative assembly of the Roman Republic—laws could only be passed by the people in a tribal assembly—but something closer to its executive, with 600 members who could raise matters of state and order the consul to take action or to draft laws to be placed before the people; once elected via the quaestorship (see **quaestor**) a man would normally remain a senator for life, unless removed by the censors for immorality or bankruptcy, hence the average age was high (*senate* derived from *senex* = old)

**tribes** the Roman people were divided into thirty-five tribes for the purposes of voting on legislation and to elect the tribunes; unlike the system of voting by **century**, the votes of rich and poor when cast in a tribe had equal weight

**tribune** a representative of the ordinary citizens—the plebeians—ten of whom were elected annually each summer and took office in December, with the power to propose and veto legislation, and to summon assemblies of the people; it was forbidden for anyone other than a plebeian to hold the office

**triumph** an elaborate public celebration of homecoming, granted by the Senate to honour a victorious general, to qualify for which it was necessary for him to retain his military imperium—and as it was forbidden to enter Rome whilst still possessing military authority, generals wishing to triumph had to wait outside the city until the Senate granted them a triumph

**urban praetor** the head of the justice system, senior of all the praetors, third in rank in the republic after the two consuls

# ACKNOWLEDGEMENTS

My greatest debt over the twelve years it has taken to write this novel and its two predecessors is to the Loeb edition of Cicero's collected speeches, letters and writings, published by Harvard University Press. I have been obliged to edit and compress Cicero's words, but wherever possible I have tried to let his voice come through. Loeb has been my Bible.

I have also made constant use of the great nineteenth-century works of reference edited by William Smith: his *Dictionary of Greek and Roman Antiquities, Dictionary of Greek and Roman Biography and Mythology* (three volumes) and *Dictionary of Greek and Roman Geography* (two volumes); these are now freely available online. *The Magistrates of the Roman Republic, Volume II, 99 BC—31 BC* by T. Robert S. Broughton was also invaluable, as was *The Barrington Atlas of the Greek and Roman World,* edited by Richard J. A. Talbert. Again, wherever possible I have followed the facts and descriptions offered in the original sources—Plutarch, Appian, Sallust, Caesar—and I thank all those scholars and translators who have made them accessible and whose words I have used.

Biographies of, and books about, Cicero, which have given me numberless insights and ideas, include *Cicero: A Turbulent Life* by Anthony Everitt, *Cicero: A Portrait* by Elizabeth Rawson, *Cicero* by D. R. Shackleton Bailey, *Cicero and His Friends* by Gaston Bossier, *Cicero: The Secrets of His Correspondence* by Jérôme Carcopino, *Cicero: A Political Biography* by David Stockton, *Cicero: Politics and Persuasion in Ancient Rome* by Kathryn Tempest, *Cicero as Evidence* by Andrew Lintott, *The Hand of Cicero* by Shane Butler, *Terentia, Tullia and Publia: The Women of Cicero's Family* by Susan Treggiari, *The Cambridge Com-*

*panion to Cicero* edited by Catherine Steel, and—still thoroughly readable and useful—*The History of the Life of Marcus Tullius Cicero,* published in 1741 by Conyers Middleton (1683–1750).

Biographies of Cicero's contemporaries which I have found particularly useful include *Caesar* by Christian Meier, *Caesar* by Adrian Goldsworthy, *The Death of Caesar* by Barry Strauss, *Pompey* by Robin Seager, *Marcus Crassus and the Late Roman Republic* by Allen Ward, *Marcus Crassus, Millionaire* by Frank Adcock, *The Patrician Tribune: Publius Clodius Pulcher* by W. Jeffrey Tatum and *Catullus: A Poet in the Rome of Julius Caesar* by Aubrey Burl.

For the general ambience of Rome—its culture, society and political structure—I have drawn on three works by the incomparable Peter Wiseman—*New Men in the Roman Senate, Catullus and His World* and *Cinna the Poet and Other Roman Essays.* To these I must also add *The Crowd in Rome in the Late Republic* by Fergus Millar, which analyses how politics might have operated in Cicero's Rome. Also valuable were *Intellectual Life in the Late Roman Republic* by Elizabeth Rawson, *The Constitution of the Roman Republic* by Andrew Lintott, *The Roman Forum* by Michael Grant, *Roman Aristocratic Parties and Families* by Friedrich Münzer (translated by Thérèse Ridley) and (of course) *The Roman Revolution* by Ronald Syme and Theodore Mommsen's *History of Rome.*

For the physical recreation of Republican Rome I relied on the scholarship of *A New Topographical Dictionary of Ancient Rome* by L. Richardson Jr., *A Topographical Dictionary of Rome* by Samuel Ball Platner, the *Pictorial Dictionary of Ancient Rome* (two volumes) by Ernest Nash and *Mapping Augustan Rome,* the *Journal of Roman Archaeology* project directed by Lothar Haselberger.

A special word of thanks should go to Tom Holland whose wonderful *Rubicon: The Triumph and Tragedy of the Roman Republic* (2003) first gave me the idea of writing a fictional account of the friendships, rivalries and enmities between Cicero, Caesar, Pompey, Cato, Crassus and the rest.

*Dictator* is my fourth foray into the ancient world, a series of journeys that began with *Pompeii* (2003). One of the great pleasures of these years has been meeting scholars of Roman history who have been without exception encouraging, even to the extent of electing me a proud if notably undistinguished President of the Classical Association in 2008. For various offers of encouragement and advice over the years I would like to thank in particular Mary Beard, Andrew Wallace-Hadrill, Jasper Griffin, Tom Holland, Bob Fowler, Peter Wiseman and Andrea Carandini. I apologise to those I have forgotten, and naturally absolve all those listed above of any responsibility for what I have written.

The two publishers who first commissioned me to write about Cicero were Sue Freestone in London and David Rosenthal in New York. Like the Roman Empire, they have both moved on, but I would like to thank them for their original enthusiasm and continued friendship. Their successors, Jocasta Hamilton and Sonny Mehta, have stepped into the breach and skilfully steered the project to its conclusion. Thanks also to Gail Rebuck and to Susan Sandon, for gallantly staying the course. My agent, Pat Kavanagh, to my great sadness and that of all her authors, did not live to see the work which she represented completed; I hope she would have enjoyed it. My thanks go to my other agents, Michael Carlisle of Inkwell Management in New York, and to Nicki Kennedy and Sam Edenborough of ILA in London. The estimable Wolfgang Müller, my German translator, once again acted as an unofficial copy-editor. Joy Terekiev and Cristiana Moroni of Mondadori in Italy have shared the journey literally to Tusculum and Formiae.

Finally—*finally*—I would like to thank, as always, my wife, Gill, and also our children, Holly, Charlie, Matilda and Sam, half of whose lives have been lived in the shadow of Cicero. Despite this, or perhaps even because of it, Holly took a degree in classics and now knows far more about the ancient world than her old dad, so it is to her that this book is dedicated.

Robert Harris is the author of nine bestselling novels: *Fatherland, Enigma, Archangel, Pompeii, Imperium, The Ghost Writer, Conspirata, The Fear Index,* and *An Officer and a Spy.* Several of his books have been adapted to film, most recently *The Ghost Writer,* directed by Roman Polanski. His work has been translated into thirty-seven languages. He lives in the village of Kintbury, England, with his wife, Gill Hornby.

A NOTE ON THE TYPE

This book was set in Elysium, a typeface designed in 1992 for the Letraset type foundry by Michael Gills (b. 1962).

Classified as an old-style typeface, Elysium was influenced by the fonts of Czech calligrapher and designer Oldrich Menhart (1897–1962). It is the calligraphic qualities, particularly noticeable in the serifs, that give Elysium its unique flair.

TYPESET BY SCRIBE,

PHILADELPHIA, PENNSYLVANIA

PRINTED AND BOUND BY BERRYVILLE GRAPHICS,

BERRYVILLE, VIRGINIA

DESIGNED BY BETTY LEW